THE NIGHT OF THE AMAZONS

THE NIGHT OF
THE AMAZONS

Herbert Rosendorfer

Translated from the German by
IAN MITCHELL

Secker & Warburg
London

Originally published in Germany as
Die Nacht der Amazonen by Verlag Kiepenheuer & Witsch, Köln
Copyright © 1989 by Verlag Kiepenheuer & Witsch

This edition first published in Great Britain 1991
by Martin Secker & Warburg Limited
Michelin House, 81 Fulham Road, London SW3 6RB
Translation copyright © 1991 by Ian Mitchell

A CIP catalogue record for this book
is available from the British Library
ISBN 0 436 42584 X

Typeset in Linotron Sabon
by Hewer Text Composition Services, Edinburgh
Printed in Great Britain
St Edmundsbury Press, Bury St Edmunds, Suffolk

Dedicated to the memory of
my father-in-law,
Rudolf Caspar (1900–1987)

Personal Description: height, 173cm

(not all that tall, then, one metre seventy-three, at five feet eight not what you would call a giant or Titan or Colossus. If, many years later, Herr Ernst Hanfstaengl, known as 'Putzi', was to describe him as a 'man-and-a-half', then that is something of an exaggeration; perhaps Herr Hanfstaengl was misled by the enchantment that distance lends.)

Hair: brown

(the colour was to play a significant role in his life).

Facial hair: red

(this colour, too, was to play a significant role in his life, albeit an altogether different one from that of the colour brown. Incidentally, 'facial hair' here refers to a moustache. There is a picture from his earlier years, in which the moustache is waxed in an upward twirl, the way the Kaiser used to do it with a satisfied 'There we have it!' Then, later, he docked the ends of his moustache, more in the manner of Menjou, for he apparently could never bring himself to adopt the snot-warmer style of his *Führer*. His hair-style: shorn up to a line well above the ears, very short on top, with a centre parting. In later years, at least on – let's call them – more lively occasions, for example at a *Fasching* party in the *Deutsches Theater*, where he had himself photographed along with *Reichsleiter* Max Amann, the *brown* hair hung in a light cow's lick over his forehead, as indeed again on the occasion of the 'Night of the Amazons'; Reich Director Max Amann, the 'jovial Bavarian', another baroque character, was the one who administered Hitler's royalties from *Mein Kampf*. But back to the whiskers: in pictures they do not appear red, but dark – dark brown? Although a red moustache does indeed

I

have something decidedly Germanic about it; did he perhaps tint his moustache with – brown – shoe polish?)

Eyebrows: arched
Eyes: blue

(so, yes, a real Teuton).

Forehead: high, steep
Nose: straight

(he always had been, and always was, somewhat prejudiced, to put it mildly, against crooked noses; crooked noses were something he always smashed in, whenever one of them appeared, unless of course the crook-nose might have hit back, which unfortunately happened all too seldom, but in such cases the straight-nose preferred to beat a hasty retreat.)

Mouth: large

(you can say that again –)

Teeth: complete upper denture

(– and that from the age of only thirty-eight years; did somebody smash his teeth in? or did a horse kick him? –)

Chin: jutting
Face: round

(precisely: a baroque figure; the pictures show flabby jowls, hanging down over his wing collar or stiff uniform tunic).

Complexion: ruddy
Build: powerful

('powerful' was a euphemism for fat that was principally employed by tailors and off-the-peg outfitters' assistants, so as not to give offence to customers whom the description fitted).

Voice: deep
Distinguishing marks: blind in left eye as a
result of a gunshot wound

(he was not averse to hinting that he had lost the eye in the war – meaning, of course, the First World War; to those who knew that he had played no part whatsoever in the war, he liked to tell the tale of how he had shot it out as a result of clumsy fiddling around with his own pistol).

Dress: yellow-grey hat

(– this probably refers to one of those hats that later became known as 'Trenker' hats after the film actor, Luis of that ilk –)

light grey trousers, leather gaiters, dark jacket

(we have to imagine this picture in greater detail: the dark jacket, a *Joppe*, mind, no mere jacket, no sports coat, no, a *Joppe*. That German, Germanic, loose-waisted short coat, the red-faced Teuton in the *Joppe*, probably with green trimmings and horn buttons, the master-race *Joppe* made of heavy woollen *loden* cloth, the red-faced, *powerfully built* member of the master-race, with the false top set and the master-race look in his eye, like an eagle, that lord of the skies, yes, aquiline, albeit a cold stare, because of said glass eye. And, *nota bene*, leather gaiters.)

The description is taken from records in Munich Police Headquarters, dated 30 October 1921. Reason for summonsing of the offender: suspicion of being an accessory to attempted murder.

Name: Weber, Christian.

*

August was rainy, but it was the first peaceful August for six years. It was Monday and the evening was already well advanced, half-past ten, and business was slow. Only the one they called the Loudmouth was sitting in his regular place in the corner under the stag's antlers, and, diagonally across from him, a tattered soldier with only one arm.

'I have,' said the one-armed man, 'an Iron Cross. First Class.'

'Let's see it,' said the Loudmouth, but quietly.

One-Arm drew a filthy bundle from the top pocket of his

service tunic and unwrapped – laboriously, with only the one hand – an Iron Cross.

'Five marks,' said One-Arm.

'They're practically giving junk like that away all over the place these days. Twenty pfennigs'll get you one.'

'That's as may be,' said the one-armed man, 'but there's something else with this one.'

'What?'

'A certificate. The citation. Signed by the general. There!'

'But the citation's blank . . .?'

'Exactly. It was awarded to me. Kind of right at the end.' One-Arm laughed. 'The general just found time to sign it before he scarpered. The clerical office, though, didn't have the time to put my name in. All you need to do is put in *your* name. Five marks.'

Slowly, the Loudmouth pulled a greasy purse from his *Joppe*, took out a silver five-mark piece and gave it to the one-armed man. One-Arm wrapped up the Iron Cross again and pushed the paper bundle and the certificate across the table.

'What's your name anyway?' asked the one-armed man. 'Just so that I know who's wearing my Iron Cross?'

'None of your business,' rasped the Loudmouth, 'just take your money and beat it.'

One-Arm grinned again, pushed himself up from his chair and left. Now the Loudmouth was on his own. The waitress had already left, only the landlord – *Blauer Bock*, the Blue Buck, the place was called – was still standing behind the bar, rinsing glasses.

'Landlord,' bawled the Loudmouth, 'another beer.'

'Cash only!' snarled the landlord.

'I'll pay you next week,' said the Loudmouth.

The landlord came unhurriedly from behind the bar, went over to the till, took out a dog-eared notebook, leafed through it and said, 'Eighteen beers, four roast porks, one with an extra dumpling, and twenty-six portions of cherry cake with whipped cream. There's all that on your slate already.'

'As a former front-line soldier I demand,' croaked the

Loudmouth, 'as a holder of the Iron Cross First Class . . .'

'Weber!' said the landlord calmly.

*

'Ah, good evening to you, Herr Dirrigl.'

'And a very good evening to you, Herr Kammerlander.'

'What vile weather.'

'Call this August!'

'I can't remember us ever having an August the like of it, Herr Dirrigl, really I can't!' Kammerlander gave a dismissive wave of the hand.

'I tell you, Herr Kammerlander, there's a reason for it all. Everything! Even the weather. It's Fate, or if you prefer, Providence. And what's behind it all? This Fate, or if you like, Providence, Herr Kammerlander? I have my own theory. No, don't laugh; the God-ordained order of things has been disrupted. You mark my words, Herr Kammerlander. The Divine Order. And the Most Exalted Royal Household is a part of that, too. I mean, where would we be if the sacred personage of the monarch were there for just anyone and everyone to, et cetera? And as if that wasn't bad enough, Herr Kammerlander: I ask you, that Kurt Eisner, a *Jewish* hack! A fine state of affairs, don't you think?'

'It wouldn't be so bad if he were just a Jew, Herr Dirrigl, but worse, much worse – from Berlin!'

'You've hit the nail on the head.'

'But he did get his just deserts, did the Jew.'

'True, true – but all the same, the Divine Order of things! Let me tell you. You'll remember my words. Ah now, your Bautzerl, what's the matter with him?'

'Ah – ah! at last . . . look at that, what a lovely little pile. He's been – I was really quite worried – he's been having difficulties with his digestion, has good little Bautzerl, but now, by the looks of it, things are moving again. And how's your Wamperl?'

'Kind of you to ask, everything's in order, isn't that so, Wamperl?'

The door of the *Blauer Bock* swings open, a man comes

5

flying out, skitters across the pavement and falls in a heap on a patch of grass at the foot of a tree. The fellow struggles to his feet, dusts himself down, he is in a state of great agitation. Dirrigl and Kammerlander step to one side.

'Heel, Bautzerl.'

'Come here now, Wamperl, come back out of the way.'

Before the fellow can start cursing and fuming, which he is obviously working himself up for, the door opens again. The establishment's doorman steps out, he has a bundle in his hand, the trench coat belonging to the man he has just thrown out. He hands him the trench coat and says, 'Here, here's your coat, and now don't give us no more of your racket, else I'll really sort you out.'

Muttering quietly to himself, the bouncer's victim pulls on his trench coat and shambles off.

'Ah, it's Herr Weber, the faithful retainer, good evening; hmmyesyes, another regular seen off the premises?'

'Ah, it's you, Herr Kammerlander, good evening. Yes – hah! A regular. Yes indeed, yes. If all our regular customers were like that one, then we'd be in a fine mess, so we would.'

'Somewhat unceremoniously dispatched!' says Dirrigl.

'Nah, well yes,' says the steward, 'it wasn't all that rough. I don't find him all that disagreeable really. They call him the Loudmouth. Adolf's his name. What his full name is, I dunno. An old infantryman, dabbles in politics now. He claims he's a painter. Mind you, not a house painter, you understand, but a painter, an *artist*.'

'Ha ha, yes, I know the type,' says Dirrigl: '"*Ah, 'tis a hard life, you couldn't see your way to lend me a couple of marks.*"'

'If he was a red,' says the bouncer, 'well, then, let me tell you – but he's one of the Nationalists. So I make sure he gets, shall we say, a soft landing. A bouncer that's worth his salt, see, he'll fire your customer out exactly where he means him to land, straight as a die. Now that one, the Loudmouth, Adolf, I always chuck him out so he'll end up precisely on that soft bit of grass there.'

'Yes, yes,' says Kammerlander, 'I understand. Who knows – these days – who knows what might become even of a former infantryman and painter. We've seen some odd ones already. And then he'll maybe thank you for it.'

'That one? Hah – nah, nah, he'll never be anything. He'll never make anything of himself, that's for sure. Anybody else, but not him. All the same, I always chuck him out gently.'

*

As a rule, a Bavarian *Barockmensch,* that larger-than-life eccentric, is firstly Catholic and secondly comes from Upper Bavaria or Lower Bavaria, in other words what is known as an 'Old Bavarian'.

So is it merely a quirk of nature that this *Barockmensch,* this *Weber, Christian,* was born in *Polsingen*?

Polsingen (today it carries the postcode 8831, is there a Christian-Weber-Strasse there? 'Maybe he did . . . well yes, but . . . nevertheless a great son of Polsingen . . . someone who is fond of horses can't be *all* bad . . . !' Or at least a Christian Weber Fountain, at which thirsty horses can find refreshment? Is the grammar school, assuming there is such a thing as a grammar school in Polsingen, called the Christian-Weber-Gymnasium? In each case it depends on whether or not the CSU, the party of the Bavarian *Barockmensch,* holds an absolute majority on the Polsingen district council). Polsingen am Rohrbach, hard by the border between the administrative regions of Middle Franconia and Swabia, in a geographical or cartographical bulge that juts out from Middle Franconian territory into Swabian. The nearest community of any size – Wemding, it can't help it if Christian Weber was born so close by – is itself in Swabia although it is nearer than the seat of local authority, the county town, Weissenburg. The county: Weissenburg-Gunzenhausen. Beautiful, cosy German (Old-Franconian?) countryside: to the west, the area on the banks of the Jagst – there you're in Württemberg already – to the south, the Danube Marshes. The land of antiquity, Roman remains, the Silver Treasure of Weissenburg. In Hohenzollern hands for centuries: Polsingen belonged to the Principality of Ansbach, the ruler was the Margrave of Brandenburg-Ansbach, with his seat in Ansbach. In 1806, the land was occupied by the French, handed over in the same year to the brand-new Kingdom of Bavaria, which officially took possession of it under the terms of letters patent dated 10 April 1810. The people of Polsingen became Royal Bavarian subjects, and in Royal Bavarian Polsingen the Royal Bavarian postman, Georg Weber, did his duty and, some time in November or December 1882, oblivious of the import of what he was doing, fathered a son, who was born on 23 August 1883: Christian Weber.

In a letter dated 1923 to a 'most respected police', by the way, Weber writes 'Polzingen', with a Z instead of an S. But, throughout his life, Christian Weber was never one for scribbling letters, and as far as spelling was concerned, he was in a state of perpetual undeclared war with it.

His mother: Sophie, née Feldmeyer (or Feldmeier, Feldmaier, or sometimes even Feldmann). Both parents were already deceased by the time, on 30 October 1921, a 'Detailed Personal Dossier' was opened on Weber in the Security Department of Police Headquarters in Munich and he was living at Aventinstrasse 5, first floor right, c/o Silberhorn.

Military connections (such is the term used in the Detailed Personal Dossier): 1st Regiment of Gendarmes, Mounted Rifles, from 1901 to 1904. Thus Weber was twenty-one years old when he was demobilised. It was 1913 at the latest when he went to Munich, for during that year the police were showing an interest in the man who was later to be Regional President and Amazon-fan, and on 28 November they directed a letter to the Polsingen local authorities enquiring whether they had any incriminating information relating to C.W. ('horse breaker'). The Mayor of Polsingen, whose name is hard to make out from the signature – Härklein? Häcklein? – replied in the negative. A 'horse breaker' is a euphemism for a groom.

On 16 March 1914, in the yard of the house at Fürstenstrasse 6, Weber was kicked by a bucking horse belonging to his employer, Göbel by name, and was taken to hospital in Schwabing. This incident, too, aroused the interest of the police – although really only as a matter of routine. In the relevant entry, dated 17 March, we read that there was no question of attaching blame to a third party, and that the injuries were potentially fatal. But Weber survived. Yet it seems that the horse did its level best. Perhaps it was then that Weber lost his eye and not in a shooting accident. (But loss by shooting has a better ring to it than 'kicked by a horse'.) Perhaps, too, that was the reason why, in 1914, and throughout the whole war, he was not called up. The Old Campaigner.

It is also possible that it was the kick from this horse that catapulted the 'horse breaker' Weber out of the career as a groom for which he had been marked out. Herr Göbel had no use for a man with one eye. But a bouncer needs no more than just the one. Even monocularly he can find the customers he has to throw out. And with one eye, too, he can distinguish those he ejects roughly from those he pilots in a gentle arc on to the soft grassy patch.

The bar-room was overcrowded. It was not an establishment of the sort from which Christian Weber expelled clients who were not to the landlord's liking, not, that is, like the Blue Buck. The *Blauer Bock* had the stamp of a tatty suburban hostelry (even though it was in the middle of town), with brown-painted tables, a flaking dado around the walls, a few sets of antlers over fading photographs of deceased regulars, the table in the adjacent room reserved for the regular meetings of the Friendly Society of the Railwaymen's Union (City Centre Branch), and that permanent hint of faecal stench, on account of how the lavatory door defied all efforts to close it properly. The overcrowded establishment on this occasion was quite different: a *Bierkeller,* a large room, much too low-ceilinged for its dimensions. The swathes of smoke from cheap tobacco began to form immediately above the heads of the customers. Almost exclusively male. (Later, that was to change, within only a few years.)

'So what do you do?' enquired Weber.

'Watchmaker,' said the man who had squeezed himself into the last vacant seat next to Weber. 'Moritz is the name.'

'A Jew?' asked Weber.

'No!' said Moritz. 'That just happens to be my name. Emil Moritz. And you?'

'Weber, Christian.'

'And?'

'Horse –' Weber paused, and then, 'dealer.'

'I see,' said Moritz, 'well then, cheers, Herr Weber.'

'You can call me Christian, you know,' said Weber, 'seeing as how the world's about coming to an end.'

Up at the front, barely visible, somebody was making a speech, somebody, if Weber had heard right, who was a turner by trade, or maybe Turner was just his name. Anyway, he was talking about 'Democracy, the Nudist Movement, unbridled naturalism and companionate marriage'.

'Can you make him out?' asked Weber.

'He's talking so softly,' Moritz said, 'and the others aren't what you'd call quiet. He's not much of a speaker. He'll never come to anything.'

'What did he say?'

'Democracy and the Nudist Movement.'

'Aha. And?'

'He's against them.'

After that, another speaker stepped up to the lectern. He was wearing a light beige trench coat and had a dog whip hanging from one wrist. He didn't have a dog with him, he was barking himself. So loudly did he bark that even Weber, right at the back, could make out some of his propositions: Germany as the victim of a world-wide conspiracy, beset from all sides, firstly by Bolsheviks, secondly by Freemasons, thirdly by capitalists, fourthly by Jesuits, all of them strategically commanded by the bloodthirsty, avaricious Jewish racial tyrants. And anyway, we didn't lose the war, either.

'An Austrian,' said Moritz the watchmaker.

'But sharp with it,' Weber said.

The Austrian barked on until he was hoarse; finally he screamed, 'Germany awake! Death to the Jews!' and every-body clinked their beer mugs and stamped their feet.

'I'm bursting,' said Moritz.

'You'll never get through just now,' said Weber. 'Piss on the floor. Nobody'll notice.'

As he left, jerking like a marionette, the Austrian swept

the room with his gaze, right and left – no doubt it was meant to look serious and grim, or perhaps resolute. With every step, a turn of the head. People were yelling; those who ran out ahead of him fussed around to clear a path for him. The turner and a few others behind him were smiling: how about that then, we've got a right lad here, eh?

'Bravo, Austrian!' shouted Weber as he passed. 'Remember me?'

But the Austrian merely stared, with his pale blue eyes, just over Weber's head. Afterwards, Weber and Moritz left to round off the evening in a brothel in the Landsberger Strasse.

*

'Ah, Herr Kammerlander, yes – and little Bautzerl, yes, Bautzerl, there's a good fellow, eh? Good boy! Well, Herr Kammerlander, how are you these days?'

'Good of you to ask, Herr Dirrigl, how is anyone these days? Miserable. Money's worth less with every day that passes.'

'It just can't go on like this, Herr Kammerlander, you mark my words.'

'Exactly my feelings – now don't pull, Bautzerl, sit, nicely. That's it – yes, exactly my feelings. It just can't go on like this. But the question is, how *is* it going to go on?'

'That's exactly the big question. Good boy, Wamperl, clever boy – do nice big dos, then. Good dog.'

'It just won't do, I tell you. In the long run, it won't do. The Divine Order has been disrupted. And do you know what I suspect? I was talking the other day to Herr Pflaum, a very high-ranking civil servant and one of my tenants; he has, how shall I put it, certain inside knowledge, by dint of his office, if you take my meaning. And Herr *Oberregierungsrat* Pflaum expressed the view that it was not right.'

'What wasn't right?'

'That the King, or if you like, His Majesty – you understand, not that you should for a moment take me for one of those Social Democrats, you know me too well for that, Herr

Dirrigl – but it *wasn't* right of the King, you know, in 1913.'

'I still don't see what you're driving at.'

'King Otto, of blessed memory –'

'A half-wit, or if you prefer, mentally deranged.'

'Well, yes. I suppose so, Herr Dirrigl, I suppose that's so. But the King, nevertheless. The Divine Order, Herr Dirrigl, the dynasty going back a thousand years, I repeat – don't pull on your lead so, Bautzerl! – I repeat, a *thousand* years. What nation can boast of something like that? Precisely. And, even if he was, hmm, well, not *quite*, et cetera, the King nevertheless. And the Prince Regent, that is, the Prince Luitpold, the Prince Regent –'

'God rest his soul!' Herr Dirrigl stressed every word.

'– he never even achieved that status. He was Prince Regent. Otto was *King*. But then, when he died in 1912 –'

'Not seven years since, and yet it seems like an eternity.'

'– then the new Prince Regent, Ludwig, the son, started right away with his plotting and scheming and before 1913 was out he had ousted his cousin from the throne, Otto, who couldn't defend himself. That wasn't right, I tell you. And unnecessary, what's more, for in 1916 Otto died anyway and Prince Regent Ludwig would have become King as a matter of course. Automatically. *And* legally! But that he should have forced his cousin off the throne – now there he committed a sin. And all that followed, the collapse, the King's flight, the Republic – Herr *Oberregierungsrat* Pflaum reckons, and he does have certain inside knowledge, as I said, he reckons it's a punishment from heaven.'

'Maybe the King should go on a pilgrimage to Altötting? D'you think? And do penance?'

'That might possibly be a solution.'

'A solution towards the re-establishment of the Divine Order?'

'Possibly.'

'Although other solutions do come to mind. As a tax payer, you understand, one does have one's views on the outrageous sums that these exalted rulers drew as allowances. Not that you should think for a minute that I'm turning Social Demo –'

'Ah, Herr Weber, good evening, Herr Weber —'

'E'nin'.'

. . .

'He's had a few more than he can manage.'

'And his fly's open.'

'Probably it's his night off, our bouncer friend.'

'Funny. Somebody that works in a pub and can't find anything better to do on his night off than get plastered in another bar.'

'Well, yes. But you can understand it in a way. All week he works in a bar, then he's bound to feel the urge to be a customer on his day off.'

'He could be a bit more polite in his greeting.'

'That's for sure. But — there you are, the Divine Order has been overthrown. The decline of values.'

'And what other possibilities do you see?'

'Well, Bürkel, the old primary headteacher, another of my tenants, he talks of the *national* one.'

'I see. Aha. The national one. And what's that?'

'Without Jews.'

'I understand. Come here, Wamperl — heel! Well, Herr Kammerlander, I think we'll have to be moving on. If I'm not altogether mistaken, there's snow in the air.'

*

By way of an addendum to the *Military connections*: the unit with which the said Weber, Christian, served was in fact one of the two squadrons of *Jäger zu Pferd*, or Mounted Rifles, which were stationed in Munich and attached to the 1st Heavy Regiment of Horse, 'Prinz Karl von Bayern'. Blue uniforms with silver buttons.

Information of a contrary nature: a local newspaper, the *Würmtal-Bote*, of 26 August 1938, celebrated Christian Weber's fifty-fifth birthday with a two-column article (with photograph): '*ϟϟ-Brigadeführer*' (newspaper and book printers had to have an extra character made, the ϟϟ, the runic symbol, if they wanted to reproduce 'SS' correctly, the way that gang wanted it; and it even turned up on some typewriters – you can imagine who used these), well then, 'Christian Weber, ⚡⚡ Brigade-Leader, President of the District Council, alderman, the *Führer*'s indefatigable comrade-in-arms.'

According to the report, Weber had attended the Primary and Vocational School in Polsingen and then gone on to study Agriculture. He was then supposed to have served as a volunteer with the Mounted Rifle Squadron in Nuremberg and to have gone into battle with the 8th Field Artillery Regiment in 1914, not returning home until January 1919, and being decorated on numerous occasions. And all that with only the one eye. 'Lest I be amazed, I refuse to believe it,' the writer Roda Roda used to say in such cases.

Curiously enough, Police Headquarters in Munich were so disrespectful as to add the cutting with the article from the aforementioned *Würmtal Courier* to the 'Pers. File: Christian Weber', ref. no. II/Pr V Wa. Obviously – and with some justification – they were extremely wary of such miscreants.

On 24 October 1921, Emil Maurice, 'single, watch-maker, b. 17.1.1897 in Westermoor', was arrested for the attempted assassination of the (Social Democratic) Member of the Regional Parliament, Erhard Auer. About his person they found 'among other items a list of the individual members of the Munich Group of the Storm Troopers of the NSDAP'. Included in the list was Christian Weber, Westermühlstrasse 23/11; *Occupation:* orderly.

*

In 1921, 24 October fell on a Thursday. At the corner of the Kost-Tor and Maximilianstrasse, two figures were hanging about, one thin and one fat. Across the street, over there under the arches of the entrance to the *Vier Jahreszeiten* Hotel, stood a group, some four in number, who were chased away by the porter at around a quarter to eight.

'Hey, you lot! This isn't a public shelter!'

'But it's raining.'

'This isn't a shelter for any old rubbish! Right?'

'I'll give you old rubbish in a minute –'

But another one gave a low whistle, hissed something, and the four men made off out into the rain.

Shortly afterwards, the Social Democrat Member of Parliament Erhard Auer emerged from the *Torggelstuben*, where a meeting of the party executive had been taking place, and, heading in the direction of Maximilianstrasse, crossed the little square with the Red Riding Hood Fountain and stepped out into the well-lit street. He paid no heed to the two figures, the thin one and the fat one.

In fact, Erhard Auer had intended taking the No. 4 tram to the Max-Weber-Platz, where he had a flat. In those days the square did not yet bear that name, indeed had no name at all, it was simply the junction of the Äussere Maxstrasse and the Äussere Wiener Strasse; Max Weber, who died in June 1920, had not been dead long enough for a square to be named after him. So Auer waited for a few minutes at the stop near the approaches to the Kost Gate, but when no tram appeared, Auer decided – unfortunately for him – to continue on foot, despite the rain, perhaps not the whole way but at least as far as the Max Monument. The meeting had been a long one, so Auer quite welcomed the chance to stretch his legs a bit. In the little park in front of the Museum of Ethnology, Auer heard a shot. At first he felt nothing and turned in alarm. The assassination of Erzberger (on 26 August of that year) flashed through his mind. Then he felt a sharp pain in the area of his right hip, which soon, with increasing speed, radiated out through his whole body. It all happened very quickly, yet, in Auer's consciousness, it seemed to spread out over a very long period, over an eternity. As he turned, Auer saw two figures, one thin and one fat, disappearing behind the round, cast-iron public convenience at the corner of the Museum of Ethnology, obviously diving for cover. Apart from them, Auer was aware of four men running diagonally across the Maximilianstrasse and then into the narrow Kanalstrasse. (In those days this Canal Street also continued north of the Maximilianstrasse up to the Army Museum.) Exactly how he fell, Auer had no idea. He simply realised – almost with a kind of bafflement

– that he was no longer on his feet but lying in the wet grass, and it was only then that the connection between the shot and his wound established itself in his mind. Shortly after that, he lost consciousness and came to – he had no idea how long afterwards – with a policeman bending over him and asking:

'Are you ill, or are you drunk?'

Auer replied: 'My name is Auer, I am a Member of the Regional Parliament. I have been . . .' then he passed out again. Auer's wound turned out not to be critical. Two weeks later he was fit enough to be discharged from hospital. At the forceful instigation of the Social Democratic group in the *Landtag*, the State Prosecutor's office reopened proceedings three days after the assassination attempt, the police having already suspended the preliminary investigation as a lost cause. The prosecutor in charge of investigations – a young man just out of training, Winkler by name – ascertained from closer examination of the files that eye-witness testimonies from passers-by were available. One of these passers-by had recognised in the thin figure a man whom he had often seen in the *Häfele* coffee shop on the Reitmorstrasse in the company of a party political orator called Hüdler. Hüdler had caught his eye at the time because he put away absolutely incredible quantities of cake and whipped cream. From photographs he had been shown, he picked out the watchmaker Emil Maurice (despite his name, not a Frenchman but a German), who was subsequently arrested on 29 October.

At first, Emil Maurice denied everything, but when he was brought face to face with the witness, who identified him unequivocally, he did admit to having been in the area at the time of the crime, but claimed that that was pure coincidence. He certainly had not fired a shot. This, incidentally, tallied with the witness' observation testifying that 'the fat man' had done the shooting. However, the witness said he had been unable to see the 'fat man' clearly, as he had been crouching in the shadow of the public convenience.

In Maurice's case, the police were dealing with a known member of the so-called '*Sturmabteilung*', or Storm Troop, of a right-wing splinter party, which had come to their attention on several occasions through their involvement in brawls and riots. They found in Maurice's possession a pocket diary containing a list of further members of this *Sturmabteilung*, complete with details of names and addresses. Further screening revealed that the fattest of all the listed *Sturmabteilung* bully-boys turned out to be a certain Christian Weber, born 25.8.1883 in Polsingen, single, horse dealer by trade. This latter was arrested on 30 October in his (new) flat in Westermühlstrasse 23, second floor left, and taken to Police Headquarters.

What struck the police most forcibly about Weber was the way he acted as if he was the policeman and the police officers the prisoners, passing 'Lotzbeck No. 2' cigarettes to all and sundry from a cigarette case embellished with a swastika in inlaid mother-of-pearl.

Weber denied everything and produced his alibi: on 24 October at eight in the evening he was at a friend's house, a girlfriend, Frau Rosa Pfandl, who lived in the Landsberger Strasse.

The prosecutor leafed through the files relating to Weber, Christian.

On 18 January 1919, a firearms certificate for a double-barrelled shotgun and a hunting rifle had been issued to this Weber, who declared himself to be the owner of a 'horse-hire business'. Weber was the holder of hunting permit No. 1399/1919.

The constable standing before the prosecutor said, 'In the case of Pfandl, Rosa, Herr *Staatsanwalt*, she's a . . . you know.'

'She's a what?'

'Well, I mean, one of *those*.'

'Would you kindly express yourself clearly.'

'She's a prostitute.'

'I see,' said *Assessor* Winkler, the prosecutor.

'Yes, it's just, I mean, one like, hm, one of those will give you anything for money. Probably even an alibi, if I might be allowed the observation.'

'An alibi is an alibi,' said *Assessor* Winkler, and Weber

was released. It was eight o'clock in the evening. On his way home from Police Headquarters to the Westermühlstrasse, he looked in at the *Hundskugel* bar and ate two pairs of hot sausages with jam.

*

'Greetings, Herr Dirrigl.'

'Ah, Herr Kammerlander, I almost didn't recognise you.'

'Yes,' said Herr Kammerlander with a short laugh, 'you have to wrap up like a mummy this cold weather.'

'It's never been like this in human memory, end of October and such a bitch of a cold spell already.'

'I don't know. For my part, I wouldn't exactly have called it a *bitch* of a cold. Would we now, Bautzerl? Rather a stupid expression, I find. If you don't mind my saying so. I'm sure your dear little Wamperl wouldn't like it either if you were to, as it were, describe it in terms of his, ah, mother.'

'Yes – er –'

'Don't misunderstand me. I don't mean it personally.'

'No, no – well, in a way, yes. We often say things like that without thinking. But I think we'd better – in here, there's a table free in the corner, I see. Just to get inside out of the cold. Come on, Wamperl, do quick wees, then Daddy'll take you into the nice café.'

Inside. It is warm, the two gentlemen have taken off their thick fur-lined overcoats. Herr Kammerlander orders a portion of coffee with whipped cream, Herr Dirrigl a tea with rum.

'Yes, just slipped out, without thinking. One of these figures of speech, you know.'

'Yes, yes, Herr Dirrigl. These things happen. I'm not immune to them myself.'

'What I really meant was a *swine* of a cold. Begging your pardon.'

'Even a *swine* is, if one wishes to be precise, not quite right either. A swine isn't cold.'

'Except when you eat it as cold roast pork.'

'Well, yes. – But even *cold* roast pork isn't as cold as all

18

that. It still has to be . . . well, it still has to be, you know, at a certain temperature, I mean, not frozen. I can remember, in 1917, my mother-in-law, she's from Vilsbiburg, well, she brought a piece of pork. A rarity in those days –'

'Yes, I'll say!'

'– and, by a stupid coincidence, my wife's sister was there too. She, just between ourselves, married beneath her station. A humble cleric in Burghausen. Ah well, never mind. Anyway, we didn't want – I suppose that's not altogether true, but just think, in '17, the fourth year of the war – we didn't want . . . I mean, my mother-in-law hadn't brought the pork for the minor priest and his family, it would have been far too fatty for them anyway. I enjoy fat, by the way, supposed to be good for you. Well, as long as the visitors were there, we had to stow it away in the loft. Well wrapped up, of course, and locked in a box. None the less, it froze. Rock-hard, I'm telling you. Once the visitors had finally left and my wife brought the pork back down – frozen solid. Of course, I was appalled, as you can imagine. I was afraid all the fat would evaporate as it thawed, or whatever. I'm not very well up on the laws of physics. So, we put the pork out on the cold balcony – it was as cold then as it is now, well, just about – out on to the balcony, so that it wouldn't thaw, and then, very carefully, so that the neighbours wouldn't notice – well of course, it had been slaughtered on the quiet, illicitly, I can admit it nowadays, all these years afterwards – we cut slices off it and ate them frozen. Horrible, I'm telling you. Disgusting. And we were sick afterwards.'

'Interesting.'

'So you see, a *swine* of a cold isn't really accurate either.'

'Yes. Hmm. So what should we say, then?'

'I've often wondered about that.'

'Devilish cold . . . ?'

'No good, no good. Devil – hell – fire – that really fits something hot. After all, we say "hot as hell".'

'Yes, you're right again there.'

'I have, as I've said, racked my brains over it many a time. I like pondering, you know. I'd suggest, a *Jew* of a cold.'

'A Jew of a cold?'

'Well, yes. The Jewish race is cold, if anything, isn't it?'

'Well, not really – rather more oriental, so, warm? Palestine, and so on?'

'Oh, now, come come. Most Jews come from Galicia, Poland, Russia. What's it like there? Cold. Blizzards, frozen taiga. And besides, the cold-hearted nature of the Jews.'

'Hmm. Well, yes, I suppose so. If you look at it like that, Herr Kammerlander. And yet – now I don't mean to contradict you – all the same, I have a lodger, on the third floor, Zwirnberg his name is, Solomon, a bookkeeper, now he's the quietest person in the whole house, and the only one that has never been behind with his rent.'

'Would you – if I may ask, Herr Dirrigl – would you like to be a Jew?'

'*Me?* What gives you that idea?'

'Exactly. No respectable person, certainly not in our circle of acquaintances, and I'm sure yours is no different, nobody would want to be a Jew, given the option. Now there's food for thought. You see, I'm very fond of musing to myself, when I'm resting on the sofa of an afternoon mainly, and then I often picture to myself: what would it be like, Kammerlander, if you were, say, an Egyptian pasha. One of those hookah things in your mouth, you know, and a fountain in the garden, with palm trees –'

'Heh, heh! And a few scantily dressed obe – odelis – oda –'

'Obelisks. Well, yes – all clean and above-board, of course. No smutty stuff – I'm too old for that. But anyway, well, why not, after all it's very warm in Egypt, not a bitch of a cold like –'

'A *Jew* of a cold, Herr Kammerlander!'

'Yes. There you are, see, it's happened to me, too. Ha ha. Good for you, putting me right on that. Well anyway, very warm, and the ladies don't need much more than a kind of veil thing – hmm, yes. That's the sort of picture I conjure up. Or I imagine I'm an English lord. In his club. Very superior, very *soigné*. You know what I mean. And the butler comes and asks, "You rang, milord? Whisky or gin?" Ah, yes. Or maybe an Indian chief. Having all my lodgers that are behind with their rent scalped. Or again, sometimes I even imagine I'm a Chinaman.'

'You don't say.'

'Oh yes. Even that has its good sides.'

'Your face completely yellow?'

'Well, I don't imagine things in all *that* detail. More sort of, well, a mandarin, you know? And a few saucy Chinese dancing-girls prancing around me, that kind of thing. Before the war, I once saw some of them at the beer festival, in a side show. But, Herr Dirrigl, what I'm saying is, never, *never* do I imagine myself as a Jew. That's quite out of the question. That would never enter my head. I would think, Herr Dirrigl, *I* would think nobody would ever fancy being a Jew.'

'I suppose the Jews themselves would.'

'No, and that's precisely the point. Even the Jews themselves don't like being Jews. They just have to. Because they are. No choice in the matter. But to *want* to be . . . ?'

'Well, yes, I suppose so, if you look at it that way. Understandable, too.'

'Exactly. And that really makes you think. Waiter, the bill. No, allow me, Herr Dirrigl.'

'No, out of the question. Let *me* . . .'

'No! No, waiter, put that on my bill, please.'

'Well really, Herr Kammerlander, you embarrass me. But it'll be my turn next time.'

The waiter says, 'Altogether, that'll be sixty billion, four hundred million and two hundred and eighty thousand.'

'There you are – call it sixty-one billion and keep the change.'

*

On 4 November 1921, a meeting of Hitlerites is broken up by supporters of the 'Majority Socialist Party'. The Hitlerites, although in the majority, are badly beaten up. Hitler himself is dealt a hefty kick in the shins and several cuffs about the head as he seeks the security of the ladies' lavatory. These are to be (unfortunately) the last instances of physical abuse he is to suffer in his political career.

The Public Prosecutor's officials and the police dutifully attempt to trace the 'thugs and trouble makers'. Investigations are in the hands of Criminal Investigation Department VI/a. In charge of the case is Detective Sergeant Bamesreiter. Herr Weber, horse trader and newspaper reporter, calls upon Detective Sergeant Bamesreiter in his office. In an immaculate SA (i.e. Storm Trooper) uniform. Offers his services as a witness, identifies several MSP members as 'thugs and trouble makers'. Those identified by Weber are arrested and beaten up. 'As a precaution,' says Detective Sergeant Bamesreiter, 'just in case they were acquitted in court.' After closing the case, Detective Sergeant Bamesreiter receives a personally autographed photograph of the Party leader Hitler in a beaten-silver frame. Detective Sergeant Bamesreiter goes to his superior officer, Chief Constable Sucheck, taking the photograph with him, and enquires as to whether it is permitted for him to accept this gift. (Correct down to his toenails, this Bamesreiter.)

'Hm, silver . . . not very heavy, that's true, but silver. With hallmarks. Hmhm. Strictly speaking,' Chief Constable Sucheck turns the picture over and over, peers at it through his pince-nez, 'well, all right. This is something different again. I can't think of any real objection to you keeping it.'

On 22 March 1922, the businessman Otto Karl Jahn, single, born in Weissenstadt in the district of Wunsiedel on 18 July 1903 – a very young businessman, in fact, just nineteen years old – is in court on suspicion of politically subversive activities. On checking his personal particulars, it is discovered that he is on the wanted list for both the Reich in general and for Saxony in particular on charges of 'embezzlement, among other things'.

Among Jahn's possessions – he is, by the way, not to be confused with the later Nazi journalist Hans Edgar Jahn, who after 1945 so adeptly turned his coat – among Jahn's possessions was found a membership card for an 'Oberland League', which at that time had not yet achieved notoriety. 'This is to certify the membership of Herr O. Jahn in Moosinning, 25.1.22.' Photograph (or 'light-picture' as it soon became known under the 'purification' of the language), rubber-stamp and signature: '*Weber, Christian. Upper Bavaria-Tyrol-Vienna Regional Headquarters.*'

The petty criminal, adolescent (in terms of the criminal code relating to minors) and alleged businessman Jahn declared in a statement relating to the *Bund Oberland*:

'We pursue three aims: 1. Rejection of the class struggle, unification of all working classes on a national basis. 2. Unconditional maintenance of the integrity of the Reich and opposition to all separatists and wreckers of the Reich. 3. Smashing the Versailles Treaty, enlightenment of the people by word of mouth and in print.'

Small fry, a nobody, really. 'And what's somebody like him supposed to have embezzled, I wonder,' was Detective Sergeant Bamesreiter's assessment.

The regional headquarters of the *Bund Oberland* were situated in Glückstrasse 9, second floor. The heads of the regional office: Christian Weber and a certain Schüssler, no further details. There was also a (higher or lower grade?) district office under the direction of a major with the strange name of Horadam.

It is as certain as can be that Weber belonged to the illegal militia, the so-called '*Schwarze Reichswehr*'.

On 22 August 1922, Christian Weber applies for a fire-arms licence for a pistol. The application is approved the very same day – amazing how quickly these things can go through. An observation, noted in high-flown language by Detective Inspector Dirscherl: 'Herr Weber is a reputable citizen and improper use of the weapon by him is therefore not anticipated.'

No. 11/6/42

FIREARMS CERTIFICATE

Herr

(the sections printed in italics are pre-printed in the certificate, the rest entered in handwriting)

Herr Christian Weber

Occupation Businessman

(sounds so much better than horse hirer or horse trader. Especially when even that young upstart Jahn claims to be a businessman.)

date of birth 25.8.83
place of birth Polsingen
Address Aventinstrasse 5/1 (right)

(so, he's moved again. Perhaps the Aventinstrasse is quieter than the Westermühlstrasse.)

is permitted to own and carry
the undernoted firearm and the appropriate ammunition:
1 Pistol
./.

Munich, 22 August 1922

POLICE HEADQUARTERS
pp Dirscherl

On the facing page

valid until 22 August 1923
Fee 23 marks
Fees Record No. F 107 78/22

In the top half is a photograph; this bears two POLICE HEADQUARTERS, MUNICH official stamps and, diagonally across it, a signature: '*Christian Weber*'.

Description of the photograph: what kind of character is this? A head as broad as it is long. The hair shaven up to well above the ears. Flattened down on top. You can just picture him, spitting forcefully on his palms and then slapping it on to this omelette of a hair-do. Hardly any eyebrows. The left eye is the glass one. Very little space between nose and mouth, and there, a brush, not much of it, but still more luxuriant than that of his bosom pal Adolf, and, most important, firmly swept from the middle out to the sides. The jowls hang down over the high collar. Striped shirt, rough woollen informal jacket (a *Joppe?*), patterned tie. Only in the enlargement is the white dot on the tie identifiable as a tie pin in the shape of a swastika.

*

'With jam, I said,' bellowed Weber.

The waitress in the *Spöckmaier* shook her head and left. The four others at the table – Maurice, Jahn, Schüssler and one they called the Stutterer – were eating roast pork or cold cuts or some other normal thing. Only Weber ate hot sausages with jam. Perfectly ordinary hot sausages (*Wieners* or *Regensburgers*), only instead of with mustard, with jam. 'Dunno who's got any objections to that? Who says you have to eat *mustard* with sausages? *I* like jam with them.' At least he drank beer with them.

'D'you put sugar in your beer too, then?' asked Jahn.

'Arsehole! Shut your face,' said Weber.

They left the *Spöckmaier*. It was 5 September 1922, a Tuesday. Weber was carrying – legally, as we've seen – his newly acquired pistol in the waistband of his trousers.

'You'd be better with a holster,' said Maurice, 'I mean, well, just stuck in your trousers . . . I don't know. If it goes off, you'll shoot yourself in the balls.'

'Arsehole! Shut your face,' said Weber.

Opposite the *Spöckmaier* was a small jeweller's shop. An elderly man in a grey dust coat and a young man, or rather an adolescent, in short trousers and braces, were busy with a razor, scraping an apparently stubbornly adhesive piece of paper, about half the size of a newspaper, off the shop window. The old man was scratching with the blade, the youngster wiping down with a sponge. DAVID HESS was the name above the shop front.

'Hold on a minute,' said Weber. He crossed the Rosental and went and stood, fists on his hips, in front of the shop. 'What are you doing?' he yelled.

'Is that any business of yours?' asked David Hess.

'The notice'll stay where it is!' hissed Weber.

'This, for your information, is *my* shop,' said Hess.

On the notice, still legible, was the legend proclaiming Germany's awakening, and death to the Jews: DEUTSCHLAND ERWACHE! JUDA VERECKE!

Hess obviously wanted to avoid trouble. He bowed slightly and said, '*Verrecke* should be spelt with two Rs. If it's supposed to be German. If you don't mind.'

Weber took one step forward, drew in his belly, then let it out sharply to propel David Hess backwards. Maurice and the others in the background laughed. Then everything happened very quickly: the youth grabbed his sponge and hurled it in Weber's face, Weber spluttered, the four others ran forward, the youth fled into the shop, the old man shouted, 'Police! Help!', Weber drew his pistol, a shot rang out, the shop window disintegrated, Hess lay on the ground, Jahn was bleeding from the back of a hand and squealing like a stuck pig, Hess was gripping the razor desperately. A policeman came running from the Marienplatz and separated the two parties – although one of them by now consisted only of David Hess.

'He attacked us with that razor,' Weber said.

'And who fired the shot?' asked the policeman.

'It was self-defence,' said Weber. 'Here's my gun licence.'

The policeman took down particulars. 'Well,' he said finally, 'I suppose, since only damage to property and –' he had a look at Jahn's wound '– minor injuries are involved, I suppose it's a matter for the civil court. I must now ask you to move along.'

Weber and the other four headed off in the direction of the Jakobsplatz. Once they were out of sight, Weber shoved his fist under Maurice's nose. 'Guess what I've got here?'

'No idea,' said Maurice.

Weber opened his fist: a ring.

'The Yid didn't even notice.'

'Out of his shop window?' Maurice laughed.

'Had a price ticket for seven hundred billion on it,' said Weber, slipping the ring into the breast pocket of his diarrhoea-coloured SA shirt.

*

'*Every* day, Herr Dirrigl,' said Kammerlander. 'It's getting so that you can hardly go out on the streets any more.'

'The best policy is, see no evil and hear no evil.'

'Certainly. But it can't go on like this.'

'What we need is a strong hand that will establish law and order.'

'How right you are, Herr Dirrigl! But where is it to come from?'

'I don't quite follow you, Herr Kammerlander, what do you mean by "where from"?'

'All these Socialists and Communists, the whole lot of them are out of the question. We don't want conditions like those in Russia. As property owners we have to reject that sort of thing as a matter of course. So they just don't come into it. The Centre, perhaps? Don't make me laugh. The Democratic Movement, Herr Dirrigl, let me tell you – the so-called Democrats are living proof of the old saying that too many cooks spoil the broth. No, no, Herr Dirrigl, with the Democrats, we'd be in a terrible state. Ha ha! Did you get the play on words?'

'No.'

Herr Kammerlander repeated it with deliberation. 'With the Democrats we'd be in a terrible *state*. See it? I didn't catch it at first either, but Bürkel, the teacher, my lodger, explained it to me. There's a double meaning hidden in there. I'm not sure how I should explain it to you.'

'Aha.'

'Anyway, it doesn't matter. Herr Bürkel could . . .'

'What about the *Bayrische Volkspartei*? The *People's* Party, after all.'

'Much too tied up with the Church. Have to pay too much heed to the Vatican's feelings. No, no, we can't look for a strong hand from that direction. We need a strong hand that'll come along and clear up the mess and protect – you see my point – protect property and the old, traditional values.'

'I couldn't agree more, Herr Kammerlander.'

'Yes, well, something along those lines. But now you must excuse me. I have to be off to my regular early-evening drinks round in the *Franziskaner*. My respects, Herr Dirrigl.'

'My respects, Herr Kammerlander.'

*

On 12 June 1922, the Reich President, Ebert, visited Munich. He spent the time from seven-thirty in the evening until shortly after midnight in the Old City Hall, at a banquet in his honour. During the President's arrival and departure, some thirty police officers were on duty under the arches in front of the *Rathaus*. A sizeable crowd of workers (presumably Socialists and trades unionists) set up three cheers for the *Reichspräsident* (around eleven o'clock), whereupon a student, standing at the corner of Marienplatz and Dienerstrasse (next to the old-established gentlemen's outfitters J. G. Meyer's), burst out in provocative laughter. The student was – for his own protection – sent home by the police.

About half an hour later, a 'nineteen-year-old trainee' (could this perhaps have been Otto Karl Jahn?), standing on the same corner, shouted disparaging remarks about the *Reichspräsident*. Out of the midst of the workers, the cry went up, 'Get that bastard! Kill him!' and a few workers armed with sticks made a threatening move towards the trainee. (This was how a police officer reported the incident to the prosecution in No. 1 District Court, Munich.) 'The police rescued the young man in the face of threatening behaviour by the workers.'

Among the workers were two trades-union secretaries, Ruf and Dichtl. They were approached by a youngish, fat man claiming to be a newspaper reporter and declaring he knew, from reliable sources, that the Reich President 'was receiving personal bribes in gold from the Soviet government in Russia', that he was having an affair with his secretary and, in addition, that he had syphilis. Shortly after, the same fat man approached the said union secretaries again, claiming to be a plain-clothes police officer, but without producing any identification. Dichtl reported this to one of the uniformed police officers, who immediately established the particulars of the alleged plain-clothes detective: Weber, Christian.

Dichtl told the policeman: 'What annoyed me most was the fact that this fat slob thought my memory wouldn't take me from twelve o'clock till noon and that I wouldn't recognise him as the same one who told me ten minutes earlier he was a reporter.'

Enquiries relating to impersonation of an official were

dropped. Weber denied everything, it was a case of one man's word against another's. (Thus the police report. They regarded the testimony of the witness Dichtl and that of the accused Weber as being of equal validity.)

The proceedings on the grounds of disrespectful whistling ('at the Reich President') were dropped on 12 December 1922. The misdemeanour under §360 Section 8 of the Criminal Code had lapsed under the statute of limitations, the relevant complaint, which had to be lodged by the Reich President for a crime of insulting behaviour to be punished, not having been brought.

*

It was the last time Wolf came to the Aventinstrasse, to Christian Weber's flat. (He came unannounced, as usual. Since he was, anyway, one of these people who were always late wherever they went, a man who was prone to go slow, in the manner of a watch, it would have been altogether pointless for him to have given advance notice. No one has yet carried out any research into what kind of deep, psycho-motor correlation exists between this 'going slow' and a weakness for sweet things. All that has been established is that people who are habitually late are always nibbling. So it was with Wolf, as is well known.)

In earlier days, Wolf had often come to Christian's place, this untidy, slovenly bachelor dwelling in which empty schnapps bottles, plates encrusted with dried-up remnants of food and ripped-open packets of contraceptives lay littered among single, hole-riddled socks. This never bothered Wolf. (In his own place in the Thierschstrasse, the scene was no different.) The more Napoleonic or even Messianic Wolf imagined himself, the more people cheered and acclaimed him, the bigger the Party grew, the fewer and farther between these visits had become. Even old friends ('old comrades-in-arms') like 'that mucky little pig Christian' were summoned by Wolf to Party headquarters if he wished to speak to them, or – a distinction in itself – to the Carlton Tea-Rooms in the Brienner Strasse, where the proprietress always kept a table with four armchairs, right at the back, reserved.

So, Christian was surprised at Wolf's arrival. Wolf had not been known as 'Wolf' for very long. Frau Bruckmann had invented, if that is the right term, the name. Frau Bruckmann, the publisher's wife. Frau Bruckmann was a famous Brünnhilde of the salons with an overwhelming bosom and size ten in shoes. She had taken Wolf – or Adolf as he still was – to her heart, firstly giving him money and secondly aiming to cure him of a few habits which she regarded as bad breeding: whenever Wolf (Adolf) arrived, late as usual, at the lady Bruckmann's musical soirées – at the piano, Putzi Hanfstaengl would already be purring his way through 'Waldweben' or 'Feuerzauber' or thundering out 'Isoldes Liebestod' – and hung his floppy hat and dog whip on a hook in the hall among the fashionable Borsalinos and silk-lapelled overcoats, Frau Bruckmann found that unrefined. Even the vulgar name Adolf struck her as unrefined, but worst of all was the unsightly smudge of moustache under his nose.

In the matter of the dog whip, Frau Bruckmann had some success: Adolf (soon Wolf) put it aside, only seldom taking it up again, and then not when in, as it were, a bourgeois environment, and, on Frau Bruckmann's recommendation, Wolf was allowed to order, and remain owing for, bespoke suits from Lotz & Leussmann on the Promenadenplatz. 'Wolf', Frau Bruckmann insisted, was the Germanic original form of Adolf – Wolf, the wild one, the loner, the dangerous one, roving through the steppe with a bold gleam in his eye. 'The leader of the wolf-pack through the steppe and into the other realm of true life . . .' (Heidegger). That struck a chord with Wolf. But the sub-nasal brush, now that was something he would not be talked out of. Frau Bruckmann tried everything, even had a large portrait photograph of Wolf retouched to show him *sans* moustache:

'Wolf, my dear, look,' she said, 'now that really sets off your steely eye to advantage.'

'No,' said Wolf.

'People all look at your ridiculous moustache, not into your eyes.'

'No,' said Wolf.

'Why not? What in all the world can that little moustache mean to you?'

'No,' said Wolf, almost in a whimper. No one ever managed to get any more out of him on the subject. (Only once, after 9 November 1923, on the run from the police, did Wolf shave off his little blotch in a fit of panic and in the belief that, by doing so, he would render himself incognito. That was in the home of Erna Hanfstaengl, Putzi's sister, in Uffing. When he was nevertheless arrested, he immediately let his mini-brush grow again.) Christian, too, had been to Frau Bruckmann's salon with Wolf. He didn't feel at ease there. Putzi's tinkling bored him, and the measures in which the drinks were served were too small for his liking. After Christian – in all innocence, as it were – had given one of the Bruckmanns' maids a slap on the backside, absolutely without evil intent, more just out of habit, Frau Bruckmann had been so appalled that she had requested Wolf never to bring 'that common doorman fellow' with him again. Christian was, if anything, relieved.

As we were saying, then, suits from Lotz & Leussmann, no dog whip any more, and 'Wolf'. 'For you, too,' Wolf told Christian categorically, 'I am, as of now, no longer Adolf, but *Wolf*.' In any case there were very few, even in the closest circles around Wolf, who were allowed to be on first-name terms. Christian was one of those few. 'The old Comrade-in-Arms.'

'Wolf – what are you doing here?' said Christian, as he opened the door.

Wolf came in, threw himself into an armchair and stared in front of him.

'What's up, then? What's the face for? You going to a funeral? – Want a beer?'

'An advocaat,' said Wolf lugubriously.

Christian went over to a small kitchen cupboard, its door already open, searched around, found nothing, went out, rummaged about, still in vain, but finally came back with a bottle containing a cloudy yellowish liquid, spat into two glasses, wiped them out with his handkerchief and poured. A thick liquor glopped like great dollops of snot into the glasses.

31

'Prost,' said Christian. 'Now then, what's up?'

'It's all over,' said Wolf.

After the murder of Walther Rathenau in June 1922, some provincial governments (among them Prussia, Baden and Thuringia) were – at long last – prepared to ban the Nazi parties and gangs of thugs. Bavaria could not make up its mind. For the fact that they remained unimpeded in Bavaria, the Hitlerites had to thank two men, Chief of Police Ernst Pöhner and the leader – since 1919 – of the *Abteilung politische Polizei,* or Political Police Department, Dr Wilhelm Frick, a native of Alsenz in the Palatinate, who not only covertly sympathised with the NSDAP like his boss, Pöhner, but was even formally a member. Many years later, on 29 March 1942, Wolf made reference (in his Lair, the *Wolfsschanze*), during his customary sanctimonious evening pratings, to both Pöhner and Frick. But for Frick, said Wolf – of the man whom he took the opportunity to promote retrospectively to the rank of Deputy Chief of Police – but for Frick at that time, he, Wolf, 'would never have got out of the nick'. The Devil had already claimed Pöhner in 1925. Frick became one of the first Nazis to take a seat in the Reichstag, in 1930 the first Nazi minister and in 1933 the Reich Interior Minister, but rather fell from Hitler's grace around the beginning of the war and became the 'Reich Protector of Bohemia and Moravia'. In 1946 he was quite rightly strung up.

There are some fine pictures of this Frick, in fact there are fine pictures of all the National Socialist figures. Faith and Beauty. But all those tiring parades! Mostly, or at least very often, these upstanding figures were photographed reviewing parades. Parading itself, that's no hardship; you just move along and stamp past, present arms or shovel or whatever, and then off for an early snifter. But reviewing a parade, now that takes hours. The 'German Salute', mechanically very awkward, arm like a lever and so on, you can't keep your arm outstretched horizontally for very long at a time. (Maybe it was a mistake to have the swastika armband worn on the left arm. Perhaps they should have ordered it to be worn to the right, on the right arm, the saluting arm, the

German Saluting arm, perhaps that would have given the many, many German Saluters the strength to Salute Germanly for much longer, that is, to extend the right arm horizontally. Perhaps then we – *we?* – might have won the war. Might have been allowed to Salute Germanly today.) Anyway, no one can manage to hold the arm stretched out horizontally for very long at a time. And you were not allowed to alternate, now the right arm, now the left . . . far from it!; only the right arm could be extended. The right arm is German, the left arm is un-German. Certain tricks were permissible: an artificial arm made of wood and inside, under the brown coat, an auxiliary mechanism, with the real arm concealed, but reasonably comfortable, under the jacket. (The way beggars so cleverly feign an amputation.) So, for hours on end, the arm would stand out, like a ramrod. And on the end, a glove. There was only one snag. The Nazi-Teuton involved had to march down from the rostrum at the end with this arm still steeply erected.

As for the Big Chief himself, *der grösste Feldherr aller Zeiten (der 'Gröfaz')* – the Greatest leader of all time (the 'Gloat') – well he, of course, chickened out again. He invented a round-arm version of the German Salute; he didn't stretch his arm straight out, but first slightly upwards, then farther and farther upwards, and upwards/backwards and, bent, arched, in a semicircle above his head – in this way the awkward lever effect was smoothed out. He always stood there looking like a waiter balancing a tray above his head – without the tray, of course.

And often they would simply stand around up there. Sports events always last a long time. Why do all totalitarian regimes have such an affinity for sport? (Because, experience tells us, sport stultifies, and such regimes welcome the turning of people into zombies? Or is it that sport and the resultant mindlessness are what really produce that substratum of the people necessary for dictatorships?) Be that as it may, sports events last an age. For hours on end, hurdles are hurdled or something of the sort. And then there are the marches into and out of the stadium, with flags waving. Why has sport such an affinity for flags? Food for thought there, surely.

33

But nobody does think about it. Folk who go in for sport don't think. Dictators value that highly. It is regarded as particularly indelicate to stick your hands in your trouser pockets during the reviewing of parades or the march-past or -in or -out of sports-club flags. That is to say, it's all right if you are in civvies, that creates a kind of English effect, which of course is also Germanic. But not in uniform. Putting your hands in your trouser pockets when in uniform is almost as bad as carrying an umbrella while in uniform. (One exception: the mess situation, officers carousing, unbuttoned tunics, champagne and ladies in net stockings . . . then, fine – for the hands in pockets, not for the umbrella, which is in any case redundant on such an occasion.) Back to our sporting march-pasts, which go on for hours: we have seen that no one can maintain a German Salute for that long, and hands in uniform trouser pockets is out. So what to do with the hands? Out of this was born the strange phenomenon whereby Nazi top brass always stood with their hands crossed in front of their private parts and were photographed in this pose. (Strange that no one has ever noticed this. As if they were wanting to keep a firm hold of their John Thomases. Beware of pickpockets!) And even the said Herr Frick (Dr Frick – what could his thesis have been about? He did his doctorate at Heidelberg), even Herr Frick is to be seen in such pictures. There's one, with *Gauleiter* Adolf Wagner and the Reich Head of Sport, Herr Hans von Tschammer und Osten. Here, Tschammer is in civvies, Frick and Wagner in uniform, studiously steeling the bored stare, keeping a firm grip on the family jewels – the Flower of the Aryans.

Pöhner and Frick suppressed – a clear abuse of power, a punishable offence, in fact – charges against Nazi bully-boys, let them off with a warning at most and, on the occasions when they had no choice but to let the police take a hand, so as not to raise suspicion, they did it too late or sent them to the wrong place.

'Well then, Wolf,' said Weber, 'what's up with you?'

'I'm Austrian,' Wolf said gloomily.

'Yes. So what?'

'Read this.' Wolf pushed a letter across to Weber. The letter bore the traces of Wolf's violent temper. It had obviously already been crumpled up, and then smoothed out again. It was a communication from the Ministry of the Interior: in the interests of public safety and public order it had been deemed necessary to deport Herr Hitler, Adolf, born in Braunau, Upper Austria, on 20.4.1889, single, writer, Austrian citizen, as an 'undesirable alien'. 'The above-named is granted the right to lodge an appeal against this decision in writing within two days, to be presented, in triplicate, to a responsible officer of the Ministry of the Interior.'

'Undesirable alien!' snorted Wolf.

'Well, now you've got it in writing,' Weber laughed. 'You enjoy being undesirable to them, our Fulfilment politicians.'

'I don't find that at all funny.'

'Sorry. You don't have to smash your glass on the floor, though.' With a grunt, Weber bent down but, fearing he might cut himself on the splinters, abandoned the task of clearing up the broken glass and simply pushed the whole mess under the sofa with his foot. At least Wolf had drained the advocaat before hurling the glass to the floor.

'And what about Frick? And Pöhner?'

'It's outside their authority. Been to them already. It's nothing to do with the police, only the ministry.'

'I'll come with you,' said Weber, slapping Wolf on the back.

'What would you do in Austria?'

'Not to Austria. To the Ministry of the Interior.'

Minister of the Interior Schweyer received Hitler and Weber in his sumptuous office on the Odeonsplatz. Naturally, both gentlemen – in so far as the term applies here – had donned civilian clothes, discreet suits. And no dog whip. They hardly had to wait any time at all in the ante-room.

'A good sign,' whispered Weber, 'we're *somebody*,' as the usher flung open the double doors and said, 'The minister will see you now.'

The tone was almost cordial. The minister stepped out from behind his desk and gestured towards some chairs round a coffee table. 'Coffee? A cigar?' Weber helped himself, quickly:

fat cigars, high-quality imports. Hitler didn't, not even then. Both accepted coffee. The minister watched, fascinated, how many lumps of sugar Hitler added. Four, five, six, seven . . . 'Does that still taste of coffee, Herr Hitler?'

Then they got down to the business in hand. 'Of course, this is not directed against you personally, Herr Hitler. We are aware that your, how shall I put it, your patriotic convictions are irreproachable.'

Hitler bowed humbly.

'It's just your people,' sighed the minister. 'That is to say,' he added hastily, 'a section of your people, *some* of your people. They do create such a dreadful disturbance.'

'They're only youngsters, Herr Minister,' said Weber, puffing at his cigar, 'difficult to keep under control. Just get carried away sometimes.'

'Well indeed,' said the minister, 'if that were all it was. I, as a politician of Catholic Christian-Democrat persuasion, I myself have no excessive sympathy for . . . for certain sections of the population, for certain . . . of foreign origin . . . ahem. If some son of Moses ends up with a few bruises now and again . . . well then. Only, Herr Hitler, the things that you preach. You know, that positively smacks of revolution.'

'It is a "folkish", a *nationalist* revolution, Herr Minister,' said Hitler.

'Revolution is revolution,' said the minister.

'Suppose we called it,' said Weber, '*National Regeneration*.'

'Now that has a quite different ring to it,' said the minister. 'If you promise me not to start any revolution, not to carry out a *putsch*, then you'll be left in peace.'

'On my word of honour,' said Hitler.

'No *putsch*?' said the minister.

'No *putsch*,' said Hitler. His eyes misted over with solemnity. 'No *putsch*. My word of honour as a German front-line soldier.'

The minister stood up. Hitler, too, sprang to his feet. Weber had rather more of a struggle. The armchair was a deep one. The minister held out a hand towards Hitler: 'Your word of honour?' Hitler grasped the ministerial hand in both of his: 'My word of honour.'

The minister breathed in deeply and sat down again. 'I take it you have no objections to a small brandy?'

'None at all!' said Weber.

The word of honour was superfluous. In the *Landtag*, Erhard Auer, the Chairman of the Social Democrats in the house, rose and stated that it would be incompatible with the fundamental principles of Social Democracy to approve such police-state measures as the expulsion of all foreigners.

He of all people.

*

'You're looking too much on the black side, Herr Blumenthal.'

'Black, Herr Peschmowitz, black wouldn't bother me one bit, or only a little. No, it's *brown* that I see everywhere.'

'Signs of the times, unfortunate aberrations, Herr Blumenthal. Just let us get inflation out of the way, let people have something decent to eat again, let a few years pass, for them to forget about the war, and then they'll come to their senses again. A whole nation, my dear Herr Blumenthal, a whole German nation cannot in the long run descend into feeble-mindedness. A whole German nation can't simply forget that it produced a Goethe and a Beethoven.'

'Goethe, Herr Peschmowitz, is dead, God rest his soul, and Beethoven too, but, against that, this Hüdlinger, or whatever he's called, I can't remember the name, he's alive.'

'They're all beating each other up. Think of what happened in Coburg. Maybe his own crowd will do him in.'

'May God grant you are right.'

'We, Herr Blumenthal, you and I, have served in the trenches like so many others. We, too, were front-line soldiers. I make a point of always wearing, there it is, you see, my Iron Cross – First Class! Awarded *most personally* by His Royal Highness, the Crown Prince Rupprecht. Now, I ask you!'

'For all that, you're still a Jew.'

'A *German* Jew, Herr Blumenthal. You shouldn't look so much on the black side.'

'*Brown*, Herr Peschmowitz, *brown*.'

*

Weber is not merely interested in horses; he has a penchant for means of transport in general. The phenomenon of the automobile begins to fascinate him. Around the turn of the year 1922/23, he submits an application for a driving licence. He undertakes the required driving lessons and sits an examination on theory, whereupon, in the spring of 1923, the driving licence is issued to him.

Discipline and organisation. Führer command, we will follow.

The Führer commanded: come to Erding. March 24, 1923. Christian Weber, holder, of some days' standing, of a permit to drive an automobile, drove the lorry. Thirty bold Teutons (in SA uniform) sat on the loading platform, holding grimly on to the sides; among them was the Teuton Fritz Petzold. Next to Weber sat the ex-officer Klintzsch. Their mission: maintenance of order in the hall at Erding.

Along the Inner and the Outer Wiener Strasse, heading out of town, all goes well. At the junction of Zamdorfer Strasse with Truderinger Strasse, there is some dubiety regarding the direction to be followed. Some of them shout 'Right!', others 'Left!' Weber, who is in any case out of his depth with the difficult steering on the lorry, apparently attempts to turn left and right simultaneously. The vehicle goes into a skid, clatters full-tilt over a kerb, there's a fearful fanfare of grinding metal, but then Weber succeeds in bringing the lorry under control and continuing straight ahead, along the Zamdorfer Strasse. Major Klintzsch looks around. If he hadn't been wearing his SA cap, his hair would be standing on end: the lorry is still there all right, but not the loading platform. It has detached itself and now lies, complete with its load of SA men, farther back in the roadway.

Among the splintered boards of the platform, moaning and cursing men were rolling and writhing about. A passer-by, an elderly man with a shopping basket full of parsnips, who himself had come within an ace of being struck dead by the flying platform, added his own imprecations. 'Stupid bugger! Driving like that – should have his arse kicked!' Storm Trooper Fritz Petzold informed Police Constable Kaspar Völk, who immediately came running to the scene, that the injured men had been attacked by Communists.

The injured (there were ten of them) were first taken to an adjacent hostelry, the Old Shooting Range in the Zamdorfer Strasse, for rough and ready patching up, then to the hospital on the right bank of the Isar. (One broken collar-bone, one fractured pelvis, several head injuries, cuts and contusions, one badly bruised abdomen, two as yet undiagnosed injuries. Fritz Petzold: fracture of both kneecaps.)

On 27 February 1934, a 'Law on Providing for the Fighters for the National Uprising' was enacted. Fighter Petzold brought along his two broken kneecaps from that occasion and the then Chairman of the NSDAP group in the Munich City Council, Weber, as witnesses to the effect that the said broken kneecaps were the result of a combat mission. Weber corroborated the theory that the only explanation could have been an act of sabotage, the bolts holding the loading platform on the lorry must have been loosened, and, in addition, that the SA men, injured and thus unable to defend themselves, had been set upon by a Communist horde.

Greater success was achieved a little later by an action carried out by the 'Fighters for the National Kneecaps', namely on 1 May 1923, the traditional holiday of the Labour Movement. Ten years later, the Nazis had the barefaced effrontery to appropriate even this holiday for their own cause, as the Day of German Labour. What is *German* labour? Naturally, not every piece of work that is accomplished on German territory (i.e. German Soil) comes under this heading. If a Jew in, say, Bad Tölz or in Mellrichstadt or anywhere in the German Reich turns out a piece of work, in so far as whatever a Yid potters about at can be in any way categorised as work, then that, it goes without saying, is in no way German. Later on, the Yids certainly did work, but more in Dachau or Theresienstadt or Treblinka. ARBEIT MACHT FREI stood over the gates at the entrance to Auschwitz. Even in the case of this labour, although it had a liberating effect, it could not be termed German labour, since it was done by foreign hands. The Yids did passive work, too. Stoking ovens. Well, being stoked . . . Conversion of Yids into energy. Haha. The *active* stoking, now that, the actual *inserting* of the Yids into the ovens, was really strenuous, they didn't go in voluntarily, they had got a sniff of what was cooking...haha...what was cooking, very good that, yes, I will have another Doornkaat, thank you, yes . . . well, the *insertion* of the Yids, that was labour in itself and, it goes without saying, as such, it was by contrast German labour. The comparative form of 'German Labour' is 'German Craftsmanship'. Zyklon B, for instance, made by Höchst. German craftsmanship. Or, of course, the V1 and V2. Oh yes, yes indeed. German labour, which is celebrated on the Day of German Labour, is any work that . . . now that's another thing: not every piece of work done by a German, a *fellow* German, a *Volksgenosse,* anywhere in the world, is automatically German labour. There are fellow Germans and fellow Germans; unfortunately. So, if a German in New York is in the regrettable position of having to sweep out the banking hall of the Yid & Co. Bank, then it follows that that is not German labour.

Is there also, let's say, French Labour? English Labour? Luxembourg Labour? Or, on the other hand, North German and South German Labour? 'Day of Middle Franconian Labour'. Nonsense. From the Maas to the Memel, from the Adige to the Belt (what in fact is that – the Belt? And where is it?), only one Germany, and so only One German Labour.

Only, as we were saying, what is it?

'To be German is to do a thing for its own sake.' So Richard Wagner is supposed to have said. A saying that makes you think a bit, but doesn't lead you to any conclusion. Is German labour a piece of work that is done for its own sake? If the office messenger Lammerschnee in Winsen an der Luhe fetches a liver sausage for his boss from the nearby village inn, he doesn't do so because the office boss is hungry or because the office messenger is duty bound to comply with the orders of the office boss, or even because the office messenger is an office messenger since he has to make a living and feed his wife and pure-blooded children; no, it is for its, the liver sausage's, own sake. The Liver Sausage *per se.* That's very German. And here we have come to the nub of the matter.

Day of German Labour. But not yet, not in 1923; for the time being it is still 'Labour Day'.

On 1 May 1923, a May Day celebration organised by the SPD took place on the Theresienwiese. After the fair had closed, a group of sixty (other reports put it at eighty) workers from the building firm of Dyckerhoff & Widmann set off in a body towards Schwabing. The group took along a red flag, a few banners and a drum. It cannot be discounted that this group of workers intended prolonging the festivities in a pub or a beer garden, perhaps Aumeister's. Presumably the landlord would have had no objections. May Day celebrations, at which a good deal of shouting goes on, are good for working up a thirst, and it's a well-known fact that there's nothing wrong with money, not even when it comes out of red purses.

Unfortunately for the Socialists, a column of SA men (2,000 – no, that is no misprint: not two hundred, but, in words, two thousand) was on its way at the same time from the Oberwiesenfeld, where, also simultaneously, a nationalist, a *völkisch* May Day celebration had been taking place. (Wolf had been hollering about 'from the Adige to the Belt' – belting it out?) They were heading for the city centre, also (it can be assumed without making any insinuations) with a beer garden, or several beer gardens, as their specific destination. No single beer garden would have that many free seats on a mild May evening, so the SA lads in their natty uniforms would have had to split up among, say, the *Augustiner Keller*, the *Löwenbräu Keller*, the *Hirschgarten* and so on.

At the junction of Hiltenspergerstrasse and Elisabethstrasse, the small group of two thousand SA lads came up against the overwhelmingly superior force of sixty (or even eighty!) beasts of the Red Front. Far from being inclined to turn tail and run, the old comrades (with Christian Weber in their midst) fell upon the reds, destroying the red flag, shredding the banners – and Christian Weber hopped on to the drum, which burst with a loud bang. That a few of the reds made off with black eyes goes without saying. The good old days of struggle. A man was still a man then. And wasn't that some bang when the drum burst! That evening, Christian

41

Weber also paid a visit to a certain Burschmann, Frieda, in the Pippinger Strasse. He brought her a ring.

The SA's roll of honour has many other notable entries besides. What are we saying, entries? Inscriptions, deeply engraved with the hard stylus of National Regeneration: 10 March 1923 – punch-up in Eichstätt; 27 March 1923 – ditto in Ingolstadt . . . and some tremendous solo efforts as well. Thus, on 7 December 1922, a certain Abraham Mysliborski, who had given vent in the Café Plendl to derogatory comments on the Nationalist Movement, was put under surveillance and, as he, in the company of a lady (what kind of a *lady* would keep company with his sort? Just wait till it's *our* turn, then anyone that tags along with a Jew we'll . . . we'll what? . . . Oh, we'll think of something appropriate), as he left the establishment in the company of a lady, the shameful nature of his conduct was pointed out to him, verbally in the first instance, as it were with refined, *völkisch* restraint. 'There's that bastard Jewish swine from the Café Plendl!' bawled Weber. But the Jewish swine Mysliborski had the brass neck to call a uniformed policeman, who immediately whistled up a second, and – you wouldn't believe it unless you'd seen it with your own eyes – all three of them, the two policemen and the Jew (with the female behind him, squawking and menacingly swinging her handbag) rushed upon the Nationalists, of whom there were only eight . . . well, in a word, the Nationalists just managed to break out of this encirclement and make off in the direction of the main station. As they did so, Weber, the wild man, got in a blow with his stick across the Jew Mysliborski's shins.

On the following day, 8 December, Mysliborski filed a complaint. In it, he claimed that three of the assailants were well known and could be easily traced, for they were frequent visitors to the Café Plendl. One of them was – claimed to be – a horse dealer. As a result, the police did – nothing.

*

'The honorary chairman of our Party –'
    Bravo! Hurrah!

'– Anton Drexler –' (Aha, our 'Mr Turner'!)
Bravo, bravo!
'– is today unfortunately unable to give his address as advertised, because yesterday he was beaten up by Marxist-plutocratic elements –' dramatic pause – 'with iron bars and –' longer dramatic pause – 'thrown out of his place of work!'
Storm of outrage.
'He is lying at home, badly injured and confined to bed.'
Hurricane of indignation.
'Since the authorities have to date taken no steps to combat this outrageous terrorism, there is nothing left but for us to take matters into our own hands. If things go on like this in Munich, then the patience of the National Socialists can be measured only in hours.'
Resounding applause.
'Despite the whining of the moral cowards, I give notice, and I'll repeat it a thousand times if necessary, that anyone who so much as attempts to carry out the High Court's warrant for the arrest of our Party Leader –'
Thunderous applause.
'– Adolf Hitler, had better bring their own coffin along with them.'
Sustained applause.
The horse trader stepped down from the rostrum. *Deutschland, Deutschland über alles.* The SA band (in *Oberländer* costume, strangely enough, not in SA uniform) is regarded, even according to opinions emanating from the Social Democratic side (summarised in a report on preliminary investigations carried out by the investigating judge in the High Court in respect of a case relating to 'Destruction of the Reich flag on the Bahnhofsplatz during the night of 13/14 May 1922'), as the 'best music corps in Munich'. Honour where honour is due, at least in musical terms. The horse dealer shakes hands all round. Then Wolf rises and makes his way up to the lectern. A breathless hush. Wolf looks all around. His steely eyes fix in a steady gaze.
'Bow-wow!'

Frenzied applause.
Circus *Krone*, 28 April 1923.

*

'Ah, Sophie, it's yourself.'
  'Hello there, Frieda.'
  'I think there's one coming.'
  'He's just passing.'
  'How can you tell?'
  'Take a look at his shoes. Anybody that wears shoes like that has no money for this sort of thing.'
  . . .
  'Hey, sweetie, how d'you fancy a while with us?'
  . . .
  'Told you, didn't I. He's not stopping.'
  'To think it's only November, and here we are, freezing our arses off.'
  . . .
  'How much do you charge these days, Sophie?'
  'Naked, or just in a doorway?'
  'Naked, for an hour, say.'
  'If there's no extras, twenty billion.'
  'Uh-huh.'
  'If you get one that pays in thousand-notes, you can hardly carry all the paper about.'
  'High time we had a sensible currency again. Especially for us.'
  'Karli – you know, my pimp – well, he says when this Hüttinger takes over, then we'll get a proper currency again.'
  'Who?'
  'Hüttinger, he's called, or something like that. Karli is sort of a pal of his.'
  'Hüttinger?'
  'Yes. Him that's always shouting the odds about the Jews.'
  'Oh, him. But his name's not Hüttinger. He's called Rittler.'
  'Well then, Rittler.'
  'Shittler! That's his name, Shittler. He's supposed to be a great speaker. And a loud one.'
  'Yes. Anyway, my Karli's his friend. Supports him, too.

44

Hee-hee. On what I earn! And when Hüttinger comes to power, then my Karli'll be a minister.'

'Don't talk a load of rubbish.'

'It's true. My Karli's even a member of that party of his. Psst. Come here. Now this is a secret. It won't be long now.'

'Till *your* ponce becomes a minister? Don't make me laugh.'

'I'm telling you. And then there'll be a hard currency. Gold marks and that. And the Jews'll have to get out.'

'All of them?'

'All of them.'

'I see. But why all of them?'

'Got a soft spot for the Jews, have you?'

'Arthur's a very nice customer indeed, that's all I can say. Practically a regular. Really treats you like a human being.'

'Arthur?'

'Arthur.'

'Is he a Jew?'

'Let's face it, in our line, we'd be the first to notice, don't you think? Hee-hee.'

'My Karli says, when I'm with a Jew, I've got to grit my teeth, choke down my disgust and double the price. But soon . . .'

'Sh!'

. . .

'Well, what can we do for you, young sir? A threesome if you like? How about a . . .'

. . .

'It's just too cold.'

'You'd almost think their peckers had seized up with this cold.'

'Well, my arse is frozen.'

'Haven't you got warm knickers on?'

'Are you crazy? If a client saw them, he'd lose the notion, quick as you like.'

'But this mate of Karli's . . .'

'Hee-hee. And you think you're maybe going to be Frau Minister? Will you stay on the game?'

'Oh, there'll be no more of that. 'Cause prostitution's going to be done away with, see? It's unworthy of German womanhood. So my Karli says.'

'What!?'

'That's what Karli says.'

'Is that supposed to mean that only these foreign tarts, that are already a pain in the neck anyway, like that nigger-woman over there, that dirty bitch . . .'

'Foreigners'll have no business here at all. Least of all darkies.'

'Prostitution banned?'

'Yes.'

'Can they really do that?'

'A clean sweep, that's what Hüttlinger, Karli's mate, says. Jews, homos, gypsies, the whole issue. All going to be done away with.'

'Does this Hüttlinger never have it off? So what does he do? Or how?'

'C'm'ere. Just between you and me. Karli now, he's in the know about this, seeing as how he's, you might say, a close friend of this Hüttler. This Hüttler bloke . . . come closer . . . Hüttler doesn't have two balls. Hee-hee. Only got one egg in the basket. That's why he's shy.'

'Like that, is he?'

'But a fiery speaker, though.'

'He'll never come to anything.'

'You'll remember it was me that told you. Soon. Soon!'

'What d'you mean, "soon"?'

'In a few days. They're going on a march. From the Bürger-bräu to the Ministry of the Interior, and then . . . You'll see.'

'Yes, well. We'll wait and see. I'm off home. Nothing doing today. Not in this cold. I'd rather get a thumping from Konrad for bringing in nothing than stand around here any longer freezing my fanny off.'

'What's he do when he wallops you if you make nothing?'

'I've to strip to the buff, he ties my hands to the bed, and then I get my backside slapped.'

'Well, my Karli, when he gives me a thrashing, he uses his SA belt.'

46

'I'd think that'd be a lot worse.'

'It's all right. It only gets nasty when he gives me a kicking and still has his boots on.'

'I'm off.'

'Good night.'

'Hey, Sophie . . .'

'Yes?'

'Prostitution banned? And what'll happen to us? And my Konrad?'

'Pimps'll be put in the workhouse. With all the queers and gypsies. You'll be taken care of.'

'Konrad in the workhouse?'

'Yes.'

'And your Karli a minister?'

'Yes.'

'That'll be the day.'

*

Munich, 28 June 1923.

To
Police Headquarters
Ettstrasse
Munich

Ref.: Request for Approval for Issue of a Shotgun Licence.

> I, the undersigned, Christian Weber, bachelor, business-man, born 25.8.83 in Polsingen, Administrative District of Gunzenhausen, nationality Bavarian, resident at Aventinstrasse 5/1 (right), here in Munich, hereby request the distinguished Police Headquarters to approve the issue of a shot-gun licence.

Reasons: My political position will already be familiar enough to the respected police as to render further details superfluous, the justification for my request seems sufficiently imperative, secondly my many journeys as a motorist, thirdly my hunting rights lies in

47

the Berchtesgaden province (Hochlenz district), which is very heavily visited by pouchers [*sic*].

My hitherto gun-licence was withdrawn last autumn, because proceedings were pending against me which I was however acquitted by the court on account of I had been actually threatened by a very large crowd of people.

I beg of the respected police a speedy processing of this my petition.

The letter, typed this far, is signed in his own hand by

Christian Weber

The mode of expression, the wayward punctuation, the logic of the phraseology, bearing eloquent testimony to the utmost exertion, prove that this document is indeed a personal concoction from the hand of the bachelor and businessman Weber. What is more, it was turned down flat by Police Headquarters, by order, 10 July 1923. To meet the costs of processing this negative decision, a fee of five hundred marks was levied, a ridiculous amount for which you couldn't buy so much as a breakfast roll, but one that Weber did not pay anyway.

(Where did Weber, Christian, bouncer and groom, get the money to rent hunting preserves? Grounds that were 'very heavily visited by pouchers'? Were these poachers perhaps Jews? Very probably. No doubt these Jewish 'pouchers', their crooked noses camouflaged with lampblack, went around shooting up the groom's hinds and stags all over the shoot in the Hochlenz District that the man had had to scrimp and save for. And very likely on the Sabbath, too. Just you wait, if I catch one of you at it, I'll let the rabbi know all about it.)

Rejected, then.

Doesn't matter.

As far as bearing arms is concerned, the National Socialist, Engl, is on record (ref. VI d. No. 1166/1223/1226/23) as declaring that the only protection of the right of assembly that was needed was the appearance in closed ranks of a considerable body of National Socialists in armbands and steel helmets. Weapons were not necessary . . .

At a later date, some weapons did in fact become a necessity. '*Am deutschen Wesen soll die Welt genesen.*' Ho yes: 'The essence of the German nation shall lead the world to its salvation.' Today Germany belongs to us, tomorrow the whole world. Originally, that had had a somewhat different ring to it: 'Today Germany listens to us, tomorrow, the whole world.' That sounds almost as if it could be the chorus from the short-wave hams' club song, has a rather arrogant ring to it, lays it on a bit thick, but on the whole quite harmless, really. (The opening lines of the song run: 'The brittle bones of all the world/Tremble at the glorious triumph's approach.') That, too, could be applied to the short-wave enthusiasts. The volume turned up too high. Granny's bones, long since crumbling, already two fractured hips behind her, next time, although nobody's to know that yet, pneumonia on top of that, and after that young Gerhardi can at last set up his amateur short-wave transmitter and receiver set in the newly vacated attic bedroom, then Granny's brittle bones will tremble no more, even Dad's and Mum's, no longer as supple as they used to be, will be spared . . . Later on, though, Gerhardi will have to dismantle his set, because the Führer doesn't hold with that sort of thing any more – well, to be precise, he does indeed set considerable store by the fact that the whole world can hear him and the brittle bones tremble as a result, the bones, for example of Churchill and Roosevelt and Stalin and all Jews and plutocrats, but he doesn't go much on Gerhardi hearing what the outside world has to say. Is the Führer afraid that Gerhardi's knees would knock then? If Gerhardi were to venture so far as to go on operating his set and to tune in to what, for instance, Radio Beromünster, the Swiss Broadcasting Corporation, was putting out in the way of hate-oozing Jewish tirades to the effect that – to take an example purely at random – in April 1943, out of the eighteen thousand tons of supplies that the kind, devoted Führer was having transported by sea from Italy to Tunisia, a good fifteen thousand tons had been sunk by Allied ships and that of the 2,500 reinforcements, some two thousand had died a hero's death by the simple expedient of drowning and that the Afrika Corps had all of sixty-nine tanks at its disposal as against the Allies' two thousand-plus and that the German supply network was quite simply in a bloody awful state of chaos and that the world was still very far removed from saving itself by the German example, then perhaps Gerhardi's knees would have been knocking, but at that time little Gerhardi was not in any position to indulge in such nonsense as short-wave hamming, for little Gerhardi had by then become a – let's say – lance-corporal in some company or other of some regiment or other of some division or other of the Central Army group in the Kuban bridge-head, and the bones of Lance-Corporal Gerhard Müller, one-time amateur radio enthusiast, were indeed trembling on account of the increasingly adjacent impacts of shells from the Russian heavy artillery and, when one such round fired off by the plutocratic-Communist-Jewish world conspiracy landed directly in his dugout, his bones were no longer trembling but flying in tiny morsels through the mild May air, '. . . steadfast in his faith in final victory, in unswerving loyalty to Führer and Fatherland', as the batallion commander, as usual from a safe distance behind the line, wrote as a matter of well-worn routine to father and mother Müller, '. . . enclosed please find the posthumously awarded Iron Cross, Class II', well, then the parents' brittle bones would be trembling, and perhaps father Müller, who by now is no longer quite so convinced, in his heart of hearts, about Final Victory, Führer and Fatherland and might even be regretting having put his cross on the voting paper against that jagged brand mark with the letters NSDAP alongside it in 1933, perhaps father Müller now goes upstairs to where little Gerhardi's amateur radio set lies gathering dust, and he actually succeeds in getting it going again, and now he hears what the world outside is saying and that Churchill's knees aren't knocking at all . . . 'Leave that alone,' says Mama Müller, 'you know the penalty for . . .' But the embittered Papa Müller doesn't leave it alone and, as ill-luck will have it, enter their neighbour, let's call him just at random Hannes Burger, a good citizen, always a pleasant 'Hello' from him, member of the NSKK, the National Socialist Corps of Drivers, well, he finds out about it and, shortly afterwards, two gentlemen in long leather coats knock at Herr Müller's door. Then Herr Müller's knees are knocking all right. But not for long. When the letter arrives, in which Frau Müller is requested to stump up the 106.25 Reichsmarks, being the fee for the enforcement of the imposed sentence, and failure to pay would mean the body cannot be released for burial, then Mama Müller's bones are trembling. Yet the world still doesn't belong to us.

So, later on, the carrying of arms was indeed necessary to a certain extent since, for some unfathomable reason, the world was not ready and willing to be cured by the German medicine. So these rotten bones would just have to be made to tremble. Manners would have to be taught. You'll see if they don't. We'll show you what's what. 'Today Germany belongs to us, and tomorrow the whole world.' What do we really want with the whole world? With Anatolia, the Kola Peninsula, with Persia, Tasmania, Tierra del Fuego, the Pescadores Islands . . . with the whole, entire world, if all over it there live only cretins with brittle bones? Or will all these bones be processed into soap? Will we possess only an empty world? Without bones? Newly resettled? Germans everywhere? 'Anybody here volunteering for the Fiji Islands?' 'Me, Herr *Ortsgruppenleiter*, sir!' Nothing but Teutons any-where. Even in the Australian outback and on Greenland's ice, nothing but blond hair and blue eyes. The entire world one vast ruin. Sorry, rune. The victory rune. Swastika. The world is saved by the German example. Beethoven's Ninth, '*Freude, schöner Götterfunke*', will be heard only with '*Die Fahne hoch*', the Horst Wessel Song, as a counterpoint.

But in 1923, not even Germany belonged to them. All that belonged to Herr bachelor and businessman Christian Weber from Polsingen was the hunting ground in the Hochlenz District, and even that was 'heavily visited by pouchers'.

*

'What day is it today? Friday? Yes. Take a billion and go down to Frau Pieger's and fetch – fetch, hold on a minute, for me, four dark crispy rolls, two pairs of wieners – do we still have enough jam there? Right – no, let's say three pairs of wieners, some brawn sausage, a slice, about as thick as my thumb, and a dozen eggs. While you're doing that, I'll put the water on to boil for the coffee. I don't fancy any beer at the moment, the stink of stale beer all night – just now the sight of a beer would more than likely turn my stomach. You'd better take two billion, over there, in the drawer. But don't think, you bandit, that I don't know there's exactly sixteen billion in that drawer. Take two billion, and get something for yourself.'

The fat man shouted all this through the bathroom door. Schelshorn opened the drawer, counted the money: sure enough, sixteen billion in hundred-thousand-million notes. Schelshorn took out two billion, stuffed them into the pocket of his grey jacket that still reeked of stale smoke, and left.

The fat man came out of the bathroom stark naked, hopped shivering across to the sideboard, pulled out the drawer, checked the money, muttered to himself and hopped back again. 'Bathroom' is hardly an accurate description. It was a little room next to the kitchen with no windows except for one small barred one looking on to the staircase. The entire pane had been rendered opaque with a smear of dark green oil paint. At one place the paint had flaked off, a spot about half the size of the palm of one's hand. The fat man scratched his backside as he peered through it. Schelshorn pulled his broad, floppy cap down over his eyes and stumbled off down the stairs. The stairwell was still in deep gloom, with the wan light of a murky November day barely spilling in through the stair window. A few dry snowflakes reeled about. 'You don't start a revolution on a day like this,' grumbled Fatso, 'a revolution's something you do in summer, when it's warm and people are out on the streets anyway and the beer gardens are full.'

In the 'bathroom' there was indeed a zinc bath, a so-called hip-bath, but not for hips like Weber's. He washed – what he would have called washing – in a washbowl mounted on a spindly trestle. A crack like thunder – Weber had farted; the single loose pane in the green-painted window responded with a gentle rattle. Weber gave an 'Ahh . . .' of relief. He liked to savour his own stench. Then he peed into the wash-hand basin, scratched his testicles. A slight erection. 'Down, boy,' murmured Weber, 'nothing doing today. Today's for the revolution. Who knows, though, maybe tomorrow you'll get a peek at a Berlin whore.'

'A revolution,' said Weber later to Schelshorn as they sat at breakfast in the kitchen-cum-living-room, 'now no sensible person has a revolution at this time of year. Put the light on. I can't even see my brawn sausage.' He spread jam over the slice of sausage.

Schelshorn got up, switched on the light and sat down again.

The coffee was steaming.

'How much change did you get out of that?'

Schelshorn laid a few thousand million on the table.

'Aha. If I hadn't asked, you'd have kept it, you crook.'

'Sorry, Herr Weber, I just forgot.'

While Schelshorn had been making the coffee, Weber had shaved and dressed. After a brief moment's reflection, he had put the SA uniform back on its hanger (it, too, stank of beer and smoke) and had put on civilian clothes, knee-breeches and a checked shirt, and a brownish-grey pullover, but not forgetting to stick the swastika pin in his tie.

'Sensible folk have their revolution in summer. But you just can't tell Hitler anything. Had a bit of a set-to with him last night. Looks on himself as Reich Chancellor already. The half-wit. Just because he fired a shot into the ceiling and the old biddies in their furs got so worked up they either cheered him or passed out. *That's* no way to run a revolution. I gave him a piece of my mind and no mistake. That Göring passed responsibility for the transport fleet on to some Lieutenant Rossbach, he did. The authority for the vehicles that are under *my* command. That's a year now I've been making sure these old crates have been kept in running order and been greased and fuelled, and then along comes this pickled Prussian, just because he was an airman in the war, and passes on "the authority" to some lieutenant or other. "Adolf!" I said – I know he doesn't like it at all when somebody calls him "Adolf". He doesn't even like anybody being so familiar as to call him *du*. But, I ask you, if I've slung somebody out

through the pub doorway, even in the friendliest way, I'm
not going to address him politely as *Sie*, am I? And then
"Adolf" really niggles him. Wants to be called "Wolf". But
I deliberately said "Adolf! Is this supposed to mean that . . . ?!
Or what? If so, then I refuse to have any responsibility in
future for the transport pool!" "To you," he snorted, "I'm
still Herr *Reichskanzler*." "What d'you mean, *still*?" says I
with a laugh, "you've only been Reich Chancellor for an
hour, and who knows how long that'll last, what with all this
muddle." "I will not tolerate . . . !" he started to shout, but I
shouted even louder, "Reich Chancellor of the Bürgerbräu!"
That was when Göring wanted to shove his oar in, but I just
drew in my belly, let it whip out again and it shunted old
Göring away like a billiard ball and then I drew the Herr
Reichskanzler aside and whispered, "Iron Cross! I. C. One!"
That cut him down to size.'

'How's that?' Schelshorn asked.

'Never you mind. Anyway, it put a stop to his shouting;
he just gave a hoarse wheeze, "What are you bothering about
a few measly vehicles for! When tomorrow you'll be Reich
Minister for Transport in Berlin!" "Aha!" says I, "very nice.
That's a different tune. Minister for Transport. And with a
racing stable, eh? I know of four of them here already, Jewish
ones that could be expropriated." "This isn't the time to go
into details!" says he. Understandable enough, too, I suppose.
"I won't forget an old comrade-in-arms!" he whispered. That's
one of the nice things about him. Well anyway. I just picked
up my beer mug and left him. But – I'm not so sure about
Berlin. Although they say there are some interesting pubs
there. And et cetera. All the same . . . *This* isn't the way
to run a revolution. You have revolutions in summer, when
the beer gardens are full. It's got to be planned. Centrally.
A warm summer's day. People are thirsty. When they've had
enough to drink, then all the bands in all the beer gardens
should strike up, at a given signal from the people at the
centre, the "Bavarian Parade March". Then, all at once, out
with all the swastika flags. In every beer garden somebody
– again, centrally planned – somebody jumps up on to a
table. Ta-ra! "And now," the bloke concerned has to shout,

"we're going to march on the Odeonsplatz. Anything you see in Jewish shop windows is yours. Tomorrow the glaziers will have their hands full, and besides, tomorrow the Weimar Republic will be over. Law and order. *Deutschland erwache! Juda verrecke!*" Or something of that sort. All centrally planned and carried out. Get them going! Then, let me tell you, then you'd see something. *Then* you'd have a revolution. And first off, the mint has to be occupied. That comes first, stands to reason. *That's* the way to run a revolution.

'But today – in *this* weather.'

Weber stood up.

'Right then. Just leave everything where it is. I'm off to the Cornelius Strasse, to the Party offices. You'll go and get the others together. What time is it now? Half-past nine. We'll meet at ten, let's say at the Isartor. On the dot. In civvies, mind! Just to be on the safe side. But with swastika armbands. You can't be too sure.'

Shortly after ten, a small procession moved off from the Isar Gate, heading towards the Ludwig Bridge, some half-dozen of them, with Weber at their head, in his trench coat, with the collar turned up. It was drizzling, with snow mixed through it. From a few houses, swastika flags were flying, or rather, they hung damply against the house fronts. Although it was a weekday, most of the shops were closed. On the Ludwigsbrücke stood a row of empty trams. The drivers and conductors hung about, shivering, rubbing their hands for warmth. A large number of policemen, standing in groups in doorways. The Isar flowed sluggishly, icy-green. Not a sound to be heard. Only from a distance, coming down from the Bürgerbräu *Keller*: the music of a brass band. The '*Badenweiler* March'.

A police officer stood in the group's path.

'Where to?'

'To wet our whistles,' said Weber. 'Morning drinkies.'

'With swastika armbands?'

'Beg pardon, we forgot. Armbands off!' commanded Weber.

The police officer, on seeing the men comply, became friendlier. 'Well, well,' he said, 'swastika fans, are we?'

'Not exactly,' said Weber. 'We just put them on . . . because you never know. We're reporters.'

'Are you now,' the policeman said.

'So what's the situation . . . ? Schelshorn,' Weber looked round, 'write down what the officer tells us.'

'What? Me? Write?'

'Shut up,' said Schuhladen, a tall, goitrous character.

'There's not much to write about, really,' said the policeman, 'nobody has a bloody clue what's going on.'

'Is there a revolution or isn't there?'

'Nobody knows. As far as we're concerned, the police that is, we're staying neutral for the moment. The Army too.'

'What about Hitler?'

'Oh, him. Still sitting around in the Bürgerbräu, he is, and nobody believes a word he's saying. If he takes it into his head to start marching, then he'll get no further than the Ludwig Bridge. But now, move on, you lot.'

'Can we get up to the Bürgerbräu?'

'We're not stopping anyone getting *out*. Whether the swastika bully-boys'll let you through, that's another matter. You'll have to sort that one out with them yourselves.'

'Did you hear that, Herr Weber?' said Schelshorn once they were on the bridge. 'Swastika bully-boys, he said. Are we supposed to stand for that?'

'Not much longer,' croaked Schuhladen.

'That all depends,' said Weber.

'On what?'

'Just *depends*, you nitwit.'

They didn't go straight up the Rosenheimer Berg, for the position there was confused. Instead, they marched some way up Lilienstrasse, following the Isar upstream, then ducked through the maze of hovels in the Au, the 'Lodgings', towards one of the steep tracks leading up to the Hochstrasse. The narrow streets between these 'lodgings' were deserted. An old woman eased a greasy curtain to one side and squinted out. Only on one single, tiny shack was a swastika flag to be seen.

'Just one!' grumbled Weber. 'Nothing but a lousy rabble that lives here anyway. Reds, every one of them. They'll all

56

be moved out. To the colonies, along with all the other monkeys.'

They managed to reach the Hochstrasse without being spotted, and now turned north again. The brass band could be heard much more clearly now.

'Just a minute,' yelled Schuhladen. 'I've lost one of my galoshes.' He ran back. Weber stopped, the others followed suit.

'A revolution in galoshes!' he grunted. 'What does he expect? Of course galoshes get stuck in the clarts, weather like this.'

'Should we put our armbands on again?' asked Ried.

'The swastika armbands will go back on when I say so!'

Schuhladen returned. His galosh was covered in muck, inside and out. Schuhladen couldn't even get it on again.

'Chuck it away,' said Schelshorn.

'Are you nuts? They cost me eight hundred thousand million.'

'That's about all they're worth, too,' said Weber. 'And now, men, forwards.'

At the corner where Hochstrasse joined the Rosenheimer Strasse stood a middle-aged man and an elderly woman. They were peering through the increasing swirl of snow across to the entrance to the *Bürgerbräu Keller*. The sky hung menacingly, like a yellow board, over the city. Lorries were parked by the pavement. Uniformed Storm Troopers were assembling their machine guns. The whole thing was like some great boulder that was ready to start rolling at any moment. The music of the brass band was going full blast.

'They're playing enough bum notes to curl your toenails,' Schelshorn said quietly.

'Course they are,' said the man on the corner, ''cause they haven't been paid yet. Not even had nothin' to eat. They're only playin' to keep warm.'

Schelshorn suddenly let out a yell. 'Heey! It's Detzer!'

Detzer turned. 'Schelshorn! Well, bugger me!'

'This is my wife, Therese,' said Detzer.

'This is Herr Weber, our . . .'

'. . . A friend,' said Weber. 'Pleased to meet you.'

57

'Old Detzer here,' Schelshorn said, 'an old mate. He's a driver too. Used to be with Cenovis.'

'Unemployed now,' said Detzer.

'Cenovis?' asked Weber. 'What's that?'

'Cenovis Cereal Products & Co. Ltd,' answered Detzer. 'Up that way, in the Schleibingerstrasse, first right.'

'You two should get off home,' Schelshorn said to Detzer, 'before things start happening.'

'Just a sec,' said Weber. 'Herr Detzer, has the Cenovis company got lorries?'

'Sure,' Detzer laughed. 'I was a driver for them, wasn't I?'

'Do you still know your way around their yard?'

'I should say so.'

'Send your wife off home and come with us. There's something in it for you. Are you in the union?'

'No!' put in Schelshorn before Detzer could answer. 'In fact, he's not a member, OK, but he's one of us.'

'*Deutschland erwache!*' said Weber softly.

'*Juda verrecke!*' whispered Detzer.

From that moment on, Weber seemed extremely ill at ease.

Right in the middle of a bar, the band broke off. A babble of voices rose inside the *Bürgerbräu Keller*, only to cease in turn, as if switched off. The Storm Troopers who until then had been standing outside, ran in. Only a few remained by the lorries. The police down at the foot of the Rosenheimer Berg began to stir. Commands were shouted. The police formed a chain, but then withdrew towards the swimming baths. The snow had stopped. The cold air was like a taut film of cellophane that threatened to tear at any moment.

'Halt!' whispered Weber. The group stood still.

A frog was croaking inside the *Bürgerbräu Keller*.

'The Führer is speaking,' said Weber.

'Is it starting?' asked Schuhladen.

'Probably,' replied Weber.

'Should we put on the swastika armbands?' asked Schelshorn. His eyes began to shine.

'Are you mad?' Weber said. 'In here.'

They slipped into the entrance to a block of flats. Weber

peered out through the dull glass pane in the heavy door.

'I've got better things to do,' muttered Weber. 'I need three vehicles. One – you'll go in it, Schelshorn – to Gabriel-Max-Strasse in Grünwald, the second – Detzer will take it – to Lamontstrasse in Bogenhausen, and the third – I'll drive it myself – to Starnberg. Two or three others will go along in each of them. Got that?'

'Yes, sure, but . . .' Schelshorn said.

'I've got to get there first. So that none of the others beat me to it. Now where did I put these bits of paper . . .' he rummaged edgily through his jacket pockets. 'Right, got them. Three slips of paper. The exact addresses. Plans of the villas. If the valuables aren't given up voluntarily, then use force. In the name of the new Reich government. And if one of the Jews in the villas ends up minus a tooth or two, well, I'll not bite off anybody's head for that. Have you got that into your skull now?' Weber smiled despite his jumpiness. 'I've got the longest journey. Out to Starnberg. I'll do that on my own. The Yid there has a racing stable, see? I've known about it for a long time. I'll take it over myself. Before that Göring gets his mitts on everything. Right then – once the operation has been completed, take all the . . . the confiscated articles of value to the Aventinstrasse. Is that clear? Schelshorn has the front-door key. Then you'll wait at the top of the stairs. You'll do all right out of this.'

'Do we take cash as well?' Schuhladen grinned.

'If it's in dollars or Swiss francs, yes. Forget the German stuff. That's only fit for wiping your arse on. Not worth it. Ready! Quiet!'

A thousand boots clattered along the cobbles of the Rosenheimer Strasse. *Three – four*. The band struck up again. '*Deutschland hoch in Ehren*'.

Weber waited for the first shots. Nothing. 'Hm,' he said, 'the police seem to have withdrawn without a struggle. Or they've come over to our side. Quite right too.' Carefully, he opened the door. The last of the SA men were disappearing round the bend at the bottom of the street. 'Let's go,' said Weber. They hurried out towards the Schleibinger Strasse.

At the gate to the Cenovis Cereal Products Co. Ltd works, the gateman Franz Huber was standing rolling a cigarette when the bunch of them trooped up. Huber, obviously frightened out of his wits, later testified that there were some fifteen people involved, whereas in fact there were only eight of them.

'In the name of the new Reich government. Show us the way to the garages, at once. We need two lorries.'

'Now hang on a minute,' said Huber, 'have you asked at head off –'

Weber drew in his belly, let it shoot out again, and Huber reeled back against the gate. Detzer snatched his keys and opened up. The others pushed the gates back.

'The wagons are kept back there,' said Detzer.

Huber ran off, but was back almost immediately with the works supervisor, Rosenberger.

'Hey! You lot! What do you think you're –' Rosenberger started to yell, and then: 'Oh, Herr Detzer, what are you doing here?'

'I require two – no, three – vehicles in the name of the new Reich government!' shouted Weber and fumbled about with some papers he took out of his pocket.

'I'll have to have a word with the management first,' said Rosenberger.

'There'll be no more talking to any management. If you don't move out of the way, I'll have you put up against a wall,' bellowed Weber.

The next to appear on the scene, alerted by the racket, was Fahrenkopf, from the admin. side. Schuhladen stuck a pistol under his nose.

'All right,' said Fahrenkopf, 'but only on production of a receipt. I was in the war too, you know.'

'Belt up!' shouted Weber.

'I know,' snorted Fahrenkopf, 'that even in wartime requisitions could only be made on production of a rec –'

'SHUT IT!' yelled Weber.

Fahrenkopf nodded to Huber to open up the garages.

'Where are the ignition keys?' said Weber.

'Fetch the keys, Herr Rosenberger, they're hanging on the board.'

'Schuhladen,' said Weber, 'go with him. See that the sod doesn't get away.'

Schuhladen, his pistol at the ready, followed Rosenberger into the building. Some terrified secretaries were watching from the windows.

'But,' Fahrenkopf stammered, 'it's not my fault, but the lorries haven't been refuelled.'

'What?' screamed Weber.

'Sorry . . .'

'Where do you keep your fuel reserves?'

'We won't get another allocation till next week.'

'What a shit-heap,' snorted Weber, 'this'll set us back hours. Where's the nearest filling station?'

'In Ruhestrasse. At the Eastern Cemetery.'

There was just enough petrol in the tanks to take the three lorries out into the Rosenheimer Strasse. Weber sent Schelshorn, Schuhladen and Ried off with jerry cans. He gave them a bundle of hundred-thousand-million notes. 'Pay only if you have to,' he said.

When they came back more than two hours later – without petrol; they had been to three different filling stations and all of them were closed – the sleety drizzle had turned to rain. Distant shots had been audible for some time now. A lorry loaded with swastika-boys came speeding up the Rosenheimer Berg. Weber signalled to it. The driver recognised him, stopped and leant out of his cab window.

'It's all over,' the driver shouted. 'Hitler's had it, Ludendorff's had it, Göring's had it. A bloodbath at the Feldherrnhalle. Finished.' He accelerated away, and the lorry disappeared round the corner of the Franziskaner Strasse.

'Let's go home,' said Weber. 'I said it right at the start. You don't have a revolution in weather like this.'

'And what about the Cenovis lorries?'

'Kiss my arse,' said Weber and, turning up his collar, made off, without once looking round, down the Rosenheimer Berg.

*

'The Jews, Herr *Regierungsrat* Pflaum, are of course human too. No two ways about it.'

'That's exactly my view, too, Herr *Oberlehrer* Bürkel – I think we should move a little to the side. There's an awful draught here. Yes indeed, I'm entirely of the same opinion.'

'Any other view, Herr *Regierungsrat*, would not be at all compatible with the, how shall I put it, the spiritual ethos handed down to us by a Lessing, a Goethe or a Kant.'

'You will not hear an epithet like "*Juda verrecke*" or anything similar pass *my* lips.'

'It would in any case be quite unworthy of an educated man, a senior civil servant such as yourself, Herr *Regierungsrat*.'

'Nevertheless.'

'I know exactly what you mean.'

'Humanitarian sentiments, headmaster, must not be allowed to lead us into losing sight of the fact that one can take such things only *so* far. There are limits!'

'Just so, just so, Herr *Regierungsrat*. That Eisler, for example . . . not that you should think for a moment that I approve of murder for political ends! But your Eisler . . .'

'From the outset I considered it . . . let's say, tactless to set a North German at the head of our state. It was simply *bound* to go wrong.'

'There's nothing I detest more than crude categorisation. A man surely can't do anything about his nose! Look at me, Herr *Regierungsrat* – now you would not describe my profile as exactly classical . . . let us be frank. But there is no denying that there *is* such a thing as physiognomy.'

'A Negro just *is not* an Eskimo, Herr *Oberlehrer*.'

'And whenever I've looked at photographs of this Eisler . . . only photographs, mind! I've never seen him in the flesh . . . there's, well, a certain something about him . . .'

'Yes. And the way they talk. Our great master of Bayreuth, in his essay, you know the one I mean? –'

'Need you ask!'

'– drew attention to the fact that this nasality, this strangulated whine in their speech is unpleasant to the German ear.'

'Outlandish!'

'Exactly. Believe me, I have nothing against them talking that way among themselves. In fact, sometimes it sounds quite comical to listen to. Exotic, in a strange way. But then –'

'They lack cordiality. Warmth.'

'Sincerity.'

'Of course, that's not given to everyone. That is not a criticism. Natures differ, that's the way it is. I recently heard on the wireless a composition by that Schönfeld – a Jew, naturally – twelve-tone. May well be very interesting, I don't understand it at all. But *sincerity*, that's what was missing for me.'

'And it isn't something that can be learnt.'

'Exactly. All the more reason why my observation is not to be taken as a reproach.'

'Nevertheless, one does have to reproach the sons and daughters of Zion for the fact that they simply will not accept this. A certain arrogance – I speak as I find, Herr *Regierungsrat* – a certain arrogance is undoubtedly characteristic of the tribe of Moses.'

'Where would we be if we were no longer allowed to say *that*, Herr *Oberlehrer*?'

'I have absolutely no objections to their being given a state of their own.'

'A fine muddle that would be. Ha ha. A Jewish state. It would just like in a Jewish *shul*. A complete shambles. Your Jew may well have a distinct talent for, well, wheeling and dealing, but administration? Legislation? Education? Not to mention military matters. Not a trace, there. Take my department, for example: the only Jew there, a certain Kalbskühn, is a senior clerk. Hasn't managed to get further than that. As for the upper echelons? There's *never* been a Jew there.'

'It's a different story in the banks.'

'Well there, yes.'

'But then, that comes from their gift for, as you said, wheeling and dealing. For money. A racially innate talent for money.'

'Coupled with a certain deficiency in professional ethics.'

'Very nicely put. But where are ethics supposed to come in, when these gentlemen have shown, over two thousand years, a preference for leading an existence *outside* our moral world order?'

'I wouldn't miss them if they were to disappear tomorrow. I mean, from this country.'

'Who knows, whether perhaps . . . all the same, though . . . that Hitler himself . . . dreadful. I've heard him once or twice. One has to keep up with the times . . . but really, that Hitler himself . . . quite unspeakable, the man is. A windbag. Wouldn't surprise me at all if he turned out to be a Jew himself. Anyway, he's more or less a write-off. Politically dead. Five years' imprisonment . . . when he comes out, nobody will remember him. But what I'm saying is, the *direction* . . . the line, Herr *Regierungsrat*, the general direction they are going is not altogether wrong.'

'I still think – ah, good evening!'

'Good effenink to you, Kherr *Oberlerrer*, a fine effenink to you, Kherr *Regierunksrat*.'

'Thank you, and the same to you, Herr Zwirnberg.'

. . .

'A quiet, affable man, really.'

'I could hardly wish for a more agreeable neighbour.'

'And yet . . .'

'Exactly.'

'One remains strangers.'

'But . . . I think, Herr *Oberlehrer*, I really must be getting along. My old student fraternity . . . Fellowship hour with the Old Boys. The Babenbergia.'

*

Temperamentally, the man is like a roller-coaster. One minute he is playing the statesman (which he never was and never will be), the next – mostly when face to face with the 'masses', in so far as one can apply such a term to the weary, bleary, beery rabble in the main room of the Bürgerbräu beer hall – he is in the grip of the usual bellowing demagogue's euphoria, and then he relapses into gloomy despair. He is still dressed in

64

the frock coat in which, the previous evening, he attempted to disguise himself as a solid citizen. He, too, had drunk rather too much beer (only later did he turn against alcohol) and eaten too many cherry slices with whipped cream. His belly blown up tight as a drum. *Meteorismus intestinalis.* He had to leave the room at frequent intervals to avoid the noises being heard. Just one such noise in front of his Teutonic followers, and any respect would be gone, literally blown away. Ah, the things a politician has to be mindful of. Did he, one wonders, take this into consideration when he decided to become one? He was to find no relief from his *meteorismus intestinalis* until a pistol shot did the trick towards the end of April 1945.

The march on the Feldherrnhalle – a necessary evil; just so that *something* happened on that dreary November day. Anything to avoid the whole thing ending in stalemate. Perhaps not such a miscalculation after all: the defeat, which was in fact inevitable from the outset, when the hordes of Storm Troopers and Militant Union followers set off with their sodden flags to march through the slush towards the Ludwig Bridge, the defeat was not as bad as an inglorious cancellation of the whole business would have been. An ignominious abandonment after the imperious shot fired into the ceiling the evening before.

He shuffled along, rather than marched. Not exactly a shining example for any close observer, but then he already enjoyed the favour of his followers to such an extent that none of them would be watching closely. At his side was Scheubner-Richter. Max Erwin von Scheubner-Richter, an 'adventurer with a turbulent past and a highly developed gift for lucrative undercover political deals . . . He was a figure swathed in mystery, yet with considerable social assurance, was something of a linguist and enjoyed connections with many industrialists, with the House of Wittelsbach, with Grand Duke Kyrill and with those in high places in the Church.' (Joachim C. Fest) Apart from Dietrich Eckart, whose plays enjoyed astonishing success, especially abroad (Switzerland, Holland, Denmark and Sweden), and brought in royalties in hard currency – on 4 November alone, fifty thousand gold marks flowed from this source into the coffers of the Munich *Ortsgruppe* – it was Scheubner-Richter's obscure sources of income which financed the Party in the 'time of struggle'.

He linked arms with Scheubner-Richter. Two comrades-in-arms. At the Ludwigsbrücke, the meagre police cordon fell back after Göring had threatened that all hostages – most of them city councillors – would be shot.

At the Marienplatz, a demonstration. It was not he who spoke, but rather Streicher who did the barking. *He* remained strangely mute throughout the whole march.

The hordes flooded through the narrow streets, Diener-strasse, Weinstrasse, Theatinerstrasse and Residenzstrasse, towards the Odeonsplatz. It was certainly not what you would call an orderly march.

At the Odeonsplatz, a police cordon blocked the way. Who fired the first shot has never been established. Seventeen dead, three of them policemen. Among the other fourteen was a completely innocent bystander, a waiter in the Café *Annast* (his name was Karl Kuhn), who had been imprudent enough to show his nose outside the front door. When, later, the funeral ceremony for 'those killed in action' was celebrated in the pseudo-Assyrian 'Temples of Honour' on the Königsplatz (under the Nazis it was renamed 'Königlicher Platz' – 'Royal Square' instead of 'King's Square'), the waiter, too, was given a bronze coffin, probably for the sake of symmetry – seven in each temple. On the brass plaque at the Feldherrnhalle, too, the name of Waiter Kuhn appeared, despite his family's protests. A reluctant hero.

Scheubner-Richter was one of the first to be fatally hit. He fell, dragging Hitler, who was still arm-in-arm with him, to the ground and as a result dislocating his shoulder (was it the right one or the left?). Ludendorff, as dull-witted as a fattened ox, marched on, erect. Which probably proved lucky for him. He, striding on, in the midst of the stumbling, retreating, fleeing rabble, he was known to everyone, even to every policeman. The 'Victor of Tannenberg'. Nobody would dare shoot at him. You don't shoot at a monument. Perhaps Ludendorff was not so stupid after all? Was this what he was counting on? He walked up to a policeman, demanded to speak to the officer in charge and surrendered his sword.

Hitler had made a swift getaway. Not exactly the genuine Teutonic way of doing things. Indeed, afterwards, it did get him into hot water with his own people. At first he defended himself by insisting that, in his confusion, he believed Ludendorff to be dead. 'But that's the very thing that should have made you stay where you were.' Later on, he said he had carried a helpless child out of the line of fire (despite his dislocated shoulder?).

So there lay the faithful Scheubner-Richter, moaning. 'Oh, Erwin, my Erwin, are you . . . ?' breathed Wolf. 'Germany shall live, even if we must die!' whispered Max Erwin with his last breath. One last gaze of Blue-Eyes into Blue-Eyes, then those of the most loyal of all were extinguished. It is well known that Wolf – stern, solitary Wolf – wept only twice in his life, once when his mother died and once when a turkey, stuffed and ready, was knocked off the parapet of the terrace into the sea by a clumsy kitchen-help – no, hold on, that was somebody else. Somebody altogether more likeable. No, the other occasion was when Germany had lost the war. Only twice. But he very nearly cried again, for a third time, as he looked into the eye, the glazing eye, of Max Erwin. 'Who is going to get hold of gold marks for us in future?' Close by, a child whimpers, paralysed by fear. Heedless of the bullets whistling around him, Wolf takes the child in his arms. 'Hush now, my boy . . .' and he brings it to its mother. The child's name must have been Siegfried, his mother's Sieglinde, of course. The fearless Wolf with the tender heart. In late 1924, Hitler even presented the child before his Party comrades. Unfortunately, the child couldn't remember a thing.

As bad luck would have it, a few Ludendorff followers had noticed Hitler, with no child to be seen, slinking along the front of a row of houses, stooped and trembling, until he got round behind the main post office and then ran off to his home in Thierschstrasse. That story about the child, Hitler said when the matter was raised, could only have been put about by the Jews. Very clever, because it was so implausible from the outset. How was a three-year-old child supposed to have found its way into the marching columns? Only so as to discredit him, Hitler, in the eyes of his own people. Typical of the Jews.

That same evening he turned up at Frau Hanfstaengl's lakeside home in Uffing, on the Staffelsee. He had made himself unrecognisable by shaving off his moustache. He was, he declared, about to shoot himself. Frau Hanfstaengl drew his attention to the fact that the Hanfstaengls' child Edgar (all the male Hanfstaengls had Christian names beginning with E) was already asleep. Whereupon Hitler refrained from committing suicide and began to grow his moustache again. Incidentally, he was waiting for the escape car promised by Frau Bruckmann to come and take him across the border. The car did indeed arrive, albeit too late, for Hitler was arrested shortly before, on 11 November. Before his arrest, he hastily pinned on his Iron Cross, First Class.

Weber turned his back on 'the Movement' around two o'clock on 9 November, or so he claimed. As well as his followers – who at first looked at each other in dismay and then dispersed – he left the vehicles 'requisitioned' from the firm of Cenovis standing where they were. After the situation had quietened down, driver Meyer and – an act of penance? – ex-driver Adam Detzer drove the three lorries back into the garage.

On 20 November 1923, in the so-called 'high-command headquarters' of the Party in the Schellingstrasse, Weber was taken into temporary custody by Det. Sgt Meyerhofer of Section VI N and immediately – at 9.45 a.m. – appeared before Dept VI/a of Police Headquarters. The charge sheet bears the reference number VI/a 653/23. Police Constable Georg Mulzer took down the – extremely verbose – statement made by the accused Weber. That morning, Mulzer must have beaten his fingers almost raw on the keys of his typewriter.

Weber opened – as is the way with all criminals – by describing at great length, in laborious detail and no doubt accurately, circumstances that were only remotely connected with the incident itself. From the outset, he emphasised that he had had only a very subordinate position in the Party and had had nothing to do with the preparations for the 'attempted coup'.

'I remained in the *Bürgerbräu Keller* until approximately two o'clock, till the first SA members returned from the city and reported that the march had been broken up and disarmed. Then I got into my car and drove to the Zeppelin Garage' (obviously a lie; if Weber had had his own car there, it would hardly have been necessary for him to 'requisition' the vehicles belonging to the firm of Cenovis, certainly not all three of them) 'and stayed there until about five-thirty p.m. At the Zeppelin Garage, I remained in the office of the proprietor, Laberger by name, with whom I spent the time chatting' (about the state of the weather, no doubt). 'Then, at half-past five in the evening, I walked back to my flat. Since Friday, 9 November 1923, I have taken no further active part in the Party leadership. All I did was to undertake the purchase of wreaths for those killed in action' (in action!) 'and see to it that the four lorry drivers were paid. I was not involved in any discussions of the high command after the *putsch*. I played, as I have already declared to various leading Party figures, for example Weiss, Dietrich Eckart, etc., a completely passive role. The sole purpose of the discussions, as far as I have been informed, was to decide upon the manner of the dissolution of the Party and/or to set up the mechanism for winding it up.' The serious matter of the armed theft of the three vehicles was not so much as mentioned by Weber. Didn't Mulzer even ask him about it?

On page 66 of the file there appears, finally, a 'note':

Within the organisation of the Nat. Soc. German Workers' Party, Christian Weber was in charge of the transport fleet. After the collapse of the *putsch* attempt on 9.11.1923, Weber emerged in a more active role. At a discussion of the provisional high command, at which Lieutenant-Commander Hofmann, Lieutenant-Colonels Brückner and Barenius were present on the eleventh of the same month, and at which a decision was reached regarding the curtailment of activities, W. attempted to propagate the idea of forming raiding parties with

the aim of harassing formations of the Imperial Army
and the Armed Brigade of the Police.

Munich, 20.11.1923
Police Headquarters
Dept VI N
Signed
(Signature illegible.)

Harassing? Were they not harassed enough as it was?
Perhaps Weber's parties were meant to raid somewhere else
altogether? Under cover of disorder? Surely the Yids don't
need to know exactly who is plundering their villas, do they?
The Red Front, for example. After all, their attitudes were
pretty sharply anti-Semitic. The only good thing that could
be said for that lot.

But what swine had landed Weber in it, had put the police
on to the business about the raiding parties? Hofmann?
Brückner? Barenius? Did they have a private score to settle
with Weber? The good old days of comradeship-in-arms.
All pals one minute, at each other's throats the next. On
21 November 1923, a document was drawn up – 'Office of
the General State Commissioner, ref. no. 3345':

I. Order.
In accordance with the ordinance of 26 September 1922,
the preventive detention of the businessman
        Christian Weber, resident in Munich,
is hereby ordered. In regard of the enforcement of this
order of protective custody, the terms of the above-
mentioned general ordinance shall be applied; this notwithstanding, any decision to rescind the order of
protective custody I reserve for myself.

II. To be issued in triplicate to Police Headquarters,
Munich, for issue of summons and enforcement.
                                        sgd *Dr von Kahr*

Weber was taken to Landsberg. A merry prison, it was.
Hitler was already in residence. A laurel wreath on the wall.
Every day, roll-call at ten o'clock before the Führer. The
prison staff did as they were told. Only one thing was not
possible – opening the gates. Probably Hitler would not

have wanted that anyway, since a spectre waited outside –
the accusation, from within his own ranks, of incompetence
and, worse still, of cowardice.

The 'People's Court' handled Hitler with kid gloves. The
speech for the defence was made by the State Prosecutor. In
effect, the defence counsel was left with nothing more to do.
The sentence: five years' fortress imprisonment, the minimum
period for high treason. Even in the speech giving grounds for
sentencing, the president of the court disclosed that he would
be released on parole after serving six months. The martyr
for the Fatherland was thus assured accommodation in the
comfortable fortress until 20 December 1924, and there he
dictated *Mein Kampf* to Hess. Despite the veil of secrecy,
the faithful – not that there were many of those left – got
wind of his imminent release, and were at the gates of the
fortress to meet Hitler.

He spent Christmas Eve – in a modestly unobtrusive blue
suit – at the Hanfstaengls' new home, *Tiefland*, or Lowlands,
in the Herzog Park.

'How marvellous to see you again, Uncle Wolf!' little
Edgar, the master of the house's son, welcomed him. Uncle
Wolf shook Putzi Hanfstaengl's hand warmly. 'I showed
him into the generously proportioned living-room which had
served my predecessor as a studio. Now a Blüthner grand
piano formed the centrepiece of the room. With a strangely
intense expression, Hitler requested me – we had hardly been
together for two minutes – "Please, Hanfstaengl, play me the
Liebestod!"' (Ernst Hanfstaengl)

And then began, in the years leading up to 1933, the
unhurried, implacable dismantling of democracy.

Even before proceedings against 'Hitler, Adolf, and others'
were opened – on 24 February 1924 – Weber, Christian, was
sentenced on 9 January 1924 by the Provincial Court, Munich
I, to four weeks' imprisonment for causing bodily harm (to
the shopkeeper David Hess). The sentence was served –
technically during suspension of his preventive detention –
in Landsberg. Weber did not so much as notice it. Apart from
anything else, somebody like Weber can serve such trifling
sentences without batting an eyelid. As a result of an order

issued on 27 February by the Ministry of the Interior, Weber was released from preventive detention on 29 February.

*

The fat man was wearing gloves. Frieda Burschmann from the Pippinger Strasse had advised him to. Unfortunately, though, the same Frieda Burschmann had omitted to add any instruction as to what one had to do with one's gloves later on when visiting refined people.

The maid at *Tiefland* took the fat man's soft, wide-brimmed felt hat and tried to help him out of his coat. The fat man, with the unaccustomed gloves still on his hands, had to struggle to get his arms out of the sleeves.

In the drawing-room sat Herr and Frau Hanfstaengl. The master of the house got to his feet. The fat man was in a quandary: should he hold out a gloved hand, or do you not shake hands when you are wearing gloves? So the fat man merely bowed, once towards the master of the house, once towards the mistress, clasping his hands behind his back. (Too late, it occurred to him what Frieda Burschmann had said on this point: Greet the *lady* of the house first . . .) The master of the house withdrew his outstretched hand.

'How nice that you could come to visit us, Herr Weber,' said Frau Hanfstaengl.

('If you haven't a clue what to say,' Frieda Burschmann had advised him, 'just say, "The pleasure's all mine." ')

'The pleasure's all mine,' said Weber.

'Please, do sit down, Herr Weber,' said Hanfstaengl.

('And if you're offered something, say, "Thank you most kindly." Even if you don't want to accept it. Got that?')

'Thank you most kindly, Herr Professor.' Weber sat down in the proffered armchair, which then sagged almost to the floor.

'I'm not a professor,' Hanfstaengl laughed.

'The pleasure's all mine,' Weber responded.

'I beg your pardon?'

'I mean, thank you most kindly. Or rather, beg pardon. I really only meant to say, Herr Doktor.'

'I'm not a doctor either. Not yet. I do intend to take my doctorate . . . oh yes. You may laugh, at my age. But our generation has been somewhat thrown off track.'

'If you gentlemen will excuse me, I'll leave you together,' said Frau Hanfstaengl, rising.

'Thank you most kindly,' said Weber.

Hanfstaengl got to his feet, too, and bowed slightly to his wife. (At this point, the fat man remembered Frieda Burschmann's words: 'And one thing you mustn't forget. Don't ever sit down before all the ladies have, and as soon as a lady gets up, jump to your feet.' Frieda Burschmann, you see, was educated, and besides, she had served as a maid to a Baron Lo Presti before she . . . before she, let's put it this way, before she opened up on her own.) Weber, too, leapt, in so far as that is possible for a man of his bulk, to his feet. The relieved springs of the armchair sang a hymn of praise.

'Please, don't get up,' said Frau Hanfstaengl. 'Can I offer you something?'

'Thank you most kindly,' said Weber.

'So . . . what would you like, Herr Weber?'

'Well now, ma'am, if you could bring me a stein of beer and half a dozen white sausages . . .'

'Oh, I see. There . . . I must admit . . . you have caught us a little unprepared,' said the lady of the house.

'My wife meant,' Hanfstaengl put in, 'tea or coffee. Or perhaps a small glass of port and a few little biscuits.'

'The pleasure's all mine,' said Weber.

'I always drink tea at this time of day,' Hanfstaengl said. 'It's a habit I picked up during my time in America.'

'The pleasure's all mine.'

Frau Hanfstaengl left. The maid brought a tray with the tea. Hanfstaengl resumed his seat, Weber likewise. When the maid came in, Weber was all set to haul himself up again, but, as Hanfstaengl remained seated, Weber, too, stayed where he was. (Obviously, the maid doesn't rank as a lady.) Weber leant back and contemplated with pleasure the maid's backside, which she had turned towards him, and tried to imagine how it would look naked.

'Please, help yourself,' said Hanfstaengl.

73

'Thank you most kindly,' said Weber.

'I think,' said Hanfstaengl, 'it might be easier for you if you were to take your gloves off.'

'The pleasure's all mine,' said Weber.

. . .

Later on, there was at least some cognac on offer. That relaxed the atmosphere somewhat.

'Old Wolf, and his book, that one he wrote in Landsberg...' Weber made a dismissive gesture. '*Mein Krampf*. What a load of rubbish. I ask you.'

'Hm, yes, I must say, I have certain reservations . . .'

'Certain reservations . . . yes, nice, that. Course, you're a distinguished gent, if you'll pardon the expression. You have *certain reservations*. I think the whole thing's a load of crap. What sod's going to read that. It's *that* thick.'

'I don't know. I've read it.'

'Well, yes, maybe. I mean I've . . . well . . . I've flipped through it. Very boring.'

'So you are – how shall I put it – you are not really all that interested in literature?'

'Me? Ha ha. No. Don't give a tinker's for that. I'm . . .' Weber tried to strike a loftier note, 'I am more of a man of action. My horses, my cars, my hunting . . . and then if there's a bit of a punch-up now and again . . . That's my kind of literature.'

'Just so,' said Hanfstaengl. 'Perhaps . . . no, indeed I'm sure, we need people like you, too.'

'If everybody was just book writers. Well, I mean. The Movement wouldn't get very far.'

'Herr Hitler thinks a great deal of you.'

'Oh yes, of course he does! We go a long way back – old soldiers. I've been around pretty well since the very start. The things we've been through together, Wolf and me.'

'You are one of the few to be on first-name terms with him.'

'You bet! A fine thing, that'd be! It would be a right joke if I had to call somebody "Herr" that I'd thrown . . . somebody I'd . . . when we've been through thick and thin . . . and thick . . . together.'

'Even within the Movement, you have, but I'm sure you'll

be aware yourself, you don't *just* have friends.'

'You mean Göring? Yes, yes. But he's just jealous of my car. I've got a Horch, see? *Eight* cylinders. Or maybe Maxi Amann? That shifty little bookkeeper.'

'Yes, yes, of course . . . I don't want to go into details. But only recently I heard Herr Hitler say that he'd stand by anybody that maintains such traditional Teutonic devotion to him as Christian Weber. Loyalty breeds loyalty.'

'You don't say. Well now, that's very nice of him. Maybe his book isn't so bad after all. You won't tell him, will you? I mean, *Mein Krampf*, and that? Maybe I just haven't understood it properly. As a man of action. I'll have to read it again, more closely. If I get the time. I've read *Der ewige Jude*. Very good. Very easy to read. Very . . . understandable.'

'You mean the book by Henry Ford? Yes, yes. *The International Jew*. That has virtually become the bible of anti-Semitism.'

'You put that very nicely, Herr Hanfstaengl.'

'Of course I read it in English. It's really . . . I mean to say . . . well, after all, it's not as if it was written by just *anybody*. Henry Ford is a big name. Translated into sixteen languages. Even into Arabic.'

'Let me tell you, Herr Hanfstaengl, if this Henry Ford was to come to Germany, we'd give him a welcome fit for a king.'

'Can I fill up your glass, Herr Weber?'

'Thank you most kindly.'

'Your good health!'

'The pleasure's all mine. Tell me, Herr Hanfstaengl, we haven't seen you and your wife at Party rallies lately, have we? You always used to be . . . ?'

'Yes. I must admit that I . . . that there have been certain differences of opinion.'

'Aha. Göring, probably. Is he jealous of you too?'

'No, not Göring.'

'Amann, then?'

'Well, since you ask so bluntly, Amann indeed. I don't know if you have heard about it . . . you see, I – this was back in the days of inflation – I gave Herr Hitler a loan. That was at the time when the *Völkischer Beobachter* was reorganised as a daily paper. A thousand dollars. In exchange, Herr Hitler made over all the printing machines and the complete inventory of the printing works to me, as security. Now, you mustn't let all this . . .' Hanfstaengl gestured with a sweep of his arm round the room, 'give you the wrong impression. Of course, we're doing nicely, my family and myself, but nevertheless – even I have to keep an eye on financial matters. Especially in recent times. We have a child who is chronically in very poor health . . . our little Hertha . . . the doctors' consultations, which, by the way, have all, absolutely all of them, proved completely fruitless, are costing us a fortune. And then I'm still studying, as it were. As I said before, working for my doctorate. Under Professor von Müller. An extremely interesting subject: Benjamin Thompson.'

'Mhm.'

'The name means nothing to you?'

'To be honest, I don't know the gentleman.'

Hanfstaengl smiled benignly. 'He has been dead since 1814.'

'Well, there you are.'

'In a word, then, at the moment – things will change, I have no doubt – but at the moment I am living off my capital. And so I would very much like to have my thousand dollars back.'

'Yes – so? Why don't you just go to Amann at the printing works?' Weber laughed. 'With a bailiff, and repossess the printing machines away from under their backsides?'

'Your suggestion surprises me, Herr Weber. How could I possibly reconcile that with my patriotic conscience?'

'With what? Oh, I see. Yes. Course you can't. Yes, right enough.'

'No, no, the *Völkischer Beobachter* wouldn't be able to appear at all. That could do incalculable damage to the Movement.'

'If you look at it that way, yes. But if they won't pay up . . .'

'I went to see Herr Amann.' Hanfstaengl sighed. 'I must say, sometimes they make it really hard for anyone to retain faith in the Movement. I had my Edgar with me. In fact, I was combining two errands in the one – taking Edgar to the hairdresser's and then, believe me, the much more difficult one of going to see Amann. He pointed at my lad and said, "Been at the barber's with the boy, have you?" "Yes, so what?" I replied. "What has that to do with my request?" "If," said this Amann fellow, and I tell you no lie, "if you can afford a barber for your boy, then your finances can't be in such a bad way after all. *Me*" – he said – "I cut my own kids' hair myself. Easy to learn how. I recommend it. And" – he went on – "if you think" – and it was the *way* he said it, you could hear the old sergeant-major coming out – "if you think you're going to get money out of the Party, then you can forget it. It doesn't have any, see?"'

Weber started laughing, silently to himself. First his head wobbled, then his neck, then his belly, then the whole fat man, then the armchair, until finally the whole floor seemed to quake.

'I don't really find it all that funny,' said Hanfstaengl. 'A thousand dollars is a lot of money.'

'I'm sorry, professor, I'm laughing because I've just had an idea. Sell it to me.'

'What?'

'You know, the thousand dollars. Your claim.'

'Oh, I see.'

'I'll make you an offer . . . seven hundred dollars. Cash on the nail. And you make the mortgage over to me.'

Hanfstaengl looked long and hard at Weber. Then he said, 'Thirty per cent commission. That's a bit steep.'

'Bird in the hand . . . two in the bush, Herr Professor.'

'Ten per cent.'

'Twenty-five.'

'Twenty.'

'Done! You'll be the ruin of me, Herr Professor. Here you are . . .' Weber twisted himself round in the armchair to reach into his hip pocket, pulled out a roll of high-value banknotes, counted out eight hundred-dollar ones and gave them to Hanfstaengl.

*

'Herr Blumenthal, if you'll forgive me saying so, you are too pessimistic. That man is a dead man. Believe me. Politically dead.'

'That may well be, Herr Peschmowitz, perhaps I am a pessimist. Do you know what pessimists have over the rest, though? They're always proved right in the end.'

'Not always, Herr Blumenthal, not every time. The world's not as bad as all that.'

'The world is much worse, Herr Peschmowitz. And it's my dearest wish that that man really was a dead one. Not politically, but . . . well, just dead. A corpse.'

'You mean, you wish, let's say, a bullet could have caught him on 9 November? Oh no, don't say that, Herr Blumenthal! I mean, it's not as if I feel sorry for the raving loud-mouthed ape. But *now*, as things are, he's politically dead; if he were dead in the flesh, if we can put it that way, *then*, Herr Blumenthal, he'd be more politically alive than he's ever been.'

'You mean, as a nationalist martyr?'

'You've hit the nail on the head, Herr Blumenthal.'

'I have my doubts. I was in the Circus *Krone* on 9 March . . .'

'What? You? You mean you dared to . . . ?'

'So why not? I'm a good six feet tall, and note, if you will, my blue eyes, not to mention my blond hair. Many an Aryan would give his eye-teeth for that. Naturally, I didn't toddle along dressed in a kaftan. No, I put on my old battledress tunic that I usually only wear for clearing out the attic or the like, and pinned on my Military Service Cross – and remember, they didn't scatter those about by the handful like you-know-who's Iron one . . . no, no, I wasn't in the least afraid. Yes, my dear Herr Blumenthal, by ten-past seven, the circus was more than half full . . . at eight, you couldn't draw a deep breath. Seven thousand the circus is supposed to hold, at full capacity, and I reckon it was in fact *over*filled. Of course, the self-important little pipsqueak took his time in appearing. Always does.'

'To heighten the tension . . .'

'Right. Just like at the opera, very casual. The band had

already played. Marches, that kind of thing, you know. But then, all of a sudden – in the middle of a bar, they broke off. A deathly hush. Then, from the entrance, shouts of *"Heil!"* *Heil! Heil! Heil!* A fanfare from the band. The crowd going mad in the circus. Little paper flags being waved everywhere – they had been selling them in advance, ten pfennigs apiece. Like Purim in a madhouse. *He* – hemmed in by brown-shirted Teutons trussed up with belts hung this way and that – comes tripping in, ruffles up his moustache, sticks out his arm . . . again it's *Heil! Heil! Heil!* Then he glares around. Doesn't just look, glares. In fact that's all the lot of them do, *glare*. Well, it wouldn't be so bad if that was all they did. But *he* goes up to the flag, kisses the flag, and at that, several women burst into tears. Then he's on the platform, glaring some more. And *then*, I'm telling you, he starts hopping around on the platform.'

'Hopping around?'

'Yes. He did. From left to right. From right to left. From one foot to the other. One step back, one forward . . . a kind of ballet. But they do it better in the theatre.'

'And he didn't speak?'

'Oh yes, he spoke all right. But he bawled and shouted so much you could hardly understand him.'

'There you are then, Herr Blumenthal. What a clown! He's no danger. Not now, I mean, now we have a healthy currency. And the big drop in the number of unemployed. Consolidation all round. You'll soon see . . .'

'Herr Peschmowitz, Herr Peschmowitz, I'd love to think I was wrong. But the man is dangerous. Look: during the time he was stuck in Landsberg, the radical-right movement pretty well fell apart. Broke up into splinter groups. They spent most of their time slinging mud at each other. The Ludendorffians, for example, they've become a *völkisch* astrological sect. And look at Ludendorff himself in the elections for Reich President – just managed to get over one per cent.'

'Exactly! Just what I'm saying!'

'Yes, but then this rat crawls out of its hole, salutes, shouts *"Heil!"*, gives a speech . . . and all, every man jack of them,

79

all the Nationalists fall into each other's arms like long-lost brothers. A riddle. And riddles, Herr Peschmowitz, can be deadly. Think of the Sphinx.'

*

Christian Weber, businessman and tenant of hunting grounds, driving-licence holder and car owner, was one of the few who held the ideal of national regeneration in high regard even when his Führer was languishing in gaol. Though all around may lose their faith, I shall remain loyal.

Extract from the *Bayerische Staatszeitung*, No. 64, of 15 March 1924:

'*Assault on distinguished businessman Herr Fränkel.*

'Over the past few days, the High Court in Munich has been hearing the case against the National Socialist, Christian Weber, who is charged with involvement in the widely reported attack on the noted businessman Sigmund Fränkel and the members of his family. During proceedings against the other accused, Weber had excused himself on the grounds of illness; now, he claimed in his defence that he had been annoyed by remarks made by the Fränkels' son.' (How on earth could anyone irritate a sick man to such an extent, when they must know how sensitive he is?) 'When this defence was refuted by the evidence to hand, Weber moved for a medical examination to establish his mental condition' (here, the journalistic language is somewhat lacking in precision: Weber was not demanding that young Fränkel's mental condition be investigated, but rather that he, Weber himself, be examined. A daring step? Regardless of all that might possibly emerge as a result of any examination of the mental state of one Weber, Christian?) 'because . . . he suffered from a certain idiosyncrasy towards Jews which meant that, as soon as he came across a Jew, he was driven to knock him down on the spot.' (Already showing quite a political talent, this Weber. Hats off to him. Or perhaps, helmets off. Not for prayer, but for silent worship under the linden tree at the Thingstead. Completely innocent, these Teutons. Nothing more or less than an irresistible genetic impulse: whenever

some lousy kike comes by with his crooked conk and kaftan
... a straightforward reflex action, uncontrollable, wallop, a
blow from a sinewy fist. Zyklon B: compulsive, *we couldn't
help it*. Saw a Yid in the street, turned on our heel, invented
Zyklon B, compulsively built concentration camps, set up
gas ovens ... *as if in a trance*. Not our fault. An irresistible
idiosyncrasy against the circumcised.)

'The court found itself unable to summon up the necessary
sympathy for these curious symptoms, but instead sentenced
Weber to sixteen days' imprisonment.' (Soon the courts will
be summoning up the necessary sympathy and understanding.
It'll take less than ten years.)

What Weber called the 'impounding' of the vehicles belonging to the firm of Cenovis on 9 November – the Public
Prosecutor's office preferred the term 'fraudulent assumption
of authority', and ought, if it had really wanted to be accurate,
to have it called 'robbery' and even 'armed robbery' – also
had its legal consequences (more like a game of consequences,
to tell the truth). The District Court of Munich-Au sentenced
Weber to a fine of two hundred gold marks, Detzer to one
of twenty gold marks. All the same, the Public Prosecutor entered an appeal, which was promptly rejected by the
Munich Provincial Court I. It had not, in the opinion of
the judges, been proven that Weber had uttered the alleged
threats.

A brief observation on the subject is to be found in the
Bayerische Staatszeitung, No. 159, of 11 July 1924, which
is of particular interest on account of an – albeit no doubt
fortuitous – association of ideas:

'*Appeal rejected in Weber case.*

'In the Munich Criminal Court, the National Socialist
businessman Christian Weber and the mechanic Detzer were
found guilty of fraudulent assumption of authority and sentenced to fines of two hundred gold marks and twenty gold
marks, or twenty and five days' imprisonment respectively,
because they appropriated, with menaces, two lorries on 9
November 1923. The Public Prosecutor entered an appeal
against these findings, and in yesterday's hearing in Court
4 of the Munich Provincial Court I, demanded additional

sentences on the accused, of one month and one week respectively, on the grounds of coercion. The court threw out the appeal . . .'

The Public Prosecutor took vigorous action, but not too resolutely. Weber's criminal act was, there can be no legal doubts about it, armed street robbery, at the very least guilt by association. If Weber had been a Jew, a gypsy or a Communist, it would have landed him with a prison sentence, and not less than five years at that. For Weber and his playmates, other criteria were applied: threatening behaviour, coercion, fraudulent assumption of authority – mere peccadilloes. The Munich Criminal Court, which in those days sat at the Mariahilf-Platz (so that the designation of 'District Court of Munich-Au' is, strictly speaking, inaccurate) treated him leniently. Despite his previous record, Weber got off with a fine. The Public Prosecutor's office stirred itself to action and entered an appeal, which was thrown out by the Provincial Court. The net result was nothing more than a suspended sentence.

The German judiciary, at least the Munich branch of it, had obviously perceived the signs of the times: eloquent testimony to the legal profession's political far-sightedness. The President of the Munich District Court at that time was Albert Singer, who took office on 1 April 1924. Far-sightedness proved its worth for him. He remained *Amtsgerichtspräsident* even after 30 January 1933, and did not retire until 1 February 1934 (at the age of sixty-eight).

The interesting, if unintentional, association of ideas? There were National Socialist leaders (later their number was to shrink to just the one Führer), National Socialist followers, National Socialist campaigners, National Socialist sympathisers, National Socialist ideologues, National Socialist bully-boys; there were even National Socialist intellectuals and probably National Socialist mental defectives.

Christian Weber was a 'National Socialist businessman'.

Autumn in the area around Berchtesgaden glows red, orange and yellow. The Bavarian sky is a pale, porcelain blue, not a cloud to be seen.

Wolf is sitting on a folding chair in front of the house, sketching. He likes drawing, and does a lot of it. Opinions as to his talent are divided. Wolf sits on his folding stool, with a board across his knees; drawing paper is attached to the board by four drawing-pins. Wolf is sketching in pencil; now and again he colours in with coloured pencils. In the grass by his side lies his rhinoceros whip. In earlier days he had had a dog whip, but since he became 'Führer' he uses something better, a rhinoceros whip. A step up. Mind you, the terms are somewhat misleading. 'Dog whip' does not indicate that the whip is made of dog hide. Wolf would never have taken such a whip in his hand: Wolf is a dog lover. Wolf is the leader, the *Führer* of Dogs, you might say, the Proto-Dog, the Dog *per se*, the Doggy's Dog, the Dog of Dogs, the Head Dog. Dog, Head Dog, Top Dog. Soon Wolf will be Top Dog. A whip made of leather that had been cut from the hide of his best friend and then tanned would be quite out of the question for Wolf. 'Dog whip' means a whip *for* dogs. Now and again, even a friend, the Under-Dog, requires guidance or correction. Lovingly, though, almost hurting the chastiser more than the chastised; but, sadly, it has to be, when the Under-Dog strays from the straight and narrow. Loving, strict, but fair.

The rhino whip, on the other hand, is made from rhinoceros hide. For rhinoceroses, however, Wolf feels no spiritual affinity.

Wolf does not use the rhino whip, in the sense of lashing out and about with it. No, no; no one has ever yet seen Wolf beating a human being, not even a Jew. (A whip made out of Jew leather? Not a bad idea, although . . . Wolf would have found it unpleasant always to have a piece of Yid dangling from his wrist.) As for a dog, that is to say, the real dog, in the zoological sense, Wolf never, but never, strikes a dog. Blondie, his most faithful companion, a German shepherd dog. Rather tending towards corpulence, mind you. Has a very sweet tooth. Suffers from constipation. Like her master. Of one heart and mind. And bowels. The dog is lying in the grass next to the rhino whip. Wolf is sketching. He is not drawing the dog, he is drawing something else. Wolf in his leisure hours. During the year in Landsberg, he got quite used to leisure, now finds it hard to get out of the habit. Is that the secret behind the fact that his public appearances are now so few and far between? That he no longer barks in beer halls is due to something else: as of 9 March 1925, he is banned from public speaking. Remarkably, he abides by this ruling. Has he perhaps really become state-fearing and law-abiding, as he solemnly swore, sealing his oath with a handshake, to Prime Minister Held in January? Word of honour? What his word of honour is actually worth, however, can be gauged from the one he gave Interior Minister Schweyer. Is Wolf holding to his word of honour now because he is afraid – after all he is still a foreigner – that otherwise he might be deported to Austria?

Nor is he sketching the *Berghof*, which he has recently rented. (Soon he will buy and extend it. Frau Bruckmann, his benefactress, has her weekend house nearby.) Although he generally enjoys drawing architectural subjects, he has, on this occasion, turned to something else. Normally he likes drawing 'imaginative architecture' – fantasy architecture!: palaces, triumphal arches, vast halls, monumental burial mounds . . . and always strangely lifeless, always inhumanly huge, always as if cut off at the top. And of course always gigantic, always exaggeratedly in perspective. They look like the drawings of a schoolboy who has just learnt the rules of perspective and cannot stop applying them.

But here in the meadow next to the *Berghof*, in the crystal-clear air of an autumn day, he is sketching something altogether different. Two screens have been erected, so that nothing can be seen from the house. The rear side is blocked off by a thick hedge. Only Wolf can see in between the screens.

Despite the ban on public speaking, he could still attend all the rallies. After all, the NSDAP has been in existence again since 27 February. Wolf has chosen the title '*Führer*' for his position in the Party. 'President' is un-German, has a bourgeois ring about it; 'Chairman', lacklustre; 'Spokesman', petty bourgeois – rabbit breeders' associations have spokesmen – the NSDAP has a *Leader*, a *Führer*. Mode of address: no longer

'Herr Hitler', but now '*Mein Führer!*' '*Mein Führer, Sturmbann* Baindlkirchen-West all present and correct!' or '*Mein Führer, SA-Standarten-Führer* Weber reporting!' (Although he, as we know, addresses him in private as Wolf and by the familiar *du*, because, to anyone he has chucked out . . . and so on, he could hardly be expected to use the formal *Sie*.) '*Der Führer*' is becoming the current scientific terminology applied to the species, even though it consists of only the one specimen. 'Adolf Hitler' is now used only in the poetic sense, as is 'lord of the skies' for eagle. He could attend Party meetings; that has not been forbidden. He could wave, could kiss children, could accept bouquets, none of that has been banned. He could draw to his bosom weeping geriatrics adorned with gallantry awards from the Great War, could stand to receive ovations – 'Führer command, we will follow!' None of that is proscribed. He could even give orders – there's no embargo on that either. Only making speeches is banned, but would he really need to speak? Doesn't everybody know already what he is always saying? He doesn't do any of this. He withdraws to the *Berghof* and draws. Has he come to the realisation that this is much, much more pleasant?

And he is not drawing the impressive panorama of the Berchtesgaden Mountains towering up all around. He is not drawing the dark spruce, stretching their tips into the skies beyond the meadow. He is drawing something else. Over one of the screens hangs a floral skirt.

On 27 February 1924 the Party was reconstituted. Wolf, whose membership number in the old party had been 555, now allocates himself No. 7. A mystical figure. Wolf has a penchant for mysticism. (The dark whisperings of the eternal Teutonic forests; Siegfried's 'Funeral March'; Entry of the Gods into Valhalla; Hail to Thee, Sun, Hail to Thee, Light, Hail to Thee, Hitler!) On the same day, the SS was founded – still as a subsidiary organisation of the SA. As a uniform, the *brown* shirt was chosen. 'Diarrhoea brown', opponents dubbed it. Wolf, who all through life suffered from constipation, took this as an expression of ridicule, and so was against it at first. But all other shirt colours had been taken, or were out of the question. Blackshirts: the Italian Fascists, whom no one wanted to emulate, not even in the colour of their shirts; Redshirts: Socialists and Commies; Whiteshirts? Quite literally too colourless. Yellowshirts? Like canaries. Greenshirts? Like frogs. Pinkshirts? (Next to the floral skirt, there was indeed a pink shirt hanging over the screen, albeit one of a different cut.) So that just left the brown shirt. But Wolf doesn't wear a brown shirt, not here. He is wearing a white shirt with a Byron collar (or, since he *is* German, a Schiller collar) and leather shorts. Leather shorts, his favourite garment. Bare knees – the male equivalent of the *décolleté*.

Wolf is sketching a flower. Not a flower that grows in the grass there, no edelweiss or gentian or Alpine rose, no, he's sketching an orchid – well, a kind of orchid – a red tongue; slender, vertical white lips; blond down.

Where does he get the money? The *Berghof* isn't cheap. Wolf's life-style up here is lavish. Does *Mein Kampf* bring in that much? No. The book was, in commercial terms, a flop. But the facts are that Wolf lives on the *Berghof* like a man of considerable independent means, or a scholar, looked after by his sister Frau Raubal and her daughter, known as 'Geli', seventeen years old; that he runs a big car, complete with chauffeur (Emil Maurice); and that he can indulge in the luxury of dispensing with any sort of regular income. Even in the Party, heads are shaken. Donations are flowing in at a substantial – a *very* substantial – rate, banks, industry and insurance firms are keeping well in with the right-wing movements. And yet the Party coffers are always empty . . .

'If I've got to sit here much longer,' groaned Geli, 'I'm going to get cramp.'

'Just a few more strokes,' said Wolf.

He held Geli's portrait at arm's length before him. (A portrait of Geli, although not of her face.)

'Can I get dressed?' asked Geli.

'No,' Wolf said brusquely, 'I want to do another sketch.'

'Ohhh, God!' said Geli, but just then Frau Raubal called down from the house. 'Wo – Wolf – a visitor!' and Geli, without asking again, dressed quickly. Wolf snapped his paintbox shut, laid the sheets of paper face-down on the grass and went up to the house.

Miscellaneous matters to be discussed. Wolf was bored by it all. Maurice had picked Weber up from the station in Berchtesgaden. Contrary to habit, Weber hadn't come by car. A keen motorist, he drove hard and with great panache. In the villages, hens scattered in panic. Washerwomen fell terrified into the trough. Weber would laugh at the sight of naked legs flailing in the air. But today he had come by train. A stupid fluke – what was that damned tree doing in the middle of that bend anyway? The whole left side of the car all to hell, cost a bloody fortune, that will. 'When our turn finally comes, Wolf,' Weber was saying, 'we're going to build one long road right across Germany, with no junctions or crossroads. And without trees on the bends. After all, we Teutons,' Weber went on, 'have always had a thing about getting around. Think of the migration of the peoples, Wolf!'

'Yes, yes,' said Wolf.

Then more miscellaneous stuff. On the previous Thursday, there had been a rally of the Nationalists, the *Völkische*. People had been lured by the promise that Wolf would put in an appearance. Till midnight the audience waited, patiently, in happy anticipation. But Wolf didn't show up.

'I told them,' growled Weber, 'that the Führer was hard at work at the Berghof. Writing the second volume of *Mein Kampf*. Then the folk gradually began to leave. Quite a few had a good moan. Was a pretty unpleasant situation.'

'I had forgotten,' said Wolf.

'You can't let that happen often, Wolf, not without offending people. I don't know if they believed the excuse I gave them.'

That brought Wolf bolt upright. 'What? They didn't believe? The National Socialist has to place blind faith in his *Führer*. These people *did* believe you. I'm telling you. *Did* believe it. They *must* believe. And they do believe. Unconditional obedience . . .'

'You don't need to shout,' Weber interrupted him, 'you're not at a rally. *Unfortunately.*'

'Thanks for the lecture,' said Wolf curtly.

'And another thing,' said Weber, 'to do with the financial situation. Amann has sent you this note: he has to find some way of entering in the books where these two thousand marks have got to . . .'

'I'm tired,' said Wolf, 'I have to have a lie-down.'

There was more than an hour to kill before the Munich train was due to leave. Weber and Maurice went out into the garden. There, Weber found the sheets of paper.

'Psst!' said Maurice.

'What's this then?' Weber laughed out loud.

'Sshh!' said Maurice.

'These are . . . they're . . . who drew this lot, then? *Him?*'

'Yes,' said Maurice.

'Well now, that's,' Weber chortled, his fat wobbling all over the place, 'now isn't that something, isn't . . . that . . . just . . . some . . . thing!'

'Geli,' Maurice said dully.

'That's Geli's naughty bits?'

'Dunno,' lied Maurice.

'Has he got something going with her?'

'Dunno.'

'When a girl lets a bloke draw *that*, and *that way*, then she's got something going with him. What are you looking like that for?'

'There's *nothing* going on with her. He's not got any-thing *going* with anybody. Not like *that*. Know what I mean?'

'So I've heard. *This* sort of thing is all he needs.' Weber began rolling up the sheets of paper.

'Hang on – what are you doing?'

'I'm taking them with me. Maybe I'll get one or two of them framed.'

'Are you off your head? He'd notice right away if they were missing.' Maurice took the sheets out of Weber's hand, smoothed them flat and laid them down again. 'I'll show you where the others are.'

'In the cellar,' Weber liked to relate later, 'there were a

hundred, maybe two hundred drawings like that in a cupboard. Signed, too.'

He took them out, one by one, clicking his tongue, licking
his lips. 'Not bad. Very true to life.' Weber laughed: '*Mein
Kampf*, volume two.'

'He hasn't counted these ones,' said Maurice. Weber took
a bundle, perhaps twenty-five of them, out of the pile and
put them in his briefcase.

'What are you looking so addled for?' said Weber.

'What do you mean, addled?'

'Gormless. Bamboozled. Thunderstruck, if you like.'

'Well, me too, I love . . .' said Maurice almost in a
whisper.

'What, the drawings?'

'No, Geli.'

'Aw, my Gawd almighty!' said Weber.

*

'He's a bit of a swine, really.'

'Your caretaker bloke?'

'Caretaker! Caretaker's good . . . he was never even a
janitor. A doorman, he was. Temporary. That makes a
difference. In fact he was really a horse dealer. He knows
a thing or two about horses.'

'And yet he's a *swine*?'

'You know what I mean – just an expression. Now he's a
businessman. And transport contractor. He's making a pile
of money. When, he says to me, when he's elected a city
councillor at the next elections, he's going to get them to
grant him a franchise for an omnibus service, from Tölz to
Munich.'

'A councillor? Him?'

'Sure. Hitler's already put his name on the Party list. They'll
easily get a dozen in, and my Weber'll be among them. You
make sure you vote for him, now!'

'OK, OK. Supposing nobody else does, if all the whores give
the NSDAP their votes they'll have plenty. And with all his
connections in – know what I mean? – *this* direction . . .'

89

'That's not all. When his friend Hitler becomes Reich Chancellor, he'll be made a minister.'

'Ha ha . . . just my idea of a minister.'

'You can laugh, Sophie.'

'And *you*'ll be a ministerial whore. First Class.'

Frieda laughed.

Then she said, 'All the same, he really put one over on him.'

'Who put one over on who?'

'My Weber. Hitler.'

'I thought you said they were friends.'

'Yes and no. Sure, they're friends, yes. But when it comes to business, so my Weber says, that's where friendship ends. In business, there's no room for sentiment. This Hitler, see, he was a bit short of cash once, it was in the days of inflation, and so he borrowed money from some Stanglhofer or . . . Hanfenstangel or whatever, a thousand dollars.'

'A fortune!'

'You can say that again. And especially then, when it was the inflation. Anyway. This Hitler didn't pay back the thousand dollars. And so this Haufenstangl, he was a professor, that is, a respectable man – or maybe he still is, I don't know him – and so, for patriotic reasons, he didn't want to be so common and take out proceedings against the NSDAP for the money, seeing as how it didn't have any money anyway. So this professor just went and yammered to Hitler that he needed to have his money back now, his thousand dollars – it was my Weber that told me all this, naturally I wasn't there myself – anyway he wailed and begged and said he couldn't get his kids' hair cut, being as how he hadn't any money and so he needed his thousand dollars back. Hitler just told him, Well, you can whine all you like. You're not getting no money from us, 'cos we ain't got any, at least nothing left over for repaying debts. And you can cut your kids' hair yourself. You can easy learn how. In the National Movement, we always cut each other's hair ourselves. So this Haberstingel or whatever his name is just had to push off empty-handed. But soon after, my Weber meets this Haberstingel, because he's a friend of his . . .'

'Your Weber is friendly with a professor?'

'Yes, why not, as a future minister . . .'

'Your fat Weber is friendly with a professor, who's a respectable man into the bargain? I can't imagine that. I can't imagine any refined and educated person that would be a friend of your Weber. No offence, but . . .'

'Yes and no. Not all *that* good friends. They don't go drinking together. Not *that* sort of thing. More Nationalist friends, you know? More political. Party friends.'

'I get it.'

'Yes. And my Weber says to him, sell me your claim, for eighty per cent, then at least you'll have that much, and leave the rest to me. Well then, that's what this Professor Haberstingel did, and my Weber – oh, yes! – he goes straight off to see Hitler. No whining from him; he thumped the table with his middle finger and said, Right, gentlemen, he said, here's the IOU, and if the readies are not making my till ring within three days, I'll be along here to shake you all till the money falls out of you.'

'Just like the Jews do.'

'Like who? Well really, Sophie – and him a real Germanic, a true-born nationalist too. A good job he didn't hear *that*. Mind you, maybe it was a bit hard, but business is business, says my Weber, and friendship is friendship, and the Nationalist Movement is the Nationalist Movement and that's all very well, but they've all nothing to do with each other, and the world of finance lives by different rules. Three days later, though, the money still wasn't there, and by this time Weber already has his document from the court, quick as you like, and has had all that lot at the *Völkischer Beobachter*'s accounts frozen, and the paper nearly couldn't come out, and so then, naturally, they all ran off and scratched together their reserves and paid Weber the thousand dollars.'

'But – *he* only gave the professor eighty per cent . . . ?'

'The rest was to cover the risk, see? For my Weber. But of course the Party had to pay him the full thousand dollars. And Weber made a killing of three thousand marks.'

'Three thousand marks? Very nice.'

'Yes, yes. He is a bit of a swine.'

'So I suppose that's the Nationalist friendship between your Weber and Hitler right down the drain now?'

'No, no. No chance of that. My Weber, see, he knows . . . well . . . he knows certain things. All of them know something about all the rest. And that, says my Weber, welds them all together into a "steadfast brotherhood". "A bond with power over life and death", that's what they call it – well, something like that.'

'Hm. But there's one thing I still find a real scream.'

'What's that?'

'The idea of the Nationalists sat in a circle cutting each other's hair.'

*

So there was, in addition to Capt. (retd) Göring, another fat man. In the south it was the fat men that stirred up trouble; in the north it was the scrawny ones. The Head Scrawny in the north did not emerge until Hitler was released from prison. He was Dr Joseph Goebbels. A fine specimen of a Teuton: about five feet one inch tall (he'd never have been let into the SS, for there the minimum height was set at five feet seven), sickly, narrow-chested and with a limp. Unfit for military service in the First World War, an intellectual Bohemian. In 1924 – he was twenty-seven years old at that time – he wrote the bombastically Expressionist novel *Michael. The Diary of a German Destiny*, so he was a colleague of Hitler the Writer. But he had a lot to hide, this Goebbels: that he had been a pupil of the Jewish Professor Friedrich Gundolf, and that he had for four years been engaged to a half-Jewess.

Half-Jewess; it is to be hoped that the reader will forgive the use in these pages of the vocabulary of Nazi terminology, but unfortunately, when one is writing about the Devil, one cannot avoid using the terms 'red' and 'black'. Half-Jew: a linguistic innovation of the National Socialists. In Innsbruck, so the story goes, there took place after the *Anschluss* of 1938 a discussion in the editorial offices of the *Tiroler Tageszeitung*, chaired by a Teutonic propaganda expert delegated by the Reich. It was decided that the Jewish members of the editorial staff – few as they were – should be dismissed on the spot. There followed a general debate on the subject of what was to be done with the Jews as a whole. The Propaganda-Teuton from the Reich made a pronouncement: the Jews would be collected together and resettled on an island. That's how humane they still were in 1938. On an island. Which island did the *Führer* have in mind? Madagascar was too big, Heligoland too German, Tahiti too small. Some island would be found all right. Whereupon one of the editors asked, with laudable courage: and what was to happen with the half-Jews? That, the Propaganda-Teuton admitted, was indeed a problem, and the *Führer* was giving it some consideration. What an enormous amount of considering the *Führer* put in, day and night! Which by the way explained why, for example, he remained unmarried. A wife would disturb him while he considered. Then we must, said the editor, assist the *Führer* in his deliberations, and I would suggest that, if the Jews are to be put on an island, then the half-Jews should be put on a half-island – a peninsula . . . (The pun does not stem from some whim of the writer, reality itself indulged in it. The occurrence is a matter of historical fact.) The *Führer* gave the proposal no closer consideration, perhaps because it was, like so much else, kept from him. Just think, incidentally, of all the things that were kept secret from him. All those bits of nastiness at *Gauleiter* and *Kreisleiter* level, all the incidences of sloppiness in the *Wehrmacht*, Göring's fiddling and wangling, the black-market dealings by the SS, all these, yes all of them, were kept from the Führer. 'If the *Führer* was to hear about that . . .' The *Führer*, isolated in his *Berghof*, is so full of good intentions, and the others hush up the difficulties. Only in April 1945 did word trickle through to the *Führer*: the Russians are at the gates of Berlin. 'What?' yelled the *Führer*, 'Why was I not told sooner?', seized his pistol, rushed outside, mowed down several hundred Bolsheviks before succumbing to sheer force of numbers and falling, the words

'Germany shall live, even if we must die!' on his lips.

The little scrawny one, who compensated for his all too inadequately marked outer Germanness by a thoroughgoing inner one, despised the scruffy Bavarian rabble down there. Those fatties, Göring, Weber and that fairy Röhm. And Hitler. Hitler, Goebbels opined in 1925, had to be excluded from the Party if they wanted to amount to anything at all, politically speaking. Later, he changed his mind. To wit, one day he was standing face to face with the *Führer*, and the latter transfixed him with his gaze – steely, yet on the other hand kindly – and then Dr Goebbels knew . . .

The corpulent Röhm. He, too, was on first-name terms with Wolf, even though he was a homosexual. Weber and Röhm were, in all senses of the word, thick as thieves. (Perhaps precisely *because* Röhm was a homosexual? 'One less rival,' Weber used to say.) Ernst Röhm, son of a senior inspector on the Royal Bavarian Railways, born in Munich on 28 November 1887. In contrast to his friend Weber, who only claimed to be, Röhm really was a front-line soldier in the First World War. He was wounded three times; one of these resulted in him losing half of his nose. This did nothing to improve his looks, but with his face – 'There's no face like Röhm' – and his figure, that hardly mattered anyway. He was short – not, of course, as short as Dr Goebbels, but so short that he always had to stretch in order to see over swastika-beflagged balconies. And he was fat. Since he was always having to stretch, it was inevitable that his belly constantly stuck out.

Röhm and Hitler got to know each other in 1919, while being de-loused in the reception camp on the Oberwiesenfeld in Munich. Röhm, too, belonged to those who were completely at a loss when confronted by the – for them – menace of demobilisation. Not only had Röhm never learnt a trade, he found Army life, particularly giving orders, more appealing than work. After all, Röhm had risen as high as captain. He feverishly searched for possible ways of prolonging the war. But single-handed he could do nothing.

But then there was Herr von Epp.

Franz Ritter von Epp, son of a painter – it is not on record whether this meant an artist or a house painter – joined the 9th Bavarian Infantry Regiment, the 'Fürst Wrede', in the same year, in fact, that Ernst Röhm was born, 1887. In 1896, Second Lieutenant Epp became a First Lieutenant; in 1901–02 he was on detachment to the German Expeditionary Corps in China; from 1904 to 1906, with the rank of captain, he commanded a company during the butchery of the insurgent Hereros in German South-West Africa. The Negroes did not want to be subjects of Kaiser Bill. This defied the comprehension of the Germans at that time. So they mowed the naked savages down with grape-shot. One man who went to mow was Captain Epp from Munich. In 1914, already a colonel and Commander of the Sovereign's Own Regiment, decorated with the I.C. Two and I.C. One, the *Pour le Mérite* and the Max Joseph Military Medal, which entitled him to bear the knightly title of Colonel Franz *Ritter von* Epp, 'Sir Franz'. He, too, was at his wits' end after the war. But he had more means at his disposal for continuing, off his own bat, to play soldiers, at least on a small scale. On 8 February 1919, he set up his own volunteer force, the *Freikorps* Epp – it was meant to be reminiscent of Lützow's *Freischar*; who could forget 'Lützow's wild and headlong charge' of 1813, which failed pretty miserably in the war against Napoleon? – and marched on Munich, where a soviet republic had been proclaimed. Just as in German South-West Africa fifteen years before, so now did Herr von Epp mow down the Bavarian anar-chists – including such anarchistic elements as the Catholic Kolping craft apprentices in Giesing. In on the act were Captain Röhm, Esq., in the role of a General Staff officer, and Lance-Corporal Hitler, Esq., who, it has to be said, was merely on guard duty back at the barracks. (For *that*, at least, a plea of extenuating circumstances can be entered at the bar of history.) On 2 May 1919, the Socialist Gustav Landauer was arrested and kicked to death in Stadelheim by Epp's henchmen. The well-known patriotic writer Ludwig Thoma from Miesbach wrote on the subject: 'These were mere preludes to more major courses of treatment which we had promised ourselves for the eventuality that the circumcised ones might get above themselves again. Then it would be no holds barred.' It was to take only a little over ten years for that to come to pass. Ludwig Thoma, however – Dr Ludwig Thoma he called himself, without justification, no doctorate was ever conferred on him – was not to live to see it.

Herr Ritter von Epp had some reservations about Lance-Corporal Hitler, notwithstanding the latter's generally impeccable attitude. About Röhm, though, he had none. He (Röhm) took part in the march on the Feldherrnhalle on 9 November, took cover in good time and subsequently was sentenced to only eighteen months, a suspended sentence at that. As early as 1924, he became, in his capacity as a representative of the German National Freedom Party, a member of the *Reichstag* and head of the *Frontbann*, a hooligan repository organisation for the members of the dissolved SA. In 1928, he resigned his seat and went to Bolivia. He exported with him the most precious thing that the German spirit has to offer: we'll soon sort out those layabouts! Down on your face! Up on your feet! On your face! On your feet! Pree-sennt harms! Basic training, or, order, discipline and cleanliness. Bolivia under President Hernando Siles was at that time arming for a war against Paraguay. Captain Röhm was an instructor. To no avail. In the subsequent conflict, the so-called Chaco War, Röhm's disciples, and with them the Bolivians, took a hammering and lost the war. By that time, though, Röhm had not only left the country of Bolivia but had also quit this earthly vale of tears. Was pushing up the daisies. A few of them, perhaps even the decisive ones, were planted by his fat friend, Weber. But more of that later.

*

The Angel of the Lord appeared unto Goebbels and spake thus: 'Dear Joseph, take off your shoes, for here you are on holy ground.'

Goebbels bends down and nervously undoes his shoe-laces. The left shoe is an orthopaedic one. The Angel looks at the deformed foot. 'Oh, my Lord and Saviour!' says the Angel, 'that does look awful.' Goebbels bows his head. 'But that in fact brings us,' says the Angel, 'to the very nub, to wit, why I've been sent to you: you've got this club foot, you're only five feet one in height; all in all, you're a stunted little weed. So, the Lord has an offer to make you: two sound, sturdy feet, shoe size eight and a half, height six feet, well above requirements, an athlete's physique.' 'Oh – my – God . . .' breathes Goebbels, 'I'll never say another thing against the Church . . .' 'Don't get carried away, now,' says the Angel. 'No no, it's true,' says Goebbels, 'I will never say another thing against the Church – or, are you not Catholic after all?' 'That would be a fine thing!' says the Angel. 'Only,' says Goebbels, hanging his head sadly, 'it just won't work.' 'Why not?' asks the Angel, 'for HIM nothing is impossible.' 'But – I mean, I ask you: if I were to appear tomorrow as Goebbels the Hun in front of Hitler and the masses, when only yesterday I was a skinny German dwarf . . . ? Nobody would believe I was really *me*. And how would I be supposed to explain it all? I don't imagine for a moment that I'd be allowed to mention your visit.' 'The LORD has thought of everything, as is HIS way. Not only will you grow by' – here the Angel does a quick bit of mental arithmetic – 'by eleven inches at a stroke, but in addition you will have always been a fine figure of a man. Everyone's memory of you will be changed. All the photographs – and so on.' 'That's fantastic,' says Goebbels, 'I don't know how to thank God enough.' 'You don't need to thank God,' says the Angel, 'you only have to fulfil one condition.' 'Anything! Anything at all!' shouts Goebbels. 'You've always been a Jew as well,' says the Angel.

*

'Morals are the basis of any state, Herr Pflaum.'

'Absolutely right, Herr Bürkel, where would we be without them?'

'The overthrow of morality was ever, Herr Pflaum, was

ever bound up with the decay of the social order. Think of Ancient Rome.'

'Exactly my sentiments, Herr Bürkel.'

'Nero, Commodus, et cetera. You know what I mean.'

'On the other hand, Headmaster Bürkel, if one thinks of the classical . . . how shall I put it . . . the undraped beauty . . . in complete . . . you see what I'm . . .'

'You mean, classical beauty *in statu naturae purae*. That was something altogether different.'

'Well, yes, of course . . . would you then have no qualms about holding up these . . . unclothed statues, the likes of the Venus de Milo as a moral example to us . . . ?'

'That's something else again. That is morality of an elevated order. Because it is classical. And anyway, the . . . ahem . . . really offensive parts of the body are usually covered by fig leaves or something similar.'

'Before going any further, I must ask you, Herr Bürkel, not to take what I'm going to tell you in the wrong way . . . or rather, I can assure you, that it was *purely* in the interests of my professional . . . recently we had four colleagues from Italy on a visit to my department. Exchange of information. Very nice people, whole-hearted supporters of the new government. One spoke good German. They were determined to . . . well, I would not have gone with them, only my head of department expressly . . . You do see what I'm getting at . . .'

'Not altogether, as yet, Herr *Regierungsrat —*'

'At first we — that is my head of department and I — were of the view that it was simply a question of innocent social . . . entertainment. I mean, after all, it *was* the first time these four gentlemen had been in Munich, for three of them their first time in Germany at all. So it was a matter of simple courtesy to look after our Italian colleagues out of office hours too. The expenses were — this is strictly between ourselves — were entered in the books under "costs arising from a fire in a waste-paper basket". That was *my* idea. My head of department would otherwise not have had a clue as to where we might accommodate these outgoings.'

98

'Were the expenses so high?'

'That's what I'm *telling* you! At first, as I said, we thought the gentlemen were looking for innocent conviviality. My head of department begged to be excused on the grounds that his gastritis required the application every evening of camomile poultices, and so it fell to my lot. I thought, I'll take the gentlemen to a typical Munich hostelry. So I went with them to the Augustiner. Although it was evening already, I ordered some *Weisswürste*.'

'Quite right. I'd have done the same. Although everyone knows that white sausages really ought not to live to hear the ring of the noonday chimes.'

'Well, the Italian gentlemen were far from delighted. One of them voiced the suspicion that the *Weisswürste* contained milk and were baby food. The others took the mustard for jam. I very soon came to the conclusion that my Italian colleagues' idea of conviviality ran in a very different direction from my own.'

'I've a feeling something nasty is going to . . . You don't mean . . . ?'

'Not exactly what you are thinking, Headmaster Bürkel, but nearly. Nearly. Do you know the Congo Cabaret in the Ainmillerstrasse?'

'Heaven forfend!'

'Still unsuspecting, I decided to take my guests, who after all were, without exception, academics, to my student fraternity house. I waved down a taxi, but we had hardly sat down in the taxi when one of them, the one who spoke German, asked the taxi driver where in Munich there was *really* something going on, and the taxi driver recommended this Congo place. What else could I do?'

'You poor unfortunate fellow.'

'Fortunately, I had brought enough money. The prices there!'

'And what, if I may ask, was on offer?'

'I couldn't possibly go through the whole list with you. It was most distressing.'

'Unclothed women?'

'Several.'

'So this is what we have come to. Purely as a matter of interest – *completely* undressed?'

'As good as, yes. At most, a few feathers or chains.'

'Disgusting. Negresses, I suppose?'

'Those too. But also . . . also white women . . . and a Chinese.'

'The world will stop at nothing these days, Herr *Regierungs-rat*. And, these ladies – in so far as one may use the term in this context – well . . . did they come on to the stage in this, ahem, costume, or did they . . . ?'

'They undressed before our eyes, on the public stage.'

'And then they danced?'

'If you can apply to *that* sort of thing a term once conse-crated to the Muse Terpsichore.'

'And, Herr *Regierungsrat* . . . I mean, how *close* – what I mean is, I hope that a certain distance, not to mention the protective cover of darkness and drapings . . . ?'

'Not a bit of it. No farther away than from here to that banister, and in the full glare of spotlights –'

'That is outrageous. And the police never intervene. Ah well, we can hardly complain if the youth of today is becom-ing more depraved by the minute. Hm. And those prices, Herr *Regierungsrat*, quite out of reach of the pocket of a normal – I mean – for someone, you know, who . . . ?'

'Barefaced robbery. For a bottle of inferior champagne, eighty marks! If I hadn't had that idea of the fire in the waste-paper basket . . . but that has to remain strictly between ourselves . . .'

'Indeed. Outrageous. But, on the other hand – it has its good side, in that it does constitute a certain constraint.'

'The sight of these ladies – my guests would have thought it very discourteous of me if I had ostentatiously looked away the *whole* time – showed me quite distinctly the gulf between that good, earthy German style, call it conservative if you will, and Romanesque depravity.'

'I suppose the Italians enjoyed themselves quite shame-lessly?'

'Precisely.'

'Oh, the noble simplicity, the mute grandeur which, as

Winkelmann so aptly noted, is the mark of an, albeit – *salve venia* – nude, Laocoon. What a sink of iniquity we live in.'

'You are absolutely right. One realises it perfectly when one has seen something like this.'

'Indeed so, Herr *Regierungsrat* – but where are the likes of us to drum up eighty marks from?'

'And then Councillor Weber arrived. You know who I mean . . .'

'Weber?'

'The groom, that used to live next door.'

'Oh, *that* Weber. Is he a city councillor?'

'For two years now. In 1926, he took over the seat that had been held by a Dr Erwin Mayer, who died. He was on the Party ticket in 1924, but missed election by a whisker.'

'The one with the enormous pot belly and the pear-shaped head?'

'The very same.'

'There you are then, Herr *Regierungsrat* Pflaum – things just *can't* go on like this. Between you and me – my wife heard this from the milkwoman – this Weber, he has a criminal record as long as your arm, and he's on the Council! Merciful heavens! I always did have my doubts about democracy.'

'Made a dreadful exhibition of himself in the Congo – he's obviously a regular there. The . . . er . . . ladies garlanded him with flowers. He ordered champagne . . . and . . . I can't bring myself to . . .'

'No need to feel embarrassed, Herr *Regierungsrat*, you know who you are talking to.'

'. . . He had a fat cigar in his hand, and finally he pulled one of the naked . . . um . . . ladies on to his lap and stuck a hundred-mark note between . . .'

'Between?'

'No, headmaster, I can't describe it.'

'Nor do you need to, Herr *Regierungsrat*, where else is anybody to . . . to a woman . . . with nothing on . . . between what . . . hem hem, I can well imagine, although I have never been in the – I mean this ironically, of course – enviable position. I imagine it was naturally the Chinese or one of the Negresses?'

'No, she was white.'

'Tsk, tsk, tsk, tsk. And these are our representatives of the *people*. What am I saying – "the people"? *I* didn't vote for him. He's a Socialist, no doubt?'

'NSDAP, Herr *Oberlehrer*.'

After a pause: 'I find that hard to believe, Herr *Regierungs-rat*.'

'But I saw it with my own eyes.'

'I really must get on with my shopping, Herr *Regierungsrat*, I've lingered far too long already. Our conversations are always so interesting. Adieu. Mhm, mhm. NSDAP. Mhm, mhm. I really don't know what to believe any more.'

'My respects, Herr *Oberlehrer*.'

*

There's something wrong somewhere. Despite all the shouting and exhortation, this Germany just won't damn well awaken. These Jews just won't damn well be damned. What's behind it all? Are the calls of those who utter The Call not loud enough? Is Germany's slumber too deep?

Only a few individuals awoke. Fräulein Anni Rehborn, for example, the German breast-stroke champion of 1924, who thanks to Emil Maurice's efforts as go-between was often a guest of Wolf's on the Obersalzberg. Apparently this did not bother her fiancé, Dr Karl Brand, in the least. It bothered him so little, in fact, that he allowed Wolf to appoint him to be his physician in constant attendance. Where did the Author from the Obersalzberg get the money to indulge in the luxury of a personal physician? Had *Mein Kampf* (there were now two volumes of it) suddenly become a best-seller? No. Sales of the book were still extremely poor, it lay like a lump of lead in the bookshops, and even more so in the cellars beneath Eher's, the publishers. Not until 1933 did sales pick up, although 'sales' is perhaps not quite the right word for it. Every couple that was married after 1933 received a presentation copy. Every child had one laid in its cradle by the local *Gruppenleiter*. (Could that have been the real reason behind Hitler's propaganda for Germanic reproduction?) Presents from the Party, the

National-Sozialistischer Deutscher Arbeiter-Verein e. V., an *eingetragener Verein*, a registered society with legal standing, whose political work was attended to by the NSDAP, bought the book from the publishers, no doubt at a discount, but the author still got a pretty generous cut. Let's take the year 1934: 1,198,350 live births in the German Reich, plus around half a million wedding ceremonies, that makes, in all, a turnover of almost two million copies. (The few who bought the book of their own free will can be left out of the calculations.) If the Party paid the publishers Eher the discount price of, let's say, ten Reichsmarks and if Herr Hitler, writer, and now in his second occupation as Reich Chancellor and national Messiah, could claim ten per cent, then that would make RM 2 million per annum. At that rate, he must have been one of the highest-earning authors ever to have written in Germany.

But where did the Party get all that money? Twenty million marks a year, for these tomes alone, that nobody read? What percentage of the NSDAP's total budget that represented is impossible to determine, for this party's conduct of its financial affairs was, to put it mildly, a dog's breakfast. But twenty million was a lot of money. (As a point of reference: the revenue from income tax, the biggest entry in the income of the entire Reich, amounted in 1933/34 to some 1.3 thousand million.) Membership fees, perhaps? At the end of 1933, the NSDAP had 3.9 million members; the membership fee stood, for the 'Unwaged', at RM 0.40, and, for members with a monthly income of over 740 marks, at RM 12 per month (the maximum level). Assuming, then, an average contribution rate of roughly RM 1 per member per month, or RM 12 per annum, this gives approximately forty-five million marks. So the Party big-wigs spent over half of that on the book . . . ? No. The Party had other sources besides, namely donations. For example, the communes were hefty contributors (from taxes, of course), and nothing could deter the city of Munich alone, the 'Capital of the Movement', from donating, between 1933 and 1945, a total of RM 27 million to Party coffers. (Mind you, only in 1947 was it revealed that a major proportion of this got snagged up in the accounts of a certain Christian Weber. If the Führer knew that – or had known. Even if the Führer had known about it, he would have said nothing, because otherwise the same Christian Weber would have . . . For Christian Weber, Munich was increasingly becoming the Capital of the Movement, for the movement of capital, in the course of which entries under 'credit' predominated quite healthily.) To sum up, then: taxes – Party donations (even at that time) – and *Mein Kampf* as a present for newly-weds, who go on to pay further taxes. So these newly-weds and future parents were thus indirectly financing the *Struggle*, at least in part, themselves.

In 1925, however, that was still all pie in the sky. Where did Wolf, on the Obersalzberg, in 1925, get all that money from? Only from Frau Bruckmann? No one knows . . . But one thing is certain: apart from Frau Bruckmann and Frau Wagner-Wahnfried (although all she contributed was complimentary tickets), there must have been many other Germans who awakened as early as 1925, otherwise Wolf would have had to get by on the Obersalzberg without a personal physician and perhaps even without Fräulein Rehborn.

Christian Weber was not one of the awakened, but of the wakeners. Nevertheless, the suspicion that the general awakening of the Germans and the general snuffing-out of the Jews constituted only a secondary aim along the road that the fat – and ever-swelling – bouncer saw ahead of him cannot be dismissed out of hand. What was his goal? It stood, bathed in a bright golden halo of light, in Weber's mind's eye: a naked girl, wearing only a helmet and astride a horse. Was *that* what Germany had to be awakened for?

Weber's excursion into intellectualism was short-lived. It will perhaps be remembered that he occasionally passed himself off as a 'journalist'. In 1925, along with the former 'Propaganda Leader' of the *Völkischer Beobachter*, Otto May, and the 'National Socialist Section Leader' – whatever that might be – Karl Eggers, he founded in Munich the weekly periodical *Europäische Zeit, Kampfblatt und Organ der deutschen Opposition zur Abwehr des Bolschewismus*, the *European Times, Campaign Newspaper and Organ of the German Opposition for the Defence against Bolshevism.* This resonant enterprise had its editorial office in No. 1 Theklastrasse. (Even in those early days, the Nazis were misusing the epithet 'European' when what they really meant was 'Fascist'. Nowadays, in this context, the talk is of the 'eternal values of the Christian Occident'.) The paper was bad, and its sales worse. Weber got out of the editorial board as early as November 1925, which, however, did nothing to raise the quality of the publication. Weber favoured more direct methods: draw in the paunch, let it out again quickly, thrust the opposition out of the way and take the money.

'I have the honour to inform you,' wrote the local civil prosecutor on 7 February 1925 to Police Headquarters, 'that C.W. has been sentenced to a fine of RM 5 or one day's imprisonment on a charge of driving at a speed of thirty-six k.p.h through the town of Pfaffenhofen.' Flashy driving was closer to C.W.'s heart than all that intellectual malarkey. Later, in a toast at a banquet on the occasion of his fiftieth birthday, the main speaker was to say, 'His' (Weber's) 'indefatigably Devil-may-care approach to the enemies of the Movement brought him before the bar of the court on 152 occasions in the space of fourteen years.' A hundred and fifty-two times – one of these in Pfaffenhofen, an indefatigably Devil-may-care thirty-six kilometres per hour. If Germany wasn't to awaken, then certainly Pfaffenhofen was – to the roar of an exhaust.

There stood Weber, then, with one foot on the bottom rung of the ladder. In March 1926 he was able to draw the second foot up behind it. An old Nazi by the name of Dr Erwin Mayer, who on all other counts would rightly have remained unremembered, died. Weber, who at the elections had missed out by one place on the Party list, moved up into his seat on the City Council. He was sworn in at a meeting of the *Stadtrat* on 16 March 1926.

As early as 1927, Weber made his first acquaintance with the big wide world. Up till then he had never got beyond the confines of Polsingen and Munich and Coburg and Erding. (He had not even been allowed to take part in the free trips into other countries organised by the King-Emperor's generals between 1914 and 1918.) On 13 August, the validity of his passport ('Weber, Christian, businessman and city councillor . . .') was extended until 20 December 1929, and he set off on his first official business trip. With several members of the *Werkausschuss*, to which Weber had had himself elected (sounds rather prosaic, but this Public Works Committee had the power to allocate public franchises; C.W. always did have a nose for where the best pickings were to be found), he embarked on a 'study of traffic problems' and visited Paris, London, Brussels, Amsterdam, Hamburg and Berlin in turn. Councillor Weber, man of the world. Just what kind of traffic can it have been that Weber studied in these cities? 'I'm off to Maxim's . . .' In London, he got to know a Mr Spratt, who took a real shine to this genuine original Bavarian character. Did Mr Spratt not notice the tiny swastika on C.W.'s tie pin? Or did he not know what this swastika signified? Or did C.W., the new man of the world, leave his swastika at home again?

On 1 May 1928 – it had not yet been declared a national holiday – Weber made his last appearance on account of his indefatigably Devil-may-care approach in the cause of National Regeneration at the bar of the court (not yet the 'People's'): indefatigably Devil-may-care, he had had three unauthorised advertising placards attached to the building at Sebastiansplatz 9 – which didn't belong to him, of course. The text on the placards – was it ONE NATION, ONE REICH, ONE FÜHRER! GERMANY AWAKE, EVEN IF WE . . . ? No? No. The legend read: CHRISTIAN WEBER'S TOURS – DISTANCE NO OBJECT. Weber was acquitted after undertaking to apply for retrospective permission for the advertisements.

The bulwark against Bolshevism. No one has ever done as much for the spread of Bolshevism as Hitler and his accomplices: without Hitler's cover behind him, Stalin would not have been able to occupy the Baltic states, there would have been no Hitler–Stalin Pact, Lemberg would not have been Russified into Lvov, Hitler would not have unleashed the war, half of Europe would not have become Bolshevik. So what's the autobahn compared to all that . . .

*

Over every happiness a shadow must fall. There's nothing worse than when one friend falls out with another, especially when it involves Teutons and loyal supporters of the cause. Wolf, and Emil Maurice. At Christmas 1927, Emil got engaged to Geli Raubal. Wolf blew his top. Himmler plucked from Maurice's family tree a few ancestors of the sort that no Teuton should have had under any circumstances. 'Moritz? Uhuh, right enough.' Hitler fired his chauffeur Maurice. Maurice had the gall to file a complaint against Hitler at the Munich Industrial Tribunal in April 1928, claiming a total of RM 3,000 in unpaid wages. The matter was settled out of court. Hitler coughed up five hundred marks, which Maurice used to set up a watchmaker's business. The engagement to Geli was broken off; nevertheless Wolf remained irreconcilable. Weber was caught with a foot in both camps, an extremely embarrassing situation for him. Maurice badgered him to intercede with Wolf and plead for a reprieve; Wolf forbade Weber any further contact with Maurice. An embarrassing situation, yes indeed. In fact, two years previously, in 1925, there had been a similar incident. But we have to go back some way to get the whole of that story.

Christian Weber, not even a city councillor at the time, was the owner of the transport firm *Christian Weber's Fernfahrten* (with the nonsensical anglicised apostrophe before the genitive S), and as such the proprietor and licensed owner of several vehicles (strange how the French borrowing '*Auto*' was later to be Germanised to '*Kraftfahrzeug*', abbreviated to Kfz, or *Personenkraftwagen*, PKW for short; why did the Nazis have such a fancy for abbreviations? Nobody has ever investigated this. NSDAP; SA; SS; NSKK, the National Socialist Corps of Drivers; NSV, the National Socialist People's Welfare; a UvD was a duty officer, an AK an Army corps, KZ a concentration camp. Gen.d.PZ signified a general of a panzer or armoured division; then there was Inf. Div., U-Boot and GRÖFAZ. An indication of dynamism? No time for frills? Brief and to the point and then straight into action? This penchant for abbreviations is incidentally something almost all totalitarian regimes have in common. So is there some underlying connection? And besides, who remembers what the abbreviation GRÖFAZ stands for? *Grösster Feldherr Aller Zeiten* – the Greatest leader of all time. The Gloat. Now who could they have meant by that?). One of Weber's cars was a Horch six-cylinder, already riddled with rust and, on more than one occasion, on the brink of giving up the Horch ghost.

'Emil,' said Weber to Maurice, who at that time was still Hitler's chauffeur, 'you know a bit about these things; take a look, will you?'

Maurice lifted the bonnet and gave an apprehensive shake of his head. 'Looks bad, does that. But I know a mechanic out on the Tegernseer Landstrasse. We could go down there together.'

However, the mechanic too just shook his head and advised scrapping it. Weber tore his hair: he stood to lose several hundred marks here, the car was still in reasonable nick and he had bought it only a year ago, second-hand mind. (It was also a pre-war model.) 'If I was to repair all that,' said the mechanic, 'I could do it – but I'm not keen, a thankless job, that – but it'd cost you . . . let's see now,' the mechanic walked round and round the car, rapping the bodywork with his knuckles, 'it'd cost you . . . let's say . . . off the top of my head, mind . . . three and a half thousand marks.'

'That's crazy,' Weber exclaimed, 'I could just about get a new one for that.'

'Exactly,' said the mechanic.

'There's something in this for you too,' said Weber as they set off on the return journey.

'I don't get you,' said Maurice.

'Yes, well, you wouldn't, would you? What is there to understand? There's something in it for you, I'm saying. I know where I can drum up the cash.' Weber rubbed thumb and forefinger together.

'I think you're going to have to be more precise.'

Weber heaved his bulk round in the passenger seat till he was facing Maurice.

'Your boss. Now his car . . . I mean, it's insured, isn't it?'

'Sure. Boss's orders.'

'Well then.'

'What d'you mean – well then?'

'If Hitler's car is insured, and you were to sort of run into mine, then the insurance'll pay up and not Hitler? Right?'

'I see,' said Maurice, and gave a quiet whistle.

'At last,' sighed Weber, heaving himself back round.

'How much?'

'How much what?'

'For me.'

'Ten per cent.'

'Ten per cent of what?'

'Of what Wolf's insurance pays him.'

'And what if Wolf notices?'

'Does he ever notice anything?'

'Not really.'

'There you are, then.'

Hitler's insurance paid out four thousand marks as compensation for the alleged accident damage to Weber. Hitler noticed nothing. When Maurice confessed to him that he had had an accident with a car 'belonging to some stranger', Hitler glanced up only momentarily from his cream cake (Maurice had chosen his moment well) and said, 'And whose fault was it?'

'Mine, I'm afraid,' said Maurice, putting on a contrite look.

'And what damage is there to my car?'

'Nothing,' said Maurice. 'I mean, not much. I've fixed it already. But the other car – a write-off. The Jew it belonged to, he was pretty peeved . . .'

Hitler smiled at that.

The accident: in those days, only a very few people knew the procedure. The two cars were set up on a crossroads as if they had just collided, and the police were called. A rueful Maurice admitted that unfortunately he hadn't noticed this gentleman had right of way . . . his insurance would take care of the whole thing. The policeman asked Weber, did he want the matter to go to court? Weber, the urbane Weber: No, not at all; you've just heard him admit responsibility, officer. These things happen. Happened to me myself. (The one element of truth in the whole story.) The fact that the drivers knew each other, that the 'accident' had been pre-arranged, never came out. And how is anybody to find out, if nobody asks? Four thousand less the four hundred for Maurice: that left 3,600. Weber sold his old car, got quite a good price for it, added the insurance money and bought himself a brand-new one.

That had been a couple of years ago. Now Maurice was sitting in Weber's new flat (no longer the sub-let in the Aventinstrasse) feeling very sorry for himself.

'I helped you out that time,' said Maurice, 'remember, with the car.' The undertones were clear for Weber to hear – that was exactly the kind of language he understood: if you don't help me, Hitler will hear about who the car belonged to, and what kind of an accident it really was. Maybe, thought Weber, this chiseller has hidden away other bits of evidence too.

Weber smiled: 'Sure . . . one good turn washes the . . . scratches my . . .'

'Deserves,' said Maurice.

'. . . another. What do you want me to do?'

'Wolf listens to you.'

'Ha ha,' Weber chuckled, 'he's got no choice.'

'I certainly don't want to be his driver any more. But I want to stay in the Party. Especially now that things are looking up.'

Weber reflected for a moment.

'Right,' he said, 'I've had an idea. I'll talk to Wolf.'

'Soon!'

'Soon.'

When Weber introduced the subject of Maurice, Wolf's face swelled up like a steam boiler about to burst, but then Weber said, quickly and as if by the way, 'It's because of the pictures, see?'

'Because of what?' barked Wolf.

'Because of the pictures. Your ones. Of Geli.'

The steam pressure subsided at once, as if it had been lanced – there was almost a perceptible hiss. Wolf's face went a greyish-brown (something like the colour later used for the uniform of the *Arbeitsdienst*).

'Who – what – how?'

'Probably Geli gave him some of them. Must have done. Saw them myself when I was at Maurice's place. Of course I don't look at . . . such, you know, intimate things . . .'

'How dare she!'

'It would be very awkward if Maurice was to sell things like that. To a Jewish art dealer for instance. Abroad.'

Wolf leapt to his feet. The steam pressure was rising again. Wolf's eyes were rolling, his mouth working, his little brush bristling, he looked to the ceiling and took a deep breath.

'You don't need to make a speech now,' said Weber, 'there's only the two of us here.'

'These . . . pictures . . . are not by me . . .'

'Signed,' said Weber drily.

At that, all the steam escaped from Wolf's boiler. His face went grey (like, later, the *Luftwaffe*'s track-suit trousers), and he began to whimper.

'Come on now, Wolf,' Weber said, patting his ashen cheek with his fat hand.

So Maurice remained in the Party. From 1933 he was a National Socialist city councillor, and later an alderman, in Munich; from 1 January 1936 Vice-President of the Reich Chamber of Trade; from 30 January 1939 an SS-*Oberführer* (that was somewhere between a colonel and a major-general); and even before that a Member of the Reichstag. Left strangely free from scrutiny after the war, he died on 6 February 1972 in Starnberg. A rich and full life for a watchmaker.

*

'What did I tell you, Herr Blumenthal? The Nationalist Movement is dead.'

'Let's hope you're right, Herr Peschmowitz, but six Nazis are sitting over there in the Town Hall, as city councillors – nine in the provincial parliament, and in the *Reichstag* there are twelve of them.'

'I see. Mhm. Out of how many?'

'Twelve out of 491.'

'Twelve Nazis among 491 Members of the Reichstag? There you are, then, Herr Blumenthal: they've become no more than an absolutely innocuous splinter party.'

'They shout the loudest, though.'

'Little children always shout louder than big ones.'

'Precisely, Herr Peschmowitz, and they grow.'

'A bad example, I admit. Little *people* shout. Take that fellow Gobble or Gobsel or whatever his name is, the one with the club foot . . . a mere shrimp, no taller than a fire hydrant, he does a lot of shouting – that, Herr Blumenthal, is because small people, well, dwarfs, since they're so easily overlooked, visually, have to draw attention to themselves acoustically. It's something of a natural law, Herr Blumenthal, and it works the other way round, too: I remember once hearing Bismarck speak – now he was a giant – and what about him? He piped in such a high-pitched voice you could hardly make him out.'

'*Goebbels*.'

'I beg your pardon, Herr Blumenthal?'

'That one you were talking about, the fire hydrant, his name is Goebbels. Dr Joseph Goebbels.'

'I never remember their names. I don't want to remember their names. I'm even proud of the fact that I forget what that riff-raff call themselves. I can't even recall the head screamer's name: Hiedler? Hügler? Histler?'

'You've got it wrong, Herr Peschmowitz, quite wrong. *They* don't need to remember *our* names. Because *we* are no threat to *them*. But they are to us, all right. The hare has to know where the hunter is, Herr Peschmowitz, which way the wind is blowing. That's the real state of affairs. Now *I'm* even keeping a list.'

'You're paying them more heed than they're worth.'

'No doubt. But I'm on the qui vive.'

'You're looking too much on the black side, Herr Blumenthal.'

'No – I told you before: as I see it, the future isn't black, that wouldn't bother me at all. It's brown.'

'A brown future.'

'God preserve us.'

'A brown future for our fatherland, Herr Blumenthal? I can't imagine that.'

'We can never visualise real catastrophes. Well, perhaps happening to others. For instance, Herr Peschmowitz, can you imagine Herr Kammerlander's wife poisoning herself, Kammerlander shooting his son, going bankrupt, being put in prison . . . and being hanged?'

'Well, I suppose . . . Herr Blumenthal . . . theoretically . . . yes . . .'

'Exactly my point. You can picture it happening to Kammerlander. But not to yourself!'

'To *me*?'

'Yes, you. We can picture disasters happening to others, but not to ourselves. At least not really. And the same applies to us collectively, too, Herr Peschmowitz.'

'A brown future.'

'Yes, there, the whole Marienplatz, full of swastika flags . . . the Town Hall full of brown uniforms. The Lord Mayor a Nazi, the Prime Minister a Nazi, the Reich Chancellor a Nazi . . . and we Jews forced to wear those yellow hats again. Those yellow, pointed hats.'

'Come now, Herr Blumenthal, we're not living in the Middle Ages.'

'That all depends on what you mean by the Middle Ages.'

'I would refuse . . .'

'Refuse? Did our forefathers refuse, in the past, to wear pointed yellow hats? – to live in the ghetto? – to knuckle under and grovel?'

'Times have changed, though. Surely.'

'Times, Herr Peschmowitz, never change.'

'But Herr Blumenthal, anti-Semitism is to all intents and purposes a thing of the past. No reasonable person . . .'

'Reasonable person?'

'I know, Herr Blumenthal, you have your doubts about what's reasonable, but, I ask you, the German people, the *good* ones . . . and . . . and . . . we're German too . . . the good ones would rise like one man and there'd be such an outcry . . .'

113

'Forgive me for interrupting, Herr Peschmowitz, but, just as an example, do you seriously believe that – good day to you, Herr Dirrigl, good day – as I was saying, Herr Peschmowitz, do you honestly believe that Dirrigl there, for instance, who has just gone past with his flea-ridden mutt, and his friend Kammerlander, who usually trails his own flea-bag about with him . . . can you see them rising as one man . . . ? Simply because, let's say, you and I were to be forced to wear pointed yellow hats?'

'But public opinion abroad . . . Germany simply can't afford such a . . .'

'Do you think for one moment that one single Frenchman, one solitary Englishman, would lift a finger for the sake of a German Jew?'

'Aren't you being . . . *overly* pessimistic, really?'

'Good luck to you, Herr Peschmowitz. But at least make a note of their names.'

'How many seats did you say they have in the *Reichstag*?'

'Twelve.'

'Out of how many altogether?'

'Four hundred and ninety-one.'

'So that's almost . . .'

'That's exactly 2.6 per cent.'

'I don't know how you remember all these things.'

'It's easy really. Twelve is an easy number to remember. A dozen. And 491 – that's the C-minor piano concerto where the beginning always reminds me vaguely of the "Musical Offering" . . .'

'What? I don't . . .'

'Mozart. The Köchel index: K 491. Piano Concerto in C minor.'

'I see. Very interesting. Is that how you memorise numbers?'

'Just a little game of mine, Herr Peschmowitz, but give a thought now and then to what I've been telling you.'

'I really don't think you're right.'

'I fervently hope I'm not.'

*

With his elevation to city councillor, Christian Weber's delinquencies also ascended, if that is the right word, to higher, more refined levels. Daring escapades. Christian Weber the dashing cavalier. (And the ladies to whom he directed his gallant overtures were increasingly drawn from better circles.) At 1.45 p.m. on 30 October 1928, Weber was driving to the City Hall in his new car (a Ford supplied by the firm of Stuppacher, which was later to play a further part in his life). Next to him sat his Party colleague and bosom pal, Karl Weiss, a fellow city councillor. In his testimony as a witness, Herr *Stadtrat* Karl Weiss declared that the businessman Wilhelm Böhm, bachelor, resident in the Blutenburgstrasse, No. 110/IV – 'very probably a Jew' – who wanted to make a left turn on his bicycle at the Thomass-Eck into the Kaufingerstrasse – 'what business has the Jew from the Blutenburgstrasse being on the Marienplatz is what I'd like to know' – gave *no* hand signal. Witness Weiss: 'Herr Weber was travelling very slowly; the injured party became unsteady and fell off his bicycle.' Just the way Jews do fall off their cycles. Can't even ride a bike properly, that lot. Now Weber, on the other hand, he's of a quite different stamp. He can even drive a car.

As luck would have it, though, there was another witness. His name was Alfred Höfer, he lived at Feldmochingerstrasse 224, and he saw that the injured man did indeed give a hand signal and that the motorist – i.e. Christian Weber – was not driving slowly at all, but more what you'd call pretty nippily. Thus Christian Weber, the Old Campaigner, stood once again at the bar of the court as a martyr to his solid National Socialist convictions. And the decision of the corrupt, Jew-riddled Bolshevist justiciary of the Weimar Republic? A sixty-mark fine with an alternative of – would you credit it! – twelve days' imprisonment.

Weber did not pay. Weber never paid if he didn't feel like it. If a Christian Weber didn't see eye to eye with anything, well, he . . . just didn't go along with it. *Paying a fine*, for something like *that*? No way. He didn't come up the river on a banana-skin, not him. It wasn't as if he was one of those that made money in their sleep. And then there was his deprived youth. And anyway. No, he wouldn't pay. The courts could take a running jump. What was that? Everyone's equal in the eyes of the law? But he's Christian Weber. That's something *quite* different. No, not paying.

It will perhaps be remembered that, back in 1923, Weber had had to stump up five hundred marks (inflation-hit marks, so a piddling amount) for the rejection notice regarding his application for a gun licence. For years some obstinate bailiff, no doubt a member of a Communist-organised union, had been on his tail. Post-inflation, the amount was amended – to 1.60 *Rentenmark*s (inclusive of accumulated interest). Weber did not pay. Every time, he had a new excuse; the bailiff was losing his hair in sheer frustration. When Weber moved up into the Council, the first thing – the very first thing – he did was to have the relevant file brought to him and to obtain a waiver from the responsible official.

But now this sixty marks. Weber didn't pay. Again, a thousand and one excuses. These went on until January 1933, by which time no bailiff's office would dare so much as to shove such a thing under Weber's nose. Weber was now ensconced at the top. Documents were *passed up* to him now. If they weren't to his liking, he scornfully hurled them back down. As a legacy of the accident, the businessman and bachelor Wilhelm Böhm was to go through life with a shortened left leg.

So maybe there is some justice after all? Wilhelm Böhm, who, contrary to Weber's assumption, came of unblemished Aryan stock all the way back to his great-grandparents, was as a result of his injuries no longer fit for military service. In 1939, when they were all marching off to where men were men and hearts were weighed in the balance, he had to stand sadly by the window and watch. In the long run, mind you, he was spared more than a few miseries.

Then there was the attack on the *Völkischer Beobachter* publishing house in the Thierschstrasse on 21 January 1931. By chance, Weber was present, a fact that led to him being questioned, on 24 January 1931, by the police, in the person of Police Constable Huber (recording clerk was Weisenberger, Clerk). (Two years on, if Messrs Huber and Weisenberger had had the temerity to summons someone like Weber, Christian, they would have found themselves, the very next day, going through purgatory – if not worse.) According to the transcript, Christian Weber behaved as a paragon of civility and patrician dignity. Apparently a vast crowd of five young men had stood outside the Nazi newspaper offices shouting '*Heil Moscow!*' and had been given a drubbing for their pains by a small troop of courageous Nazis from the building (there were fewer than twenty-five of them). Whereupon one – presumably Jewish – police officer (Sergeant Pflügel) had insolently forced his way into the building in order to take the names of those national heroes who had done the fighting. In doing so, this Jew Pflügel (the very name – typically Jewish) threw the whole works into confusion, coming within an ace of delaying the prompt delivery of the following morning's edition of the *Völkischer Beobachter*, which would have caused incalculable damage. Strictly observing the formalities, he, Weber, had said to Pflügel, 'You could not possibly take the consequences of hampering the work of this company, for you would never be able to afford compensation for the damages.' (And with that he had suddenly let out his belly and bowled the policeman, who had single-handedly confronted a threatening mob of a couple of dozen Nazi bully-boys, some of them armed, right out of the building. Weber did, however, omit to make mention of this in his evidence.)

Preliminary proceedings were instituted against Weber. But it was Police Officer Pflügel's word against that of the entire Nazi works staff, and the Public Prosecutor's office – among them *Assessor* Winkler, a name we seem to have come across before – recognised the mood of the times. The proceedings petered out. According to a memorandum, Weber had entered an 'objection' (presumably to an order for a summary fine) on 1 September 1931. A further note in the files, dated 30 January 1932, reveals that at that time the case had still not been concluded. A year later to the day, the case was finally settled. Other matters were also settled. Herr – now State Prosecutor – Winkler became a member not only of the National Socialist League for the Preservation of Justice but also of the SS.

On 27 August of the year 1928, two days after his forty-fifth birthday, Weber had moved house: away from the Aventinstrasse and into more appropriate accommodation in a most salubrious area. Sebastiansplatz 9, second floor, tel. 27728. This was something of a return to his roots: outside his flat, the Blumenstrasse leads into the Viktualienmarkt. On the corner, there – still – stands the *Blauer Bock*. Directly next to that, going towards the Jakobsplatz, is Sebastiansplatz 9. Wasn't it in the same Blue Buck that a certain Weber, Christian, once discovered his devotion for the Nationalist Movement? Whenever Councillor Weber passed by and the landlord, still the same one, happened to be standing at his door, then he would bow deeply and say, 'A very good evening to you, Herr *Stadtrat*, will you be doing me the honour of your custom one of these days?'

Weber would return the greeting affably with a wave of his hat, saying, 'Sure, sure, all right. If I get time. Oh God, pressures of office, pressures of office!'

He never frequented the *Blauer Bock* any more. He much preferred the Congo.

Then again there was the great rally, when people converged on Nuremberg from all points of the compass for the '1929 Reich Party Convention', from 1 to 4 August. Up for competition were prizes like the 'Adolf Hitler Challenge Trophy' and a 'Distance Prize', put up by Munich's National Socialist city councillors. 'All enquiries relating to the Rally . . . should be addressed directly to the Rally Administrative Headquarters, Munich office, Sebastiansplatz 9/II, no later than twelve noon on 1 August.' Thus ran the lavish advertising spread in the *Völkischer Beobachter*, and then, below that, 'At the car park in Nuremberg, pump facilities for petrol and benzol are available, as are grease, oil and spark-plugs and a mobile repair workshop.'

In Munich, there were facilities on hand that could be pumped for other things – not everyone had access to them, just a select few. And greasers were in attendance, too. Well, two of them at least. Their names were Weber and Röhm. In those days, they attended rallies together.

On the occasion of this particular rally, something must have occurred, for on 24 September 1929 the Nuremberg

District Court issued a summary punishment order against Weber on the grounds of 'two violations, both of them relating to §21 of the Motor Vehicle Regulations of 3 May 1909, and to §§ 27 and 21 (II) of the Road Traffic Regulations'. A fine of RM 10 with the option of one day's detention. Weber did not pay this either. (In the face of oncoming traffic, one must drive on the right. Weber had been driving in the middle, apparently needing the whole road to himself.)

On 8 December 1929, the last – for the next sixteen years – City Council elections in Munich took place. As far as the NSDAP was concerned, the results did not match up to expectations: the Party won only eight of the fifty seats. But Weber was elected; that is to say – and has to be said in defence of the people of Munich – he was placed so high on the NSDAP list that he gained entry into the Council. A vote of confidence, from which one might deduce any degree of popularity, it was not. Weber most certainly did not, as the modern-day expression goes, maintain a high profile. In plenary sessions of the Council in the years up to 1933, he kept himself very much to the back benches. No intervention on his part is recorded in the minutes. But his attendance record was almost perfect. He wrought his good works mostly in silence. Good, that is, for Christian Weber. In June 1930, Max Amann resigned his seat on the *Kreistag*, the County Council. Amann, too, was a short, fat man. He had been a junior NCO in the unit (the 16th Bavarian Infantry Reserve Regiment) in which Hitler had served as a lance-corporal. For a lance-jack, an NCO, however junior, was little short of a superior being. That stuck in Hitler's mind, and remained stuck. With unswerving loyalty he stood by Amann, who was thick but cunning. Compared with what this Amann managed to purloin, even Weber's acquisitions were very small beer. From 1921, Amann had been Managing Director of the *Völkischer Beobachter* and from 1922 a director of the Central Publishing House of the NSDAP (formerly Franz Eher, Publishers) and paid horrendous fees for Hitler's literary contributions. Hitler returned the compliment: post-1933, he allowed Amann a free hand for his series of piracies throughout the world of newspaper publishing. By the end, Amann held sway over seventy, if not eighty, per cent of the German press, a newspaper empire beside which the Hearst one paled by comparison. Amann's annual salary in 1934 was RM 108,000, in 1944 RM 3.8 million, yet for all that he successfully declined to contribute so much as a single pfennig in income tax. After the war, Amann had the effrontery to maintain that he had been nothing more than a businessman and had in fact had absolutely nothing to do with the Party. It is a rare glorious page in the history of Bavarian post-war justice that this, at least, was given no credence whatsover. Amann was given ten years in a labour camp and died penniless – and rightly so – in Munich in 1957.

Up to 1930, Amann was also a city councillor and a member of the County Council. In June 1930, however, he resigned these offices in order to devote himself full-time to accumulating a fortune. (On the side, he also managed, for a cut of five per cent, Hitler's royalties from *Mein Kampf*.) Weber then slid into Amann's place. As can be seen, then, the nimbus around Weber's head was growing: city councillor and Member of the *Kreistag*. (In those days, the *Kreis* was what is now called a *Regierungsbezirk*, the primary administrative division of a *Land*, or province, as in *Kreis Oberbayern*. On the other hand, the *Landkreise*, or rural administrative districts, were called *Bezirke*, regions. The Nazis turned the designations around at the end of the '30s, and the Free State of Bavaria has retained this terminology to the present day.)

On 15 May 1930 a new passport was issued to Weber, valid for five years. The passport photograph shows the city councillor in a choker, a stand-up collar with down-turned peaks, and overhanging jowls. 'Personal description: *Build:* solid, medium height; *Face:* round; *eyes:* grey-blue; *Hair:* d. brown; *Distinguishing marks:* left pupil slightly dilated.' The right eye was the glass one.

Christian Weber the pioneer. Not merely a pioneer of the Nationalist Movement, but also a pioneer of loutish behaviour in public places; the extension of his trick of shooting out his gut by other – namely, motorised – means: a note in the files of the Munich Police Headquarters, dated 16 March 1931, ref. no. 1760 Ia/Ic 5:

> *Re*
> Weber, Christian, bachelor, city councillor . . .
> for insulting & threatening behaviour, committed
> against Jules Dührenheimer, Merchant

(so, Pflügel . . . and Böhm . . . and so forth . . . it may well be that they were *not* . . . etc. . . . but *Dührenheimer*! Not to mention *Jules*! and *Merchant*! – well, if that doesn't add up to a Yid).

> *Address*: Ainmillerstr. 37/0.
> *Facts of the Case*
> At approximately noon on 6.1.1931, Dührenheimer was driving his vehicle along the secondary road between Krünn & Mittenwald. A vehicle following him indicated by means of horn signals that it wished to overtake. Owing to the poor condition of the road surface, it was impossible for Dührenheimer to pull over and give way immediately. Despite the fact that this must also have been evident to the driver of the pursuing vehicle, he continued to sound his horn in repeated and sustained blasts, with the result that Dührenheimer was forced to drive into a pile of snow, from which he was later able to withdraw only with considerable difficulty. After the other car had passed, the driver stopped, alighted from his vehicle and subjected Dührenheimer to verbal abuse. At the same time, the accused also got out of the vehicle & shouted: 'You Yid, you Czechoslovak! Haul him out of there and sling him in the Isar, the bloody Jewboy!' & he attempted to open the car door and to do physical violence to Dührenheimer. Only the latter's completely passive behaviour prevented violence of any kind being committed.
> On 14.2.31, Dührenheimer registered a complaint through his lawyer, Levinger, on the grounds of slander and threatening behaviour and instituted legal proceedings.

The Public Prosecutor in Munich I, in a letter dated 23.2.31, directed that the case be investigated.

Investigations established that Weber's car was being driven by Franz Raila (married), a lorry driver, of Ludwigstrasse 3/I. He claimed that Dührenheimer could have pulled over sooner, since the snow was only 20 cm deep and tyre tracks to the side of the road indicated that vehicles had already been travelling well over towards the edge of the road. When he had finally succeeded in overtaking Dührenheimer, the occupants of his vehicle had ordered him to stop. Weber and Esser had then alighted and walked back. He had heard animated conversation, but had not been able to make out what they were saying to Dührenheimer. The two city councillors had been annoyed because they were in a hurry, and Dührenheimer had refused, over a distance of some 4 km, to give way, despite repeated warnings.

The upshot of these proceedings, too, is unknown. What became of the merchant Jules Dührenheimer after 1933 is, unfortunately, not difficult to surmise.

The Teuton Hermann Esser, Weber's fellow councillor, is worthy of some passing attention. Esser distinguished himself by dint of an astonishing physical resemblance to friend Wolf of the Obersalzberg, which he heightened further by the cultivation of an exact replica of the sub-nasal brush. As a result of an inner conversion, the Radical Socialist Esser veered off into Drexler's German Workers' Party, the *Deutsche Arbeiter Partei*, even earlier than Hitler, and, as an Old Comrade, he collected so many items of information of the grubbiest and most intimate nature concerning his comrades-in-arms that, despite a personal record of corruption and squalid exploits that was appalling even by Nazi standards, he could neither be jettisoned by Goebbels, the Strasser brothers or Rosenberg, nor neutralised by Hitler himself. Esser, who must rank as pre-eminent among all the despicable excrement in the annals of the NSDAP, was from 1928 a member of the District Council of Upper Bavaria, from 1929 Chairman of the NSDAP Party group in the Munich City Council (and so a predecessor of Weber's), held a similar post in the Bavarian provincial parliament from 1932, became a member of the *Reichstag* in 1933 and soon after a Vice-President of the *Reichstag* and thereupon Bavarian Economics Minister and Head of the State Chancellery.

The compromising details about the Nazi bosses that were known to Esser ran the gamut of all aspects of life, one might say from the purse to the penis. If he had blown the gaff, the Nazi government would have disintegrated like the piece of rotten fruit it in fact was. A rotten apple that was held together only by the hands of the Old Comrades. All for one, one for all. If one of them had taken his hand away, then the filth would immediately have gushed over the hands, arms and bodies of all the rest.

It would have been intriguing to learn exactly *what* information Esser had, but of course it remains unknown, for nothing like that is ever committed to paper. Only one thing is certain: Esser was in on the blackmailing of industrialists who were obliged to contribute to Party and (subsequently) state coffers. These blackmailing imbroglios had implications that went far beyond the borders of Germany. The crafty NS-mafioso Esser may well have forestalled the risk of being silenced by a long knife by having put his information down in black and white and deposited it in a Swiss bank vault, with instructions to a Swiss lawyer to forward the documents, in the event of the demise of the depositor, to the *Weltwoche* magazine. Presumably the whole lot is still reposing in the bank vault, for Esser probably revoked the relevant powers of attorney before his death. In fact he did not die until 1981, having been released from prison as early as 1952. What did he live off from 1952 onwards? Perhaps the said industrialists continued to provide for him in his old age, even after 1952. As we have said, he died only in 1981. The Bavarian Prime Minister, Dr *honoris causa* Franz Josef Strauss, sent his widow a telegram of condolence.

*

A balmy summer evening. A gentle breeze wafting along the Prinzregentenstrasse, stirring the trees under which stands the monument to Richard Wagner. Two fat men emerge from the door of the house at Prinzregentenplatz 16, where Wolf now lives on the second floor.

'It's perfectly simple, Ernstl,' said the First Fat Man, 'you see, it's because you stink.'

The Second Fat Man gave the First Fat Man a long, hard stare, but before he could recover sufficiently from the momentary inner paralysis occasioned by this remark to give due consideration to the question of what he should do next (ask for clarification? just not believe him? assume he had misheard? punch him straight in the mouth?), the First Fat Man went on, 'As one friend to another – well, I don't exactly mean you *stink*, I mean you smell too nice.'

'You've lost me now, Christian; do I stink, or do I smell nice?'

'*Too* nice. I suppose it's that . . . what is it? . . . Brazilian perfume.'

'Bolivian, not Brazilian. Brazil and Bolivia are two completely different countries.'

'Brazilian, Bolivian – it's six and half a dozen. Old Adolf doesn't like it when a man smells of perfume. And you were giving it off in clouds.'

Franz Raila, the chauffeur, came up to Weber, snatched his cap from his head – the city councillor, conscious of the respect due to his status, had trained his chauffeur well – and asked, 'Does the Herr *Stadtrat* wish me to bring his car here, or does he wish to walk to the car?'

'Tell you what,' said Weber, 'we'll stretch our legs a bit and stroll on down as far as the Isar. Franz,' he said to the driver, 'you drive on ahead to the statue of the Angel of Peace and wait for us there.'

'Very good,' said Franz Raila, replacing his cap and setting off towards the Neherstrasse, where Weber's car was parked.

Röhm had just arrived back from South America. No one had reckoned with that any more. Even less expected was the fact that Hitler – who by this time was associating with such respectable people as Hugenberg and Kirdorf, in other words with the kind that sat in leather armchairs, smoked imported

Havana cigars, could distinguish six different brands of cognac by their colour, and whose word really counted in the world of politics and economics – would take up again with this sleazy arse-bandit.

'In those days,' said Röhm, as the two fat men slowly moved off down the Prinzregentenstrasse, 'I wouldn't have given Adolf and his party a cat in hell's chance.'

'That's just where you were wrong,' said Weber. 'The rise of the People's Movement is irresistible. Let me show you: while you were away in – where was it again?'

'Bolivia.'

'In Bolivia . . . in that time, I've become a city councillor. You've no idea the advantages that brings. You know what strings to pull. I've got two companies belonging to me: Christian Weber's Tours and *Blaubock-Tank*.'

'*Blaubock-Tank?*'

'Yes – haha. A distant reminder of the Blue Buck. Omnibus companies. Six buses and a staff of twenty-eight. They toe the line all right! Obviously. Otherwise they'd be out on their ear, quick as you like. And well they know it! With four million unemployed, there's plenty out there just desperate for the chance to come and polish nuts and bolts for me. Eating out of my hand, they are.'

'But you only take on convinced National Socialists, I suppose?'

'Wouldn't dream of it. Just the opposite. For *my* lot, it's *me* that gives the orders, nobody else. And then, as you've seen, a car with a chauffeur. The city pays his wages, what's more. Ho yes. When you sit on the Trade and Commerce Committee, like me, you know the right wires to pull.'

It had been Röhm's introductory visit to Hitler. Weber had gone along with him, for it had been Weber who had put in a good word for him with Wolf. 'A poofter he may be, but that's neither here nor there, Wolf, he's still a GOS.'

'A what?' Wolf had asked.

'A Genuine Old Soldier.'

So Wolf had consented to embrace once again – metaphorically speaking, of course – the fat man with half a nose. In

125

actual fact, Wolf had kept him at arm's length, at first even addressing him formally as *Sie*.

'Because you gave off such a stink with your Brazilian perfume, of course.'

'Bolivian,' said Röhm.

They stopped.

'So who's he, then?' asked Röhm.

'Who?'

'Him up there on the monument.'

Weber went up to the plinth and read, 'Richard Wagner.'

'Oh, I see,' said Röhm.

'That's another thing; I'm going to Bayreuth this year,' Weber told him.

'Where?'

'Where Wagner is. Well, *was*. It's his daughter-in-law that's there now. A friend of Wolf's – same calibre as Erna Bruckmann, more or less. And fat! You've got to keep your wits about you when she comes towards you, so's you don't get steam-rollered. But we get the tickets for nothing.'

'You mean you go to the opera there?'

'Yes,' sighed Weber.

'Is it funny?'

'That would be the least of it, the fact that it's not funny. But – long! God, is it *long*! Very long. And there's no yawning there, mate. If Wolf was to catch you having a yawn, not to mention this Winifred – that's the daughter-in-law's name – you'd be *right* in it.'

'And you're going to that?'

'Well, you see,' said Weber, 'everything's changed while you've been away. It's all more a question of propaganda now. Carefully targeted. The four million unemployed, says Wolf, the bankruptcies, the starvation, all that, Wolf says, suits us just fine. Then the National Socialists come along as the saviours.'

'And . . . what about the punch-ups at meetings . . . I mean . . . you know, the good old . . .' Röhm's eyes were beginning to light up.

'No chance! Not any more. We're practically respectable now.'

'I never did trust that Bruckmann bitch and her little, thin teacups. The day Wolf began to swop his beer mug for one of these teacups –'

'Wolf doesn't drink any alcohol at all now. He's strictly teetotal.'

'Anybody that's teetotal,' said Röhm, 'sooner or later sinks to the depths – vegetarianism.'

'And you're not allowed to smoke in his presence, either.'

'I can't see this working out,' said Röhm.

'What are you talking about – working out or not working out? Me, I don't give a tinker's. I'm a city councillor and I've been elected for five years. I've got my nice little number. Nobody's going to take that away from me now.'

By this time, the two fat men had reached the Stuck villa. The evening sun was playing on the bronze Amazon that adorned it. Weber stopped.

'What a fantastic specimen of a woman,' said Weber, 'get an eyeful of that! – I know you're not very interested in this sort of thing, but you must admit . . .'

'Suppose so,' said Röhm.

'What a fantastic piece of womanhood. Starkers on horseback. Would you feast your eyes on that! And a marvellous horse as well. Have a good look at that head.'

'What d'you want with a naked female made of tin? And what about a cigar for me, too?'

'Sorry,' said Weber, 'forgot to offer you one.' He drew his silver cigar case from his pocket and held it out to Röhm. 'One mark apiece, those. Smoke it with reverence!'

Röhm sniffed at the imported cigar, then bit the end off and stuck it in his mouth. Weber gave him a light. His gaze was drawn back up to Stuck's bronze Amazon.

'Isn't that really something! What a fantastic bit of stuff! And stark naked on a horse! Tell you what – what's the time? Eight. The Congo'll be open by now. Come on.' Weber stuck two fingers in his mouth and whistled. A skinny shoe shiner came running from one direction, an emaciated porter from another, and started grovelling. Weber swung a kick at them. Up ahead, Franz Raila had heard the whistle and drove up at speed. The two fat men got in. As they moved off, Weber cast one more glance through the back window at the Amazon.

*

'Never again!'

'What?'

'When you look back, Sophie, it's got its funny side, but, I can tell you, while I was sitting in there . . .'

'Had a row with your caretaker, Frieda?'

'He's not a caretaker, I've told you a thousand times. Takes care of people all right – as a bouncer. Well, he used to. Now he's a city councillor.'

'In the City Hall?'

'Of course in the City Hall. Where else?'

'But how can a bouncer become a city councillor?'

'I tell you, Sophie, *two* of them in the *same* car, and both of them out to reform the world! Never again! And me – going absolutely *doolally*.'

'I don't follow what you're driving at.'

'Driving at is right. One of them was a driver – an engine driver. Hirsch, he's called – you know him, he often comes to me. A bit of a fiery type, but then, just when he's getting there, he runs out of steam.'

'Oh, that one. Didn't know he was a railwayman.'

'*And* a city councillor, too.'

'Well! I'll tell you this, under the King, that would never have happened – bouncers and railwaymen as city councillors. And is this Hirsch in the NSDAP too, or what?'

'No. Just the opposite, that's just it. Hirsch is a Communist. I suppose *that*'s why he gets the droops just when it matters. All he ever thinks of is world revolution. Whenever he . . . well, if he does manage . . . now, I'm not one to blab out intimate secrets about my clients, but . . . *if*, then afterwards he always moans out the Party song, "*Brüder, zur Sonne, zur Freiheit*".'

'And your bouncer? What does he serenade you with? "*Deutschland erwache*"?'

'Him? He gives me a slap on the backside and lights up

128

a cigar. Then I've to sit naked astride the arm of the sofa and pretend I'm on horseback. That works him up so much that he . . . well, you know what. Costs him extra, naturally. And with Hirsch, the Communist, it costs him extra when I promise to believe in world revolution. But I think I've lost him as a client. It was stupid of me, I suppose. I'd fixed up Weber for half-past ten, and, going by past experiences, he's always finished – with everything, even the horse-riding – by about twelve. So what did I do? Only made an appointment for Hirsch for half-past twelve. Well, I ask you, Sophie, in hard times like these, where so many of the girls are queuing up at the soup kitchens, *two* tricks like that on the one day – that's worth a whole month's turnover for one of them!'

'Sure. Go on.'

'Well, the rendezvous was the usual, the Café Capitol, in the Bayerstrasse.'

'For both?'

'Yes, but one at half-past ten and the other at half-past twelve. Two hours apart.'

'All the same, a bit careless.'

'It's easy to be wise after it's happened. I went a bit queasy when half-past ten came and Weber hadn't turned up, nor even at eleven. I was just about to go when he got somebody to telephone and say he'd be a bit late but I was to wait. I thought and thought, What should I do now? . . . what a mess! . . . and so on. And then Weber finally did appear. Quarter-past eleven it was by then. I tried to hurry him, come on, quickly, let's go *now* . . . but oh no, our Weber has to have his white sausages and strawberry jam and get a couple of beers down him . . . and then . . . it seems that Hirsch, who used to be on the Works Committee at SB II . . .'

'SB what?'

'I dunno – signal block, something to do with the railways anyway. Hirsch is at daggers drawn with the reformist unions. Always gives me the whole story. And on that day he had had a meeting, but only thirteen of *his* people showed up, but fifty of the reformists, and they shouted him down, so he took to his heels and made for the Café Capitol in the Bayerstrasse to see if maybe I was already there . . .'

'And not only were you there, but so was your bouncer.'

'Right.'

'Hee hee. *Two* gentlemen of the City Council.'

'Nazi and Commie. And not only that, but at the last Council meeting, or the one before that, Hirsch had threatened Weber he'd bring one of the oak chairs down on his skull.'

'Is that the way they go on?'

'Yes, well, no. It's not as bad as it sounds. That's the only kind of talk that Christian Weber understands.'

'So – which one did you take to your place, then?'

'Both! Neither of them would give way. So before there was a scandal in the Café Capitol, I waved down a taxi, bundled the two of them into it and, to be on the safe side, sat myself down in the middle, between the pair of them. And that's how we drove out to Pasing.'

'And then?'

'Luckily I had a bottle of really strong Slivovitz at home. Real powerful stuff it was, though. A regular client brought me it, a highly respectable businessman from Belgrade. He visits me every time he's in Munich. Well then, when these two, Hirsch and Weber, had knocked back enough of the Slivovitz – too bad, but more than half the bottle had to be sacrificed – then . . . well, I won't go into the details, but by the finish they were arguing again – about who was going to foot the bill. Each one insisted on paying for the other. But – look at this.'

'What is it?'

'A newspaper cutting. Yesterday's *Münchner Post*, 8 May. You won't believe it. Read it. The whole story, down to the last dot and comma.'

'Right enough.'

'The only thing I can think of is that the taxi driver must have recognised both of them.'

'Pst. Here's one coming. Hello, darling – how about us two, then?'

'For a small supplement, we'll make it a threesome, eh?'

*

130

The mid-point of life. A man's best age. Fifty years. In his prime: born in 1883, so fifty years old in 1933, Christian Ludwig Weber (where he suddenly acquired the 'Ludwig' from is impossible to ascertain; a distinctly baroque – or Bavarian? – embellishment of the all too spare, always rather Prussianly aloof-sounding Christian?), Christian Ludwig Weber, city councillor and entrepreneur, member of the NSDAP, GOS (Genuine Old Soldier). Now arrived at the zenith of his life, fifty years old. A round figure, and a round figure of a man. Or has he not yet reached the zenith? Are new shores still to beckon? What's this 'still'? This is just the beginning now, when, in this same year of 1933, the National Regeneration has at last . . . yes, how should one put it, dawned? broken out? has been *implemented*? Or perhaps better: in the year in which the National Regeneration has been fulfilled. Or: in which the Nation has regenerated itself. *Völkische Erneuerung*, National Regeneration – a new Nation. If the government is found wanting, the Nation dismisses it and elects a new one for itself. The old *Volk* no longer exists, it has abdicated, it has blossomed anew, the withered one has fallen away, it has shed its skin, it has purified itself, it has become an altogether different one, and Hitler is Reich Chancellor. First, the *Bohemian* corporal rose in the eyes of Hindenburg to the much more respectable level of *Austrian* corporal; then the Reich President, approaching senility at the gallop, declared that he had no wish ever to appoint this man, namely the Austrian corporal, to the post of Imperial Army Minister and Vice-Chancellor, when, a year before, all he had not wanted to appoint him was Minister for Postal Services. For a whole week, Wolf was a senior civil servant, a *Regierungsrat*, in Brunswick. (Curious, that: Brunswick – Braunschweig; *braun – schweig*: brown – be quiet; but the brown ones were not being quiet, they were shouting the odds all over the place.) In January 1933, there were secret talks between Hitler and Oskar von Hindenburg, the – as the word was at the time – 'constitutionally unforeseen son of the Reich President', and Hitler threatened to expose the Hindenburg family's scandalous tax evasion connected with their acquisition of the Neudeck estates, whereupon Oskar persuaded his father that he had to make the Bohemian-Austrian-Brunswickian corporal and *Regierungsrat* Reich Chancellor. And so it came to pass.

*

Bismarck's lip-smothering hand-brush had shrunk to Wolf's scraggy toothbrush. *Heil! Heil! Heil! Ein Volk! Ein Reich! Ein Führer! Heil Hitler!* (In rather more refined tones, after Hitler's celebrated speech to the Düsseldorf Industrialists' Club on 26 January 1932, the industrialist Fritz Thyssen shouted, '*Heil* Herr *Hitler!*' A variation which, it has to be said, did not catch on.)

A year of change, a year of fulfilment, also, it goes without saying, for Herr *Stadtrat* Christian Ludwig Weber. Although, mind you, the weight had shifted – not Weber's weight, no, that, if anything, and if such can be said of weight, just put on weight; no – the weight of *events* had shifted, from Munich to Berlin to be precise. But Weber remained in Munich. In fact, all the GOSs remained in Munich: Maurice, Röhm, Fiehler, Amann, Esser, Wagner; in Berlin it was these Göring, Rosenberg, Ribbentrop characters, and above all that obnoxious Goebbels, who were throwing their weight about as if they owned the place, monopolising the Führer and the political scene and making a start on the reordering of Europe. The New European Order was of no interest whatsoever to Christian Weber, so long as no one called into question his New Order for the Sebastiansplatz and the surrounding streets.

Councillor Weber, who to date – and it was all of seven years now – had been most economical with his rhetorical talents in plenary sessions of the Council, asked permission to take the floor on 26 April 1933, after Fiehler had been elected 'Acting Senior *Bürgermeister*': 'It is with pleasure that we note that our Party comrade, Karl Fiehler, has now been elected to the honorary post of Senior Burgomaster of the State Capital City of Munich . . . I now call upon my party group, as a demonstration of their approval, to join me by engaging in three cheers. *Siegheil! Siegheil! Siegheil!*'

The party group did indeed 'engage in' the triple *Siegheil*. (Weber had been Party leader since March, leader of what was soon to be the only party group. The Brown Army Faction.) In fact the whole (new) nation engaged in the *Siegheil* – the new, the regenerated, the nationalist nation regenerated by National Regeneration. The only strange thing was that the faces had remained the same. Without closer inspection, you could quite easily have mistaken the new nation for the old one, the new *Volk* for the same old folk.

The agenda for this meeting of the Council included, among other items, 'the conferment of the freedom of the city upon Reich Chancellor Adolf Hitler; conferment of the freedom of the city upon Reich Governor General Franz Ritter von Epp; Brienner Strasse to be renamed Adolf-Hitler-Strasse; Promenadeplatz to be renamed Ritter-von-Epp-Platz; issue of official telephones and free tram passes to city councillors'. During the vote on the question of the freedom of the city for Hitler, the Social Democratic group walked out of the chamber. They would have been better not to. On the other hand, if they had remained there, they would have been better not doing that either. In fact there was absolutely nothing left for the Social Democrats to do that they would have been better not doing. The next meeting of the City Council took place on 9 May 1933.

Steadfast, nationally regenerated, adorned with their – henceforth – Teutonic sleeve protectors, the stenographers dutifully took everything down in German Standard Shorthand: 'Meeting opens, 9.44 o'clock a.m. Excused from attendance: Cllr Wimmer, on account of sick leave; Cllr Dichtl, who is in protective custody for the time being' – for the time being. That's rich! – 'and Cllr Rauch.' Then: 'Cllr Amann (on a point of order): I wish, on behalf of my group, to make the following statement. In the last session of this council, during the honouring of Herr Reich Chancellor Adolf Hitler and Herr Reich Governor Franz Ritter von Epp, the Social Democratic group demonstratively left the chamber. This conduct constitutes an outrageous provocation directed not only against our party group and our movement but against the entire population of Munich.' So, not 'it *is* a provocation', but 'it *constitutes*' one. Well, did you ever! And against the *entire* population. Even including the Communist Party Councillor Dichtl, 'for the time being' in protective custody? If Amann says so, then he, Dichtl, in his otherwise no doubt elegant protective custody, must have writhed in agonies of provocation. 'We reject any further cooperation with these Marxist traitors to the working class and demand that the Social Democratic group clear off out of this chamber for once and for all.' (The National Socialist councillors *engage in* shouts of 'Out! Out!') 'Acting Senior BM Fiehler: In the present situation, I feel bound to request earnestly that the Social Democratic group, in its own interest, leave the chamber forthwith.' Magnificent, that man – a man of sophistication: feel bound . . . request earnestly . . . in its own interest . . . that's the kind of people *we*, or rather *they* were . . . well, really, when you think of all the mud that has been slung at them, and still is today . . . (Cries of 'Out! Out!' – members of the National Socialist group move into the seats of the Social Democrats.) Acting Senior BM Fiehler: the session is adjourned! (Adjournment of the session at 9.47 o'clock a.m.) Acting Senior BM Fiehler (9.55 o'clock a.m.): I declare the session reconvened.'

In the intervening eight minutes, the Council stenographers leant back in their chairs, straightened up their sleeve protectors, closed their eyes, waggled their fingers to keep them supple. Nothing was committed to the records. If anything had been recorded, it might well have read something like this: 'Cllr Weber moves over to the Social Democratic group benches. Cllr Weber seizes Cllr Uebelhör. Cllr Weber draws in his stomach and lets it out again abruptly. Cllr Uebelhör crashes against a bench. Cllr Weber engages in a triple kick. Cllr Uebelhör leaves the chamber in the interests of his own safety. Cllr Weber smiles. Cllr Weber: And now a beer would go down a treat. Cllr Weber resumes his seat and lights a cigar. The National Regeneration of the City Council has been implemented.'

In an atmosphere of complete calm, undisturbed by Marxist subversion, the cleansed and purified City Council turned its attention, at nine-fifty-five o'clock, to the weighty matters before it:

1. Penzberger Strasse: Provision of funding for drainage
2. Reich small-scale housing estates in Unterföhring: Laying of water mains preparatory to extension work
3. Perlacher Forst Cemetery: Allocation of a support grant

. . .

7. National Regeneration

During the session on 23 May 1933, the title of *Oberbürger-meister* was conferred on Senior Burgomaster Fiehler. This National Socialist titular creation has been retained by all Munich's municipal heads since 1945, too. Secondly, the two Social Democratic district councillors, Fiederl and Uebelhör, had finally got it into their thick skulls: they had directed letters to the City Council containing the following information: 'I hereby declare that I wish to renounce the exercise of my office as a member of the City Council of the State Capital City of Munich.' The letters were read out, and the records contain the reference, 'Duly noted.' The other, incorrigible, Marxist-plutocratic subhumans insisted on their (alleged) rights. In vain. The National Regeneration soon steam-rollered over such democratic fiddle-faddle.

Thirdly (yes, sorry, but there's more): 'I would further like to announce,' said the (now) *Oberbürgermeister* Fiehler, 'that our Führer Adolf Hitler, today our Reich Chancellor' – unfortunately he was still that the next day, 24 May, and still again on the 25th – 'has expressed to me personally, verbally, his sincere thanks for the honours bestowed on him in the first session of the Council, namely the conferring of the freedom of the State Capital City and the renaming of a street in his name, but at the same time he has requested that the decision to rename a part of the Brienner Strasse should not be carried out on account of the historical significance of the buildings on the Brienner Strasse and of the historical significance of the Brienner

Strasse as a whole within the context of the building programme of that era. I think that no discussion and no special
decision of the Council will be necessary to enable us to
comply with this wish of our Reich Chancellor. The decision
taken at that time will, in any case, not now be implemented
and the Brienner Strasse will retain its present name along
its full extent. An occasion will no doubt present itself at a
later date to rename a suitable street after Adolf Hitler.'

'Duly noted.'

No occasion did arise at a later date, and none has up to the
present day ... What would have been the most suitable street?
The Prinzregentenstrasse, where, on the square at the far end,
Fräulein Braun would in due course stand at the window, drawing the curtain slightly to one side and having a surreptitious
look as she waited for the swain who was not to play groom
to her bride for another twelve years? Or the Dachauer
Strasse, perhaps, leading out to the famous council housing
estate where obstinate members of the national community
were to undergo a course of persuasion by the National
Regeneration? Perhaps one side of the Dachauer Strasse,
the one taking you *out towards* Dachau, could retain that
nomenclature, while the inward side, on which the spiritually
purified would walk, could be renamed Adolf-Hitler-Strasse.
Or, again, the Theatinerstrasse, because there are quite a few
renowned cake shops there? Or the Thalkirchner Strasse,
the one leading out to the slaughterhouse? Or maybe, even
better, the Viktualienmarkt, the vegetable market, because
the Führer, the lone Wolf, was a herbivore?

Alas, 'twas not to be. But even without a street, even
without a monument, His memory is still alive in the hearts
of many, and no passage of time can erase His image.

Fourthly: 'Grosslapen Sewage Works. Funding for the
voluntary labour service.'

Fifthly: 'Construction of a gallery for art exhibitions' (which
was later to be known as the 'House of German Art', or, in
the vernacular, the 'White Sausage Temple', because of its
ill-proportioned, chalky columns).

Sixthly: 'To conclude the meeting, the Party once again
engaged in a triple *Siegheil!*'

Christian Ludwig Weber, since March not only Chairman of the NSDAP group in the City Council but simultaneously also President of the Upper Bavarian Regional Council – '. . . my name is Weber, you will address me as *"Herr Präsident"* . . .' – had not shied away from the effort required, on 9 March 1933, to squeeze his enormous bulk into the lift in the City Hall tower and to ride all the way up, and then to climb up even farther, grunting and gasping, with a roll of red cloth under his arm. After making sure that the parapet was safe, he had stepped out and unfurled a huge swastika flag. Single-handed. 6.05 p.m. A crowd of Müncheners numbering in the tens of thousands cheered enthusiastically and sang patriotic songs. David Hess, in Rosental, had no song on his lips. He had, as a precautionary measure, lowered the shutters in front of his shop window. Much good it was to do him.

*

Münchener Neueste Nachrichten, Saturday 26 August 1933:

BIRTHDAY CELEBRATION FOR
CITY COUNCILLOR WEBER

To mark the occasion of his fiftieth birthday, a large number of friends gathered last night around the President of the Upper Bavarian Regional Council and leader of the sole party group, City Councillor Christian Weber, that intrepid and unflagging veteran campaigner for the National Socialist Movement, in a simple celebration in the Blue Room of the Café Fürstenhof, which had been transformed into a veritable flower garden.

Prominent among the guests attending were Ministers of State Wagner and Esser, as well as *Oberbürgermeister* Fiehler. The well-wishers on this happy occasion were also joined by Reich Treasurer Schwarz, Managing Director Amann from the Central Party Publishing House, former Justice Minister Dr Roth and numerous other companions in hardship who had, in times past, been in Landsberg Prison along with Christian Weber. A table laden with presents, and, above it, draped around with swastika flags, a portrait of Weber facing that of the *Führer* Adolf Hitler, enhanced the festive atmosphere.

Dressed in the brown of the League of German Girls, Gabriele Steinacker presented the birthday boy with a handsome bouquet and recited some verses appropriate to the occasion composed by Steinacker *père*. The coffee-house proprietor, Councillor Otto Seeländer, followed suit with a beautiful china sculpture. Councillor of State Mantel offered his congratulations to Christian Weber as one hunting friend to another. For his part, the man at the centre of the festivities expressed his thanks with some witty words and further regaled the company with some reminiscences, especially concerning his sojourn in Landsberg Fortress – Weber made no fewer than 152 court appearances on account of his activities in the Movement.

With pithy phrases, the Head of the State Chancellory, Minister of State Esser, congratulated the indefatigable campaigner who, from the very moment of the foundations of the Party, was the first to come to Adolf Hitler's side, and who, since then, has been one of his most fearless and loyal supporters. With a *Siegheil!* to Christian Weber, the minister wished to pay tribute at the same time to all the other Old Campaigners for the Movement. The ensuing hours of merry sociability were given added spice by the delightful artistic offerings, both light-hearted and serious in tone, provided by Herr Rehkemper, the celebrated singer, Maria Wutz of the Dessau State Theatre, Karl Steinacker and Hans Denk.

Happily, the poem rendered by the little maid in the brown dress and emanating from the pen of the never-to-be-forgotten People's Actor Karl Steinacker has been preserved in the City Archives (under the index number BuR 1611):

Congratulations
(To Herr *Stadtrat* Weber on his Fiftieth Birthday)

High summer 'tis! – And golden ears
stand harvest-ready, full of grain,
each garden lies ablaze with cheer,
oh, may its like return again!

Nature's resplendent gifts, her flowers,
has she bestowed – 'tis but its due! –
on summer, zenith of the year,
adorning it in lavish hue.

This simple bouquet from that great
and bounteous storehouse now I bring,
loving token, birthday greeting,
fifty times fifty, praise I sing!

Entwined within this bouquet's heart
not only have I wishes bound;
these blooms I give into your hand
our heartfelt gratitude expound!

Of brave campaigners you are one,
who true and hard and long have fought
till in the face of darkest pow'rs
you home the final vict'ry brought!

The way you long strove to prepare,
on which now marches German Youth
towards the Germany, new and fair,
respecting honour, love and truth!

That youth to you its thanks presents,
here in this hour of celebration.
With guileless words a German maid
speaks love from a grateful nation.

Five decades may have come and gone,
and life may long have passed from Spring;
its Autumn yet far distant lies
when vibrant Summer holds the ring!

My wishes all I summarise
in one: may now from ills and strife
the good Lord you protect and keep,
on your still valiant way through life!

May He in gen'rous measure send
you years with satisfaction filled,
to gaze fulfilled and proud upon
th' eternal works you helped to build!

Siegheil!

And indeed the good (German) Lord did, for some years to come, protect the celebrator of that summer jubilee from almost all ills, with the exception of one tiresome little matter in 1934, and a sizeable abscess on the sweat-gland in his right armpit in 1943. All the same, the wish that he be sent 'years in gen'rous measure' was not to be fulfilled. Nevertheless, twelve of them, almost exactly twelve, were still earmarked for him, and sunny, magnificent years they were to be. A well-rounded, replete life.

Yes, of course, the menu (or should we say, eschewing all foreign taint, the 'order of courses'), that too has been preserved:

Swedish Appetisers

Oxtail Soup, served in bowls

Young Partridge with Sauerkraut
and Potato Purée

Prince Pückler Ice in a glass
Fürstenhof Style

and that morning, at the meeting of the City Council, Weber's seat was 'decorated with a splendid basket of flowers'. *Oberbürgermeister* Fiehler sent, on behalf of the city, five bottles of wine.

Five. Not fifty. What kind of thing is five – in figures: 5 – bottles of wine to send to a President Weber! Always did keep a tight fist on the budget, that Fiehler. What about, say, a racehorse? A noble (brown!) racehorse. Now that *would* have been something. But *five* bottles of wine. Pathetic! In the flat on the Sebastiansplatz lay, nicely arranged and classified, eight hundred bottles, each with notes on its provenance and vintage, matters on which an office-bound pen pusher like your Fiehler would not have the slightest clue. And just wait, when the time was ripe, there would be . . . well, he knew exactly where the best wine cellars were. In *Commerzialrat* Solomon

Goldglück's house, for instance. Just you wait, when the time was finally ripe, then the National Regeneration would get its fingers into the alien Goldglückian wine cellar, and before you could say 'Cheers!' the whole lot would find a new home in the flat on the Sebastiansplatz. And then the visitor's gaze would be able to wander at liberty over not eight hundred, but eight thousand bottles. *Five* bottles! Was this whey-faced girl in her dowdy brown duds never going to get to the end of her poem? Herr *Präsident* felt a belch coming on. Keep a smile on your face, though. A poem of twenty-five strophes – cata-strophes! Weber undressed the girl in his mind. A good mount. Yes, it would have been no bother at all to . . . admittedly the festivities would have had to be transferred to the parterre (in plain language – none of your foreign rubbish – ground floor) of the building, so that the Amazons could come riding in. Now *that* would have been something appropriate to the occasion. But *five* bottles of wine!

Just wait, Weber, patience, not long now . . .

The *Völkischer Beobachter* did not let the event pass unnoticed either. From the article 'Festivities on the Occasion of the Fiftieth Birthday of Party Member Christian Weber' in Edition No. 238 of 26 August 1933, we glean the additional information that '. . . the function suite was bedecked overall with fir branches and twigs and had been transformed into a veritable flower garden'. It concludes: 'The evening's further offerings scaled lofty heights of artistry and finally bubbled over into hearty conviviality . . .' And then again, the Monday afterwards (No. 240 of 28 August), the *Völkischer Beobachter* doubled up with a further report. 'Erna Ruhland's singing and playing', it ran, 'was a joy, and Hans Denk, who marched on after midnight along with Käthe Delheim, the well-known lady yodeller, and the Vom Platzl Band, contributed his unique brand of soldier songs, to his own zither accompaniment, markedly heightening the mood of the evening.' This report on the contribution of unique soldier songs appeared in the column headed 'News from the Munich Movement'. The small print at the foot of this column is remarkable: 'Publication in this column is open only to contributions bearing the official stamp of the District Administration, and in addition, in the case of cultural events, that of the League of Action for German Culture.' Did this contribution bear both official stamps? That we shall never know. For sure it carried the *Gauleiter*'s imprimatur – a rubber-stamped contribution, a rubber-stamped Movement, a rubber-stamped National Regeneration, a rubber-stamped Nation. The significance of the rubber stamp in totalitarian regimes. Woe betide anyone without a rubber stamp in his hand. And woe betide anyone whose papers did not bear a stamp, or even bore a negative one (a J, for example). God turned His face from the German people and cast an ink-pad down upon the Earth.

It was long past midnight. The unique soldier songs had long since been contributed, the last cries of '*Siegheil!*', which had been engaged in in multiples, had long since died away. The luxuriant fir-drapings were wilting in a pall of smoke, half-empty wineglasses stood all around, the ice was melting in the champagne buckets, waiters, yawning surreptitiously behind their hands, hung around, hoping to be able at last to clear up.

'Hey, Wagner . . . heh-heh.'

'All right, who was it? Who let one go?'

'Pfraarftt!'

'Dirty piggy!'

'Hee hee, Weber, old pal!'

'Come on, there's still something left in that bottle.'

'Esser! Esser! Whassamarrer?'

'I don't feel well.'

'I think he's going to puke his guts up.'

'Let Amann sleep in peace, so long as he don't pee hisself.'

'Heeheehee –'

'Chrr – chrr – hnmph –'

'Waiter!' bawled Weber. 'This champagne's warm. D'you think you might see your way to bring us a new one – at the double?!'

'Very good, Herr President.'

'President! Haw haw haw –'

'What's so funny about that, then?!'

'You old bugger! And now you're President!'

'Vrrroomph!'

'Quiet!'

'But it was great, though.'

'The good old fighting days. Oh, yes.'

'Cheers.'

'Brraarfft!'

'*Sieg* – er . . . what was it . . . can't 'member . . . oh yer – *Siegheil!*'

'*Siegheil!*'

'Cheers!'

'Cheers. Y're on'y young once.'

Weber heaved himself from his armchair. Amann rolled under the table with a certain finality.

'Somebody button up the *Gauleiter*'s flies,' Weber croaked. 'Waiter, lead me to m'car. I godda drive t'Pasing.' Frieda would be waiting to add her own brand of congratulations.

The aforementioned article in the *Völkischer Beobachter* concluded with these words:

'Long into the night, the old friends sat together, steeped in memories of the difficult, and yet so happy, days of the beginnings of the Movement, of their great *Führer*, Adolf Hitler, and united in the silent vow to serve the newly risen Third Reich as loyally and unswervingly as they had served the Movement from the very first day on.'

*

'Well, well, Herr Dirrigl.'

'Ah, there you are, Herr Kammerlander.'

'Yes, and there's little Wamperl, too. And how's Wampi-Wampi, the good boy then?'

'Bow-wow!'

'And yourself, Herr Dirrigl. How are you?'

'Thank you for enquiring. And your good self?'

'Can't complain, Herr Dirrigl.'

'Joined the Party too, have you?'

'One must move with the times.'

'You're right there, Herr Kammerlander, otherwise, well, hm, otherwise the times pass one by.'

'I'm ah – we've known each other long enough, my dear

Herr Dirrigl, I know I can speak frankly with you – I'm not altogether in agreement with everything . . . indeed I never *was*, as you know . . . and certain things . . . now, I admit . . . you can't make an omelette without breaking eggs, and after all, these SA people, they're all young. Unfermented wine, so to speak. One must make allowances. And besides, you understand – unemployed, so they have to work off their aggressions somehow. After all, we were young once too, weren't we?'

'You're so right, Herr Kammerlander.'

'And if, I must say quite without fear or favour, if some hare-brained disciple of world revolution or some Solomon or other comes out of it all with a black eye, then – I must be honest – then my sympathy for him is by no means unbounded.'

'I've always said, it's better for them to be running around in their uniforms than having their heads full of heaven knows what kind of silly ideas. They certainly seem to be clean and presentable.'

'A bit of discipline and order never did anyone any harm. I consider this Labour Service that's just been introduced to be no bad thing at all. There's many a one who previously, on the strength of his dole money, fought shy of work, and now he knows at last what a shovel looks like. And nobody yet died of blisters on his hands.'

'True, very true. My son, mind you, is unfortunately in-dispensable to the firm. But he does go out with his collecting tin of a Saturday.'

'My son sadly suffers from what they call "trumpeter's chest". It's some sort of malformation – nothing outwardly noticeable, thank heavens, but the doctor told him –'

'Dr Rosenzweig?'

'No. We always consult Dr Flacher now. You see, he lives a little closer to hand. More convenient, you know.'

'And so your son is unfortunately not able to . . .'

'Unfortunately.'

'And of course, all that anxiety is a thing of the past. It was such a worry last autumn, having to live virtually every day with the fear of civil war breaking out. Your actual plebs,

Herr Kammerlander, now your plebs – not afraid of civil war, nothing to lose, after all. But I –'

'And I too!'

'Exactly. I went to ask my lawyer –'

'Herr Bernstein?'

'No, I'm now a client of Dr von Singelmann; he's younger, more astute, I feel.'

'And you asked . . . ?'

'Yes; do you know that in the event of civil war the insurance companies will pay nothing on broken windows! That would be a disaster for householders.'

'And another thing. It'll do foreigners no harm at all to take a bit of notice of us. And I'll tell you this, Hitler's going to manage it, he's going to get back Alsace-Lorraine and even the colonies.'

'It wouldn't surprise me in the least.'

'You know, I will admit quite frankly that I do *not* feel, now let me stress, not *altogether* easy about the man, I freely admit it . . . but one thing you have to say for him, whatever he goes after, he achieves it. Now that's something in itself.'

'Undoubtedly.'

'And then again, the Herr Reich President is still there after all. And Vice-Chancellor von Papen. And Privy Councillor Hugenberg. All of them, and I mean *all* of them, honourable men. Why shouldn't we let the wild dog off the leash for a few months – a few years, for that matter – so that he can show the rest of them once again that we Germans are not after all the lowest of the low? And then, he can be brought to heel again. Wouldn't you agree?'

'Well certainly they're beginning to whistle a different tune abroad, from what we hear.'

'Now, your Frenchman, coward as he is by nature, he's beginning to knuckle under, your crafty Englishman, it's in his character always to go along with the stronger side, and as for your Russian – what a shambles they're in over there! – well, he's not worth wasting breath on.'

'All in all, Herr Kammerlander, I must say I somehow feel a bit easier in my mind.'

'Absolutely. And so does my Bautzerl.'

'Bow-wow!'

'Yes, that's right, isn't it, Bautzerl? Bautzerl! Where's the Jew-boy? Where is he, then?'

'Grrr!'

'Ha, ha, ha.'

'And he's also supposed to be a great dog lover, our Herr Reich Chancellor, or so I've heard. Apparently he keeps several dogs himself.'

'Can't be a bad sort, deep down, then, can he?'

'Well, with those few words, Herr Dirrigl.'

'Yes, well, a very good evening to you, Herr Kammerlander.'

'And my respects to your good lady.'

'And to yours, too. Been a pleasure meeting you again.'

*

The Region – as from 1939, the District – of Upper Bavaria had a regional parliament, the *Kreistag*. Even prior to 1933, this legislative body was virtually devoid of authority, and after 1933 it was completely so. Nevertheless, the Nazis did not dissolve it, it being their way not to dismantle the legal structures of the Weimar Republic and its provinces but simply to hollow them out into empty shells. The posts remained in existence so that, for example, Genuine Old Soldiers who were too stupid, too crude, too corrupt, or all of these together, to be exposed to public gaze in the new aura of power in Berlin might be appropriately and comfortably provided for. For instance: Herr Businessman Christian Ludwig Weber, President of the *Kreistag* (as of 1939 *Bezirkstag*) of Upper Bavaria. The centralisation of the Reich – which never did come about – was to be achieved by another means, namely at Party level.

The Führer and Reich Chancellor, soaring ever upward to those heights where only eagles dare, did not like to be reminded of his past. It was something of a dilemma: on the one hand, the constant ranting about unconditional loyalty, Teutonic same; on the other, the very sight of that former bouncer, who insisted on addressing one in the familiar *du* (at least he had settled for 'Wolf' and had dropped his damned 'Adolf', not to mention 'Adi' or 'Dolfi'), was a constant and painful reminder of the provenance of the effectively modest Iron Cross First Class on the chancellorial breast. And of divers other things.

Munich must have been for Hitler something like a nest to which the dried-up faeces of youth still adhered. And in which the GOSs lived, who had in the mean time hatched out of the eggs to become not eagles but vultures, snaffling everything that wasn't firmly nailed down and, contrary to all proverbial truths, intent on gouging out each other's eyes at every opportunity. Hitler conferred on this filthy nest the title 'Capital City of the Movement' (this description was one of the exceptions, in that it was not retained after 1945, but replaced by the semi-official epithet 'Metropolis with Heart'), had his architect Troost disfigure it with a few of his buildings, and lingered there as little as possible, in fact virtually only when he was on his way from Berlin to Berchtesgaden. So he left the GOSs in Munich to muddle along by themselves. And muddle along they did. On 14 November 1933, just a few days over ten years after that march on the Feldherrnhalle, Herr *Präsident* Weber moved into official offices and apartments in – implausible as it may seem – the former royal Residency. *From the Kaiserhof to the Reich Chancellory. A historical account in diary form* was the title of one of Goebbels' concoctions, published in 1934. (By '*Kaiserhof*' he did not mean the Imperial Court in Berlin, but the Hotel *Kaiserhof* in the Wilhelmstrasse, where Hitler was in the habit of putting up in the years immediately leading up to January 1933.) 'From the Blue Buck to the Residency' was the whisper that went round Munich about Weber. The *Kreistag* President's official rooms and adjoining apartments were on the ground floor, facing the Fountain Courtyard. Later on, even this accommodation no longer seemed prestigious enough to the bouncer, so he wanted the whole wing facing on to the Court Gardens and had the brass neck to demand the removal to another place of the Egyptology Collection.

(Pharaoh Weber: the soft tones of harps, played by girls, naked or merely draped in the most diaphanous veils, naked slave-girls, adorned only with a broad necklace, waving palms. A cool tankard of beer. Crawling on their bellies,

147

servants, underlings, officials approach to beg for the orders of the day. Incense fills the air. The Pharaoh gives a gracious wave of the hand – or, sometimes, ungracious, as the case may be. Work is well in hand on the colossal statue, carved out of a single, hundred-metre-high monolith, its gaze directed towards the rising sun over the Max-Joseph-Platz (now the Pharaoh-Weber-Platz). The glass eye, one enormous diamond, which flashes in the sunlight and illumines the Weber City of the Movement.)

He did not manage to get quite that far, however. It seems that even Weber's power was not limitless, because of course he was not the only GOS in Munich, and each GOS had staked out his territory, and intrusions were not always without their perils. So Weber had to make do with the Residency in the *Brunnenhof*. King Christian Ludwig I, affable and close to his people. Still took himself out to Pasing from time to time, although, with the passing years, Frieda was not getting any younger either. More youthful ladies were now summoned to the Residency. The President also retained his flat on the Sebastiansplatz. A *grand seigneur*; just a pity that it was not reflected in his behaviour.

Over and above all this, the *grand seigneur* bouncer was a man of many parts: member of the Reich Transport Council, member of the Executive of the Convention of German Community Councils, member of the *Deutsche Reichspost* Advisory Board since 1934 and member of the *Reichstag* since 1936. And from all sides there were expense allowances, subsistence payments, attendance money and bribes, and then official trips and diversions, opportunities to see the world. Frieda's Berlin opposite number was called Wilma, and she had her, shall we say her studio, in Dahlem. And then of course Weber was the bearer of the Golden Insignia of Honour of the NDSAP, which Wolf invented in 1933 to be awarded only to GOSs (or IOSs – Indefatigable Old Soldiers) with Party membership numbers below 100,000. And the holder of the Insignia of Honour of 9 November 1923, a.k.a. Blood Order, also established in 1933: a silver medal, its obverse showing in profile an eagle, strangely hunched up inside the rim and holding a wreath; inside the wreath, the legend 9 NOV, the eagle's beak pecking at the letters MUNICH/1923/1933. Awarded – in Weber's case – for the daring provision of three automobiles (in good, untainted German, 'Kraftfahrzeuge') from the firm of Cenovis in the Schleibingerstrasse. Oh yes, and Honorary President of the Company of Bavarian Mountain Bloodhounds.

By comparison, Ernstl was a nonentity. Ernstl – the gay Röhm. There was no getting away from the fact that the SA had become surplus to requirements. Wolf sat firmly in the saddle, after the death of the ramshackle Hindenburg, who by the end had finally turned into dust; he crowned himself Reich President and outwitted the Papen–Hugenberg–Schacht pack. Rampaging brawls, the domain of the SA, were now undesirable. It was plain for all to see that with the Nazis, for the first time in German history, the room-and-kitchen fug of boiled cabbage, the German carpet slipper, the petty-bourgeois, comfy camaraderie of the regular pub card-school had seized the upper hand, but the room-and-kitchen faction was playing power politics, and foreign powers were playing along. Lord Rothermere had written in the *Daily Mail* as early as 1930 that 'it would be best for the welfare of Western civilisation if there came to the helm in Germany a government permeated by the same healthy principles with which Mussolini has renewed Italy in the last eight years'. Now these healthy principles were coming to the fore, but the splendid punch-ups were a thing of the past. Instead of merrily singing and slugging their way down the street, letting the cosh wallop down wherever the Red Front or Judaism raised its head, they were now behind bars. No, the SA had not been locked up; locked up were the Red Front and Judaists, as were bellyachers and trouble makers and intellectuals, but their guards were no less behind bars, albeit with better food and board, and with evening passes available. The merry avant-garde of National Regeneration suddenly found themselves on permanent assignment as prison warders. Was that to be their reward?

'Come and sit down, Ernstl, you old bugger!' bawled Weber.
Röhm sat down and looked around.

'Nice place you've got here.'

'Well, yes. Fortune favours the brave.'

'President now, are you?'

'I am that. What can I get them to bring you? It's great you could come and see me again. Look – all I have to do is press this,' Weber gave a bell a clout with his fat paw, 'and right away . . .'

An SS man entered, cracked his heels together and saluted. 'The Herr President wishes?'

'Dismiss,' said Weber.

The SS man disappeared again.

'See? Right. What d'you want? Wine? Beer? Champagne? A cigar? Or maybe a little fork lunch? It's just gone eleven anyway, time I had a bite, so the empty space between break-fast and lunch doesn't get too long. Well . . . ? Champagne? When an old friend like you does me the honour after all this time, you won't catch me skimping.'

'Yes, OK,' said Röhm, 'I don't mind. Just whatever you're drinking.'

Weber clobbered the bell again.

'The Herr President wishes?'

'Lay two places, because the Chief of Staff is going to have a fork lunch with me. Let's say, cold chicken –'

'Cold chicken.'

'– eight white sausages, with raspberry jam for me –'

'Eight white sausages with raspberry jam.'

'Mustard for me,' said Röhm.

'– and a few crispy rolls and a helping of caviar and a bit of smoked salmon – and so on.'

'And so on. Very good, Herr President.'

'And champagne. And see that it's properly cold, right?'

'Properly cold, very good, Herr President.'

The fork lunch was a protracted one. They chatted about old times. 'My God, d'you remember . . . !' 'Yes, right, Coburg 1922 . . .' 'Come on, old fella, you're only young once.' Tears of emotion welled out of Old Soldiers' eyes and trickled down podgy Old Soldiers' cheeks. 'Cheers. Great to see you again.' Thumps on the bell. 'The Herr President wishes?' 'Can't you see there's nothing but fresh air in that bottle, you bonehead?' 'At once, Herr President. If the Herr President will permit me, may I remind him that the District Council meeting has already begun.' 'The Herr Knucklehead hasn't noticed that I'm in the middle of a meeting with the Chief of Staff of the SA. Eh? So you'll just have to telephone over and say I've been held up. No. Wait. I'm indisposed.'

'Indisposed. Very good, Herr President.'

'Cheers, Christian.'

'Cheers, Ernstl.'

'Maurice told me – hope you don't mind, Christian, but... – he says you've got some drawings.'

'Drawings?'

'Yes – drawings of Wolf's.'

'Me? Drawings of Wolf? I've got a big photograph of Wolf, in a silver frame, autographed, for my fiftieth.'

'No. Drawings of Wolf's. Drawings *he drew*.'

. . .

'Oh, I see. Ha ha. You old shyster. I get you. Yes, sure. So, so. And Maurice told you that.'

'Supposed to be very interesting drawings.'

'You wouldn't be interested in *that* kind of thing, you old bugger. Or would you? You haven't suddenly started playing the other field, have you?'

'Have you still got the drawings?'

'Sure.'

'Wouldn't mind a squint at them.'

Weber clouted the bell.

'The Herr President wishes?'

'Close the curtains. As of now, the Chief of Staff and I are not to be disturbed. Scram.'

'Very good, Herr President.'

Weber heaved himself up off the sofa, went to the door and turned the key in the lock. Then he also locked the door to the rear, fished a small key out of his waistcoat pocket, pushed a picture – a large oil painting of 'Diana in the Bath' which he had 'organised' out of the galleries of the Old Pinakothek – to one side. This revealed a safe. Weber stuck the small key into the lock, turned it once to the left, once to the right –

'Hell's teeth! Think maybe I'm not as sober as I was . . .
now . . . just a minute . . . not once to the left, once right,
but right and then left . . .'

Röhm regarded the sketches with no great enthusiasm.

'Geli Raubal,' said Weber. 'Mind you, the meat you see
on her there, the worms've had that long since.'

'Does Wolf know you've got these?' Röhm asked.

'Could be,' said Weber.

'Hey,' Weber exclaimed, 'time for lunch – we very nearly
missed it. Right, what's it to be, Ernstl, will we get ourselves
driven to the *Walterspiel*, or will we partake of a small
sensation here?'

'Here's better,' laughed Röhm. (He didn't really laugh, he
just made a pretence of it.)

After the meal, Weber fell asleep. He was lying on his back.
His paunch swelled up almost as high as the bottom edge
of the picture of Hitler hanging above the sofa. With each
sawing breath, the upholstery creaked and groaned. After
about twenty such thunderous blasts, Weber woke up again,
turned his head – now the cheek on top was squashing his
nose – and gazed at Röhm. He was sitting, or rather hanging,
in an armchair, with all four limbs extended. He belched.

'You sleepin' too?'

'Rhnyeah,' wheezed Weber. 'Plezzm –'

'Plezzm – what?'

'Plezzm . . . I d'no . . . plezzm . . . you know wh' I m –
urp! mean.'

'Nch – krrff.'

Snoring.

'Dreams,' murmured Weber. 'Plezzm dreams, a's wha'
wannid t'say.'

'S'm t'you,' snored Röhm. He wasn't really snoring, only
making a pretence of it.

When Weber awoke around half-past six, Röhm had
already left.

*

'Good evening, Herr *Senatspräsident*. Would the Herr President permit me to join him?'

'Please do, Herr Winkler, I'm always happy to have young people around me.'

'Thank you. If I may be so bold as to enquire after your state of health?'

'Ah, Herr Winkler, as I always say, I'm not ready to be put out of my misery, not just yet. Ha ha ha. But seriously, I can't complain. A twinge here and there, as one gets older, but there are others worse off. And as far as work goes — but then, I don't want to talk shop during the happy hour. The usual, though, too much, too much, as you well know yourself. But where are you now, Herr Winkler?'

'In the Public Prosecutor's office — Munich I, the Political Department.'

'Oh, very interesting indeed. You'll not be short of work there since the new — ahem — legal arrangements.'

'That's for sure, Herr *Senatspräsident*.'

'I was once in the Political Department, too. A long time ago. Things were very different then. Sadly. Not to my taste *at all*. You've got things easier nowadays.'

'Much, if I may say so, has become a good deal easier.'

'Of course, officially I've nothing to do with that, I head a civil senate, as you know, but naturally I also take an interest in the latest developments. I've read the new law. The provisions are *very* flexible.'

'On the whole, a workable instrument.'

'That's my impression, too. And long overdue.'

'Exactly my feelings.'

'Your health, dear colleague.'

'Here's to yours, Herr President.'

'Mmm. There's nothing to beat the evening's first mouthful. Do you find that too? You have to savour the first draught with great reverence. You can drink as much as you like all evening, but that . . . that . . . now how should I put it . . . that virginal freshness of the first taste . . . it just doesn't return. So, with reverence, the first swallow. Not to be rushed. Yes. And now the second.

'And tell me, Herr Winkler, how do you like it then, in the Political Department?'

'Very much indeed.'

'In spite of all the work?'

'I've been in the judiciary for twelve years now, and, in all the departments I've worked in, I've never yet been happy to see the workload increase. Until now.'

'That catches the spirit of the new era.'

'You know, Herr *Senatspräsident*, when one is on the track of some petty thief, or, for that matter, a bigger fish, or a swindler or a pimp or a homosexual, and then, my God!, he gets off with a few months, or it might be a few years, then he's released and starts all over again – and when one of them snuffs it, there's always another to take his place – well, there's just no satisfaction in that. *Now*, Herr *Senatspräsident*, now I have the feeling that this is not a bottomless pit. *Those* ones are not propagating themselves now. Here I see – at long last – some success in my work. *I* certainly don't yearn for the days of the Old Order.'

'Who does?'

'Well . . . a few . . . colleagues.'

'That was certainly a bad business about Herr Fichtelbaum. Four children, the fifth on the way . . . promotion to Provincial High Court judge due at any time. Very highly qualified. I wouldn't have been at all averse to having him in my senate . . . but . . . !'

'What's he doing now?'

'Strictly between ourselves – come a little closer – I saw him recently: auxiliary postman. But he's to be dismissed even from that any day now. Terrible. I wondered for a moment whether I should slip him a tip . . . but . . . not really done.'

'Yes, yes. Terrible. I knew him. But there you are, you can't make an omelette without breaking eggs.'

'That's the way it goes.'

'The nation, I always say, the people, that's the element in which I live. It's from the *Volk* that my ancestors sprang, it's among the *Volk* that my descendants will take their place.'

'Beautifully put.'

'Read it somewhere recently. Found it tremendously inspiring. Well, damn it all – begging your pardon, Herr *Senatspräsident* – you have to have something you can depend on. If I never do anything but brood – how am I to get to the root of things? I never thought Hitler – I mean, our *Führer* – well, in the past, I didn't think he was . . . you know . . . *quite* . . . You understand. But now, he's doing all right, these days. And so are we, along with him.'

'You know, my dear young friend, I don't bother my head about all that. What is the justiciary there for? It's not there to make the laws. The justiciary is there to apply the laws. Who makes laws, how laws come into being, that has absolutely nothing to do with us. My judicial oath, which I take very seriously, binds me to the law. If that law is called "Law for the Protection of the People and the Reich", can anybody hold that against me? Certainly not. Cheers, my friend.'

*

On 26 March 1934, a diplomatic passport was issued to *Kreistagspräsident* Weber. His Excellency Weber. (Sadly, the title was no longer in common use. Besides, the stiff formality of the other diplomats, the consuls and ambassadors abroad, almost all of them throwbacks to the Old Order whom Hitler seemed strangely hesitant about replacing, well, their manner left a deal to be desired.) On 12 June 1934, the expense allowance for the Chairman of the NSDAP group in the City Council (there was no other party group by now) was set at three hundred Reichsmarks; a lot of money in those days, a month's wages for a skilled worker. Office expenses: a further three hundred marks. On top of that, his parliamentary allowances as President of the District Council and, from 1936, as Member of the *Reichstag*, plus all the other little jobs that carried a remuneration – on the Reich Transport Council, on the Executive of the Convention of German Community Councils, on the Postal Advisory Board and then as Brigade Commander in the SS and Inspector of the SS Riding Schools, Chairman of the Munich Exhibition Grounds Association, Administrative Councillor for the Munich Estates . . . – all in all, the bouncer must have been pulling in a monthly income of three or four thousand Reichsmarks. (In terms of purchasing power, we can multiply that by ten for today's

– 1989 – equivalent; on DM 30,000–40,000 a month – and, *nota bene!*, tax-free – you can live quite comfortably.) On top of all that, at least two transport companies, *Christian Weber's Fernfahrten* and the *Blaubock-Tank Co.* The firms were flourishing. Weber had the knack of exploiting his position in the administration in order to snuff out competitors. On 7 April 1936, Weber forced through a decree forbidding taxi drivers from offering city sightseeing trips for tourists. Weber wanted this monopoly for his own 'Long-Distance Tours' firm. The Chairman of the taxi drivers' guild ('Reich Transport Group – Vehicular Trade') wrote a letter of protest. Weber reported the Chairman to the State Prosecutor's office and it was not until the said Chairman had withdrawn his complaint and apologised to Weber in person that Weber expressed his forgiveness; and Weber's cash register went on ringing. Weber's transport concern ran – on a monopoly basis – the bus service on the route between Dietramszell and Munich. Anyone wanting to travel from the Haching Valley, from Sauerlach, Diesenhofen, Taufkirchen or Unterhaching to Munich, to the fruit market, say, or anywhere else for that matter, had to pay the price of his ticket into Christian Weber's pocket.

There was in those days a young lawyer in the Department of Economics, his name was M. Ferid, and he can recall numerous complaints entered by Herr President Weber; he kept a perpetual sharp look-out, you see, and if anyone did anyone else a good turn by giving him a lift anywhere along Weber's bus route, then the President would report the motorist concerned for a violation of the regulations governing the conveyance of passengers. On that stretch, only Weber had the right to convey; and to cash in. We must have order. After all, *order* was the highest principle of the National Regeneration. Order and discipline: marching in fours, German women do not smoke, Labour Service, sorting out the sheep from the goats, two, three, four, sing, Party Committee of Investigation for the Protection of National Socialist Literature (founded: 16 April 1934), Führer command, we will follow . . .

But back to President Weber: that was by no means all.

He also knew how to come by indirect income, wealth that did not appear on paper as belonging to him, but over which he had sole right of disposal. This took the form mainly of estates, stables and horses, horses and more horses: the *Isarland* stud farms, the *Buchhof* Estate near Percha and the neighbouring *Heimathausen* Estate, the *Empl* Estate (Munich, Empl-Ring 8), the *Eiderhof* Estate in Riem, the *Borm* demesne in Feldafing Am Schluchtweg. In part, these estates nominally belonged to the City of Munich, and so Weber had control over them as its business agent, or they belonged to the 'Brown Riband of Germany Club', a registered association, whose President was Weber. We shall come back to that one. How much of the proceeds from these estates trickled its way into Weber's bank account cannot be verified. In those days, he was not required to render account to anyone.

Clause 11 of the NSDAP's manifesto of 24 February 1920, revised and expanded by Hitler on 13 April 1929, reads: 'Therefore we demand the abolition of any income earned without work or effort.'

'Firstly,' the shade of Christian Weber would reply to this reproach, 'firstly, I know nothing of this manifesto. There might well be something like that in it, and then again there might not. I haven't read the bumf. I'm not a great one for reading.

'Secondly, God knows what all there is in this programme, from what I've heard. I have, as I said, never read it. But there's supposed to be a whole lot in there that Adolf would never have dreamt of putting into practice. For instance, the thing about the big department stores. All the big department stores, so the nutter wrote in that thing, were to be divided up into booths and these were to be allocated to small local traders. The milkwoman from Sebastiansplatz No. 4 went along on 3 February 1933 to the Tietz store on the Bahnhofsplatz and wanted to pick her stall. A load of crap, naturally. All that happened was that Tietz was renamed, because Hermann Tietz was a Jew. "Hertie" it was called from then on. And still is today, from what I've heard.

'Thirdly, in order to enforce the abolition of unearned income, or "earnings without work or effort", you've got to have people to do that. And that's us. Us in the NSDAP. And that takes effort and work, or am I wrong?

'And fourthly, the others were no better than we were either.'

That's true; starting with the highly to be admired and respected Reich President, Herr Field Marshal Paul von Beneckendorff und von Hindenburg, the Victor of Tannenberg, from whom Hitler wrested consent for his appointment as Reich Chancellor, as has already been mentioned, by dint of his threat to let the tax swindle surrounding the acquisition of the Neudeck Estate hit the fan. Later, the making over to himself of another, neighbouring manor and the Preussenwald Forest, on which all debts and liabilities had been written off at public expense, was Hindenburg's price for keeping mum on the subject of the Enabling Act, after which the Reich President was even prepared to perform the touching and historic handshake at Potsdam on 5 March 1933. In fact he generally spoke in increasingly friendly terms about Herr Hitler, for whom he seems to have developed a real fondness. In July 1934, when Hindenburg had finally turned into a spiked helmet and already had his feet in the stirrups for the ride to Valhalla ('Go now, O dead Commander, and enter into Valhalla!' Hitler ended his valediction before Hindenburg's sarcophagus), the Reich President even addressed the Chancellor – albeit we have to accept it as a slip of the tongue – as 'Your Majesty'.

And Göring, the biggest black-marketeer in the Third Reich. His salaries as Reich Marshal, as Reich Aviation Minister and as Prime Minister of Prussia would never have been sufficient to finance the building of the hundred-million-mark 'Karinhall' project. Göring trafficked in foodstuffs in the grand manner. His rival here was Himmler. For instance, after the occupation of Czechoslovakia, Himmler had a monopoly over the mineral springs there, and merely from supplying the German Army he made more than a tidy fortune. (In those days, the mineral water was known in Army slang as 'Himmler champagne'.)

And what about the *Wehrmacht* itself? It was always something of a riddle as to why the generals, otherwise always so much on their high horse, capitulated so ignominiously, as early as February 1933, before the Bohemian, now Austrian, Corporal Adolf Schicklgruber. (No later than in 1934, General von Blomberg – without so much as an order from Hitler and therefore in an act of obliging courtesy – introduced the swastika as an emblem of the *Wehrmacht*.) It was very simple: Hitler bought the generals off. Leeb, Rundstedt, Milch, Keitel, Raeder, Hube, Hossbach, Brauchitsch and even the aged Mackensen cleaned up, in cash or in kind (lordly estates – for example, Field Marshal von Kleist: the Hünen Estate; General Guderian: Diepenhof Estate). Hitler's secret budget for such sweeteners, kept quiet from the Auditor General's office, amounted to 3.3 million in 1935, and rose by 1945 to forty million Reichsmarks. Hitler's standard concluding banality – for instance in his letter of 30 March 1942 to Field Marshal Milch (incidentally he was the only non-Aryan among the generals; it was to him that Göring's words referred: 'I decide who is or isn't a Jew') – ran '. . . may perhaps, on the occasion of your fiftieth birthday, be of some assistance in the structuring of your private life. With sincere greetings, Your devoted Adolf Hitler.' The cheque, in this case, was made out for RM 250,000.

'And you want to get on to me,' the probably none too insubstantial shade of Christian Weber would say, 'about a few bits of loose change?'

Herr *Präsident* Weber made ample use of his diplomatic passport. In March 1935 he travelled to Hungary, in December to Paris, in February 1936 to London, in May 1938 to Rome, then on to Bucharest, to London again and to Switzerland. There will be more to be said later about his travels post-1939. All of them on official business, of course. In the cause of National Regeneration – and of buying horses. And the fact that everywhere that Herr *Präsident* Weber turned up with his entourage a high old time was had by all really seems hardly worthy of special mention.

*

The old, and still – with all due respect – corpulent gentleman sits in an armchair behind a small table, taking occasional sips

159

from a modest glass of wine (for some years now he has had to be careful – the liver, you know!), but he still enjoys his cigars. Minister of State (retd) Weber, founder member of the CSU after the war – admittedly there were a few incriminating matters, but the de-Nazification process has now been concluded, and others, the Federal Chancellor, federal and provincial ministers, ambassadors, professors and who knows what all, well, they were also . . . 'De-Nazification': according to the literal sense of the word, that means 'making free of Nazification'. Something like, for example, 'de-iced'. Free of ice. Anyone who has been de-Nazified is no longer a Nazi. And besides, a man can change his mind. One can even change one's views, one's *beliefs*. One sees the light. It's never too late for that. How old was Weber in 1945? Sixty-two. By no means past the age for changing one's views. Sudden change of heart – instantaneous, even. The mists lift. Day breaks. It is as if the scales have fallen from one's eyes. What was it that's supposed to have happened to the Jews? Gas ovens? Appalling! One sees pictures, one sees films: quite incredible! First I've heard of it. If I'd known *that*, then I'd have thrown my Party Badge in Gold straight in the fellow's face . . . I had *no idea*.

How is Weber supposed to have known anything about it when the whole German people knew nothing? After all it's a well-known fact; it turns out that nobody, not a soul, not a single one, knew about the concentration camps, the gas chambers . . . certainly not the military, they were all *out there*, having to shoot, to save their own skins. They knew absolutely nothing. Yes, sure, there were rumours, let's be honest, Dachau and the like . . . but there were all sorts of rumours about all sorts of things! That that Hitler could do such filthy, disgusting things – incredible. But he's dead now. He certainly must have got up to these nastinesses all by himself, because, as we've said, no one in the Whole German Nation had so much as the remotest idea of it all. Least of all Herr Christian Weber, who, let's face it, was no more than a mere nobody. A fellow traveller – fine . . . opportunist . . . perhaps. Who wasn't?

Germany, or Blue-Eyed Innocence. They always were

unworldly romantics; all the more reason to believe them when they say they really knew nothing of the shameful deeds of this Hitler – who, in any case, was an Austrian! Well, there you are, then! That has everything to do with having had nothing to do with it. 'Literally nothing to do with it.' So help me God.

Reconstruction has to start somewhere, with somebody to set it going. We can't fire all the experts. If we're to become once again upright members of the family of nations, then we must establish contact somehow. Schacht, now, he understands a bit about money, and Weber, he knows a thing or two about horses . . . expert knowledge. The kind of expert knowledge that has nothing to do with politics. Are we supposed never to perform the '*Meistersinger*' again, just because that . . . what was he called again? See, now we've even forgotten his name already.

De-Nazified. Rehabilitated. Slipped quietly in through a side door. Founder member of the CSU. Purification. A democrat. Slimmed down a bit. Secretary of State. Minister of State. Now 'retd'. An elderly gentleman.

No, of course not all of that is true. Not everything, that is, that has been said about Weber in the foregoing section. Weber did not become a founder member of the CSU. He didn't survive 1945, but more about that later. If, however, he had lived beyond 1945 . . . well, I wouldn't bet my life on it. Let the cross-examination take place in Valhalla. GOS Department. The advantage of this is that Weber remembers everything.

'The business with Röhm? Haha. He was . . . how should I put it . . . well, to cut a long story short, I didn't really notice right away. Only a few days later: he must have – this was while I was having a snooze after lunch – sneaked the little key out of my pocket, opened the safe and taken the drawings out, pocketed them and scarpered. As it turned out a few months later . . . well, turned out is maybe not quite accurate, as exhaustive investigations revealed, he passed the pictures on to a Swiss SA man who was absolutely devoted to him. Absolutely devoted! Haha. Devoted to Röhm . . . you get my drift. Wolf, well, Adolf, Hitler, he originally

intended to get rid of the *Wehrmacht* and set the SA up as
the people's militia in its place. But, as often happened with
Wolf, suddenly he dropped the whole idea. The splendour
of the Army! You see, a corporal, a corporal that has bought
his Iron Cross, First Class – he's a mug for that sort of thing.
The beautiful Army. Those *uniforms*! Those *flags*! Generals,
field marshals, battleships! Bands playing. You have to try to
imagine it: a corporal's-eye view! Compared to that, the SA:
that degenerate load of crap in their shit-brown rig-out. And
then the others, the entire *Wehrmacht*, with all its medals and
its braid, was suddenly lying at the corporal's feet . . . well,
you can forget Röhm and his tuppenny-ha'penny outfit right
away.

'Yes, well, all of a sudden Ernstl, old Röhm, finds himself
standing there in his shirt-tail, and Wolf, I mean Adolf, Hitler,
he's saying, Right, forget the truncheons, get a collecting-tin
in your hands. Thanks very much, says Ernstl, but we're not
a charitable organisation but Storm Troopers, in case you had
forgotten. "*Rrraus!*" howls the Wolf. And that's when Ernstl
started going on about the "Second Revolution". About the
real revolution, the SA Revolution.

'Between ourselves, though, nothing but hot air. Röhm
would never have mounted a *putsch*. Anybody else, yes, but
not him. Hitler could have whipped the entire SA away from
under his arse and Röhm wouldn't have so much as noticed,
so long as he had been left his little brown nancy-boys. But
for him to pinch these drawings from me! Let me tell you!
You don't do that to a Weber and get away with it! And me
lying there defenceless on the sofa.

'All right, it was hardly the height of chivalry or refinement,
the way it was done, I'll give you that, but what else could I
do? I went to Wolf and I said to him, Wolf, I said, Röhm was
at my place and he's planning a revolt to get rid of you, and he
wants me in on it, but in my heart there's nothing but Teutonic
loyalty and I've no time for despicable treachery, and besides
Röhm said about you, Wolf, anybody that's a vegetarian will
even sink low enough to become a teetotaller.

'Well, you should have seen old Wolf. He was up out of
his armchair like a jack-in-the-box, gnashing his teeth and

all the rest. All right, you know what happened after that. The Night of the Long Knives. June 30, 1934. *I* wasn't there, mind, not me. In Bad Wiessee, Wolf personally hauled Röhm and his clique out of their beds. They butchered a few of them on the spot, Röhm was shot in Stadelheim.

'"That," Wolf said to me afterwards, "I won't forget, never."

'"One act of loyalty deserves another," I said.

'"Name your wish!" says he.

'"The Brown Riband of Germany," says I.'

*

'Well now, Herr Peschmowitz, life still treating you well?'

'Please God, Herr Blumenthal.'

'You know, Herr Peschmowitz, I'm curious about when we're finally going to take some action –'

'What? How's that? You mean, now that general mobilisation has been brought in again? When we're going to take back Alsace-Lorraine, West Prussia and the colonies?'

'*We?* Herr Peschmowitz, you said "we"? Were those ever *our* colonies?'

'From who else were they, then?'

'They were the colonies from the Germans.'

'Are you not a German, Herr Blumenthal?'

. . .

'Ah, I understand, Herr Blumenthal.'

'When I say *German*, I'm not thinking of *us* any more.'

'That sounds very bitter, Herr Blumenthal.'

'And Hitler, he's sweet. So we keep hearing.'

'But what do you mean then by "when we're finally going to take some action"?'

'Yes, *us*. Us, the Jews.'

'We Jews? Take action? Merciful God! When we should just be happy they've left us in peace this far.'

'Left us in peace. That's a good one. Have you read the new laws? No, of course you haven't. You ought to read them, though. Here you are, the *Law Gazette*, I always have it on me.'

163

'Where did you get that?'

'You can buy it anywhere. Didn't you know that? Even a Jew can. In any bookshop. Look, here you are – "Reich Civil Law" of 15 September 1935, and here, "Law for the Protection of German Blood and German Honour" of the same day, and then the Enforcement Orders of 14 November 1935. You have to admit, Herr Peschmowitz, the Germans – now, hear me right, the Germans, not *us* – are a very orderly people. We, the Jews, are to be done in only after the creation of nice, tidy legal conditions. Not just out of hand, like in the Soviet Union . . .'

'And that's the law?'

'Go on, read it. You can keep it. There, Article 2, § 1: "Only nationals of German or generically related blood may be deemed citizens of the Reich" . . .'

' "Generically related"?'

'Exactly. *You*, Herr Peschmowitz, you are not generically related. Well, to me, maybe. But not to Hitler.'

'Thanks very much for that, I must say.'

'You are probably generically very unrelated to Hitler. Oh, and here, you have to admit, it's very nicely put: "Imbued with the consciousness that the purity of German blood is the necessary prerequisite for the continued existence of the German People . . ." I'm asking myself, Herr Peschmowitz, why "blood" is not written with a capital letter, as "People" is. Now me, I would have had the "blood" in "German blood" with a capital B.'

'And you can make jokes about it?'

'Anyway, you and I don't have pure blood with a capital letter or with a small one, and we are in consequence not German. So, when you are talking about the Germans, you may not say "we".'

'The whole thing is quite terrible.'

'There's only one article I really like. Here, Article 4: "Jews are forbidden to raise the Reich and national flags and to show the Reich colours." You see, that doesn't matter a hoot to me. I never hoist the Reich flag anyway. I have completely lost the urge to do so. But – read on, in Section 2: "On the other hand, the showing of the Jewish colours is permitted. The exercise of this right is protected by state guarantee." '

'What are the Jewish colours?'

'Now that I don't know either. Perhaps Hitler knows? You'd have to ask him. And if even he doesn't know – for myself as a Jew, I'd choose a delicate pea green and a nice rich violet.'

'But seriously, Herr Blumenthal . . .'

'You want seriously? Right, well, here's seriously – read, if you will, Article 4; carefully, though. Don't let anybody claim we Jews have no rights here in Germany. My dear fellow, of course we have rights. And what rights! We can show our colours of pea green and violet! That's even protected by the state! And you're still complaining? The dear, kind Führer has given us his guarantee.'

'I have to admit that I . . . that you, Herr Blumenthal, have been sceptical for years . . . but, what should we have done?'

'The Grau family, you know them, the ones with the little haberdashery in the Westenriederstrasse? Right? They've gone off to Trieste, they have relatives there. The Silbersteins have gone to America. They have relatives there.'

'I've only got relatives in Bamberg. Yes – and a cousin in Cracow . . . but would you want to go to Cracow?'

'We'll take action.'

'You're talking in riddles again.'

'Yes *we*, the Jewish International Conspiracy.'

'The Jewish *what*?'

'I do believe you don't listen to Hitler . . .'

'God forbid!'

'You should, you know. The Jewish world-wide conspiracy. It's a threat to the Aryans, and especially to Hitler. Aren't you a member, Herr Peschmowitz, a member of the international conspiracy? Do Herr Peschmowitz and his good lady wife not eat any Aryan children? You don't? Ah well . . . so Hitler is mistaken then?'

'Herr Blumenthal – what rubbish. There is no Jewish world conspiracy . . .'

'Oh, I see. So that's what you think, is it? In glaring

contradiction to the Herr Reich Chancellor? Oh well, that's it then. So the Jewish world conspiracy can't intervene to ensure our salvation. And there was I, hoping again and again that the Herr Reich Chancellor was right.'

'What baffles me is, what do they have against us?'

'They are Aryans. So they say. And we are Jews.'

'Fair enough, but . . .'

'We belong to an inferior race.'

'Herr Blumenthal – I am a flour wholesaler – still. I can tell inferior grades of flour from superior grades. All I need to do is stick my finger and thumb in. But how, I ask you, is Hitler to know what an inferior race is?'

'Perfectly simple: the Jewish one.'

'You're trying to make a fool of me: Jewish because inferior, and inferior because Jewish. Where's the logic in that?'

'Now, Herr Peschmowitz, you're getting closer to the nub of the matter. It has nothing to do with logic.'

'So with what, then? Are they envious of us? What for? There are rich Jews, admittedly, but a lot more poor ones . . .'

'Of course they're jealous of the rich Jews. But that's not it. Look, Herr Peschmowitz, I've heard Hitler's speeches, I've even read *Mein Kampf* – both volumes! There's probably hardly one Nazi who's done that, but that's neither here nor there. Your Hitler, Herr Peschmowitz, has no political strategy. Never did have. Nor can he have. If he *had* had a political strategy, he would never have got so far. A dictatorial movement catches on much faster the more overblown its arguments are. The masses don't want to think, the masses want to feel. Look: of course there have been NSDAP programmes. Declarations of intent, plans, campaign broadsheets . . . all of them changed a hundred times over. With every change in the political situation, Hitler has adapted his plan to suit. If he himself were to read, today, his 1920 programme . . . his little quiff would stand on end. Now that would be a comical sight. Do you see no significance in the fact that he has even forbidden the newspapers to print or to quote from the NSDAP programme? That he has even banned them

from quoting from *Mein Kampf*? Just like the Christians in the
past with the Bible. Herr Peschmowitz, you never, never unite
the masses *for* something. The masses can always be united
against something. And, in this case, we are unfortunately
that something.'

'But surely they can't – surely not all Germans are so
stupid . . .'

'Richard Wagner.'

'Beg pardon?'

'He started it. Have you never read him either?'

'Read, no – but heard, of course . . . marvellous music.
Tristan, Tannhäuser –'

'Hitler is more a fan of Léhar; with Wagner, so they say, he
is secretly bored, just pretends he'd like to like him. The main
thing is the *writings* of said Wagner. Here you are, Reclam
paperback . . .'

'You're a complete walking library.'

'*Judaism and Music*, published in 1850. The seminal work
of German anti-Semitism. I read it very attentively, because
I wanted to know what it is, in real and concrete terms,
he's got against us. Something comprehensible, something
tangible.'

'Well?'

' ". . . instinctive repugnance", he says.'

'That's rather feeble.'

'Exactly. His second argument: "The Jew talks the modern
European languages merely as learnt and not as mother
tongues . . ." '

'Even Heinrich Heine?'

'Third argument: the Jew is heartless, and he "never was
driven" – I'm quoting you his very words, see, here – "to
speak out a definite, a real and necessary thing . . . he just
merely wanted to speak, no matter what".'

'Was it really the same man who wrote that as composed
my *Tristan*?'

'And now the fourth argument, the really devastating one
against all Jews: ". . . and therefore, when as artist he reflects
them back upon us, his adaptations needs must seem to us
outlandish, odd, indifferent, cold, unnatural and awry, so that

Judaic works of music often produce on us the impression as though a poem of Goethe's, for example, were being rendered in the Jewish jargon".'

'And that's all?'

'That's all.'

'Nothing else?'

'Not a thing.'

'Can you imagine, Herr Blumenthal, a poem by Goethe being recited in the *Saxon* "jargon"? Does that make the natives of Saxony outlandish, odd, indifferent, cold, unnatural and awry?'

'Presumably no one thought of taxing Wagner with that one. Yes indeed, Herr Peschmowitz. Just imagine it, the Saxons with the right to display only the colours of Saxony. Black, green and yellow, I believe.'

*

Of course Wolf kept his word. One act of loyalty deserves another. He always kept his word. His word of honour as a German. So long as he hadn't changed his mind in the mean time. But he had no second thoughts on the Brown Riband, and already Christian Weber's visions were beginning to emerge from the mists of mere fantasy to become flesh on the firm terrain of reality.

As of 1 October 1935, the bouncer gloried in another title: Weber became, with his 'appointment to full-time status as a civil servant, an alderman of the Capital of the Movement. Signed *Adolf Hitler*.' On 1 April 1935, the new system of local government laws came into force, uniform the length and breadth of the Reich, which, while not exactly abolishing municipal and local government organs, nevertheless reduced them to insignificance *vis-à-vis* their respective *Bürgermeister* (the leadership principle!). All that local councillors were left with was 'to advise the burgomaster in his autonomous capacity and to ensure public sympathy for his measures'. A set-up which was just made for Weber, of course. The City Archives have preserved a whole bundle of missives, most of them postcards:

Christian Weber, Swine

A clown, a cripple and a morphine-head
(Hitler) (Göbbels [*sic*]) (Göring)
preach to the Germans what's pure-bred.
It's with people like these the ex-bouncer of the
Blue Buck Herr Chr. Weber is in cahoots.

Drunken sot!

. . . you're getting fatter and fatter . . .

Cobbler! Stick to your last!
Bouncer! Don't you get too brash.

These expressions of sympathy were of course almost all anonymous, only the last-quoted letter bears a signature – no doubt fictitious: Alois Weidemann. Wherever you may be, whether still in the land of the living or elsewhere, Alois Weidemann, hats off to you, even if your rhyme doesn't quite match up to the loftiest criteria. Nevertheless, these little messages niggled Weber, which is obvious from the fact that he repeatedly tried to get the police to sniff out the anonymous senders.

The bitter pill of the relegation of the local councils to the role of mere figurehead (and former Party members' welfare) bodies was – in so far as municipal councils were concerned – sweetened by the conferring of the title 'alderman'. 'Alderman' – an aura of patrician nobility wafts around this title: oak-panelled rooms, late-afternoon light through bull's-eye windows, heavy tankards on massive tables, a gold chain reposing on the contours of a prosperous *embonpoint* – the authority to appoint to aldermanic status was (in line with the already mentioned centralisation policy of the Party hierarchy) restricted only to a 'commissioner of the NSDAP', which in the case of smaller and medium-sized communities generally meant the *Kreisleiter*, and for towns and urban districts the *Gauleiter*. Only in the case of the Capital City of the Movement, the nest he had flown, did Hitler reserve for himself the right of appointment, which is why Weber's official scroll bears the Führer's signature.

Let no one suggest that Mr Alderman President Weber was an uncultured man. No indeed! That would be to do him an injustice. He even devoted his attention to cultural events in which the ladies appeared fully clothed. From as early as June 1935 (perhaps even before that), Weber had been Chairman of the official New Studio Theatre Society. He made more of a dent in, than an impression on, the theatre business, and appointed Paul Wolfrum – at that time still his friend and boozing companion – who was also an alderman and an SS-*Sturmbannführer* to boot, to the post of managing director of the Studio Theatre, thus ensuring the harassment of the theatre manager, Falckenberg. Wolfrum – and, now and again, Weber himself – liked to stride the boards in SS uniform and satisfy himself during rehearsals that the theatre was being artistically run according to the tenets of National Regeneration. At any suggestion of rebelliousness from members of the ensemble, he would utter the simple word 'Dachau', and if that did not produce the desired effect, the complaining mouths would be stopped up with salary raises and assurances of major parts. Wolfrum's artistic thinking ran along the lines of 'Actors are men who can march . . . not a bunch of effeminate, spineless characters', or – a motto that must have been very much after Weber's own heart – 'Art, for me, is Siegfried and naked females'.

In July 1938, Weber attempted to fuse the two concepts of the theatre and the horse in perfect harmony. The occasion was the performance of a festival production as part of the 'Riem International Race Week'. The comedy by the widely unknown playwright Fritz Schwiefert, entitled *Derby*, was reworked on Weber's instructions and emerged on the Studio Theatre's stage as *The Brown Horse*. The direction was nominally in the hands of Wilhelm Holsboer, but Wolfrum, who apparently now felt called to direct, joined him in the producer's chair and had his say. The third act was enriched by the introduction of female students of the masterclass in the Fashion School ('naked females' . . .); the set and props all satisfied the requirements of even the critical eye of that connoisseur of stables, Weber. Originally, live horses were supposed to feature in the action, but this idea foundered on the steep flights of steps leading up to the stage. So the actors were merely roped in to ride a horse a few times round and round the courtyard of the Studio Theatre before representatives of the press. 'To set the mood.'

Criticism – in the sense of artistic criticism – was regarded as un-German. That's perfectly logical: no one has ever heard of Teutonic art critics. Caesar and Tacitus reported on everything to do with the Germanic tribes, but there is no mention anywhere of art critics. 'Yesterday's gathering of the border tribes in the Thingstead suffered, as was only to be anticipated, as a result of the indisposition of the Bard, Sigiswald, who, in any case, as has frequently been noted in these columns, greatly over-estimates his own vocal range . . . The harpist, Kunihild, in her performance of "The Spring Roundelays in Reykjavik", took the triplets in bar sixteen perceptibly slowly, which meant that the sociological fragmentation in respect of the lateral impact on the two-dimensional tonal landscape . . .' No. There was nothing like that. So criticism is un-Teutonic. In any case, the most malicious critics in the days of the Old Order were Jews. One of them once criticised Goebbels' novel *Michael*. Now, instead of criticism, there was only reporting. Besides, the word for reporting, *'Berichterstattung'*, was a good German word, whereas *Kritik* stems from the Eyetie Latin. (*Berichterstattung*, later also *Kriegs-Berichterstattung* – war correspondence, which makes everything perfectly clear; *'Kriegs-Kritik'*?: 'Colonel von Kriechnuckel und zu Brotmergel proved during yesterday's attack on enemy lines that he has not yet recovered his past peak form. The left flank, normally his forte, became bogged down in the kind of all too gentle, lyrical tones which one might more readily have expected in some minor skirmish set against the backdrop of an undulating, hilly countryside in its pre-springtime hues, but not, it has to be said, when heavy Russian artillery . . .') Quite out of the question. The *Völkischer Beobachter*, in its *Berichterstattung* of 27 July 1938, was hard pushed to find a word of praise for the play. (How it would have been savaged if there had been such a thing as a *Kritik* hardly bears thinking about.) Financially, the production was a disaster. (Even a totalitarian system has its limitations: you cannot simply have everybody who does *not* go to see a nationally regenerated play arrested and locked away in Dachau.) The incident came to the ear of Goebbels, the Nazis' top culture boss. He had detailed reports sent by confidants in Munich. For a long time now, the Munich GOS clique had been anathema to him, and this artistic and financial flop was the perfect excuse for teaching that clique a lesson. Within the Party, he blew up this wash-out to scandal proportions and went straight to Hitler to raise a stink. On 1 September he summoned *Oberbürgermeister* Fiehler to the *Berghof* and ordered Wolfrum's dismissal as commercial manager. Weber, however, remained on the board of administration, but from then on he kept a distinctly low profile in matters artistic.

Anyway, soon there were other things to be attended to.

Back in 1934, shortly after Hitler had given the go-ahead, Weber had founded the 'Board of Trustees for the Brown Riband of Germany'. Horse-racing was to be Germanised in grand style. Weber dreamt of a 'World Arena', which he intended building at the northern end of Lake Starnberg, and which would become a Mecca for all horses and riders. On 16 May 1936, Weber presented before the Registrar's Court of the Munich District Court the constitution and rules of the 'Brown Riband of Germany' Club, which had grown out of the Board of Trustees. These were registered the very same day under the reference number VR 3733, thus earning legal standing and the suffix '*e.V.*' – the club was now an 'incorporated association'. A few weeks later, on 12 June, the club was granted the designation of a 'Reich Organisation': that is to say, it more or less achieved the status of a public company. Founder members included, apart from Christian Weber, such figures as a certain Dr Josef Hölzl and one Herr Hans Kleeblatt, fellow alderman Paul Wolfrum, the full-time professional city councillor Ernst Schubert and Eva Braun's brother-in-law, SS-*Gruppenführer* (i.e. Lieutenant-General) Hermann Fegelein. Club President was, it goes without saying, Christian Weber.

From 1936 until the outbreak of war, the race for the 'Brown Riband of Germany' was held every summer. Since the World Arena on the Starnberger See had not yet been built, they had to make do with the racecourse in Riem.

('Christian van Riem' was the nickname attached – discreetly, of course – to the Herr President from then on.) But the extravagance expended by Weber on this event was enormous. He saw to it that everything that went on in Munich during those few days revolved around the race meeting. Weber himself gleamed greasily in his black SS uniform, complete with aldermanic chain. Banquets for diplomats and other prominent foreign guests and, of course, high-ranking Party members ended up in convivial get-togethers in intimate groups. It was no problem for Alderman Weber to have the Capital City of the Movement dressed overall with flags (a motion to this end, dated 1 August 1937, is extant), while Adviser to the Reich Postal Service Weber pushed through the issue of a special set of stamps to commemorate the occasion. Naturally, Weber took part in the races with his own stables – in its heyday, two hundred gallopers, racing colours 'Cornflower Blue' – and the crowning glory was the victory of his stallion, Wild Lad, in the main event in 1938.

That, and the Night of the Amazons, of course, which finally dawned – or dusked – in the wake of the Brown Riband.

*

'A pity,' muses the shade of Christian Weber in Valhalla, 'a pity that Wolf never came. Three Nights of the Amazons there were. In '36, '37 and '38. We were always lucky with the weather – for instance in '36: that day, I remember quite clearly it was a Monday, 27 July, and that afternoon a tremendous thunderstorm hit Munich, a real cloudburst, with hailstones, and we all thought, That's it, a wash-out, but then, towards evening, it suddenly cleared up, and it turned into the most marvellous summer night. And the year after, in 1937, that was when the festival was on a Sunday, 31 July, and before it there was a downpour and then it turned fine again. Only in 1938 had we had a long, persistent period of fine weather beforehand.

'But Wolf didn't turn up. Not once, even though he wasn't in Berlin, but on the Obersalzberg at the time, if I remember rightly. Just didn't show up. A shame. If he had seen that, seen something as beautiful as that . . . he'd have realised right away, who needs a war with all this? He'd have been bound to see that. There's just nothing finer.'

'Naked and beautiful, the girls have to be,' so Christian Weber 'who was in overall charge of the festivities' was supposed to have said. The situation regarding sources for remarks like this is of course somewhat unclear. The time in question is not so far in the past that it should simply have trickled away into the general stream of history, but, on the other hand, so many years have elapsed that the memory of those that partook of the experience has become clouded – or transfigured by the enchantment that distance lends. In connection with the Night of the Amazons, transfiguration is more likely.

There were three such galas in all; all three were put on in connection with Riem Race Week, with the race for the Brown Riband of Germany to be precise. And it appears that all the festivities were organised and financed by the city of Munich. There was only one single piece of documentary evidence to be found in support of this assumption. (In the City Archives there is nothing under 'Night' nor under 'Amazons'.) This one document is dated 16 September 1936 and had somehow found its way into the file marked WEBER, CHRISTIAN, ALDERMAN – even though he is not specifically named in it. It is a letter from the American Express Company, Munich office, to the city, re – Night of the Amazons, and is signed 'American Express/With the German salute/*Heil Hitler!/R. Molck-Ude*, Manager.' The letter contains the information that the Ballet Russe of Herr Iskoldoff of London had been engaged by telephone, via American Express, to come to Munich (presumably to plug a gap caused by some other attraction having dropped out), and that the city was requested to agree to pay the – unspecified – additional expenses. The city agreed to nothing of the kind.

That, as has already been said, is the sole piece of solid evidence. Other than that, there are only a few newspaper reports available, and the transfigured memories of those who were there at the time, for Weber did not have the girls of the BDM, the League of German Women, prance about for his own solitary amusement; he let the population, already taking in the National Regeneration (or perhaps already taken in by it), have their share, so long as they were prepared to buy tickets. An advert in the *Münchener Neueste Nachrichten* of 27 July 1936 reveals that there were advance-booking offices at, for instance, the Max Hieber music shop (in those days at Marienplatz 18) and at the Bavarian General Tourist Bureau, Ritter-von-Epp-Platz 12 (that is, the Promenadenplatz). Fifteen thousand spectators were prepared to come up with the cash for a ticket to have a look at the Amazons; the price of admission is not stated. At the first performance, it was found that the acts could not be clearly viewed from all seats, which explains why in 1937 and 1938 only twelve thousand tickets went on sale. Both of these performances were sold out. Herr President Weber, of course, had a perfect view, even the first time the show was staged, for he was sitting in the VIP seats in the midst of the guests of honour, who in 1936 included the Reich Governor Ritter von Epp, Prime Minister Siebert and Lord Mayor Fiehler, along with pretty well every single general stationed in the Munich area. The second festival was, according to the records, also graced by the presence of the Royal Romanian Ambassador, General Coumeu, and the Mexican Ambassador, General Azcarate. Ali Khan, too, it is said, was among those present.

There are a few photographs: one shows the Director of Munich's *Deutsches Theater*, Paul Wolz, at rehearsals with four 'Amazons' and two horses. The producer – in discreet grey suit, with tie, Hitler moustache and spectacles, he looks more like the custodian of the petty cash – is hard at work with one of the Amazons, the sight of whom is well worth a second glance, trying to recapture exactly the pose of that original model in front of the Stuck villa – inclining slightly backwards to launch her spear. The other three Amazons are watching with interest (or pretending to do so), the horses appear serene and indifferent. Two of the girls are completely naked except for their helmets, one of the equestriennes is wearing knickers and the other a kind of narrow sash, which has the effect of being more of an accessory than an article of clothing. The helmets look like the sort of thing a costume designer of only average talent would imagine ancient Amazon helmets to look like. Those of the two girls looking on beside the horses are oversized and obviously made of cardboard. The more ample of these two foot-soldier Amazons is not in fact completely bare, but has on a belt, which in turn has the effect of making her appear even more naked than the altogether nude one standing next to her. A total of sixteen mounted Amazons took part, or so it is said. Legend has it – although where legend got it from is not clear, but it does sound plausible – that there were problems: firstly, despite the mildness of the July evening, the undraped BDM equestriennes felt distinctly chilly and in the intervals between their appearances they lay down, flat as flounders, on their pedestals, which were lit (and thereby somewhat warmed) from beneath; this apparently had a distracting effect, but nothing like as distracting as the extraordinary bouncing momentum developed by the unfettered breasts – threatening an oscillatory disturbance, a resonance overload, of seismic proportions – during the gallop-past. In the end, they had to make do with a trot-past.

There were eight items on the programme for the delectation of Weber and his guests: 1. a mounted troop of SS (in a state of full dress – Röhm was no longer around) under the command of *Obersturmbannführer* Ballauff received the guests of honour. 2. A 'Dance Display' at the park fountain, for which the (also fully clothed) State Opera Ballet and State Orchestra had been called into service; this was not a new production for the occasion – the ballet corps of the opera merely danced the Venusberg scene from *Tannhäuser*. 3. 'Venetian Carousel 1700', performed by the Military Academy under Captain of Horse Pönicke, accompanied by the Corps of Trumpeters of the VIIth Intelligence Corps, under the baton of Staff Director of Music Kiessling. 4. *The Golden Lion Ride*, an equestrian play from around 1700, directed by Lieutenant Fegelein (not, of course, to be confused with the previously mentioned brother-in-law of Eva Braun). 5. *The Gladiators*, also presented by the *corps de ballet* of the State Opera, production by Ballet Master Ornelli.

6. 'Quadrille in Homage of the Great Prince Elector' (Elector Christian Ludwig of the Blue Buck), danced by sixteen officers and sixteen ladies, which probably involved the first entrance of the Amazons. 7., considered by the anonymous journalist in the *Münchener Neueste Nachrichten* to be the highlight of the evening, 'Night-Dance of the Shepherds and Shepherdesses', followed by 'Wild Mounted Shepherds' Games', performed by the combined forces of the State Opera Ballet (Ornelli), the aforementioned Iskoldoff Russian Ballet and other, unspecified, 'Baron Wrangel Cossacks'. The eighth and final turn saw the staging of another *Amazon Play*, which merged into a 'Baldaquin of Fire', to quote once again the frenzied gushings of the reviewer, by now almost beside himself with enthusiasm, a 'symphony in the heavens', which presented two thousand completely new products of the pyrotechnic arts.

It seems hardly worthy of special mention here that the generous and genial *spiritus rector* of this extravaganza of *völkisch* jubilation insisted, after the show, on mingling with the cast of Amazons – 'Can we get dressed now?', 'Don't you dare! You've to be presented to the Herr President first', 'But we're freezing', 'Well, lie down on the searchlights for a minute. And anyway, you can keep your helmets on' – and on expressing his admiration of each and every one of them with a hearty handshake (or rather, a hearty laying-on of his shaking hands wherever Christian Weber deemed fitting to the occasion).

*

'It is,' croaked SS-man Staudigl, 'a rather private matter, Herr *Obersturmführer*.'

'Yes? Well? What is it then?'

'I don't know, Herr *Obersturmführer*.' SS-man Staudigl was making a great effort to stand to attention, but he was in such inner turmoil that he swayed like a tree in a gale.

'You're quite green about the gills, Staudigl,' said the major. 'Are you feeling sick?'

'I wish that was all it was, Herr *Obersturmführer*.'

'At ease!' said the major.

Staudigl relaxed a little, bending one leg slightly forward. It was obvious that Staudigl was on the verge of having to hold on to the *Obersturmführer*'s desk for support.

'It's because,' said Staudigl, 'I can trust you, sir. That is,' he spluttered on hastily, 'I trust my other comrades too, of course, and because . . . and . . . we're all in this together, I know, and all the other officers . . . only . . . but it's . . . because I feel, as it were . . . I can confide in you on a direct, man-to-man level, if I may say so . . .'

'Good God, Staudigl! Pull yourself together! You look as if you're about to blub any minute now.'

Staudigl gave a loud sniff.

'Permission to blow my nose, Herr *Obersturmführer*?'

'Sit yourself down first.'

'Thank you.' Staudigl blew his nose. Then, 'Excuse me, this sort of thing should not happen to an SS man, but . . . if you . . . I don't know . . . whether I can ask . . . because . . .'

'One thing at a time, Staudigl, one thing at a time. What's eating you?'

'I'm engaged,' Staudigl squeezed the words out.

'Aha!' said the major knowledgeably and leant back into his armchair. The back of the chair was decorated with a large runic life-symbol, carved into the wood.

'Perhaps,' said Staudigl, 'it's not so much that I *am* engaged, maybe I *was* engaged.'

'Thought as much, thought it'd come down to that. I've always said, an SS man should always . . . hm! . . . the example of our *Führer* . . . but we'll drop that. Now then, your intended has run off with somebody else, has she?'

'No,' said Staudigl.

'No? I see. *You*'ve found another . . .'

'No. Not that either. It's . . . because my fiancée is in the BDM and can ride a horse.'

'Don't tell me the young lady has –' the *Obersturmführer* let out a dirty laugh, but stifled it abruptly when he saw that SS-man Staudigl was not in the mood for jokes – 'with a stallion . . . I'm sorry . . . just a joke, no offence meant . . . well, what's up, then?'

'I don't want her,' Staudigl blurted out, 'to become an Amazon.'

'Amazon?'

'After all . . . I'm . . . and my family . . . and her family . . . it's not as if . . . as if . . . I mean, they're not Bolshevik swine who . . . who . . . she's a respectable German girl, Herr *Obersturmführer*, and – I don't want you to get the idea that it's for any religious reasons, oh no, obviously we both left the Church long ago, but, before the wedding . . . you understand. She would never allow it. Ilse. Ilse's her name.'

'I still don't see what you're driving at.'

'Although we've been to Youth Camp together, on Langeoog, and . . . not that there wasn't plenty of opportunity, in the Youth Camp, we were always together out in the dunes, in the moonlight, and really, all we did was sing songs . . . I had my accordion with me . . . and although . . . well, *she* always went back to the girls' tent and I went to the boys' one . . . and now! She's an Amazon! And I wasn't even asked, *me*, her fiancé. Even though we swore, that night in the moonlight on Langeoog, that we would present the Führer with at least six children. But only after we were married, you understand. And then I played the old ballad, "*Wir wollen zu Land ausfahren*", on my accordion, and Ilse laid her head on my shoulder . . .'

'Before taking herself off to the girls' tent.'

'Yes. And now she has to ride around naked as an Amazon. In the Park. Herr *Obersturmführer*. I, her fiancé, *I've* never seen her naked. We wanted to keep that for the consecration of our physical love after the wedding, Herr *Obersturmführer*, and now she is simply detailed for riding around, in front of ten thousand people, Herr *Obersturmführer*, naked – stark naked, with only a helmet . . . I can't stand it, Herr *Obersturmführer*, it isn't right!'

The major gave a growl, fumbled for a cigarette in his cigarette case embellished with the death's-head symbol. 'One for you? Staudigl?'

'Thank you, no, I don't smoke, Herr *Obersturmführer*. Just like the Führer.'

The major stood up, paced a few steps up and down, then

stopped by the window and gazed out.

'Amazons,' he said after a while. 'I'm with you now. The "Night of the Amazons". But surely there are several of them skipping around naked there? Quite a crowd of them, from what I've heard.'

'I don't care about the others,' said Staudigl. 'It's my Ilse I'm bothered about.'

'Hm, hm,' said the major, 'and your Ilse herself? What does she have to say about it?'

'I'm afraid,' Staudigl's voice dropped almost to a whisper, 'she rather enjoys it.'

'Would it help at all, Staudigl, if I were to get you a free ticket for the show?'

'Am I to be a spectator at my own disgrace as well?'

'You're over-reacting. Look at it this way: Faith and Beauty. A Teutonic maiden of pure blood has nothing to hide –'

'I'm not concerned with racial purity. Have you ever seen Herr President Weber? Have you? There you are, then. So have I. He sits up there, and stares . . . and stares . . . at my Ilse too . . naked, as even I have never –'

'You're starting to blub again, Staudigl! Don't forget you're an SS man.'

'I beg your pardon.'

'I can't do anything to help in this, you know. You'll just have to get over it. It's not exactly as if she's been deflowered in the course of it, your Ilse. Pardon the expression. You've still got that to look forward to. And if Herr President Weber, who after all is a Genuine Old Soldier –'

'A Genuine Old Sod –'

The major laughed. 'I'll pretend I didn't hear that. You'll see, once you're married, in a few years' time, you'll have forgotten all about it. Or you'll both look back and laugh about it. Maybe I can fix it for Herr President Weber to be best man at your wedding . . . wouldn't do your career any harm if . . .'

Staudigl leapt to attention. 'Thank you. No.'

'Suit yourself.'

'If Ilse . . . as an Amazon . . . then . . . marriage would be quite out of the question.'

'Now you're beginning to rave, Staudigl.'

'So you can't help me, Herr *Obersturmführer*?'

'I've no idea how I could. I can't forbid the Herr President . . . I ask you, one of the Führer's bosom friends.'

'Thank you, Herr *Obersturmführer*,' Staudigl saluted.

'Now don't do anything reckless, Staudigl.'

'I know, Herr *Obersturmführer*, what an SS man has to do in a situation like this.'

However, SS-man Staudigl did not, after all, go out and shoot himself.

*

One might be forgiven for assuming that dictators encourage immorality. (Well anyway, what our Christian ethics proscribe as immorality, which is pretty well everything that gives people pleasure. Political immorality has never been condemned.) One might in fact think that dictators would cast 'unbridled licentiousness' – or whatever other term is used to describe anything that provides mankind with any enjoyment with even the remotest sexual tinge to it – before their people like so much bait, for there is nothing they would snap up more quickly. Give the masses pleasure, and they will dispute no dictator's claim to power . . . One might imagine that to be the way dictators' minds work. Not a bit of it. Beginning with the theatres, Cromwell's revolution banned everything that was even reputed to be entertaining. The French Revolution was almost more steeped in morality than in blood; compared to Robespierre, Calvin was a raving degenerate. Mao banned music, Khomeni banned laughter, Stalin countenanced only diversions of a patriotic nature, and we need not even go into the record of the Christian churches. It would seem that state or social terrorism is inconceivable without terrorising people's minds. What is the reason for this? What made Ceauşescu believe his first duty was to protect his people from the sight of naked female bosoms? It is incomprehensible why dictators make things so hard for themselves. What is the link between the prudery of dictators and their lust for power? To be sure, many dictators, particularly dictators of conscience, are old men, who will not grant others what they themselves are past enjoying any more. But that is not true of all dictators: if you think of Mussolini who, to put it in discreet terms, was not averse to loose living (at least in secret). Put less politely, he was one of the randiest skirt-chasing lechers in world history. Is it perhaps because dictators can't accept that there might be one sphere of the lives of their subjects that they cannot regiment? Or are they too stupid to recognise the advantages here? Or is it some merciful quirk in the scheme of things that thus ensures against the perpetuation of dictatorships? For in the long run puritanical antagonism to pleasure has never yet succeeded in conquering mankind's sensual urges, and even noble Christianity has – let us not delude ourselves – failed, because its priests backed the wrong horse of sexual repression, for which there is no justification to be found in the Gospels.

National Socialism, too, was anti-pleasure. Asceticism had been put about as the watchword. It took on solid form as an ideal, epitomised in the figure of Führer Schicklgruber, the solitary, lugubrious Wolf, who – to pile metaphor upon bogus metaphor, as was the manner of those times – like some stony eagle hovered above his people, restless yet serene, guarding against filthy Jewish-Bolshevik-plutocrat tentacles attaching their rapacious suckers to . . . The solitary Wolf, high on his storm-buffeted *Berghof*, his defiant gaze piercing the far distances, ever-brooding, all-envisioning (not omniscient, for the Führer unfortunately did not know everything, but anyway all-envisioning, all-envisioning Adolf, it has a much more Germanic, almost Wagnerian, ring to it: 'aquiline All-Father, all-envisioning Adolf') – it is the icy chill of duty alone that encircles him. True enough, the devoted disciples, the seasoned, strife-seared soldiers, rally round him in droves: the gold-greedy Göring, the high-hearted Himmler, the rambling, rabbiting Ribbentrop, but earthly love, the flickering fire of female fervour is eschewed by the valiantly virility-vanquishing Wolf, his only consolation coming from the prattling passion of his people proclaiming their patriotism . . . Asceticism. In reality, Schicklgruber was a lazy rascal who, hardly had he become Reich Chancellor, concerned himself only with ensuring that all those around him were sufficiently jealous of one another, so as to prevent any one of them becoming strong enough to constitute a challenge to his power; whose earthly love – which was not without its problems – was called Eva Braun; who, up on his *Berghof*, had cheap, kitschy-sentimental films and music from Léhar operettas played to him and devoured mountains of whipped cream. Besides which, his eagle eye was decidedly short-sighted, and only his chronic bouts of flatulence assured him of temporary solitude. And anyway, he was a clown: he postured and grimaced in front of a mirror, gnawed carpets on receipt of bad news and hopped about like Rumpelstiltskin in response to good. But no one was to know about that. Outwardly, the watchword was asceticism. The function of sexual intercourse was not to satisfy lust but to serve the National Regeneration. Only in one respect did National Socialism differ from other Fascist dictatorships: nudity was permissible. Konrad Ziegler ('the Master of German Pubic Hair'), Paul Matthias Padua ('the Führer's favourite painter') and Josef Thorak ('Reich Marble-Block Leader') wallowed in breasts and arses and muscles, but of course all that did not come under the category of 'sensuality', but of 'Faith and Beauty'. An Aryan need conceal nothing. Blond-haloed, shining figures of racial purity. Even the nipple points the way upwards to sunlight and Aryanism.

All this had deep roots – well buried even in those days – reaching down ultimately to the hyper-Germanicism imbuing the origins of the Naturist Movement around the turn of the century: all those sun worshippers cavorting in the dew, those flimsily clad sons and daughters of the soil, those undraped spring roundelays in the groves of 'Free Body Culture' by a Diefenbach or a Fidus were basic fundamentals – unacknowledged but none the less not to be underestimated in their influence – of Pre-Nazism, and they found expression, by way of Fra Jörg Lanc von Liebenfels (i.e. the renegade monk Adolf Lanz), in a magazine entitled *Ostara* after the Germanic Goddess of the Earth and the Spring, the flagship publication of the *Heldlinge und Arioheroiker*, the

Young Valiants and Aryo-Heroics, to which Adolf Hitler was a subscriber, as also was a certain Werner von Bülow, who later founded the Edda Society in Munich, what might be described as an Aryan salon in the *Walterspiel* restaurant, frequented by Frau Bruckmann and the Hanfstaengl family. The tangible remnants of the Aryo-heroines cavorted about in Christian Weber's Amazonian nights and were thus perfectly compatible with National Regeneration.

By way of a parenthesis: no man is endowed with *only* bad taste, not even Hitler. He did not have only kitschy films shown, he was also an admirer of Charles Chaplin. The connection between these two men who, regrettably, have to be mentioned in the same breath, is an extraordinary one. They were of the same age, almost to the day; Chaplin adopted Hitler's little moustache as part of his make-up, long before he can have become familiar with it; but stranger still is the fact that the aforementioned scheme of things, the poor old *Weltgeist*, already pretty badly knocked about, called forth in Charles Chaplin a direct antipode to Hitler: where the one was an idle buffoon who attempted to play the serious national leader and statesman, the other, who always played the sad clown, was a great, tireless, serious artist, perhaps the true Shakespeare of the twentieth century. That Chaplin should, at the peak of his artistic career, have slipped into the mask of Hitler has a certain inevitability about it and indeed is one of world history's greatest strokes of luck. No film documentary reveals Hitler's ludicrousness more sharply than Chaplin's inarticulate speech in *The Great Dictator* or his celebrated bit of business with the inflatable globe. In one's contemplation of the ways of the world, there is some consolation to be derived from the knowledge that Hitler saw this film. He was consumed with the wrath of the unmasked hypocrite. From that moment on, Chaplin's films were struck from the repertoire for his private viewing.

The Nights of the Amazons in 1937 (on 31 July) and 1938 (on 30 July) were if anything even more glittering and the girls even more naked than in 1936. In 1937 a cast of 2,800 took part, the Nymphenburg Park was illuminated by 1,200,000 candles. 'The lively pace of the sequence of events affords

the fifteen grand tableaux every possibility for development,'
wrote the *Münchener Neueste Nachrichten*. A photograph
shows a few bob-haired Amazons in a kind of tin brassière
and holding shields and spears, although only on foot '. . . for
the narrow entrance allowed tantalising glimpses of all the
activity of a colourful masque, of horses tripping delicately
among scantily clad girls . . .' 'At the instigation of President
Christian Weber, who is in overall charge of the festivities,
producer Paul Wolz assembled this magnificent spectacle . . .'
'. . . wondrous clusters of searchlight beams . . .' '. . . and
already the final scene is upon us, a bewildering, raging,
exciting struggle, the Battle of the Amazons, whose equestrian
mettle stole this whole night. Tender nymphs, wreathed in
the flowing billows of their magical veils, helmeted Amazons
with clashing shields . . . half naked in their panther-skins
. . . until the victory celebration of the virginal combatants
brings the battle to a close and a victorious Penthesilea is led
in amidst a triumphal procession.' There is a photograph of
this, too: a large flat cart is being hauled by strapping Party
members in rococo livery and plaited wigs. On the wagon,
picked out by gold and silver lighting, similarly costumed
musicians are bowing and blowing away, and above all this in
a somewhat asymmetrically adorned frame the naked Diana,
with nothing but a thin wisp of a veil around her hips – was
this a technical hitch or a particularly cunning piece of erotic
direction by producer Wolz? The veil, which in any case was
far too flimsy to conceal anything, was not draped round that
part of Diana's loins where the centre of feminine sexuality
is located, but higher up, round her hips. And her hand is
raised in the German salute. Faith and Beauty. Nationalist
Faith and Aryan Beauty. Presumably the Amazon Queen is
about to be paraded past Herr President Weber. What would
the Nazis have said about this kind of a spectacle if it had
been presented in, say, a Paris cabaret, and produced by a
Jew?
     The third and – although no one could know this at the
time – last Night of the Amazons: again, twelve thousand
spectators, six bands, curtain up at nine p.m., theme 'The
Wedding of Prince Elector Max, "thus interweaving in the

play equestrian skill with grace and beauty"'; '. . . flower goddesses enter on gleaming coaches, and Heracles is in combat with doughty warrior Amazons, battling for the queen's sash . . .' (this, thanks to Paul Wolz's production, her one and only garment), '. . . and so a vanquished victor lies at the feet of the beautiful Amazon Queen as she drives on her lofty chariot past the Prince Elector and his guests . . .' This report, too, is embellished in the *Münchener Neueste Nachrichten* with a suitable photograph. But let us turn the page: a bronze Amazon, on horseback and naked but for her helmet, in the act of launching her spear, the way she is to be seen in front of that villa, only smaller, on a tall marble plinth: 'On behalf of the members of the Board of Trustees for the Brown Riband of Germany, *Gauleiter* and Minister of State Wagner presented this token of esteem to President Weber in recognition of his unparalleled contribution to the advancement of German horse-racing and of the breeding of German thoroughbreds. The figure represents Stuck's Amazon.' Amazons, everywhere you looked. And there, in the midst of the Amazons, Weber, the Happy Weber. (An appalling thought flashes across the mind: what if Franz von Stuck hadn't actually been an Aryan . . . ? But he was indeed Aryan. Phew!)

So what was next? How much higher? Was there any other goal for him, Christian Weber, to aim for? Still more riches? Still nakeder Amazons? Impossible – they were stark naked already. There to be viewed from fore and aft, lit up by 1.2 million candles or hundreds of floodlights. And you couldn't find a better seat in the house than his box – so how much higher? Could anyone be more blissfully, repletely happy? For a while, it is claimed, Weber toyed with the thought of ousting that colourless desk jockey Fiehler and becoming *Oberbürgermeister* himself. ('One word from him,' Fiehler testified before the De-Nazification Commission after the war, 'and I would have been out the very next day.' Admittedly, we have to remember in connection with this testimony that of course the surviving Nazis themselves did everything they could to palm off all the principal blame on to the dead ones, but in the light of all that is known about Weber, and of all that Weber knew about Hitler, it does not sound altogether far-fetched.) But he let it be. He knew – yes, sometimes even a bouncer is that clever – that in totalitarian systems the real power is exercised behind the scenes.

But what has become of the beautiful bronze replica of the Amazon presented to Weber on that 30 July 1938? Did she fall victim to the bomb that blew Weber's Residency apartment to smithereens? Is she lying buried in the rubble under the foundations of the new replacement for the block at Sebastiansplatz No. 9? Or did he rescue her? Was she stashed away along with the other valuables in Otterfing in 1943, where he had also moved his fleet of vehicles? Did she figure among his estate? For, in Weber's case, the county court dealing with the so-called 'objective proceedings' (that is to say, the de-Nazification proceedings against dead Nazis) set the material value at 9.6 million Reichsmarks. How much is that Amazon worth? Was she auctioned? Did she land up on a stall at the fair in Au? Is she perhaps standing today in the living-room of some art-loving latter-day *Barockmensch*? I'd love to know.

Christian Weber's star at its zenith . . . star sign: Amazon. A few days after the third bout of festivities, Weber reached his fifty-fifth birthday. And again, *Oberbürgermeister* Fiehler sent him five bottles of wine . . . *Five.*

*

'I tell you, Herr Dirrigl, this is not the way things were meant to be.'

'I couldn't agree more.'

'You are more or less my age, aren't you? Born in '79, I believe?'

''78. I'll be sixty this year.'

'Well, just about the same. Now, I served the flag, of course – 1st Field Artillery Regiment, the "Prince Regent Luitpold".'

'And I in the 8th Infantry Regiment, the "Franckh".'

'Aha. Yes. But I assume that you, like myself, ahum, we did not have the good fortune to be able to wear the King's uniform on the field of battle.'

'Unfortunately not. My stomach trouble, you know . . .
and in 1914 I was already over thirty.'

'We did not lose the war.'

'What do you mean, Herr Kammerlander . . . ?'

'We were robbed of victory. Look, once the Prussians start
ruling the roost in the General Staff . . . I've always said –
but we'll let that pass. What could our brave Rupprecht,
I mean His Royal Highness the Crown Prince, what could
he be expected to achieve? When the Prussians lost their
nerve? Wouldn't you agree? Russia was already prostrate in
defeat, victory over the western powers was within reach,
Herr Dirrigl, within our grasp . . . all we had to do was stretch
out a hand . . . one final effort . . . and then the Prussians lost
their nerve.'

'And then of course the scandalous goings-on in Kiel.
Et cetera.'

'Yes. And Austria. I ask you – they start the whole war
and then suddenly they've had enough. Of course, all these
foreign peoples, united under the Imperial and Royal crown
. . . bound to be a problem. But they knew perfectly well from
the start that you can't depend on these Slavs and Hungarians.
I mean, look, our milkwoman's daughter, Prielhofer's her
name – Sonja . . . well, up pops a fiancé . . . I said to Frau
Prielhofer, the mother that is, a very respectable woman,
"Frau Prielhofer," I said, "not with a bargepole," I said. A
Serbian. Yes indeed. Name's Naprovitch or something like
that. Just not right at all.'

'But Serbs are Aryans, aren't they?'

'In theory, yes, of course. But Slavs all the same. And that
counts as alien too. And, Herr Dirrigl, unreliable. One day,
then, he . . . just imagine, the old Prielhofer woman was so
trusting, she left him *alone* in the dairy. And it happened,
Herr Dirrigl, as happen it must – off, gone. Took the whole
lot and absconded.'

'Took all the milk?'

'No, of course not. Not the milk. Even a Serbian isn't
that stupid. The *money*. You know, the contents of the
till.'

'I see.'

'And the engagement ring he had given the milkwoman's daughter turned out to be pretty worthless. Tin and glass.'

'Absolutely disgraceful.'

'And that is the sort of thing that calls itself a victorious power. Well now, I ask you, Herr Dirrigl, wouldn't you say we ought to do something? What with victory having been *stolen* from us?'

'I couldn't agree more.'

'All the same, I must say, I put my faith in the Führer. You know, when the whole world, and especially the Jews, you know what I mean, when your Jews are cursing and fuming at the Führer, then that alone tells you the man must be all right. Fine, fair enough . . . there may be certain – come a little closer – there may be certain things going on in the Movement that aren't altogether to my liking. For instance, the fact that that . . . that *bouncer* fellow – you know who I mean, that bouncer from across the way – I don't want to point – well that that bouncer fellow is now . . . and so on . . .'

'You mean . . .'

'Ssh. Of course.'

'But he's an old front-line soldier.'

'Well let me assure you, the Führer knows nothing of his wheelings and dealings. He can't be expected to take care of everything, now can he? After all, he has *major* tasks ahead of him.'

'I have to admit, Herr Kammerlander, it was a great relief to me too, the way he, now how shall I put it, the way he brought that Röhm and the SA into line.'

'A gang of thugs.'

'Right. It's obvious that the Führer isn't going to shy away from sweeping out his own ranks, and with a pretty stiff broom, if the need arises.'

'That's exactly it, Herr Dirrigl, and let me tell you, we're on the right lines. But I must be going now, otherwise I'll be late for my NSKK regular round in the *Torbräu*. *Heil Hitler*, and my respects, Herr Dirrigl.'

'*Heil Hitler*, Herr Kammerlander.'

*

President Weber had a brown uniform: NSDAP. He also had a black uniform: SS. He had a red uniform, that is to say, he had a knee-length red coat, white breeches, black boots and a black cap: his riding dress. (It was all a pretty tight fit, and the President looked like a stuffed sausage.) And he had a green uniform as well: for hunting. President Weber was not only a hunter and owner of hunting grounds, he kept the whole German, nationally regenerated art of hunting under his protective wing. Reich Master of the Hunt was, admittedly and regrettably, Hermann Göring. Nothing could be done about that. Weber saw himself restricted to the Bavarian hunting grounds, which lay somewhat outside the Reich Marshal's purview. Nevertheless, in the long run, President Weber was to serve his country proud in this area.

A certain Count Arco-Zinneberg (this was probably the Royal Bavarian Chamberlain and Lieutenant, retd, Commander of the Chapter of the Royal Bavarian Order of St George and Squire of Schönburg by Pocking, Count Maximilian Konstantin Friedrich Alfons, born in 1850 and a rather distant uncle of the man who murdered Eisner) had nothing better to do with his time than assemble a collection of sets of antlers. These antlers (there were hundreds of them) adorned the Arco town house – town palace! – on the Wittelsbacherplatz. Everything in the house, including the chandeliers, was made out of antlers. In 1933 there was a threat of this collection being sold to a Dutchman. Weber the patriot intervened and prevented this national antler treasure going abroad. The NSDAP gave an advance of 110,000 Reichsmarks and Weber bought – deducting a certain commission, let it be said – the collection from the Arco family heirs and established the 'German Museum of Hunting'. Göring, it's true, tried to shoot down this scheme, but scored only a near miss. All the Reich Master of the Hunt managed to get out of it for himself was the Prince Leopold Palace in Schwabing, which Weber had originally earmarked as a suitable home for this, his second favourite baby (after the Brown Riband), and Weber had to content himself with the west wing of the Nymphenburg Palace. On 16 November 1934, Weber had also become President of the German Museum of Hunting (like the Brown Riband, legally constituted as a registered society), and on 16 October 1938 the museum was ceremonially opened. A procession in hunting and traditional costumes marched under the banner of ONE THOUSAND YEARS OF HUNTING – ONE THOUSAND YEARS OF STRENGTH from the Nymphenburg Palace to the Theresia Meadows. There a programme of racing and trotting was put on, and a firework display rounded off the day's festivities. It would not have been a Weber festival if scantily clad Dianas and bare-breasted Amazons had not been on hand to embellish the parade.

It goes without saying that they did not stop at the acquisition of the contents of the noble Count Arco's antler collection. The museum was further enriched by a painting by an artist, Prof. Hommel by name, depicting Reich Master of the Hunt Göring with a red deer. Seven feet by six feet. This format was only just big – or at least wide – enough. Albeit with ill grace, Weber was obliged to grit his teeth and hang the picture. He had fewer problems with Hitler's present, a 'Diana in the Forest' by one Prof. Richard Klein, not quite as large (six and a half by four). At least the Diana was naked.

However, despite his many official duties and despite his tireless commitment to National Regeneration, President Weber paid a good deal more than mere lip service to the noble art of hunting. Put another way, in the few leisure hours that the indefatigable President allowed himself, he was never happier than when he was out in the open countryside, where he drew strength from the German forests to enable him to cope with his mighty tasks, which, as we have seen, required of him superhuman – no, *sheer* superhuman – strength. In addition, he was ever ready to make himself useful, as can be seen in a letter from the Herr President to the *Oberbürgermeister* dated 25 September 1939 – barely a month after the outbreak of war:

Re
Annual leave, 1939.

In the last application for annual leave for 1939 submitted by me, the period from 1 to 15 October was included.

Since considerable stress has now been laid on the necessity for ensuring that the permitted quotas for shooting deer and other game be fulfilled one hundred per cent this year, and since part of the staff in the hunting sector has been called up, I shall be required to make particular efforts, during this year's rutting season, to shoot quite a large number of deer and to make them available for the supply of food to the population.

I therefore request that you grant for this purpose the leave I have applied for from 1 to 15 October.

Heil Hitler!
Weber

Must have made the population very happy.

November 9, 1936, saw the approach, for the thirteenth time, of the anniversary of what the Nazis called the 'March on the Feldherrnhalle'. One thing you have to give Christian Weber – he never missed a single excuse for a celebration. He organised a 'March of Remembrance'. In solemn, dignified manner, with muffled drum-rolls, the original march was recreated. Obviously not exactly repeated, not on the scale of 1:1. For instance, the child rescued by Hitler was missing, and nobody dislocated Hitler's shoulder . . . But seriously, it was a dignified, moving ceremony, with the old combatants of those days – sadly some of them, for example Chief of Staff Röhm, were no longer in the land of the living – in the simple jerkins of the old days, and with the blood-drenched flag of those days at their head . . . President Weber, meanwhile, was in attendance in the Schleibinger Strasse, where, to right and left of the entrance to the firm of foodstuffs suppliers Cenovis & Co. Ltd, pillars had been erected surmounted by blazing flames of remembrance, and naked BDM girls held garlands of honour high above their heads, while President Weber, deep in contemplation of the memories of those hard yet wonderful times of struggle, then confiscated three lorries and drove off with the BDM girls to the *Walterspiel* restaurant where a special room had been . . .

No. Weber in fact had the brass neck to march along with the others. What was going through the mind of Hitler, who added his own two feet to the parade? Did he have a poor memory? No, Hitler's memory was far from bad. Perhaps it would have been better for the course of world history if Hitler had had a bad memory, and to that extent his almost proverbially excellent memory (the good memory typical of dictators) is indeed a bad memory, but we shan't go into that here. We can proceed from the assumption – as legal eagles like to put it – that Hitler knew, or at least ought to have been aware, that the Old Soldier Christian Weber, back in 1923, had really been the Old Skiver Christian Weber. Nevertheless, neither Hitler nor the other 'bearers of the Order of Blood' raised any objection to his marching commemoratively with them. Far from it: Christian Weber was made the official 'Organiser of the Memorial Marches of 9 November' (that was his official, albeit in the light of the plural not strictly accurate, title). The reason for this is a simple one: it arises from the endeavours of the Nazis (which they have in common with all Fascistic systems and all dictatorships) to smooth out underlying realities for public consumption. (Hegel: 'if reality does not correspond to the idea, then tough luck on reality'. Hegel, the father of Marxism and National Socialism (in alphabetical order) and also of anti-Semitism.)

That the Old Soldier Christian Weber had marched on the Feldherrnhalle shoulder to shoulder with Hitler simply *had* to be true. (Anyway, this was a mere trifle, other matters were far and away more difficult to bend into the right shape; for example, what Hitler said about the expropriation of big businesses: 'If the Führer said anything in the past which is no longer correct today, then it follows that he never said it. Got that?' 'Yessir, Herr Area *Jungvolk* Leader, sir!')

Right then, so Christian Weber marched along with the rest in the memorial parade. Not in the front row, that's true – if he had, then those few who claimed to be there as of right might have been malicious enough to *remember* – but in the second. Besides, the parade did not follow the historic route, but headed for the Temples of Honour on the Königsplatz. Nor were Hitler's memorial shot fired into the ceiling of the

Bürgerbräu Bierkeller and the tankard of beer he was holding in his hand at the time recreated on this occasion.

So, there was Christian Weber, now Organiser of the Memorial Marches. A great organiser. In the course of the years from 1933 to 1945, the word 'organise' underwent a decisive change of meaning. It is altogether remarkable how National Socialism, for all its other instances of linguistic ultra-Germanness, maintained such a penchant for foreign expressions. (The very fact that Hitler allowed himself to be termed a 'Messiah', since that in fact comes from the Latin, although it does sound perilously close to the Yiddish.) On the one hand, a vehicle became a *Kraftfahrzeug* instead of an *Auto* and *Radio* became Germanised to *Rundfunk*, and then there were such beautiful neologisms as *Amtswahrer* for an office bearer; a stew, with everything being cooked in the one pot, became an *Eintopf*; petrol was no longer *Benzin* but *Treibstoff*; the national *Emblem* became a *Hoheitszeichen*; and a ski was translated into a *Schneeschuh*. On the other hand, what about *Propaganda, Armeekorps, Organisation, Grenadierbataillon, Feldgendarmerie, Protektorat* . . . ? The very name of the association (which, in legal terms, is what the Party in fact was) – three-fifths of it contained foreign borrowings: *National-Sozialistische* Deutsche Arbeiter *Partei*. Then there was the organisation itself, a prime example. There was even a *Reichsorganisationsleiter*: his name was Dr Robert Ley and he was an industrial chemist. His involvement in the public sphere arose from the fact that he had been fired by Bayer in Leverkusen in 1928 on account of his alcoholic excesses. In the NSDAP, he founded and headed (organised) the 'German Labour Front', a kind of incorporated, nationally regenerated, unified trades union, within which he never tired of preaching abstinence from alcohol. He himself remained one of the most significant consumers of champagne within the whole Nazi hierarchy. He invented the '*Kraft durch Freude*' or 'Strength through Joy' Organisation as well as the term 'soldier of the economy' for 'worker'. He also invented the Ka-De-Ef car, later to become the *Volkswagen*, so the 'people's car' went from KDF to VW. Of course, he did not invent the car, the construction, the technical things, that is. Ferdinand

Porsche looked after that. Ley invented the organisation. The soldiers of the economy were required to have a proportion of their wages voluntarily deducted, in return for which they would then – on the day of the first blue moon, but they were not to know that – receive a beautiful, brand-new, nationally regenerated KDF car, complete with spare wheel and five tyres. Ley pocketed the savings contributions. Not one single KDF car was ever delivered. Thus the Reich Organisation Leader organised a not inconsiderable personal fortune. Somehow or other, the whisper must have gone round, for the word 'organise' sank to somewhat lower levels of meaning. One did not *steal* potatoes from the fields at dead of night; one *organised* them. One organised the corrugated-iron roof off one's neighbour's garden shed. One organised butter from the farmer. And ultimately one Army unit organised petrol and ammunition from another Army unit. One great big, beautiful, general, national organisation. Weber organised horses.

*

'Very pleased to meet you,' said Weber. Fräulein Bogner held out her hand, slightly bent at the wrist. Fräulein Bogner was wearing a floor-length skirt made of blue linen, very coarse blue linen, almost coarse enough for a hair shirt, and a loose-fitting white blouse with very full sleeves.

'Would you sit here, please, Herr President,' said Herr Weidenmann. Herr Alfred Weidenmann had on a brown velvet jacket that hung very smoothly, in his lapel was a Party badge and on his head a broad floppy beret.

Weber grunted as he squeezed himself into an armchair. He put his fingers in his mouth and whistled. A batman in SS uniform leapt to his side.

'Two bottles!' hissed Weber. The SS batman leapt off again.

Fräulein Bogner had her black hair cut in a bob. 'Saucy', they would have called it in those days. Her bare feet were stuck in heavy wooden clogs.

'So this,' smarmed President Weber, 'is Franzi Bogner.'

'Herself, Herr President,' said Weidenmann. 'Her hair . . . now that, as you can imagine, will not stay as it is, of course.'

'Aha,' said Weber.

Franzi Bogner slipped out of her heavy clogs and nipped off towards the back of the room. Soon afterwards she reappeared, blonde. Blonde is in fact an understatement: she returned wearing a practically corn-golden wig with bulging plaits, like some illustration from L. F. Clauss's standard work *Race and Character, Part I* (1936). In the mean time, the SS batman had also appeared and was opening the first champagne bottle.

'A little refreshment,' Weber said. With his own particular brand of grace, and with his own fair hand, he passed the filled glasses to Fräulein Franzi Bogner – who was still in her bare feet – to Herr Weidenmann and to all the others who were standing around, taking the last glass for himself. Cowed and uncertain, the SS batman looked at him. Weber gave a wave of the hand, a gesture of gracious generosity, and then the batman poured himself a glass too.

'Well then, your good health!' said Weber.

They all drank.

The fire in the open grate flickered and then began to subside.

'Is nobody going to bank up this fire?' shouted Weidenmann.

A man in a grey dust coat rushed out through the doorway (which had been assembled out of roughly, not to say crudely, hewn beams), pausing only to stand his champagne glass on the equally rustic sideboard, on which already stood, next to an earthenware dish and a matching jug, a bouquet of cornflowers, poppies and ears of corn.

'So,' Weidenmann was saying, 'and now, quiet everybody, please! Franzi – all set?'

'Sure,' said Franzi, 'I don't have any lines here anyway.'

'Forty-five – take one!' shouted an assistant.

'But just a minute,' piped Franzi Bogner, 'how are we going to do the bit with the water? I mean, you surely don't expect me to actually stick my head in it.'

The man in the grey dust coat came in with an armful of logs and built up the fire.

'I think I'm going crazy,' Weidenmann yelled, 'no! no! no! no!'

'But surely you don't think –?'

'Is this all part of the scene?' asked Weber.

'Herr President,' said Weidenmann, 'now you have some notion of the difficulties facing a producer.' (Here, he favoured the title *Spielleiter*, another nationally regenerated neologism, rather than *Regisseur*.) 'We are going,' sighed Weidenmann, turning again to Franzi Bogner as if he was having to talk to a sick cow, 'to film the water in the tub in the wide shot from above, then Bodenhammer will tip out the water – chalk-mark there, please – right?, so that it goes back in exactly the right place, and then you stick your head into the empty tub. You can manage that, I hope? Hmmm?'

'I think I can deal with that,' said Fräulein Bogner acidly.

'Is she going to have a bath in this scene?' enquired Weber.

'No,' said Weidenmann, 'she's doing herself in. The screenplay is based on a short story by Kolbenheyer. I think. Anyway, it's called "The Girl from the Mountain Farm". But the film's to have another title. *The Girl from the Mountain Farm* has no shape, doesn't grab you. For the moment, the working title is *The Lasting Blessing*.'

'And Fräulein Bogner is the girl from the mountain farm?'

'Yes. She's called "Moid".'

'Uhuh.'

'Yes. Has a kind of hard, robust ring to it – *Moid*. And yet tender, soft. *Moid*.'

'And why's she doing herself in?'

'The farmer has got into serious difficulties through no fault of his own and has fallen into the clutches of the Jewish usurer. He's sucking his blood – metaphorically speaking, that is. Takes everything in hock, then he squeezes the farmer dry. The way the Jews did, in fact. Yes, well then, once the last cow has been driven out of the cowshed, the farmer suffers a heart attack while a thunderstorm rages and lightning strikes the barn. We've already filmed that, outside shots. Yes, and then, next morning, once the storm has cleared and the mountain sun is shining again, the farmer's wife –'

'Moid . . .'

'Yes, Moid, buries the dead farmer with her bare hands under a gnarled oak tree, for she doesn't have any money left for a coffin –'

'With her hands?'

'Well, yes – no, she's got a shovel, of course. Yes, and then comes the third scene, the one we're filming now: Moid goes back into the kitchen. The despair on her face has given way to an earnest, solemn determination. She takes the washtub, fills it with water, puts it on the floor – first, though, and I'd like you to note this, she wipes away a few splashes that have landed on the floor beside the tub, she couldn't bear it if anything was left untidy when she takes leave of the world – and then she pushes her face down into the tub and under the water . . . and dies.'

'Marvellous,' said President Weber, 'but, I mean, where's the "Lasting Blessing" in that?'

'The film is set in the days of the Old Order, obviously, when your Jew could still hatch out his dirty tricks and the Party was banned. But the local *Gruppenleiter* of the Party, who's working in the underground movement, gets wind of it, comes up to the farm, finds Moid dead, there's nothing he can do in the circumstances, comes out of the house, gazes out over the sublime mountain scenery and shouts: When is the time going to come when this kind of thing, et cetera, you understand, and at that moment an eagle soars up and circles over the valley. You see the symbolism?'

'Yes. Aha, yes.'

'And now,' Weidenmann turned to his team, 'let's have quiet. Forty-five – take one. Franzi – and don't forget, the despair in your expression gives way to an earnest, solemn determination – perhaps . . . just a minute . . . maybe you could look out of the window one last time . . . yes, that's very good . . . yes, and back to the tub . . . don't forget . . . wipe up the splashes.'

'With my apron, or should I take a cloth?'

'A cloth's better. Yes . . . that's good . . . very good . . .

we can shoot that straight off . . . yes . . . and now – let's cut to your face first – and now to the tub . . . closer . . . yes, very nice . . . great. And now, pan slowly down . . . but *don't* – don't take your head out of the tub, slowly down *over* the tub . . . otherwise it'll look comical . . . Yes . . . that's the way . . . very good. Yes. Like that. Exactly like that, all right? Then we can go for a take on the whole scene –'

'Herr Weidenmann!' whispered an assistant.

'Well? What is it?'

'It won't do like that, Dr Gerstl said.'

'What won't do? And who's Dr Gerstl?'

'The doctor. The doctor that was here earlier for Promeisl and his arm that got crushed.'

'What? What's that? I think I'm losing my mind. Here am I in the middle of shooting, and I'm supposed to bother myself with Promeisl and his squashed arm . . . I don't even know who this Promeisl is!'

'No, no. The doctor was listening to what you were saying. He says it won't work, on medical grounds. You *can't* drown yourself that way. Because –'

'What? Why not?'

'I'm only telling you what Dr Gerstl told me to tell you . . .'

'I think I'm going crazy, I'm going off my head . . . hold me down before I commit murder. Where is this doctor? Why didn't anyone tell me this earlier?'

'Excuse me, Dr Gerstl is my name, I didn't want to interfere, only – well, this suicide is, from a medical and physical point of view, impossible. As soon as she loses consciousness, she falls over backwards or sideways and so her head comes out of the water and she gets air again and comes round . . .'

'I see,' said Weidenmann dully.

'Yes,' said Dr Gerstl, 'I just felt it was my duty to bring it to your notice.'

'I see,' said Weidenmann dejectedly, 'it was *my* idea.'

'Sorry,' said Dr Gerstl.

'So what do *you* suggest, then?' Weidenmann asked menacingly.

'Please don't misunderstand me,' said Dr Gerstl, 'I don't want to interfere with your screenplay . . .'

'How kind of you.'

'The farmer's wife would have to get right into a bigger tub and weigh her head down, with something like a stone . . .'

'Maybe a millstone round her neck,' said the assistant.

'Shut up,' said Weidenmann.

'If I might make a suggestion,' said Weber, 'I reckon that's not altogether a bad idea. First, the farmer's wife carefully folds up her clothes and her underwear, which she has taken off, and puts them on a chair –'

'Not with me, you don't!' shrieked Franzi Bogner.

'I'm afraid that won't do, Herr President, the film has to be suitable for young people, for reasons of political education.'

'Oh well, in that case,' said Weber.

'Of course we could . . .' Weidenmann was thinking aloud as Dr Gerstl slipped away, 'if the *Ortsgruppenleiter* was to find not the farmer's wife's corpse, but . . .'

'And he marries her, after all she's a widow now,' said Weber, 'and the eagle can rise up just the same.'

'Where's the doctor?' asked Weidenmann.

'Gone,' said the assistant.

'D'you know what?' yelled Weidenmann. 'To hell and buggery with it! We're going to shoot it with her head in the tub. It's all right in a film. Right, that's it. And I bet you hardly anybody will notice. Places, everybody. Camera!'

'Camera's rolling!'

'Sound!'

'Action!' bawled Weidenmann, and Franzi Bogner, with the despair on her face giving way to earnest, solemn determination, stepped forward to the tub. Herr President Weber's offer to assist her afterwards while she changed in her dressing-room – with another bottle of champagne – was declined. His dinner invitation for the following evening was accepted.

*

So who was this Weber, that anyone should want to write a book about him? One of 74,827,000 Nazis? Seventy-four million, eight hundred and twenty-seven thousand: the population of the German Reich at 1 January 1938 (already including – the statistical year-book was being a little bit premature – Austria). No. They were not all Nazis. So how else are we to calculate the number of Nazis, real Nazis, in the Germany of 1938 – when Weber had just turned fifty-five? In the financial year of 1937/38 for the 'Winter Aid Scheme for the German People', the WHW, donations to the tune of RM 297,318,038 were received. All that was achieved with the collecting can. If we assume that everyone who had a collecting tin stuck under his nose gave ten marks (which is putting it on the high side), then that works out at some 29.7 million donors – 29.7 million Nazis? No, not all Nazis. Many people simply collected the WHW badges that came out in various shapes. At the end of 1933 – when enrolment was closed until 1938 – the NSDAP had 3,900,000 members. All of them *genuine* Nazis? The NSDAP was divided up into forty *Gaue* (and one 'Foreign Organisation'), or administrative regions, and these regions into a total of just under seven hundred *Kreise*, or districts. Each *Kreis* was headed by a *Kreisleiter*. Leaving aside the almost innumerable *Ortsgruppenleiter* in charge of local groups, that gives 740 *Gauleiter* and *Kreisleiter*, plus the *Reichsleiter, Stabsleiter* (there had to be a staff level, too), *Organisationsleiter, Reichspropagandaleiter*, the 'Führer's Representative for the Supervision of the Overall Intellectual and World-Philosophical Education of the NSDAP', the Head of the Reich Department of Agricultural Policy (incidentally, another foreign borrowing, in fact a double one – '*Agrar-Politik*'; why was this *Leiter* not given a title like *Reichsschollenleiter*' – Reich Leader of the Sod? Probably because there was no Reich Leader for the Germanification of Vocabulary), the *Leiter* of the Reich Legal Department and finally the NSDAP party group in the Reichstag – let's say, roughly another 740 Nazis, genuine Nazis. That makes 1,480 in all. And the Gloat himself. We can safely count him among the genuine Nazis, Schicklgruber-Greatestleaderofalltime. So, 1,481.

And Fascism? Fascism: a state system (or even any other

social system, a church, for example), which maintains that it represents the one and only correct and the one and only salvation-bringing doctrine; that is, it claims exclusive truth. That is common to all Fascist systems. Farther down the scale, they tend to fan out a bit: either they sing about class warfare or they dream of old empires or they want to populate the world with battery-bred pedigree blond creatures. And all of them become corrupt, from within in fact, for no human being can fulfil the lofty demands of a fascism. The German brand of Fascism was the most unappetising of all. It was perverted right from its inception. From the very outset, German Fascism stank of potato peelings and dried vegetables; from the very first day, German Fascism screamed for early rising and washing out mess-tins; from its very emergence, German Fascism dressed in loden-cloth and jerkin; in short, German Fascism was the incarnation, on the political front, of the ideals of the kitchen-cum-living-room. Talentless painters and sacked bouncers formed the (Teutonic) spearhead of National Regeneration. Woe betide, if untalented (and snubbed) artists and sacked (and avaricious) bouncers come to power! The almost amiable charm of the Night of the Amazons should not blind us to the fact that in this Weber we find the meeting point, the focus, of all those characteristics of inhuman petty-bourgeois attitudes and brazen brutality that are the distinguishing features of German Fascism. And what about this Weber? Was he in fact a Nazi at all? Or just a grease stain that the ill-will (for him, goodwill) of the universal spirit expectorated into History, Dept Bavaria? Is writing a book about him doing him more honour than he merits? Yes. Undoubtedly. But as long as there are those around – and there are enough of them – who are only too ready to find something to say in favour of the running sore of National Socialism that carries the scientific appellation 'Third Reich', it is better that we talk about it and that we write about it.

*

'We are living, Herr Kammerlander, in great times.'
   'Well now, to be honest, Herr Dirrigl, they could, for my money, be a little, just a wee bit less great.'

'But, my dear fellow, surely you haven't joined the ranks of the grousers and malcontents?'

'Not at all. Only, you see, I can't understand how . . . I really don't know how to go about this . . . so that you don't get me wrong . . . take eggs for example. I have no idea exactly how many eggs we are allocated each week on our food coupons. My wife knows more about it than I do, of course, but all *I* know is, it's too few. In the old days, I mean, before the war, I used to go into the grocer's and say, A dozen eggs, please, and the grocer's wife would sell me a dozen eggs, and if I had said, Two dozen eggs, she would have sold me two dozen eggs, and if I had said, A hundred eggs –'

'A hundred eggs, Herr Kammerlander, come now! What normal family gets through a hundred eggs in a *week*!'

'It was meant only as an illustration, Herr Dirrigl, all I'm trying to say is, were there actually *more* hens before the war? It's not as if the hens have been called up to the forces, have they? Or is it just that the hens are laying fewer eggs? Because there's a war on? Do the hens *know* that?'

'Hm.'

'Exactly!'

'Hm. Probably everything's needed to supply the *Wehrmacht*.'

'You mean the Army's firing eggs?'

'If I were you, I'd be more careful with such would-be biting sarcasm.'

'Surely we can still have a joke. But seriously, though: the people that are now eating eggs as members of the *Wehrmacht*, surely they also ate eggs as civilians, previously. It's six of one and half a dozen of the other.'

'You're quite right, really – I don't *quite* understand it myself. Maybe it's that imports from abroad are no longer available.'

'Talking about imports. As far as I know the German Reich is not at war with Cuba, and yet my Doña Clara Havanas are no longer to be had anywhere. Why, I'd like to know.'

'Enemy submarines.'

'Torpedoing my cigars? Well, I must say, Herr Dirrigl, this is not what I imagined the National Regeneration would be like. The mind boggles. Do you really believe enemy submarines go around torpedoing ships loaded with cigar imports? Anybody knows salt water is very bad for cigars. Well, that really is the last straw. I ask you, why doesn't our Navy do something about it? Take a look at this – look at the kind of weed I'm smoking now – *Deutsche Ehre*. "German Honour", thank you *very* much! Just take a sniff, if you would, Herr Dirrigl. And that's what they palm off on me! Someone who always smoked only Havana Doña Claras! And even these German Honour things you can only get on smokers' coupons.'

'After the final victory you'll get your Doña Claras again.'

'Final victory?'

'Yes. Final victory? Why do you ask?'

'I only hope you're right, Herr Dirrigl.'

'Oh, now look. Look at how things stand! Poland defeated. Denmark and Norway in our hands. France is down and out. Any day now and the invasion of Britain will start . . .'

'Fine. But . . . it seems to me as if there are some folk who can walk across the food market . . . across the same market where you used to be able to buy anything and everything, and they pick up a lettuce here and a whole cheese there, and a hundred rolls here and four bunches of flowers there . . . they just lift this and pick up that until their arms are full, and then they take something else and . . .'

'. . . and then they drop the lot. Yes, true enough. But the Führer, I always say, knows exactly what he's doing.'

'Are you sure?'

'Absolutely. You'll see. Once England has been beaten, we'll get our colonies back, and a few more besides . . . maybe even Cuba. Then your Doña Claras will be called "Frau Klärchens". Has a much better ring to it, don't you think?'

'And – how long, do you reckon?'

'Herr Bürkel, the headmaster, who keeps such a sharp

eye on how the war is progressing – you know who I mean, Headmaster Bürkel who lives in my block, and who has papered his whole flat with maps and sticks in little flags after every *Wehrmacht* bulletin on the wireless and recently bought himself a trumpet so that he can join in the fanfare that introduces every special announcement . . . Headmaster Bürkel says another six weeks, three months at the outside.'

'Up to Christmas, then?'

'More or less.'

'Can he play the trumpet?'

'No. He's learning.'

'In six weeks?'

'He hopes to be far enough on in a fortnight. For the moment, though, I have to admit, it sounds awful.'

'Well, Herr Dirrigl, I must be off. Just look at that, though, German Honour, it's gone out again. Completely useless. Pure sawdust.'

'Stick it out, Herr Kammerlander, stick it out. Another six weeks, and then you'll have your Havanas again. And your Bautzerl, too, isn't that so, boy –'

'Bow-wow!'

'You'll get good din-dins again.'

'Let's hope so.'

*

He is supposed, according to legend, to have said on the outbreak of war, 'Would you believe it! Now, *now*, just when we've got everything ticking over so nicely, that half-wit starts a war.' That's what Weber is reputed to have said. In all the German Reich, only one single GOS could have had the temerity to call Hitler a half-wit. Another version has a rather milder, more resigned ring to it. According to this one, Weber is supposed to have said, 'We've got everything we need, so why did the Führer start the war?' Once, during the war, when the champagne was doing the talking, Weber is reported as having come out with the following toast: 'Right, mates, drink up, we're goin' to lose the war, an' I'm already gettin' the horrors at the thought of what we'll get to drink after it.' Naturally, such utterances are not backed up by documentary proof. That's the cross we have to bear with history: the interesting things are usually not supported by documentary evidence, because there was always someone or other interested in sweeping the details under the carpet. Documented history is, for the most part, insipid stuff. Not only is it insipid, it's wrong. When politicians talk, they lie, and when they write, they lie even more. Bismarck's *Reflections and Recollections* – now there's a pack of lies. If you take that off the shelf, don't be surprised if the pages curl. Out of sheer embarrassment. If anyone tells the story of the history of mankind based on the documents that have been handed down, you can be sure that *that* can't possibly be the way it happened. So what is (historical) truth?

The utterances as quoted would nevertheless have fitted in with Christian Weber's character, although the third one, again according to shining legend, did not come from Weber but from Wagner, Adolf Wagner that is, a proud name (in those days). Adolf Wagner was from Lorraine, an officer in the First World War and one of the original louts around Hitler (a GOS). From 1929 *Gauleiter* for Upper Bavaria, post-1933 Commissioner of State, then Minister of the Interior and Deputy Prime Minister, and later Minister for Education and the Arts. This completely bald bull-terrier with the pinched mouth was the architect of Dachau concentration camp and, along with his close buddy (in the early days at least) Weber, he saw to it that it was kept full; in addition, Adolf Wagner invented, on 9 November 1938, 'Spontaneous Popular Outrage', which set the synagogues alight and ransacked the windows of Jewish shops. (Which is, of course, not backed up by documentary proof either: legend has it that Christian Weber, naturally well aware that the meticulously prepared Spontaneous Popular Outrage would erupt spontaneously on 9 November 1938, was already off the starting blocks and executing a precise plan of action aimed at steering, partly with his own fair hand and partly with the aid of a gang of NS-ruffians on his payroll, Jewish cash, jewellery, antiques and – it goes without saying – racehorses in the direction of National Regeneration. Where does it say that legends always have to be wide of the truth?) Further, it is said that the cocky toast had also been Wagner's, but proposed in Weber's presence – now *that* Wagner should not have done, for in the spring of 1938 a certain matter – again, of course, not fully documented – occurred. Apparently, Christian Weber tried to meddle in some banking transactions by the *Bayerische Vereinsbank*, and as a result seems to have poached on Adolf Wagner's preserves. In any case, there is a letter extant from Bavarian Minister of the Interior and *Gauleiter* Wagner to the respected Party Comrade *Oberbürgermeister* Fiehler in which Wagner does not mince words in suggesting that District Council President Alderman Party Comrade Christian Weber should kindly keep his nose out of the affairs of the management of the Bavarian *Vereinsbank*, since that institution was not a municipal, but a state bank. '*Heil Hitler, Wagner.*' Apparently Weber thereupon received a dressing-down, as can be read between the lines of a letter of apology written by Fiehler to Wagner on 15 July 1938. At the foot of the copy of this letter preserved in the City Archives, there is simply '*K.g.* [contents noted], *Weber.*'

'Go on! Sign it! Get on with it!'

'But . . .'

'Sign it, I'm telling you! What's got into you? The *Vereins-bank*?! Don't you know that only Wagner . . . et cetera? Well, go on! What are you waiting for?'

A character like Weber is not strong, he is always just stronger. If someone takes him on head-on, then a Weber will draw in his horns and climb down. The flab on Weber's hand wobbled as he reached out for the pen: '*K.g., Weber.*'

'And don't let me hear of anything like that happening again!'

Let's spin out the legend a little farther. So then stupid old Adolf Wagner commits the gaffe of coming out with that toast in Weber's presence. Weber has a telephone, Wolf has a telephone. It goes without saying that not any old

Party comrade Tom, Dick or Harry can simply ring up the Aquiline One, but there are indeed those and such as those who know the number where Eva Braun in person will lift the receiver.

In 1942 Adolf Wagner was relieved of virtually all his posts of responsibility, and in 1944 he died. The pomp that marked his funeral would indicate that Adolf Wagner was wiped off the slate by his own comrades: Hitler came to Munich in person – this was to be one of the last occasions – and decorated the DOS (Deceased Old Soldier) with the 'Gold Cross with Oak Leaves of the German Order', and then, by way of the Temples of Honour on the Königsplatz, next to which he was buried, the warrior Wagner, Adolf, entered Valhalla.

Weber had taken his revenge. Admittedly, he never sank his talons into the *Vereinsbank* again, but President Weber more than made up for that by helping himself in generous measure from the Municipal Savings Bank. As early as 1936, he had succeeded in getting his clutches on the *Wagner-Bräu* brewery and the Hotel Wagner, both of which were up to their necks in debt to the Savings Bank, and in 1942 the same thing happened to the Hotel Sonnenhof. These occurrences, too, are only sparsely documented. One thing is sure: up to that point, the Hotel Sonnenhof had belonged to the Savings Bank. Weber seems to have contrived a scheme whereby this hotel was to have been sold first to the German Theatre Co. Ltd and then on to a front-man and finally back to the Savings Bank. In all of these deals, a percentage of the purchase price was meant to find its way into Weber's bank accounts. But the fiddle had got no farther than the sale to the German Theatre Co. Ltd when Weber crossed swords with his old pal Wolfrum. Wolfrum, alderman and *Obersturmbannführer* in the SS, was on the management committee of the German Theatre Co. Ltd, and apparently, at a meeting of the City Council's Finance Committee on 31 July 1942, he asked some embarrassing questions (not minuted). We have to assume that Wolfrum, himself a prominent figure in National Socialist corruption circles, had other plans in mind for the

Hotel Sonnenhof. The closing stages of the meeting were minuted:

> Alderman C. Weber: Right, that's enough, get to hell out of here . . . (Alderman Weber threatens Alderman Wolfrum with physical violence.) Get yourself off to the front line! (Alderman Wolfrum leaves the chamber.)

This very Weber-like document, the only one in which his animal brutality is preserved in writing, is in the safe keeping of the City Archives. It is surprising that anything of this nature was minuted in those days. Did the recording clerk sit there on the sidelines, grinning to himself, and take everything dutifully down in shorthand?

'What's he writing there?'

'I'm taking the proceedings down in shorthand, Herr President.'

'Oh yeah.' Weber, still short of breath from 'threatening Alderman Wolfrum with physical violence', gives a snort: 'All right then, let's have a look. Oh, I see. Shorthand. Read it out!'

The recorder reads it out.

'So who told him he was to shorthand that?'

'The rules are that I have to take *everything* down.'

'Everything! Everything! Everything doesn't mean all. Or rather, all isn't everything. Got that? It's obvious. You can't just – what a thickhead! These are internal matters! They've nothing to do with the minutes, right? Right!'

'Very good, Herr President.'

But he went ahead – thankfully – and wrote up a fair copy in longhand, and Weber forgot to have it shown to him. So documented Historia does now and again lift a hem of her full, flowing gown to give us a glimpse of her true figure. In this case, of her rump.

Alderman Wolfrum had obviously overestimated his own power and his position *vis-à-vis* Weber. On this occasion, Weber was higher up in the pecking order. Wolfrum, who had been at the front during the Polish campaign (not too far forward, certainly not, he was an officer after all) and had been posted back unfit for combat duties because of an eye complaint, did in fact have to report for duty again on 9 October 1942 – at Weber's instigation – and was thus removed from the path of the latter's gravy train. On 18 November, Weber applied for leave 'for the purpose of fulfilling targets in respect of nutritional supply programmes' and went hunting. During that same time and farther to the east, the Soviet major offensive on the Don was opened, leading to the encirclement of Stalingrad. Two hundred and fifty thousand men, eighteen hundred pieces of artillery and ten thousand vehicles were being thrown into the melting pot (which is a bit of a joke in view of the Russian winter), in order that, among other things, Herr President Christian Weber might be assured of just under three more years of comfortable living, or, in the jargon then current, to enable him to carry out in peace and quiet his responsibilities towards the 'fulfilment of targets in respect of nutritional supply programmes' in the snow-covered paradise of the mountain forest around Berchtesgaden.

And so it was that the nutritional-supply-conscious huntsman Weber went striding around in the forest. It is not only by dint of one's income that one becomes rich, but also by dint of what one does not spend – perhaps that more than anything else. In Mittenwald, too, Weber had leased hunting preserves, as long ago as 1937. As a result, the community of Mittenwald incurred a bill for damage caused by game to the tune of RM 427.20, for which, by law, the leaseholder was liable. But one thing Christian Weber had never been able to accept was that the law also applied to him (except where that was to his advantage). He did not pay up. The parish of Mittenwald went through the prescribed channels and approached *Oberbürgermeister* Fiehler with the request to prevail upon Alderman Weber to pay his debts. Weber explained frankly and openly to Fiehler that he was not going to pay and they could put out a seizure warrant if they wanted. (Any bailiff that had dared to carry out such an order would have found himself in Dachau the next day.) The letter from the Mittenwald community authorities is dated 27 December 1937. To this day, it is still waiting for its RM 427.20.

But as the business with the *Vereinsbank* (viz. Adolf

Wagner) demonstrates, Weber was not always quite accurate in his assessment of the pecking order. In 1939, Historia raises her skirts once again, albeit somewhat furtively. The balance of Weber's criminal record tipped, if we can put it that way, in 1933. Up till then, all his convictions and bookings – apparently some 150 of them – had been honourable scars sustained in the struggle for National Regeneration. With the coming of 30 January 1933, Weber became, as a matter of course and overnight, a man of honour and irreproachable integrity. From that day on, the criminal record of Councillor and President Weber bears only one official stamp per year, NOTHING TO RECORD or NO CHANGE. On closer inspection, nevertheless, it can be established that the page for 1939 has been pasted in and that the stamp with which NOTHING TO RECORD has been recorded was one that had in fact been withdrawn from use some years before. Someone has therefore been fiddling the books, and only Weber could have stood to gain from that. The only reason the page would have been substituted would be if there had been something on the original one. What was it then? Did Weber commit some act of such hair-raising vileness in 1938 that, even for him, the Public Prosecutor and the courts could not but . . . ? 'Dear Herr *Oberbürgermeister (Strictly Confidential!)* It is with regret that, in the light of the extremely serious nature of this case, the State Prosecutor's office finds itself with no option but to institute proceedings. You may rest assured that, in paying all due regard and respect to his standing as an Old Campaigner, everything will be done to spare Herr President and Councillor Weber as much embarrassment as possible. However, it will be inevitable that . . .'

What can it have been? Fraud in the grand manner? Probably not, for he carried out all his swindles under the guise of official duties, so he was well covered there. Did the dashing motorist knock down and kill someone? Or did the lousy shot bring down a beater or some little old dear out gathering berries? No, someone like Weber would have had no trouble at all in wiping that sort of bagatelle from the nutritional-supply policy slate. Had he perhaps fallen in love with a Jewess? Was there in his flabby body and in his flabby heart some fibre or some chamber that was capable of love, genuine love, at least for a few days? And did he, let's say for argument's sake, during the carnival festivities of *Fasching* in 1938, at the ball in the *Deutsches Theater*, meet a young soubrette (let's call her Sylvia Nordborg), whose charm and beauty penetrated all his layers of fat like a bolt of lightning? Was the name Sylvia Nordborg only a stage name, and was the young thing in reality called Lea Fischl? Such a constellation of events would not have been altogether impossible even in the spring of 1938. And then – God forbid – did the President commit the racial desecration of having sexual relations with a non-Aryan? No. That, too, is highly improbable, for in such a case the still-applicable principle would have been applied: '*I* decide who is and who isn't a Jew.'

Such trifles as getting a fourteen-year-old apprentice-girl pregnant, accessory to abortion, embezzlement, usury or arson, being drunk and incapable, persecution of the innocent or tax evasion were the sort of thing a Christian Weber could settle as easily as falling off a wall. It must have been something else altogether, something that touched a raw nerve in the Movement; either he throttled Eva Braun's favourite fox-terrier or blew up one of Göring's black-market lorries or – most likely – he went in for currency fraud on such a grand scale that the affair could no longer be kept quiet from his own fellow gangsters. Smuggling foreign currency was indeed regarded as a crime punishable by death. In the five years between 1933 and 1938, Weber had amassed a private fortune amounting to millions. It was as clear to Weber as to anyone that Hitler wanted a war, he was hell-bent on it. One thing you have to give Weber: he had an almost animal nose for what was about to befall. Even if the utterances attributed to Weber earlier were no more than imputations, it can be safely assumed that Weber knew or at least suspected that the approaching war could not be won by Hitler. Since, on the other hand, someone like Weber cannot conceive of the laws of nature being any more applicable to himself than the laws of society and the state, neither could he envisage the collapse of the system bringing about his own destruction.

'I can see other people's blood unmoved, my own makes me flinch,' Ochs von Lerchenau sings in the opera set by the Aryan Strauss to the words of the Jew Hofmannsthal. Weber could conceive of anyone's demise, but not his own. So he had to make provisions, and how did one provide for eventualities in those days? By illegal transfer of cash to Switzerland. It would seem that Weber had the bad luck to be caught in the act. There can be no doubt that he was convicted in 1939, for only a conviction would be entered in his records. No doubt he then put the comradely loyalty of his friend Wolf sorely to the test. Very probably he had to lick his (jack)boots – no problem, really, for someone so given to satisfying his own vanity as to be wholly devoid of self-respect. A pardon, a deletion from the criminal records, by secret order of the Führer – more than a deletion, a falsification of the records 'on official instructions'. 'And I swear to you, Wolf, on my honour as a German, that I most deeply regret my transgression. It will never happen again, so long as I live.' 'All right, Christian. You always were an impulsive fellow.' Christian sobbing. 'Wolf, d'you remember, back in the old days, when we . . .' Wolf sighing, 'Yes, yes.' Christian, overwhelmed by gratitude, spontaneously seizing the Führer's hand and kissing it. Deeply moved, the Führer, whose heart is all too seldom touched by feelings of human warmth in the midst of all the political turmoil that confines him to the icy peaks of world history, can feel the burning tears of the old campaigner coursing down his hand, and he too, the Führer, the otherwise so hard, iron-hard hero of the National Regeneration, he too averts his steely-blue eye heavenwards, as a deep sigh is wrung from his lips.

Weber's subsequent deals were transacted only after meticulous and intensive planning.

*

It was about ten o'clock when the sirens howled. The first bombs fell almost at the same time; the early-warning system had completely failed yet again.

There was snow on the ground. The sparse anti-aircraft

defences fingered the night sky with their few searchlights. In their beams, the ominous shapes of the RAF bombers were silhouetted like crosses. The anti-aircraft guns fired. It was pathetic. Bombs fell on the city that night, 903 tons of them. Not one single bomber was touched by the flak. The night fighters did not even leave the ground – petrol shortage. One car was not short of petrol; blacked out according to regulations, with hoods over its headlamps allowing only slits of light to emerge, it drove along the Prinzregentenstrasse towards town. Mark you, 'petrol' we said, none of your methyl alcohol rubbish, distilled from wood.

'I can't understand,' said Weber to Fräulein Gerda, 'what they're still dropping bombs for. It's pure wastefulness. I mean, everything's blasted to bits already.'

Weber had met Fraülein Gerda only the previous evening. In fact, she was a ballet dancer at the Theatre on the Gärtnerplatz, but all the theatres had been closed since Goebbels proclaimed his 'total war' (not a soul could have told you what that was supposed to be), and Fraülein Gerda had been conscripted for labour – naturally, essential to the war effort – in the N. gear-wheel factory in the Holzstrasse, which did not suit the ballet dancer in the least. She had got a few days off, because the film director Luis Trenker had offered her a minor part in a new film, and that was regarded as even more essential to the war effort. Fräulein Gerda had to hop a few times round a linden tree in blossom, all in all half a minute of film, but never mind, and it meant she didn't have to go to the gear-wheel factory for four days. Yesterday, shooting was completed, and Director Trenker threw a little farewell or closing party, to which that patron of the arts who was obliged to Director Trenker in so many ways, Herr President Weber, was also invited. And so it was that Weber had got to know Fräulein Gerda.

It was not exactly as if the gross Weber, looking in his dinner jacket as if he had been pumped into a sausage-skin, was the type of man Gerda yearned for in her dreams, but Weber had been so soulful with his 'Fräulein Gerda – such little hands, such dainty feet . . . a factory is no place for these. That's a sin. Just you let old Weber take care of things, Fräulein Gerda . . . or may I just call you Gerda?'

So it was that Fräulein Gerda was permitted to spend the night of the 16/17 December in the Town Hall (ever since Weber's apartments in the Residency, as well as his flat on the Sebastiansplatz, had been reduced to rubble by the bombs, he had been resident in the Town Hall), and as from today, 17 December, the category of Fräulein Gerda's war-work duties had been redesignated: she was no longer an auxiliary worker in the gear-wheel factory but a secretary in the transport firm – essential to the war effort, too, it goes without saying – of Christian Weber's Long-Distance Tours. Over a year previously, in November 1943 in fact, Weber had evacuated his fleet of vehicles to Heigenkam, near Otterfing, out Holzkirchen way, where there was no fear of bombs falling.

'Just to let you have a look at your place of work,' said Weber on the morning of 17 December, 'we'll take a drive out there. Climb in.'

In Heigenkam, on a plot of land in the woods that had been *organised*, Weber had built several large corrugated-iron garages, all well camouflaged. It had not been easy, even for him, to get hold of the corrugated iron. Parked there were a number of omnibuses and lorries and two private cars, and there were also stocks of tyres, spare parts, jerry cans and all sorts of other items. A shack served to house a heavily armed farmer's lad whom Weber had had released from military service and who mounted guard on his treasures here.

'Otherwise the lot would be organised away before you could so much as look round,' said Weber. 'But Arnulf here, he's a good lad, isn't that right, Arnulf?'

'Yes sir, Herr President.'

'And remember, shoot on sight if anybody suspicious comes snooping around. Shoot him down on the spot, it'll be no loss. None of them's any loss.'

'Yes sir, Herr President.'

'And! Just *one* screw missing because you weren't on the look-out, and you're back at the front line the very next day.'

'There's nothing missing, Herr President.'

Weber gave Arnulf a cigar, then walked once round the site with Fräulein Gerda.

'So what about the coach tours? Where do they go? I mean, if they're essential to the war effort?'

Weber grinned. 'Nowhere's where they go. For the time being. Not until after the . . . um . . . Final Victory.'

They drove on to Lake Tegern. Weber and Gerda pulled in at a large hotel, which now housed an Army hospital. In a back room, a table had been set for two. The hotelier himself did the serving. He was on first-name terms with Weber. There was soup with liver dumplings, followed by a smoked trout, roast pork with potato salad, cheese, pear Hélène, ground coffee and a Kirsch liqueur. Between the soup and the smoked trout, Weber also put away four white sausages with strawberry jam. With the fish a light Moselle, and with the roast a hefty Burgundy, and after that a bottle of champagne.

'And that's real coffee, from beans?' asked Gerda.

'Course,' said Weber, 'drink up, lass.'

'I thought you couldn't get that any more.'

'You just didn't know the right people.'

Instead of paying, Weber had a quiet word with the land-lord. Then the President withdrew with Fräulein Gerda, she more than just a little tiddly, to one of the bedrooms, and around nine they set off back towards Munich. Weber was able to keep up a fair speed despite the covering of snow, for there was not another car out on the roads for miles around. They were on the outer reaches of the Prinzregentenstrasse when the sirens took them by surprise.

Gerda was frightened. There was a constant rumble of bombs exploding. Weber pulled in at the right-hand kerb and turned off the engine and the lights.

'It's over there, across the Isar, isn't it?' whispered Weber.

'Don't ask me,' breathed Gerda.

The sky was hung with the famous 'Christmas Tree' flares, columns of flame spurted up, well in towards the city centre though. But the earth was quaking. Muffled figures ran past, weighed down with bundles and suitcases; just up ahead was a surface air-raid shelter. A child was crying, its mother dragging it along behind her. Again and again a glaring yellow and red mushroom – 'That's the station,' said Weber – shot into the air. Garlands of incendiary bombs rained down. A red glow was spreading along and up from the whole horizon, and there was a cracking like breaking ice.

'You'll be all right with me, lass,' said Weber.

'What makes you so sure of that?'

'Nothing's going to happen *here*,' Weber replied.

'Here? What d'you mean, here?'

'Up there, on the Prinzregentenplatz, that's where Wolf has his flat.'

'And who's Wolf?'

'Wolf is Wolf. The Führer. Who else?'

'Well, what d'you mean, "Wolf"?'

'Close mates that are on first-name terms with him call him Wolf.'

'You're on first-name terms with the Führer?'

'Course I am.'

A crash that drowned out all the other explosions shook the street. At the same time, a wave of fiery-hot air bent the leafless trees on the Prinzregentenstrasse almost double; simultaneously, every window in the house splintered and a whirlwind of sparks swept down the street. Then broken slates and lumps of wood and all manner of rubble rained down. And a moment later, the same again.

'Now it's *here*,' screamed Gerda.

'Stay in the car,' yelled Weber. 'Bloody hell! They wouldn't dare!'

A third detonation; dust enveloped everything.

'They wouldn't – not when the Führer's flat is just over there –'

'Why shouldn't they?'

'We didn't bomb Churchill's house, did we?'

The explosions were now coming in quick succession. Even Weber's colour drained.

'I have to puke,' said Gerda.

'Right then, let's go,' said Weber, 'up there, into the shelter.'

There were a few moments' respite, like between heavy rain showers. Weber and Gerda ran to the shelter. Weber hammered on the door. A fat old woman opened the tiny window, more like a spy-hole, next to it.

'Well?' enquired the old woman.

'Open up – can't you see, we've got to get into the shelter.'

'The shelter's full,' said the old woman.

'Don't fart about, granny,' bawled Weber, 'or else you'll –'

'Block warden's orders. When it's full, it's full, 'cause of the oxygen.'

Weber gasped for air.

'Please, let us in, please,' begged Gerda.

'Him!' yelled Weber, 'him! I don't give a bugger about your shitty block warden!'

'No need to be vulgar,' said the old woman.

'Where is – where's – where –?'

Yet another explosion. Gerda began to whimper.

'Don't I know you,' the old woman said to Weber, 'aren't you –?'

'No!' screamed Weber.

'Aren't you that bloke what used to be the bouncer at the Blue Buck?'

A crash, the likes of which the world had never heard, swelled and threw both Weber and Gerda to the ground. For an instant everything was as bright as the mouth of a furnace. Then lumps of a shattered wall went hurtling past horizontally. That one must have landed close by. The old woman opened the door, Weber barged in, Gerda after him.

'Well now,' said the old woman, slamming the door again, 'I thought at first you were President Weber.'

'You said something different a minute ago,' said Weber, beating the dust off his suit. 'Blue Buck, you said something about.'

'Not that I remember,' said the old biddy. 'If you had been that Weber, I wouldn't have let you in. But you're not Weber. If you were, you'd've at least been wearing your Party badge.'

The place was packed with people. Nobody gave Weber or Gerda so much as a second glance. There were bundles and bags piled all over the place. A candle was burning. A group in one corner was praying loudly. 'Jesus, who died for us on the cross . . .' one of them chanted. 'Pray for us,' came the full chorus. The old woman sat down on the steps and joined in the praying.

'Where are we supposed to sit, the young lady and me?' Weber asked, his old sharpness now restored. But the old woman remained unperturbed and merely gave a slight nod towards the steps. Weber sat down with a curse and took the still trembling Gerda on his lap.

After a time, when the group of prayers paused for a break, Weber turned to the old woman.

'Tell me, what I'd like to know is *why* you wouldn't have let President Weber in?'

'Well, 's obvious. 'Cause the shelter was full. And it's strictly forbidden to let any more in. On account of the oxygen, the block warden says. And I wouldn't be wanting to break such a strict rule in front of President Weber, now would I?'

Weber turned away. 'Far as I'm concerned,' he hissed to Gerda, 'they can drop all the bombs they like, till the whole bloody shower are blown to hell.'

Soon after, the all-clear sounded. One whole side of the street lay in ruins. Weber's car still stood there, as if it had been deliberately spared. Covered in dust but untouched. And the building in which Wolf's flat was situated remained unscathed.

*

Reality is impossible to describe in words. Pictures do it better. Should we perhaps add pictures to this book? Naturally, there are pictures of Christian Weber, unspeakable pictures, photographs, the state archives look after them. It is not known whether Christian Weber was ever painted, done in oils, by Professor Hermann Kaspar or by Professor Paul Matthias Padua or by some other professor, or perhaps even by some simple – but of course Aryan and non-degenerate (undegenerate or deungenerate?) – painter, not, or not yet, a professor but just a Member of the Academy, or for that matter a painter without a 'Member of the Academy' to his name. From what we can judge of President Christian Weber, he would not reckon it worth his while having himself painted. Weber never spent good money on anything like that. But it might well have happened that some young Member of the Academy did approach Weber, '. . . therefore I would consider it a great honour to be allowed to paint you, Herr President, and I hasten to add, sir, that this would, of course, not involve any expense on your part . . .'

And perhaps Weber did feel flattered – after all, all the top Nazis had themselves painted, Göring especially loved it. Hitler as well: the finest picture of Hitler is the one where he is represented as a sardine. The master intended to portray the thing the Führer is welded into as a suit of armour, but it has come out looking like a sardine tin. Staring resolutely out of the hole in the top of the monstrous armour, palely shining and bristling with spikes, is Schicklgruber himself, complete with his little brush of a moustache. The very fact that this picture (it was titled 'The Führer keeps watch over his People!' or something of the sort) was hung in the House of German Art and the painter was honoured instead of quartered proves that Hitler had no eye for art whatsoever.

So how should Weber be portrayed? One possibility: on horseback. By the way, he could not ride a horse. After all, he had never been a horseman as such, only a groom, and quite apart from that he had always been much too fat for riding. There are all manner of photographs of him, but not one single one showing him riding or even just sitting on a horse. For someone of his vanity, the only possible explanation for that is that he simply could not ride. Leading a horse by the bridle, now, he was photographed in that pose from time to time. Leading a horse by the bridle is something that grooms are supposed to be able to do. So, on horseback in oils? That would actually have been the ideal opportunity . . . as the model, you don't even have to get on a horse, just sit astride a chair. Weber the horseman – as an Amazon? No, of course not, but perhaps surrounded by Amazons, naked ones naturally, with one of them offering up to him her bosom, no, sorry, a cornucopia. Or dressed in a panther-skin? No. What about riding dress: red coat, black cap, white breeches, brightly polished boots? Or, another definite possibility, as a huntsman, his foot on his bag, a wild boar. Or maybe in tails, with medals, top hat propped against his hip, in his office (the 'Randy Dandy in the Residency' was a secret honorary title bestowed on Weber by Munich's gossip-mongers, even though, while *der Stenz von der Residenz* may well rhyme nicely, this represents a misapplication of the term *Stenz*; a *Stenz* in Munich suburbanite parlance is a good-for-nothing wastrel all right, but one with irresistible charm. Weber was no *Stenz*, but a fat bigwig, a *Bonze*. But *der Bonz in der Residonz* loses something in the transformation). Or, again, in the black uniform of the SS, with the death's head on the cap? Or in the brown uniform of the Party?

If ever such a picture did actually exist (to find out, one could leaf through the old catalogues of the exhibitions in the *Haus der Deutschen Kunst*), not a soul now knows where it has got to. The Finance Ministry has in its safe keeping – serves it right! – hundreds or perhaps even thousands of paintings which the Americans confiscated but, ten years later, handed back, or rather, wanted rid of. The tax officials don't dare throw the junk out, because it still is state property after all, and, who knows, when it's as old as the pyramids, maybe no one will notice that it's trash and all of a sudden it will be considered art. But of course neither do they dare exhibit the pictures. So it might well be that, somewhere between 'German Soil' by Werner Peiner and 'This was the SA' by Erik Eber, the 'Portrait of President Weber at Sunset' by Knud-Siegebold Daubsplasher lies gathering dust.

The photographs of Weber do not flatter so much as expose; his passport photo has already been described, but we have pictures like: Weber in frock coat with Erna Sack, the diva, Weber in tails with Max Amann (both slightly the worse for drink) in the company of a couple of saucy dollies at the *Fasching* ball in the *Deutsches Theater*, Weber with Fiehler, Councillor Ulrich Graf and Emil Maurice (all in black SS uniform) on their way to the opening of the 1938 *Oktoberfest*,

Weber at the inauguration of Brown Riband Week, Weber at the official opening of the Museum of Hunting, Weber with sporty representatives of the League of German Women, Weber in jovial conversation with Richard Strauss, Weber and Furtwängler giving the *Heil Hitler* salute . . . everywhere you look, this Weber; and always the word that immediately springs to mind is *rotund*. Low-slung, bulging rotundity, a robust, stunted, straining rotundity. If he had reached old age, say seventy or eighty, he would have become a wrinkled, slack old omelette, but in those days, at fifty, sixty, *robustly, tightly rotund*. Or, another line of thought: *puffed up*, as if he had a valve at the back, attached to a compressed-air pump, inflated, nipped quickly and plugged. In the pictures he always has his lips tightly pursed, as if to stop the air escaping. (In the evenings, when the air is let out, President Weber lies on his bed like the skin of those white sausages that he so enjoys with strawberry jam; in the morning, he'll be pumped up again by one of his SS adjutants.) Or again: *rising fat*. The fat comes pushing up from below, splays the arms out till they protrude like fins, it presses the shoulders upwards, squeezes out the jowls from below, until they hang over on to the collar-bones, the area round his mouth looking as if the Herr President is about to take a deep breath and, a moment later, to emit a piercing, locomotive-like whistle.

Are pictures truthful? Truer than words? Or rather, since 'true' does not readily assume the comparative form, less untrue? What is truth? Documents never reflect the whole truth. Documents are always drafted to the benefit of one side or another, or to someone's disadvantage, always biased. Granted, documents are indispensable, but to follow the course of history we have to read between the documents. Can we discern the true figure of Christian Weber between the lines of paper archaeology? Some of it, no, much of it, no, most of it, is genuine, documented, as they say. For example, Weber's shared taxi trip with the Communist Party councillor and the whore . . . Other incidents have been invented, the gentle ejection of Hitler at Weber's hands, for instance. But there are certain things which simply have to be invented because the facts would otherwise be less credible than the invention. Those things cannot have happened any other way. The fact that Weber betrayed his ex-pal Röhm was a strong rumour that was going the rounds even in the Nazi era; that Hitler sketched the most intimate parts of his sweetheart and niece Geli Raubal's anatomy is historical fact; that such drawings found their way abroad and were bought back by Hitler in exchange for the price of a battleship, that too. That Weber had a hand in the sale and – very probably – even in the buying-back, well, that's the only way it could have been.

And the disproportionately high incidence of faecal expressions in this book. The close association of Nazism with faeces is quite simply too overwhelming, and not only because of the Movement's favourite colour.

'What have you got back there, Herr *Oberscharführer*? A diesel engine backfiring? Or a snorting dragon?'

'Neither, Herr *Sturmbannführer*, that's just Herr President Weber sitting on the lavatory.'

*

'I tell you this, Herr Dirrigl, it's not good enough! Just not good enough! And to think that the Führer himself, as everybody knows, is a dog lover. Not . . . good . . . enough! I sometimes ask myself, Herr Dirrigl, just where National Regeneration is taking us, or for that matter what use it is and so forth . . . I mean, after all; and then this pen pusher in the Town Hall says to me, he says, Well, he says, it's up to you to see how you feed your mutt. You can hardly credit it, this jumped-up bureaucrat telling me . . . I have abso*lute*ly *no* intention of bandying words, me, a rate payer and tax payer, not to mention member of the National Socialist Drivers' Corps since . . . since practically . . . well, to all intents and purposes practically an Old Campaigner, as you know, Herr Dirrigl, I have no intention whatsoever of bandying legs –'

'Words.'

'– yes, words, of course, bandying words with him, whether he's a chief clerk or a department head or for all I care an area office manager, for me he's nothing but a pen pusher, Herr Dirrigl, that's what *I* call him. And he has the effrontery to tell me, cool as you like, It's up to you to see how your feed your mutt. Mutt! I ask you. "I do believe," I said, "my ears are deceiving me, but I think I heard you say mutt." Well, of course, he backed down a bit at that. "Maybe, and then maybe not," he said. "I would like to point out to you that I am not prepared to tolerate that," I said – I was boiling with rage, and I can tell you, Herr Dirrigl, if the *Oberbürgermeister* in person had come through the door just then . . . "And now!" I said, "now I'd like to have a meat ration card for my Bautzerl." After all, Bautzerl is seventeen years old. A *German* rough-haired dachshund. There you are! Seventeen years old, to all intents and purposes, a venerable old gentleman! And when you look at him, Herr Dirrigl, a physical wreck. Yes indeed. It would make you weep. A physical wreck. That's the Fatherland's thanks for a pure Aryan rough-haired dachshund's seventeen years of loyalty. He's to starve to death. Oh, yes indeed! The gratitude of the Fatherland. And all I ask is a meat ration card for my dog. And to think the Führer himself is a dog lover. And do you know this – now brace yourself for this –'

'You're quite out of breath, Herr Kammerlander –'

'That I am, but I've good reason for my agitation, don't you think? Now brace yourself, Herr Dirrigl, his reply was, "Well, feed your dog on vegetable scraps. The Führer's a vegetarian, too."'

'Outrageous!'

'"Here!" I said, my voice steady, yes, but inside I was trembling with rage, "here you are, my NSKK driver's licence. And there, my badge. I resign. And here, I also resign from the National Socialist People's Welfare, and here, you can have the NS Patrons of Culture as well, and the badge of the Reich League of Large Families, you can stick that where you like, and the same goes for the Self-Denial Ring, and you can strike my name from the list of sponsor members of the SS, and there's my Labour Service merit badge – here you are! And I hereby resign from the People's League for German Culture Abroad, and the League for the German Eastern Territories, it's on its last legs anyway what with the Russians practically at the gates of Berlin, and that's me out of the German Reich League of Physical Culture as well, and the Kyffhäuser League of Veterans of the German Reich . . . oh, yes indeed!" Well, you should have seen the look on the pen pusher's face – and when I reckon it all up, Herr Dirrigl, what I've been paying every month in membership fees! With that money I can afford to feed my Bautzerl on the black market.'

'So did you get a ration card for your dog?'

'No. Of course I didn't. But now I'm going to write to the Führer himself about this whole business.'

'I fear, Herr Kammerlander, you won't get very far.'

'I'm afraid so myself.'

'Do as I do. My Wamperl's been eating potato peelings as it is.'

'Do you know what I think? This whole war was a piece of nonsense. That's what *I* think. All this talk of a people without living space, living space in the east . . . don't talk to me about it. What are we supposed to think of a system that leaves a faithful, seventeen-year-old dog to die of starvation?'

'Now I too . . . I've – come closer a bit, we've got to be especially careful now that the rats are getting desperate, what with having their backs to the wall . . . come closer – I'm sure I can say this to you, I had my doubts right from the start. As you well know. I said back in 1939, it'll all end in tears. And now look at us! Practically the whole city in ruins, half of my house fallen victim to the flames, and in my own flat, evacuees from the Sudetenland! Talking in a dialect that would set your teeth on edge. And on top of all that . . . ! My Wamperl has been living on potato peelings.'

'By the way, how is your Headmaster Bürkel getting on with his trumpet?'

'He's able to play the signal for special bulletins now, but he seldom has occasion to do it these days.'

*

The celebrations surrounding his sixtieth birthday, in August 1943, seem to have been somewhat less lavish than on previous occasions. In the days preceding it, Sicily had been lost, the Russian Army had retaken Kharkov, and British airmen had dropped 1,765 tons of bombs on Berlin. In the files, there is no note of *Oberbürgermeister* Fiehler having again sent Party Comrade Weber five bottles of wine. Things were palpably going downhill.

In 1940, in the delirium of victory which had probably gripped even Weber, despite his scepticism born of peasant shrewdness, it had all looked very different. On 22 June the cease-fire had been concluded, on 28 June General von Falkenhausen had been appointed Commander-in-Chief of the forces in occupied France. July and August passed with Hitler and his generals poring over plans for the invasion of Britain and for a campaign against the Soviet Union. The plans were secret, of course, yet that did not stop someone like Weber getting wind of them. And perhaps someone like Weber also suspected that these were all military adventures whose outcome was questionable. So the pickings had to be assured beforehand. On 1 September Weber was, 'under orders from General Command S' (whatever that was – S for Stallion?), 'transferred to occupied France'. Weber requisitioned (organised) horses. It can be safely assumed that he did not stop at Jewish riding stables. (The wording quoted above is taken from Weber's application for leave dated 31 August.) Weber undertook further 'inspections' of horseflesh between 16 and 26 September and again for 'approx. ten to fourteen days' from 22 or 23 October. Around the same time Weber, as a member of the Finance Committee, leased to Weber, as a member of the National Socialist General Corruption, the estate at Planegg and the municipal hunting reserve in Forst Kasten. From the Italian Consul, Grisi, the Brown Riband of Germany Association Ltd (i.e. Weber) bought the *Königshof* Hotel on the Stachus. By way of rounding off the Planegg Estate, and indeed the whole Weber empire north of Lake Starnberg, where, it will be remembered, the World Arena was to be erected after the final victory, Weber leased some meadows and a stable from the supreme ruling dynasty. Prince Ludwig of Bavaria recalls the Herr President's offer of terms for the lease: 'I have had an area of your property surveyed with a view to erecting new stabling accommodation. The value is estimated at . . . Reichsmarks. By the by, the name of Dachau will no doubt mean something to you. *Heil Hitler! – Weber.*'

Of course, Dachau did indeed mean something to Prince Ludwig. It meant something to every German, although not after 1945. The prince leased his land.

In 1941 Weber went off to review horses in France again, albeit for one last time; this was for some ten days starting on 4 June – that is, a few days before Hitler's attack on his ally Stalin.

But Weber was active – and successful – in other economic spheres too. Although his Christian Weber's Long-Distance Tours company was no longer carrying out any long-distance, or for that matter short-distance, tours, Weber was still drawing supplies of petrol for this firm, essential to the war effort as it was. Dating from 1942, there is an earnest representation made by 'Department S' (i.e. Weber) urging against any cuts in petrol allocations. Weber was trafficking in petrol. The returns on this much-coveted commodity were most gratifying. In 1944, a new source of income opened up for the industrious Weber: for men coming home on leave from the front, there were special 'Food Coupons for Personnel on Leave'. While these coupons were in fact issued by the Army, they were distributed by the city authorities. There was a special kiosk set up for this purpose at the main railway station. In the notorious bureaucratic disarray that prevailed in the German *Wehrmacht*, this represented a crevice through which food coupons seeped away. Weber knew of this crack, and held his hand under it. Food coupons were even more precious than petrol. The returns were again very gratifying. It seems, however, that the local garrison commander, General von Kieffer, got wind of Weber's little scheme, as also did Paul Wolfrum, who had been packed off to the front by Weber but had made a very speedy return, and who consequently had a bone to pick with him. No scandal of any significance ensued, however. Weber seems to have smoothed over the whole affair by cutting both Kieffer and Wolfrum in on the enterprise – the most elegant of solutions, it has to be conceded.

Overall, though, these were somewhat troubled times. The file marked DAMAGE TO THE PROPERTY OF CHRISTIAN WEBER in the City Archives refers to bomb damage in the Residency, losses suffered by his pool of vehicles, casualties among his racing stables and even in his fishing waters. This nasty, nasty war. They were even bombing Weber's carp. What was he supposed to have for Christmas dinner in 1944, then?

Weber moved into the – very cramped – conditions of the City Hall. He managed to make up for other losses by personally acquiring the various properties belonging to the missionary Benedictines when their assets were confiscated by the state (where were they going to be doing much missionarying these days anyway?). On 2 May 1944 (shortly before the Russians' decisive assault on Sebastopol began) Weber moved into a remote retreat in Feldafing, the house at No. 22 Schluchtweg (tel. – well of course the war-essential Regional Council President and alderman got a line installed immediately – 0257 251).

What went on in the mind of a Weber who – in so far as he paid them any attention whatsoever – had access to the things that were omitted from the cosmetically improved *Wehrmacht* bulletins – the fact, to take just one example, that a hundred thousand men of the defence force in the Crimea could no longer be shipped over to Romania because the Greatest Leader Of All Time had been too late in giving the order to evacuate? The virtually unarmed hundred thousand were beaten to death by the Russians with their rifle-butts. Was Weber knocked all of a heap? Or another one: the fact that the Allied air offensive of 12 May 1944 had paralysed the production of synthetic fuels, reducing it in the Leuna works in Merseburg by sixty per cent, in Böhlau by fifty per cent and by the full hundred per cent in Tröglitz and Brüx? The German air defences had shot down a laughable forty-six bombers (less of a laughing matter for the bomber crews involved), the majority of the German fighter crews were sitting in air-raid shelters because of a lack of fuel and their only counter-offensive measure was a loud grinding of their teeth. But Department S got its petrol supplies.

But we'll leave it at that – we mustn't get tangled up in the friend/foe constructs that were being put about at that time. Only the German shot that missed was a good shot, and only the German deserter was a hero. Every daring military action, whether by Rommel or Kluge or Molders, merely served to prolong, among other things, Christian Weber's opportunities for sinking his teeth into pheasants' legs and women's buttocks.

How did Weber envisage the end? That the end of the lost war would also mean the end for the Nazi system, and that the war had long since been lost, must have been obvious even for somebody (like, presumably, Weber) whose foresight would not take him past the end of his own nose. Did Weber believe in miracles? In wonder-weapons? Was it his belief that someone who exerted such an enormous body-weight on the earth's surface could not simply be swept away? Did he consider himself immortal? Or perhaps: 'Excuse me, Mr De-Nazification Officer, I'm Weber, I'm not Hitler or Göring. In fact, I was always against that Göring, I always found him extremely dis-agreeable. And I never did *anything* to *anyone*. I was only interested in horses. That's not forbidden, is it? I had nothing to do with *race*, except when it was a question of breeding thoroughbreds. The Jews? The Jews? Never really bothered about them, there's no such thing as Jewish horses. And the Amazons, back then – you don't think that had anything political about it, do you? Anyway, I can prove that in 1938 I was against them . . . on the night in question, you know what I mean, or rather, afterwards, I can prove I wasn't in favour, I assure you I can prove it, when the city of Munich . . . um, ah . . . bought . . . um . . . well, let's say, took over . . . Jewish properties.' In fact it can indeed be proved. There is one source available, a lawyer, a Law student at that time, in the Estates Department of the City of Munich, whom *Oberbürgermeister* Fiehler wanted to assign to Depart-ment S to keep an eagle eye on Weber. (That would be around 1942, '43. Weber's all-too-liberal dealings in pet-rol coupons had become too obvious even in terms of the general Nazi corruption scene.) The observation had to be undercover. The Alderman-President, insisted the *Oberbürgermeister*, absolutely had to have a 'Personal Adviser'.

The young lawyer presented himself in Weber's office one forenoon around eleven-thirty. Weber was sitting in front of a tankard of beer and six pairs of white sausages with strawberry jam. He invited the young Doctor of Laws to have a beer with him before dismissing him and sending word to the *Oberbürgermeister* that he had his SS adjutant to fetch his beer for him and what he needed a personal adviser for he could not imagine. Thanks, but no thanks. The *Oberbürgermeister* did not dare make an issue of it.

That once-young lawyer, nowadays an old gentleman, can testify as a witness that it was Weber of all people who stopped the city taking over the confiscated Jewish lands and property. A noble attitude? One inspiring respect? I would maintain that there is only one explanation for it: Weber wanted these properties for himself. That's the only way it could have been; anything else would have been out of character.

Until shortly before the end of the war (and his own end as well) Weber was making plans for his World Arena on the northern shore of Lake Starnberg. He amassed one parcel of property after another, rounding off his *imperium*. This was done by means of either straightforward expropriation or compulsory exchange. Sometimes a farmer would put up a fight, as in the case of old Liebhart in Percha, of whom the local party-group leader was only too ready to report that he never greeted anyone with a '*Heil Hitler*'. After extensive, systematic harassment, Liebhart had been softened up in 1944 and agreed to the exchange of a large, self-contained piece of land (this was valued at nine thousand Reichsmarks) for a few scattered plots offered by the Brown Riband (and assessed at RM 12,000). Liebhart had to pay the Brown Riband the difference of RM 3,000, which brought him to the verge of financial ruin. After that, he no doubt made sure he never greeted anyone with a *Heil Hitler*. The notarial attestation of the exchange took place on 11 May 1944. One year later to the day was to be a date of special significance for Weber.

We have already dealt in some detail with the extent to which Weber was apparently convinced that the end of the war would not impair his own well-being, and that this cessation of hostilities might well cost the Beloved Führer, his friend Wolf, his head – and in addition (here a gleeful rubbing of his hands) Göring, Goebbels and other henchmen too – and might also bring about the downfall of the Great German Reich, of the National Regeneration, of the NSDAP, et cetera, but not of an idea of such far-reaching import as the Brown Riband of Germany, e.V. Probably Weber was looking confidently forward to the day when Eisenhower approached him and said, in his nasal whine, 'Oh, Mr Weber, nice to see you. You'll see to it that the famous Brown Riband goes ahead again as soon as possible. OK?' 'OK, Mr Eisenhower,' Weber would reply, 'and you'll be coming along to the next Night of the Amazons, won't you? Hey? But take a tip from me – leave your good lady at home.'

As we have already reported, the Brown Riband of Germany Association was founded as a registered society in 1936, its President was, it goes without saying, Christian Weber, its Vice-President Councillor Ernst Schubert. Schubert was elected first for a limited period, up to 1 February 1939, and then as from that date for life, only to be voted out at a general meeting of the association on 13 April 1945 and replaced by a Capt. (retd) Arthur Holzmann, estates manager in Gutharting, nr Grabenstätt on the Chiemsee. The meeting took place in Dorfen. On 13 April 1945, Münster in Westphalia, Frankfurt am Main and Karlsruhe were in Allied hands, Königsberg had capitulated, and on that same day Vienna fell. In Dorfen, Weber invested his new Vice-President. And if that were not enough, a week later, on 20 April – Wolf's birthday, celebrated by only a very few – Weber held a further general meeting of the members of the Brown Riband (the venue is not indicated in the minutes). On that same day, the Americans were marching into Nuremberg and Leipzig and the Russians were making a start on the shelling of the city centre of Berlin. On the agenda was an amendment to Article 10 of the association's constitution. Up till that point, Article 10 had laid down that in the event of the dissolution of the Brown Riband the association's assets (which in property holdings alone amounted to millions) should pass to the Capital City of the Movement. Now Weber amended Article 10: the assets were to accrue, in the event of the Brown Riband being disbanded, to the German Museum of Hunting Association *e.V.* President of Munich he was not, and never would be (this was no doubt Weber's line of thinking), but President of the Association for the Museum of Hunting he most certainly was, and the Museum of Hunting was, after all, an extremely unpolitical item.

Was this something of a premonition? During the night of Friday 27 and Saturday 28 April, the day on which the US Army pushed forward as far as Augsburg, a courageous officer, Capt. Rupprecht Gerngross (in private life, Dr Gerngross, solicitor) attempted, along with the Company of Interpreters in Army Sector VII and sections of the 19th and 61st Grenadier Reserve Batallions, to render the SS units grouped around Munich harmless and to surrender the city to the Americans without resistance before any further disaster could befall. The venture unfortunately failed. Captain Gerngross named his rescue attempt 'Operation Free Bavaria', and the password was 'Pheasant Shoot'; in the popular vernacular, which of course emerged only from the corner of the popular mouth, 'Golden Pheasants' was the name given to bearers of the Party Badge in Gold and similar bigwigs. One of the few pheasants to be caught was Christian Weber. Among the buildings occupied by the men of the liberation operation, one happened to be the City Hall, which was however deserted – except for Weber.

*

The fat man was sitting on his bed. It was cold. Granted, the neo-Gothic Town Hall in Munich may well be considered beautiful, but it is uninhabitable. A cold April morning. The ante-room, actually intended for the secretary, is the President's office, the room to the rear his bed-sitter. That it should have come to this. The fat man was sitting on his bed in a flannel vest and long flannel underpants. He had pulled on one sock before he had a wheezing fit.

'Zinser!' he bawled.

Zinser failed to appear. Normally Zinser put on his socks for him, Zinser, his SS batman.

'Zinser!'

Nothing moved. Weber braced himself against the bed and heaved himself to his feet with a groan, took a step forward and let out a howl – hell, but that stone floor was icy-cold! The heating hadn't been on for days now.

'Flaming arseholes,' muttered Weber, 'a man could catch his death here.' He hopped towards the door, trying to keep his considerable weight as much on the stockinged foot as possible, and yelled into the outer office, 'Tipflinger! Where are you, you bitch?' But Fräulein Tipflinger, Weber's secretary, was not there either. Weber hopped back in, turned the radio on again: solemn music, something that Weber was not familiar with. (Weber knew only folk – in the Nationalist, *völkisch*, sense – songs like 'Come, Black Gypsy' or 'Cornflower Blue'.) Weber summoned up all his strength, forced his will-power to fight its way through all his fat, and teeteringly set about trying to reach his second foot with the other sock.

'Attention! Attention! We are interrupting this programme of music to bring you an important announcement. This is the Reich Broadcasting Station in Munich. This is Operation Free Bavaria. The time has come. Bavaria is about to liberate itself; we call on everyone to help throw off the last yoke of Nazi subjugation! Our beloved Bavaria is acting with one accord. Liberty and our native land will once again be ours! Act decisively and remain united! Be prepared to take action for the noble cause of Operation Free Bavaria! Our homeland will be spared the ravages of war, soon the bells of peace will ring out. And now, here is the proclamation issued by Operation Free Bavaria, consisting of ten points: 1. The eradication of the bloody tyranny of the National Socialist regime. 2. The abolition of militarism, which in its present form has brought nothing but endless misery upon the German people. Militarism is fundamentally incompatible with the character of the Bavarian people. 3. The German people shall once again become a member of civilised humanity, enjoying equal righ –'

'Shut your trap,' growled Weber and switched off.

Early in the morning – for him, at the crack of dawn, which meant something like nine o'clock – Weber had already heard a similar announcement. He had been feeling pretty rough anyway, last evening's white wine had tasted corked and sour and was now burning its way back up his gullet, and the goose-liver pâté (the third-last tin) was some way past its best. In addition, he had hardly slept – about five in the morning there had been the thunder of artillery coming from the west. When, around nine, Weber, tormented by heartburn and bellyache, had woken with a jerk – startled by what? by nothing? by the unaccustomed silence in the huge building? – he had turned on the radio, and that was when that announcement had come.

A man of Weber's ilk is incapable of making any sense of a catastrophe immediately threatening his own person. His capacity for understanding does not go that far. The tidings of disaster were left hanging in the room uncomprehended, unbelieved. It's like someone trying to put one hand round a lump of concrete ten metres long. The mind – and especially a mind like Weber's – lags behind, gives up trying to comprehend, gives up even beginning to try to comprehend.

Even the blackest news, right down to the thunder of artillery drifting over from Augsburg, had not really disturbed Weber, snuggling down in the security of his cosy little nest of privileges, provisioned as in peacetime, but now his own personal shell had landed right at his feet and was threatening to go off at any moment. On the shell were the words IT'S OVER.

Sleep was out of the question now. Weber sat up in his bed, pushed the black-out curtains aside: rain-sodden ruins, with the rain turning to snow.

Weber still had only one sock on when footsteps echoed through the corridors outside. Boots. Weber pondered for a moment and eyed the cupboard, but a knock at the door stopped him short.

'Weber!' a voice called, 'Open up, we know you're in there.'

Weber tried to shout 'Come in,' but phlegm blocked his gullet. The door was thrown open, two soldiers – *Wehrmacht*, not SS – entered, a lieutenant and a corporal. The lieutenant drew his pistol.

'I'm not . . .' gasped Weber once he had noisily cleared his throat, 'I'm not . . . I'm just the batman . . . Weber's gone . . .'

The lieutenant laughed. 'I've seen you too often. I know who you are.'

'Anyway,' said the corporal, 'a bloated swine like you – there couldn't be another one.'

'Do you mind!' breathed Weber.

'Get dressed!' said the lieutenant.

'What for?' Weber enquired.

'Now there's a stupid question,' said the lieutenant, 'or would you rather come along in your underpants?'

'Where to?'

'You'll soon find out.'

Weber was trembling. Slowly, slowly, his limited intelligence began to grasp the significance of the 'It's over' that was throbbing around the room. He tried to pull on the second sock, but he was quaking so violently he could not manage it. The lieutenant nodded to the corporal.

'Matter of fact,' muttered the corporal, 'he should be shot in his underpants. No more than he deserves.'

'Give him a hand,' said the lieutenant. 'We're not savages. *We* don't want to be like him and his kind.'

'Shi . . . sha . . . shot?' stuttered Weber.

'Hanged would be better,' said the corporal, helping him into his trousers.

'I've got to go to the lavatory,' whimpered Weber.

'Not worth it any more,' said the corporal, 'save it up till you get to hell.' He snapped Weber's braces over his shoulders.

'Wi . . . withoutaf . . . thoutafairt . . . without a fair trial,' panted Weber, 'you can't do that . . . please . . . I demand . . .'

The corporal shoved Weber's arms into the sleeves of his jacket. 'Of course, without a fair trial. In half an hour at the outside you'll be with Old Nick. He's stoking the fires already. He's going to need a big pot for you.'

'Herr Lieutenant,' Weber whimpered, 'I've never done you any harm, as far as I can remember. I don't even know you. I'm only – mnonly . . . I've only . . .'

'Get yourself into your shoes, or else!' barked the corporal.

Weber was crying softly.

'Should I put a tie on him?' the corporal asked the lieutenant.

'Hardly worth while at this stage,' said the lieutenant. 'Wait, though. This'll do.' The lieutenant picked up the Party Badge in Gold from the bedside table, stuck it in Weber's lapel and waved his pistol towards the door. 'Out.'

Weber had to go first. Outside in the office, Weber said, in a slightly steadier voice, 'There, in the safe.'

'What about the safe?' asked the lieutenant.

'May I, gentlemen . . . I mean . . . the key's in there in the bedside table drawer . . . might I offer you gentlemen two hundred thousand marks – each? They're in . . . I mean . . . if you gentlemen could find your way . . . it's there, in cash . . . if you could find your . . . would refrain from . . . could forget about taking me to . . . to . . .' Weber gulped, 'It's in there in cash.'

'Get a move on, march!' said the lieutenant coldly, jabbing his pistol in Weber's back.

'Wait!' wailed Weber, 'I'd be prepared . . . in Swiss francs, they're in there too . . .' his voice rose to a whine again, '. . . they're in there too.'

'We'll come back for them later,' said the lieutenant. The corporal fetched Weber a kick.

'Hey!' snapped the lieutenant, 'what d'you think you're doing?'

'Whenever *they* arrested anybody . . .' said the corporal.

'Maybe *they* did. Not us,' said the lieutenant, and, to Weber, 'Get your hands up!'

Weber raised his hands as far as he could, which was not very far. His fins pushed his shoulders upwards, his shoulders pressed his cheeks higher, so that Weber could hardly see. His mouth swelled outwards, his scrubby moustache bristled. In that state, he went out.

*

The Bavarian Liberation Operation had no intention of stringing Weber up. Captain Gerngross was too decent for that. He had absolutely no intention of shooting or hanging anyone at all. Maybe he should have done, maybe then his coup would have succeeded.

Weber was taken to the Company of Interpreters' barracks and locked in an attic room. By the evening of 28 April, it was clear that the liberation campaign had failed. Weber had got away with it again. The SS, who came to search the barracks, released him. All the same, the first thing Weber did was to remove the Party Badge in Gold from his lapel.

*

'No, not a wound, an accident.'

'Accident?'

'Yes.'

They went on shovelling.

'Nearly twenty years ago. A car knocked them down. On the Marienplatz, Thomass's corner. That's why I never got called up. What about you?'

'I've only got half a stomach. Anyway, I'm a tailor.'

'Tailor? So digging ditches isn't exactly your line of work then either.'

'No.'

'A tailor? Don't tailors have to go to the Army?'

'Strictly speaking, yes, but not me.'

'Because of the half-stomach?'

'That too, but . . . but I'm a cutter. Chief cutter. With Kielleuthner's.'

'Kielleuthner's?'

'Doesn't the name ring a bell? Kielleuthner's, Maximilian-strasse. Top-class gentlemen's outfitting.'

'And just for *that* . . . ?'

'We make . . .' the tailor lowered his voice, 'we make uniforms. Göring, Ribbentrop, Keitel . . . know what I mean? Well, we *made*.'

'I get it. Ha ha. And of course you . . .'

'Hey, you two! When you've quite finished your little chat,' shouted the SS man who was sitting on a park bench and was in charge.

'OK, OK,' said Wilhelm Böhm, and then, quietly, 'Don't get all het up. Soon be all over for you lot.'

'Careful,' whispered the tailor.

There were about two dozen of them, tearing up the road surface at the eastern end of the Reichenbach Bridge, piling up the stones and digging skimpy little ditches to make what the SS man chose to call 'tank traps'. For the two dozen old men and invalids there were no more than nine spades, and one of them was a child's sand spade.

'What did you say? I heard exactly what you were saying!' barked the SS man, who with one jump stood right at Böhm's back.

'What? What d'you mean?'

'You said – something about it being "all over".'

'Yes. Of course. The war will be all over. Soon.'

'Is that so?'

'Sure. Look – these ditches we're digging, and the tank traps, well, the Yanks'll not get past them, then they'll give up in despair . . . and pack it in.'

The SS man eyed Böhm suspiciously.

'Or?' asked Böhm. 'Or maybe you don't believe in final victory?'

The SS man exhaled with a snort.

'Get on with it,' he said after a moment, went back to his bench and set to work on a crossword puzzle.

Like an apparition from another world, a car hove into sight at the city end of the bridge. The SS man leapt in the air. The others stopped working. The car moved gingerly across the bridge. No Army vehicle this, but a private car (about as scarce as ground coffee), and in fact it wasn't one run on wood-gas either. A bigwig, then. The SS man moved forward. A fat man leant out of the car window: 'What's going on here? I can't get through!' The SS man shouted some orders, the men quickly removed a pile of stones that was giving particular offence. The fat man slalomed his car through the road-block.

'At your service, Herr President!' called the tailor from Kielleuthner's and shouldered arms with his shovel.

The fat man put his foot down and drove off along the strip of the Ohlmüllerstrasse that had remained clear of rubble, heading out of town.

'He got stuff made up by us, too,' said the tailor. 'He's even got a hunting/dinner jacket still lying in the shop – green, with horn buttons – only been for a first fitting.'

'It'll lie there for a while yet,' said Böhm.

An old woman emerged from what was left of a house at No. 2 Ohlmüllerstrasse, shouting, 'The *Wehrmacht* bulletin! They've just said in the *Wehrmacht* bulletin, old Hitler's kicked the buck –' Catching sight of the SS man, she hesitated and, lowering her voice, went on, 'The Führer is dead.'

The SS man's jaw dropped.

'Right! That's it, then,' said Böhm, rammed his shovel into the ground and limped away.

*

There are various versions of the story of Weber's last days going the rounds, contradictory ones, at least in part. Unfortunately, the rumour that still persists to this day in the area round Starnberg is inaccurate: Weber was supposed to have been beaten to a pulp like a fat rat in the last days of the war. No, he wasn't beaten to death. He did manage, shortly before the Americans took Munich, to flee to the Tegernsee, where he is supposed to have holed up with a friend. The friend was called Stuppacher and was a car dealer, a Ford agent. Weber was a customer of Stuppacher's. However, it seems he then left Upper Bavaria and headed north, to Percha in fact, near Starnberg, the site of his future World Arena. On 4 May the half starved, and for some time past ammunitionless, unit that bore the somewhat extravagant title of Army Group G, the remnants of the 1st and 19th armies under Infantry General Friedrich Schulz, surrendered in Haar, near Munich, whereby the National Regeneration in Bavaria came to a halt. The National Degeneration took over.

In the confusion that reigned in these days, Weber apparently succeeded in making his way from the Tegernsee to Starnberg, where he hid in a barn on his *Buchhof* estate. Whether out of revenge for some injustice Weber had done him or in order to curry favour with the new masters, one of the employees on the estate, some minor administrator or other of the stud farm, betrayed Weber's hiding place to the Americans, who immediately hauled the trembling fat blob out of the hay, to the accompaniment of enthusiastic applause from the watching peasantry.

According to another legend, Weber is supposed, while being transported by lorry through the devastated city of Munich, to have suffered a stroke, brought on by shame and disgrace. That's not true either. Or again, he is supposed to have fallen off the lorry – did he fall or was he pushed? This is in fact somewhat closer to the truth, for there is an eye-witness account which describes Weber's end. According to it, Weber was first taken to a camp or a prison in Ulm. From there, he was to be transferred to Heilbronn:

SWORN STATEMENT OF KETTERER Dr. Emil.

Before me, William J. Aalmans, ASN 102885 Neth. Army, Interrogator-Investigator, attached to War Crimes Group 7708, Dachau Detachment, APO 205, U.S. Army, personally appeared KETTERER, Dr. Emil, No. 29-11510, 31-G-6 603 667, a German prisoner, who, after first being duly sworn by JOHN. W. BROOKS, o-112697, Major, Infantry; and after being informed by me about the reason of the interrogation, made and signed the following statement.

In the night of 10–11 May 1945, there was a transport of P.W.'s, Civilian internees etc. from ULM to HEILBRONN. A convoy of 16 big army trucks left ULM and approx 10–12 K.M. before the convoy reached HEILBRONN, the 8th truck in the convoy did not keep the road and drove down a bend, turned over, killing 3 (three) of the people riding on it and wounding many of them. I was sitting on the floor of the back of the truck together with:

WEBER, Christian, (sitting next to me)
ZOEBERLEIN, Hans (a writer)
ILZHOEFER (an SA Oberführer)
BLUEMLER (an SA Brigadeführer)
CHRISTOFFEL, Adam

and many other people, who are all unknown to me. I was buried under the truck, as well as WEBER, but due to help from the occupants of the other cars, we were released pretty soon. I was wounded and had a slight brain-concussion. WEBER was severely wounded; had probably a broken back and other injuries, which caused his death within, approximately, 10–15 minutes. A German Wehrmacht-physician, who was in the convoy, gave WEBER an injection, trying to save him, but he died shortly afterwards. I had – although I was myself in a bad condition – a look at WEBER, but nothing could be done to help him because he already was completely blue. Two other severely wounded P.W.'s and I were then taken to the University-Hospital at HEIDELBERG. I never heard what happened at the scene after I left.

I do not know what happened to the body of WEBER, nor what happened to the other dead and wounded people. I assume, that they were taken to the P.W. Camp near HEILBRONN, resp. to the cemetery at HEILBRONN.

The above testimony was made by me, voluntarily and without any threat or coercion, at DACHAU, Germany, Camp 29, on the 30th January 1947, and read to me in the German language before I signed it.

I swear by God, that it is the truth, the whole truth and nothing but the truth, so help me God.

(signature) *KETTERER, Emil.*

Subscribed and sworn to before me, at DACHAU, Germany, this 30th day of January 1947.

(signature) *JOHN W. BROOKS*
Major Inf.
Chief screening Section
DACHAU Detachment.

Remember the accident involving the lorry in the Zamdorfer Strasse on 24 March 1923? The bouncer's fondness for various means of locomotion: horses, cars . . . ? It is not, therefore, without a certain poetic justice if Weber did lose his life as a result of a road accident. But why could it not have happened on 24 March 1923 instead of only on 11 May 1945? This would not have made any difference to the course of world history, but at least one swine fewer would have done his National Socialist wallowing in the murky sludge of the German Fatherland. But can something, out of which that sort of thing can grow, be called a fatherland at all? Can it keep on shedding its skin until the swastikas no longer show on the pelt?

*

'My, my, Herr Dirrigl. Ah, you're here too?'
'Well of course, everybody has to be. Horrible.'

242

'Yes, horrible indeed. I'm really not sure it's right to . . .'

'In some ways, yes, but in others, no it's not. What's past is past, I always say. And anyway, they should show us, who have been through so much, something a bit more cheerful, more constructive. Marika Rökk, for example. And not these concentration-camp films.'

'I couldn't agree more. Nobody would go in there of their own free will.'

'To see Marika Rökk, they would.'

'I for one wouldn't have gone to see this film if it hadn't been for – well, the official stamp, you know, to get ration cards. Although it's enough to put you off food altogether, looking at that. Those skeletons! Those piles of corpses . . . the gas chambers . . .'

'Most of the time I just didn't look, Herr Kammerlander, just couldn't look.'

'I was exactly the same. But sitting there with your eyes shut all the time, it does get boring.'

'And anyway, Herr Kammerlander, it's all wrong, of course, forcing all these starving people in to see that film. It's the others that should have to watch that. The Nazis.'

'Precisely.'

'But what's the use of talking about it? The world is in a bad way no matter who is in power. And as a householder you're absolutely at the bottom of the heap. An aerial mine blew my roof right off, and as if that wasn't bad enough – twenty-eight refugees billeted on me. I ask you, Herr Kammerlander, just try to picture that. Twenty-eight refugees! And six of them toddlers. It's barefaced Communism, that.'

'And again we've just to keep our mouths shut.'

'By the way, that young Herr Davidsohn came back. You remember, the son of the Davidsohns that . . . well, up to 1938 they lived on my third floor. Now he calls himself Davies, he's an officer, but still talks – very funny, really – with a strong Munich accent. Little Davidsohn. Was a sweet little lad in those days. Good Lord, how time flies.'

'Were they not the ones with the nearly new refrigerator that you . . . um . . . relieved them of for five marks?'

'Yes, yes. That's as may be. Anyway, he came to visit me, did little Davidsohn – I mean, Lieutenant Davies, a beanpole of a fellow now, a handsome young man, – asked me if he might take a look at his parents' flat. Of course, please do, said I – suited me fine, because that way he got a look at the conditions: twenty-eight refugees, six of them toddlers, and all of them started screaming at once.'

'And he didn't ask about the refrigerator?'

'I don't know why you keep going on about the refrigerator, Herr Kammerlander; if *I* hadn't . . . taken it off their hands, somebody else would have. Or, worse still, it would simply have been taken from them. Be fair!'

'What actually became of the Davidsohns?'

'I've just told you, he's called Davies now and he's a lieutenant – a "lootenant" – and when he's demobilised, he's going to go back to Cleveland . . .'

'I meant the *old* Davidsohns.'

'Ah, I see. Yes. Well no. They – I really have no idea. In 1938 they went . . . they were positively delighted that I took the fridge off their hands, because – I mean, you can't take a refrigerator to . . . you couldn't very well drag a fridge along there, now could you, but ready cash . . . I tell you, they were positively delighted . . .'

'Did you never hear from them again?'

'No. You see . . . it was very early in the morning when . . . they left very early. I don't get up that early. And I didn't want to ask Lieutenant Davies whether he knows anything about his parents. It might . . . I didn't want to open up old wounds. Anyway, he clambered over all these refugees, looked out of the window very pensively. His parents packed him off to his aunt in Austria in 1935, you see, and later he went to America with this aunt. He looked out of the window deep in thought. "The house opposite," he asked me, "or rather, the house that used to be over there, that's where Maxl, Maxl Sellmaier, used to live, that sat next to me in school, isn't that right?" "1943," says I, "Pavlograd." "Ah," that was all he said, but very pensively too. Do no harm for him to know, I thought, that we too . . . and so on. Yes, and then he passed chewing gum round the refugee children, and sort

244

of pink sweets that looked like cotton wool – and he gave me, Herr Kammerlander, he gave me a whole unopened tin of Nescafé and two cartons of Lucky Strikes. Yes indeed, they were always quiet, respectable tenants, the Davidsohns.'

'If we had only realised –'

'What do you mean?'

'You know, what we've seen in this film. Such horrors.'

'Dreadful. Inhuman. Those SS, absolute hyenas.'

'And yet to look at them – all right, that death's head on their caps, but we just took that for . . . well, as just another badge, instead of an eagle or the like . . . but that they could . . . take young Kernpichler, for instance, a nice, friendly man, well set up, very handsome, for a while it looked as if he and my Gisela . . . my middle daughter, you know . . . they were practically engaged . . . he was in the SS. I had no *idea* what went on in that man's mind.'

'Nobody had any notion.'

'Nobody could have had the faintest idea, Herr Dirrigl.'

'Well I, Herr Kammerlander, *I* – I can swear to this – *I* knew absolutely nothing, nothing of all these atrocities.'

'No more did I. And you more than anybody, Herr Dirrigl, can testify to that. All right, so I was in the Drivers' Corps, the NSKK . . . very well . . . I joined that only so as not to have to go into the Party itself . . . and the fact that my wife received the Mother's Cross from the *Gauleiter* . . . but I mean *inwardly*, Herr Dirrigl, I was always against them.'

'I too.'

'I believe, Herr Dirrigl, that – especially in Bavaria – absolutely nobody was in favour of them. Not a soul. Except, of course, for a few bigwigs, like Fiehler, Giesler, Esser, Weber, and then only because they stood to gain some advantages from it. For *respectable* folk, Herr Dirrigl, especially in Bavaria, National Socialism was suspect right from the very start.'

'You're absolutely right.'

'And, Herr Dirrigl, I can tell you one thing. If we had had even the *remotest* idea of these atrocities, then the whole population would have come out quite openly against it.'

'Exactly.'

'We just had *no* idea.'

'Not till now.'

'And it's too late now. But of course the Americans won't be able to understand that.'

'One thing we mustn't do, Herr Kammerlander, we mustn't allow them to tar us respectable Germans with the Nazi brush.'

'That's very true. Now, though, I must get off home. My Wamperl has to get out for his wee-wees.'

'Quite right. And – by the way, if now and again you have something you want stored for you, well – I mean, now and then one does manage to get hold of something, something perishable, and would like to . . . well then, just you bring it over and put it in our refrigerator. It's still working perfectly and it's in a safe place. The refugees can't get near it.'

'I'll be glad to avail myself of it, Herr Dirrigl. Thank you very much.'

'Don't mention it. We have to stick together in times of trial.'

*

'I just don't believe it!'

'Herr Blumenthal?'

'I've been on the run, half-way round the world, for ten years, and here in New York there are – how many million inhabitants? And here on – how manyth Street is this? I still haven't got my bearings – here I run into none other than old Peschmowitz. What brings you here?'

'Exactly the same as you. I've been on the run all the way round the world too, only maybe the other way round.'

'Do you have a few minutes, Herr Peschmowitz, or are you already so much of an American that you're forever rushing about? Shall we go in here for a coffee?'

'With pleasure. We'll have a cup of what passes for coffee here.'

. . .

'Have you any intention, Herr Blumenthal . . . of going back?'

246

'Ask me something easier.'

'Did you – did your family . . . have you lost a lot of your relatives?'

'Only myself. I mean, my family has lost *me*. I'm the only one left.'

'Yes. Yes, I see.'

'And what about you?'

'My sister got out. Nobody else apart from me. She's now living in Los Angeles. But she wants to go, as soon as it's possible, to Palestine. Israel, as they call it now.'

'Palestine . . . Israel, God forbid, Herr Peschmowitz, but I suppose that could be a possibility for folk like us too. But, do you know Palestine? Israel? The desert?'

'No, of course not.'

'I always say, Herr Peschmowitz, if the British want to make us Jews a present of a country that doesn't belong to them, why don't they give us Switzerland?'

'What about back to Munich? No notion of that?'

'And you?'

'Hm.'

'What I will never be able to forgive that – I will not do him the honour of letting him haunt my memory even as a name, which is why I always insist I've forgotten his name, that Hündler or Fitler – what I can't forgive that shmuck for is that he has put me right off Germany.'

'Germany I could cope with all right. It's the *Germans* I can't stomach any more, I'm afraid.'

'And yet that's what we are ourselves. Germans, I mean.'

'Germans? Not Jews?'

'Now don't get philosophical with me. In real life, as we know only too well, that is just no help at all.'

'Always the pessimist.'

'Does have the advantage that you're mostly proved right in the end.'

Acknowledgements

I am greatly indebted to the following books for the information I have used in this novel: Joachim C. Fest, *Hitler*; Ernst Hanfstaengl, *Zwischen Weißem und Braunem Haus (Hitler – The Missing Years)*; Karl Ploetz, *Auszug aus der Geschichte*; Andreas Hillgruber/Gerhard Himmelchen, *Chronik des Zweiten Weltkrieges*; Robert Wistrich, *Wer war wer im Dritten Reich (Who's Who in Nazi Germany)*; Kurt Preis, *München unterm Hakenkreuz*; Martin Broszat/Elke Fröhlich (eds.), *Bayern in der NS-Zeit*; Helmut M. Hanko, *Kommunalpolitik in München*.

Occasionally I have consulted the curious encyclopaedia *Schlag nach!* (Leipzig, 1939), and *Der Neue Brockhaus* (Leipzig, 1938/39). In addition, I made use of the documents relating to Christian Weber (mostly unpublished) in the Bavarian State Archives, in the Munich City Archives, the Institute for Contemporary History, the Monacensia Department of the Municipal Library and those belonging to the Munich District Court and the Museum of Hunting in Munich; to the curators and staff of these institutions I owe a debt of gratitude which I am happy to acknowledge here.

For valuable advice on the Nazi era in Munich and on the man, Christian Weber, and his activities, I am grateful to: Prof. Dr Murad Ferid, my dear and respected teacher, Dr Otto Gritschneder, lawyer, and ex-Town Clerk Dr Oskar Vetter. To my colleague Josef Darchinger, my thanks for his assistance with the initial, and crucial, research work on Christian Weber, which proved so invaluable that I can say that, without that help, this book would not have been written.